**There was something behind the glass, behind her reflection
and the wash of clouded sky above her.**

She gazed past the surface, as though she were looking deep into
clear water, ignoring the ripples and movements on the surface to
search out what lived beneath. A tree, she realized, bending in a faint
breeze, draped with purple leaves like streamers. Pure-silver flowers
winked and sparkled in the deep foliage, swinging gently like bells,
though Alaine couldn't hear anything. She gazed deeper, drinking
in the beauty of a silver mist of moss on the ground, of a tangle of
pale branches woven into knotwork unnaturally symmetrical, down
to thorns bowing deeply to one another in vine-wrought curls.

Something moved in the purple-and-silver forest, a figure, sliding
like mist through the boughs. A woman—Alaine started. She was
tall and slim, shaped more than anything like a birch tree, with the
same silver-pale gleam. Her hair was loose behind her, wound
through with purple flowers, painfully bright against her fair waves.
She looked up, gazing right at Alaine, almost meeting her eyes—

And then the mirror shattered in her hands.

Praise for Rowenna Miller

"A gorgeous weave of romantic fantasy and urgent politics."
—Anna Smith Spark, author of *The Court of Broken Knives*

"Miller places immigrant ambition and women's lives at the heart of her magical tale of politics and revolution. I was utterly enchanted by this unique, clever, and subtly fierce fantasy."
—Tasha Suri, author of *The Jasmine Throne*

"Miller deftly weaves a thrilling tale of revolution and turmoil in a complex fantasy world."
—Cass Morris, author of *From Unseen Fire*

"Miller caps off the Unraveled Kingdom trilogy with a seamless blend of magic and heart, all under the cloud of war and revolution. Smart, thrilling, and full of charm, *Rule* is the perfect sendoff for the tale of Sophie Balstrade."
—Mike Chen, author of *Here and Now and Then*

"A delight, woven through with rich detail. Magic, sewing, and an achingly good romance—what's not to love? A deeply satisfying read. I'm dying for the next one!"
—Alexandra Rowland, author of *A Conspiracy of Truths*

"One of the best novels I've read this year! *Torn* is masterfully written—full of fascinating politics and compelling characters in a vividly rendered, troubled city. Sophie is a believable, layered, and wonderful heroine; her journey from ordinary to extraordinary is a joy to read. I absolutely loved this book!"
—Sarah Beth Durst, author of *The Bone Maker*

By Rowenna Miller

The Fairy Bargains of Prospect Hill

THE UNRAVELED KINGDOM

Torn

Fray

Rule

THE FAIRY BARGAINS OF PROSPECT HILL

ROWENNA MILLER

REDHOOK

Copyright © 2023 by Rowenna Miller
Excerpt from *The Magician's Daughter* copyright © 2023 by H. G. Parry

Cover design by Lisa Marie Pompilio
Cover illustration by Arcangel and Shutterstock
Cover copyright © 2023 by Hachette Book Group, Inc.
Author photograph by Emily R. Allison

Redhook Books/Orbit
Hachette Book Group
1290 Avenue of the Americas
New York, NY 10104
hachettebookgroup.com

First Edition: March 2023

Redhook is an imprint of Orbit, a division of Hachette Book Group.
The Redhook name and logo are trademarks of Hachette Book Group, Inc.

The publisher is not responsible for websites (or their content) that are not owned by the publisher.

The Hachette Speakers Bureau provides a wide range of authors for speaking events. To find out more, go to hachettespeakersbureau.com or email HachetteSpeakers@hbgusa.com.

Orbit books may be purchased in bulk for business, educational, or promotional use. For information, please contact your local bookseller or the Hachette Book Group Special Markets Department at special.markets@hbgusa.com.

Library of Congress Cataloging-in-Publication Data
Names: Miller, Rowenna, author.
Title: The fairy bargains of Prospect Hill / Rowenna Miller.
Description: First edition. | New York : Redhook, 2023.
Identifiers: LCCN 2022032675 | ISBN 9780316378475 (trade paperback) |
ISBN 9780316378574 (ebook)
Subjects: LCGFT: Novels.
Classification: LCC PS3613.I55275 F35 2023 |
DDC 813/.6—dc23/eng/20220711
LC record available at https://lccn.loc.gov/2022032675

ISBNs: 9780316378475 (trade paperback), 9780316378574 (ebook)

Printed in the United States of America

LSC-C

Printing 1, 2022

For Heidi,
who went on ahead,
and for Jenna and Erica,
who stayed behind for now.

1

Where flowers bloom unfading
And leaves are ever green
Fortune's winds are shifting
By fairy touch unseen
                    —Folk song

WHEN THE MADISON Railroad laid the tracks at the base of Prospect Hill, there were no roads cleaving the thickly forested slopes and no houses overlooking the distant river. A few farmsteads were nestled into the beech woods on the other side of the crest, out of view of the rail workers driving spikes through oak ties into untouched clay. Horatio Canner was one of those rail workers, and when he looked up into the tapestry of boughs, he thought it was the most beautiful place he'd ever seen.

He took his lunch breaks at the edge of the clearing for the railway, shorn saplings and ragged trunks of great oaks and walnuts crowding the space where sunlight ended and the shade of the forest began. Horatio sat on a walnut stump, feeling a bit like a trespasser. And then he heard a soft rustle and saw a shimmer of light in the shadows of the branches.

A girl. Not a girl, exactly, he amended, as he stood hastily and swept his hat off his close-cropped hair. A young woman, hovering on the edge of adolescence, eyes wide and thin lips parted to speak. Instead she turned and slipped between the trunks. After a moment's

hesitation, he followed. It seemed almost as though she led him on purpose, slowing when he lost the pale form of her white dress through the trees, hastening again when he came too close, until she stopped beneath a linden tree in full blossom.

Horatio Canner was not a country boy, or he might have paused to wonder why a linden tree was blooming in the first fits of spring warmth. He had been born out east, and had never pressed into the thick forests and still-wild places beyond the mountain ranges until he took work with the railroads. He could be forgiven, then, too, for assuming that the plain white dress the girl had on was what country folk wore, so unlike any fashion he'd seen back home or in the out-lying towns along the river as the steamboat chugged past. Horatio Canner didn't consider any of these things as the girl met his eyes, held out her hand, and finally spoke.

"What do you offer, and what do you ask?"

Horatio blinked. "I reckon I—that is, I don't quite know what you mean," he said.

She cocked her head. Her neck was as slender as a swan's, Horatio thought, and the plain dress skimmed a figure that could have been one of the saplings circling the tree. "You followed me to the gate, but you don't mean to ask for anything? Well." Her smile was sharp and tight. "Perhaps, still, you've something to offer, and I could tell you what it's worth."

Horatio still didn't understand, but he dug into his pockets any-way. "I've got a bag of tobacco, and the pipe for it," he began, and she winced and pulled away. It stood to figure a young lady wouldn't be interested in smoking, he chided himself. "And this kerchief." He dug out the red printed cotton and held it out.

Her eyes shone. "You'd part with it, then?"

"I suppose." He took a step closer, but she held up a hand.

"It's dear enough," she murmured, eyes still on it. "A true red." She scanned him up and down, and he felt read for the simple man he was. "If you could ask for anything, what would you want?"

"A parcel of Prospect Hill, I suppose," he said with a laugh. "Fifty acres. I've the will to tend it."

She plucked the kerchief from his hand. In her pale fingers it looked somehow more real, more solid. "A most unorthodox transaction," she said, amused. "But as you will."

The girl stepped into the tree and disappeared, leaving Horatio Canner gaping at nothing.

"And that is how Orchard Crest came into our family," Papa Horatio finished with a flourish, tipping back his coupe of sparkling wine made with the grapes from the north slope.

"I didn't realize I was marrying into a fairy-favored family until we'd said the vows," Jack Fairborn said with a wink at his wife.

"You ought to have guessed," Alaine replied, playfully swatting his arm. "After all, how do you think you managed to end up on my dance card for the waltz every ball of the season the year we got engaged?"

Alaine Fairborn had heard the story of her grandfather's encounter with the Fae a hundred times if she'd heard it once. He'd never seen the pale woman again, and no one else in the family had ever seen one of the Fae. Still, the fairy-woman kept her end of the bargain. Within two months, he bought a farmstead at the crest of Prospect Hill for a song, the seller shaving fifty acres off a sprawling tract of land to pay off a gambling debt. It was a stroke of luck of a magnitude Horatio had never had before and hadn't had since.

The other story she'd heard a hundred times if once was how a disoriented Horatio, wandering away from the blooming linden tree between the Fae and human worlds, had stumbled upon the Riley family farmstead and met a plump, tanned, very human girl feeding a flock of ruddy chickens. Gran had always laughed at this when she told her side of the story, that she knew that her husband had perfection on his mind from that Fae woman and she could never live up to it. And then Papa Horatio would flush red and protest that Lilabeth was the loveliest woman in the world, in any world, and that he'd never been happier than their wedding day.

"That's enough, Papa," Alaine's mother said with a sigh, swiping

his glass before he could refill it. "You have to leave us a few bottles for the wedding. I've been wearing my fingers to the bone for two weeks, getting the garden ready. I won't have a last-minute wine shortage to account for, too."

"Having it in the garden—I never heard of such a thing. Me and Lilabeth got married in the church, proper," Papa Horatio said with a sly twinkle in his eyes. "And so did you and my son, Iris. And now my granddaughter gets married in the garden?"

"It's fashionable to be married at home!" Delphine protested. "Besides, is there anyplace in the world I love better than Orchard Crest?"

"Hardly," Papa Horatio said. "But it doesn't rain inside the church."

"It won't rain," Del replied. "Alaine will see to that."

"She paid the best attention to Lilabeth," he agreed. "Still, no guarantee like a roof over your head."

"When will the Graftons be here on Saturday?" Mother asked for the fifteenth time.

"At eight o'clock in the morning," Delphine replied. "And the ladies in the wedding party can get ready in my room, and the fellows in the study."

"Is Emily allowed in with you?" Alaine asked. "She's talked of nothing but her flower girl dress since last week."

"Of course!" Delphine said, a genuine smile breaking the tension in her jaw. "She's my best niece."

"Only niece," Mother corrected.

"So she's clearly the best." Delphine grinned. "The judge will be here at ten so we can begin by eleven. And then luncheon at noon."

"Judge!" Papa Horatio shook his head. "The Graftons have some pull, getting the damn judge to officiate."

"You might forget that we have some pull now, too, Papa." Mother stood, her silk taffeta skirt rustling as though punctuating her point.

"*Some* pull," he said. "Hardly Grafton pull. Oh, Alaine, I keep getting mail delivered up here for the farm—something came from the bank." He rifled in his jacket pocket and produced a rumpled envelope.

"The bank!" Mother chided. "That's hardly after-dinner talk."

"Is this the Waldorf-Astoria? Are we at a formal dinner party? Have we had the sorbet course already? Here I thought I was in my own dining room, Iris." Papa Horatio laughed. "I'm sure it's nothing to worry over, but—"

"But I'll worry about it if it is," Alaine said, taking the papers. She traced the sealed envelope fretfully. Probably another notice. "We should go soon." Alaine laid a hand on Jack's in a silent signal. No letting Papa Horatio draw them into one more story, no letting Mother finagle Jack into looking at a leaky pipe in the kitchen. His glance went from her hand to the envelope in her lap. He gave her a barely perceptible nod, understanding. "It's almost past Em's bedtime as it is."

"Is she still out in the garden?" Delphine turned to look out the bay window, lithe neck encased in a high collar of lace. Alaine could have been jealous of her sister's fashionable gown and the filmy white lace if it hadn't looked so mercilessly scratchy at the seams. She smoothed her own practical wool skirt, the plum color hiding several jam stains.

"She would spend the night there if we let her," Alaine said. "But not tonight."

"Not any night!" Mother said, appalled until she realized that Alaine was joking—at least, mostly. Mother had always reined in Alaine's penchant for the woods and wilds, trying to teach her flower arranging and piano and, one disastrous summer, watercolors. Alaine took the opposite tack with Em, indulging her preference for an open afternoon of exploring the forest, tattered hems and muddy shoes notwithstanding.

Alaine followed Delphine's gaze out the window. Emily was hanging upside down from the low-hanging branches of a crab apple. Delphine fought back a grin. "I'll call her in."

Alaine watched her sister go with an odd tightness in her throat—even crossing the family dining room of Orchard Crest, where they'd eaten thousands of breakfasts and dinners, played thousands of games of checkers in the hollow of the bay window, spent thousands of afternoons reading in its long swaths of sunlight, Del was graceful.

Alaine's little sister wasn't just grown up—she was an accomplished lady who had mastered all the genteel arts their mother had tried to impart on them. Flower arranging, piano, and especially watercolors. Alaine had long ago stopped begrudging her that.

Delphine brought Emily in by the hand, the six-year-old's face beaming with admiration for her aunt. She had once told Alaine that Aunt Del must be a princess. Alaine had very little argument to the contrary.

"Time to go, love. Say good night to Grandmother and Papa Horatio."

Jack and Alaine let Em skip in front of them on the dirt road that wound through the orchard on one side and the woods on the other, linking Orchard Crest to their cottage, tucked away near the back ridge of the hill. Papa Horatio and Grandma Lilabeth had built a small cabin on their fifty acres when they were first married, a rustic square of hewn logs and mortar. It still stood where the trees thinned near the ridge, but even Alaine, with her staunch loyalty to every piece of the family farm's history and especially anything Papa Horatio had made, had to admit it was cramped and dark. When the orchard had made its first profits, Papa Horatio built the house facing Prospect Hill and named it Orchard Crest. He raised a family there, and Alaine and Del had grown up there, too.

When Papa Horatio had offered the strip of land along the ridge to her and Jack, she knew she could never tear down the cabin, but they had built nearby, a lavender Queen Anne with white gingerbread trim and windows tucked into sloping eaves that, as they approached from the lane, even now gleamed with the lamps inside.

If she was honest with herself, Alaine had always assumed that Delphine would do the same when she was married—take the offer of a parcel of land, build a cottage as fashionable and pretty as she was, and keep the little world that was Orchard Crest spinning along as it always had. Then Pierce Grafton had come along and knocked the perfect balance off-kilter. Alaine wasn't sure how to right it again, how to imagine the family farm without part of her family.

"You're thinking deep thoughts," Jack teased softly as they rounded the curve in the road and Emily ran ahead to catch up with the chickens foraging in a tangle of blooming multiflora rose.

She snorted. "Hardly." She held back a sigh, and it stuck in her throat, tight and painful. "No, the opposite. I was thinking about the wedding and—well, I suppose anything I could say sounds petty or childish."

"What? Don't you like Pierce Grafton?" Jack's blue eyes pinched at the corners, half laughing but not entirely.

"Oh, it's not that." Alaine caught herself. "Not that I *don't* like him, of course." It was an open secret between her and Jack that she didn't care for the Perrysburg glass magnate, with his impeccable manners and his thin moustache and his bellowing laugh, but she still never said it out loud. "It's that she's going away. Doesn't that sound silly? Like something Em would say."

She pushed back a sudden urge to cry, the feeling gumming up the back of her throat.

"I don't think it's silly at all." Jack caught Alaine's hand and slowed their pace, turning to face her as they stopped. "You've both lived at Orchard Crest your whole lives. I thought you must have some sort of secret sisterhood blood pact to never leave," he teased lightly, but the furrow between his eyes deepened. He sensed her fears, her griefs, even if she hadn't articulated them.

"Maybe we should have." Not, Alaine thought with a flush of anger, that Delphine wouldn't have broken it anyway. For Pierce Grafton, for the new house in Perrysburg's best neighborhood, for the chance to be the wife of the sort of person who had season tickets to the opera and invited the mayor for dinner parties. Alaine felt her ears getting hot, and she clamped down on her runaway thoughts, shamed by her selfishness. There was nothing wrong with Delphine wanting any of that, she reminded herself, even if Alaine couldn't see why. But she couldn't shake a feeling that, somehow, Delphine was turning her back on something more important than both of them. Especially now, with the bank sending notices every other week.

Jack squeezed her hand. "It's only Perrysburg. Hardly anything

on the train. Maybe we'll get you one of those electric motorcars that so many ladies seem to favor."

"I don't want an electric motorcar, thank you very much." Alaine sighed. "Del's really leaving the farm," she added in a whisper.

Alaine stopped herself, but she knew what she meant, at its core—that she had thought the farm was as important to Delphine as it was to her. That, just like her, Delphine felt the rhythm of the orchard pulsing in her blood, that she would do anything for the fifty acres on the slopes of Prospect Hill. And now Delphine was leaving, without a glance behind her. Alaine felt the sting of deep betrayal.

Jack settled an arm around her shoulders and pulled her closer. "It's a hard change for us. We're used to Delphine at dinner and Delphine helping in the orchard on harvest days and Delphine's jam thumbprint cookies for teatime."

"And now someone else gets to have Delphine at dinner, and Delphine's tea cookies," Alaine said, fully aware that she sounded petulant, but unable to tell even Jack what she really thought. "But one thing is sure—Delphine is still going to help at harvest."

"Was that the blood pact?"

"No, but try keeping her away." Alaine smiled, pretending for the moment that she believed Delphine would come back for the autumn harvest. "Listen," she said, reining in the tremor in her voice, "I've got one more thing to do before we turn in. There's the election tomorrow for the Agricultural Society to think of."

Jack grinned. "First woman to run in the county."

"In the lower half of the whole state," Alaine retorted. "Howard Olson is running the organization into the ground, and Acton Willis right along with him. The two of them are businessmen, not farmers—preying on farmers, more like."

Though Olson managed a granary and Willis owned a transport company that catered to farmers, they weren't truly integrated into the community. And, after last year's dismal harvests and Olson's lukewarm response, it was clear that the Agricultural Society needed better leadership. When Alaine looked around the stuffy fellowship hall of the Free Methodist Church and didn't see anyone else raising their hand, she couldn't stop herself. Someone had to push the Society out of the slump Olson had driven it into, and if no one else would volunteer, she'd be damned if she'd sit idly by.

"It did have to come right at the same time as the wedding," Jack joked. "I'm sure Olson is running the old campaign wagon around town, and you're tied to the house, making macaroons for the reception."

Alaine laughed, but she tasted bitterness in the joke. Her sister's wedding was a trump card over her plans. The oncoming cherry harvest, the bank's demands on the mortgage, the health of the Agricultural Society—these were more important than the cake or the flowers or the dress for the wedding, but Alaine found her attention dragged time and again back to this one day, this pretty picture Delphine was painting. She didn't want to resent Delphine, but there were other things in her life to tend to.

"I think I still have a good shot at it. Olson sunk himself raising prices at the granary in the middle of the worst harvest we've had in a decade." She raised a conspiratorial eyebrow. "Besides, I've got another plan."

"A bargain." Jack's mouth pursed, the way it always did when he was thinking. Usually when it pinched shut, it was over a legal contract or a political editorial in the paper, and Alaine knew he had a thesis-length torrent of thoughts percolating on the subject. "I don't recall one for local elections."

"It's not for elections, specifically. Lands, imagine if it worked that way, picking a side to win!" Terrifying, actually—thank goodness bargains didn't work like that, or the political parties would have commandeered them long ago. "It's just an extra pinch of good luck. It may or may not work—I haven't tried it before." Her hand hesitated over her pocket, grazing the black soutache trim along the opening. "I'll only be a moment."

Jack gave her a curious look, but didn't press. Unlike most Prospect Hill newcomers, he didn't tease her about bargains or question their efficacy—he'd seen enough for himself. But he considered them her domain, just as much as she considered the law firm where he was primed to make junior partner his territory. Respected, but foreign.

She fished out a length of scarlet ribbon and another of white weighty silk pooling like liquid in her palm. She threaded both through a pair of silver rings so that when she spun the rings the ribbon alternated white and red, red and white. A bargain for change, for switches, for reshuffling the cards. As Gran had said, it would take the first and make him last, and the last, first—and more efficiently than the preacher at their white clapboard church ever had.

Alaine stopped at the garden gate, hanging the ribbon and rings in a loop over the latch. Then she slipped a paper copy of the ballot into the latch, too, the Agricultural Society seal partially hidden by the silk ribbons.

"Silk and silver," she whispered, remembering the words Gran had taught her, though she'd never used them, "chance and curse, favored and spurned, now reverse."

Alaine left the bargain wedged in the creaky latch of the garden gate. It was a less clear-cut bargain than she'd employed before—it didn't ask specifically for no rain or an averted snowstorm or more eggs in the chicken coop, but something intangible, applying a bit of reversed luck to her particular circumstance. She hoped her meaning was clear enough. Gran had instilled in her a healthy distrust of Fae logic, warning her that they'd use a bargain to their own ends whenever they could. Still, this was one of Gran's bargains, tested and safe. She let the gate swing closed behind her.

2

Coin in the door for a visitor welcome
Bit of old leather for a welcome farewell
—Traditional bargain

"HAND ME ANOTHER rose—no, not the white, the pink," Mother said, the color rising in her cheeks and her voice clipped. Delphine stripped the thorns from another pink rose and handed it to her mother. She assessed the vase of flowers silently, eyeing the flush of color from deep pink to pale. It needed more white to balance the colors, but it wasn't worth arguing. She probably, Delphine thought with a smile, wanted to highlight the fussy centifolias that were the pride of her garden.

"There we are. Another vase, and we'll have the flowers quite settled." Mother smiled, painting over the nerves Delphine knew she harbored about the wedding. Delphine didn't demand perfection from her wedding day, but Mother did. She didn't remember her being this fractious over Alaine's wedding, but then again, Alaine hadn't married into one of the richest families in the county.

The Perrysburg society pages didn't write it up when Alaine Canner married Jack Fairborn, just another boy from another Prospect Hill family, and not even an old family at that. A respectable family, a well-liked family—but not the family that owned the largest glass factory in the state like the Graftons.

And, Delphine allowed, Alaine wasn't her mother's baby. It wasn't that Mother didn't love both of her daughters, but while Alaine had tagged after Father and Papa Horatio in the orchard and copied every one of Grandma Lilabeth's charms, Delphine had taken to her mother's tutelage, soaking up all the beautiful things she knew how to do. It was clear, early, that there would be no boy to take over the family farm, so Alaine willingly filled the role, one replete with torn skirt hems and muddy stockings. Delphine lingered closer to home—and closer to Mother.

"Now, I'm going to clean this up. You should freshen up before Pierce arrives." Mother swept loose leaves and clipped stems into her hand. Delphine picked up the dustpan to help and promptly gouged her hand with a stripped thorn. "Oh, dear! Don't go bleeding on your dress! You needn't bother with this—I can do it." Delphine let Mother shoo her out of the kitchen, dabbing the blood from her thumb with her apron.

She caught her reflection in the hall mirror and smoothed a few loose hairs. In only four more days, she would be Mrs. Pierce Grafton. The thought sent a shiver running though her limbs, right down to her bleeding thumb.

Marrying Pierce Grafton. She could never have imagined it when she'd first been introduced on a visit with her friend Mary Porter. He'd swept like the west wind into the parlor, upsetting everything she'd assumed about herself with his generous smile and his expansive presence. He was outside her sphere then, a wealthy man from a wealthy family in a city she visited only sparingly—and yet by luck contrived from fairy bargains and some inscrutable magic of the universe, here they were. Delphine still couldn't quite believe her good fortune, that a man like Pierce Grafton could want to marry a farm girl like her.

And wrapped entirely with marrying Pierce, another desire, to move to Perrysburg, to stretch and reach and taste and see more than Moore's Ferry could offer. She loved Prospect Hill and Orchard Crest nestled into its ridges, but she had memorized it like a piece of piano music, its details practiced until her fingers knew the positions on the keys by rote and she didn't have to think. Perrysburg was like a stack of new sonatas and concertos ready to be studied. And perhaps she could find more purpose there than Moore's Ferry and even her family home could offer. If Alaine was the queen of the orchard, Mother was chatelaine of the estate, and Delphine was left the bored spinster in a tower.

That would change in Perrysburg. She would have a place there, and a role that she could excel at. There would be charitable societies to helm, art exhibitions and music series to sponsor, the game of local politics to play—and the not insubstantial job of managing her husband's social calendar and home. Pierce had built a new house for them, the height of style in the most fashionable neighborhood, three stories of limestone with nods to the new "Prairie School" of architecture. Pierce had hesitated over that, unsure if it was too daring or too modish, as Delphine had showed him photographs and sketches, but the resulting symmetry of pillars and piazzas and windows was striking yet still classic. Now he beamed when he showed it to friends, complimenting his fiancée's good taste and keen eye. They would host dinners in the expansive dining room, teas in the parlor, parties on the piazza. She could imagine carriages and automobiles lining up beneath the porte cochere and laughter wafting from the gardens.

A new life, her life, that she would build. But it meant leaving Orchard Crest behind.

It would have been easy to fall into dime novel dramatics over it, imagining that she hated farm life, that she was desperate to escape a horrible fate, but the truth was, she loved her family and her home. Still, as much as she would miss quiet winter evenings in the parlor and languid summer afternoons in the garden, she wanted more than Prospect Hill, craved it like cool water on a hot day. It was why she spent so much time on watercolors and sketching; she could explore something more, express something new. She had never been content with the rhythm of farm life, the repetitive tasks in an endless cycle, looping year after year.

Her sister loved it. She always had. She loved the feel of dirt on her hands, the confidence of knowing what chore came next and exactly how to execute it. Alaine could see the harvest in the spring bloom and calculate how many barrels of cider were ripening on the trees. Delphine's interest in the orchard ran in contrary currents.

Watching the trees bloom in a riot of pink clouds in spring, the red-gold sunrise in the skin of an apple, the shadows mingling on the moss, the moments of novelty and beauty hidden in the repetition—this was the orchard that captured Delphine. She tried to catch its movement in sketches and coax its colors into painted landscapes. And she knew, intuited it from the quietest, deepest part of herself, that there was more of that novelty and beauty waiting to be discovered. Waiting for her.

In any case, even if she had wanted to stay on Prospect Hill, there wasn't any room for her. Not really, despite Alaine's hopeful nods to running the orchard together. There could be no equanimity, no real partnership with Alaine, through no fault of her sister's or her own. Alaine not only breathed and bled the orchard, she covered it, enveloped it, her ambition and surefooted strategies overtaking even the need for Papa Horatio's oversight. But while Papa Horatio could slide into an easy retirement, the country sage in the rocking chair, there was no room for Delphine except in her sister's shadow.

A knock at the door startled her, and she quickly stripped her apron and balled it into the umbrella stand in the foyer as she swung the door wide.

"Delphine, you look lovely! My sister was a wreck the whole month before her wedding, but here you are, looking as fresh as a daisy." Pierce planted a chaste kiss on her cheek. She closed her eyes, briefly, inhaling cologne water and relishing the fleeting touch of his fresh-shaven cheek. His gray eyes, set deep under studious brows, caught hers as he pulled away, and she tamped down the sudden heady nerves that still accompanied his every touch.

"Mother has things well in hand." She ushered Pierce into the parlor, the afternoon sunlight spilling in from the bay window. Orchard Crest may not have been as fine a home as the Grafton mansion in Perrysburg, but the light—the light was incomparable.

"I've brought the last of my things for the wedding—those shoes needed a good polish. Now. Are we quite alone?" He dropped his voice and leaned toward her, brushing her lips with his. The sudden intimacy made Delphine flush warm. It strained against propriety, but she leaned into his neatly pressed suit and felt the steady rise and fall of his chest under her hand as he kissed her.

He brought out a bold desire in her, had ever since the first time she had met him on that trip with Mary. He was the center of every room, the dominant voice in every debate, a commanding presence that left Delphine speechless, but he made room for her. He softened his voice to ask her thoughts, he left the orbiting crowd and sought her out. He was important, and his mere attention made her feel important, too.

"I brought something for you, too." He pulled a folded bit of newsprint from his jacket pocket. "There's an art studio opening downtown that's going to offer lessons. I thought you might enjoy that—you seem to like painting here at Orchard Crest."

Delphine took the advertisement, torn from the *Perrysburg Gazette*, a grainy image of a spacious loft full of windows and bold type promising expert instruction to students of all ages. "I think I would," she said slowly. "I've never done much but watercolors, but I'd love to try oils someday."

"My mother says a young lady needs a hobby or two. Even after children come along, to give her something to talk about with the other ladies at parties." He laughed, the expansive bellow filling the parlor. She loved how it took over a room, how his jovial mood could enliven even the dourest of parties. "I'll look up the particulars after the move."

"The move—is the furniture all in?"

"Quite nearly. The dining room set is still on the way from Chicago, but we shan't really need it right away, do you think?"

Delphine shook her head. There was a breakfast room upstairs, already outfitted with a fine maple table and chairs, small and comfortably intimate for lunches and suppers, just the two of them, for the first few weeks. "I can't imagine wanting to host a dinner party until well after the honeymoon."

"My father wants us to host the board before fall. I think he sees it as a sort of a signal that I'm taking over as executive officer." Pierce grew somber, his gray eyes narrowing, almost troubled. "Can't disappoint the old man, can we?"

Delphine rushed to reassure him. "Late summer shouldn't be any trouble. We'll be well established by then, won't we?" She smiled, and Pierce's cheerful demeanor returned. "And plenty of time to get settled after getting back from our trip."

"About the honeymoon—I know we'd planned on Chicago and I'd ordered theater tickets already, but I've got a bit of business I need to manage for the glassworks." Delphine tried to keep her face neutral to erase any sign of disappointment. When they'd first become engaged, Pierce had suggested first a tour of the continent for their honeymoon bookended by voyages on a luxury liner, then a train trip to the West Coast, then a trip to Niagara Falls and New York City, his plans drawing ever more abbreviated and closer to home before settling on a week in Chicago. "Father wants me to take care of it, as the new face of the business, you know. There's a copperworks in Kentucky that wants to partner with us to— Well, I needn't bore you with the details."

"I see," Delphine said, measured. She swallowed. "It's important to—"

"Now, I'm not giving up on the idea of a honeymoon completely. There's French Lick down in the hills near the Ohio River—one of those places folks go to take the waters, you know?" Delphine nodded. "I could arrange to meet them there, and we could spend the rest of the week as we please." He hesitated, catching her hand in his. He pressed on the fresh cut on her thumb, and she bit back a wince. "It could be nice, I think, not having to travel as far?"

He watched her, waiting, she could tell, for reassurance that she wasn't disappointed despite the hard edges of his family's and the glassworks' expectations already wedging themselves into their lives. He was making the best of the situation, Delphine told herself, and she couldn't fault him, though she wondered how his father could even suggest he abandon his honeymoon to tend to brokering a new deal for the glassworks. There were plenty of others who could have handled it—but no, it must be very important for Pierce, for his career. This was part of her new life. Her husband's career would come first.

She pasted on a smile. "Of course! It sounds like a lovely place."

"And first, a wedding." He leaned forward, clapping his hands on his knees as though he had just closed a business deal, any unpleasantness of negotiation or disappointment now in the past. "Mother is quite worried about rain, suggested we rent a pavilion of some kind when I told her it was too late to move the wedding indoors. She's still miffed we didn't hold it in Perrysburg—I think she wanted to show off their renovated ballroom." Delphine began to apologize, but Pierce stopped her. "No, no—I told her that the bride and her family get to make the decisions about the wedding, and that's all there is to it. Goodness knows she orchestrated everything about Stella's wedding. But..." He hesitated. "What about rain, Del? Your folks' place isn't big enough to hold that many people."

"It won't rain," she said confidently, even though she knew Pierce didn't—couldn't—share her conviction. The veil was thin on Prospect Hill—it allowed bargaining that wasn't possible in Perrysburg, or even in most of Moore's Ferry, for that matter. How to explain it to an outsider, she asked herself for the hundredth time if the first? That it was so simple, that she and Alaine would put a charm in the garden gate, and that was all there was to it? It wasn't mechanics and it wasn't science, but it was a bit like business—a transaction with the Fae, well established. But she found that, under the scrutiny of his earnest, intelligent gray eyes, she couldn't explain it. "I promise. Papa Horatio knows the weather patterns around here inside and out, and he says it won't rain," she said instead.

"If you say so," said Pierce, unconvinced. "I suppose if worse comes to worst, we'll all cram into the parlor, by hook or by crook. Now, how about some tea?"

Mother would be hovering in the kitchen, waiting to put the kettle on, so Delphine agreed quickly, pushing down a vague annoyance with herself that she couldn't acknowledge fairy bargains with her future husband.

3

A coin given to the Fae is ten saved on misfortune.
                                                    —Folk saying

"WELL," JACK SAID as he dried the last of the supper dishes. "Are you going to open that letter Papa Horatio gave you two days ago, or are you going to leave it in the desk, hoping it grows feet and runs off?"

"I prefer the latter," Alaine replied, letting the weak joke cover her fears. She hung up her apron and rifled through the desk drawer where she had stashed the envelope. Between the wedding preparations and the elections at the Agricultural Society meeting, she had managed to pretend the letter didn't exist, even as it nagged the perimeters of her thoughts. Even when Maisie Freeman tallied and reported the results of the election, Alaine winning by a wide margin over Howard Olson, and as the fellowship hall of the Free Methodist Church erupted in applause for her, she pasted a congenial smile over the simmering anxiety. She was quietly thrilled to discover that the unusually ambiguous bargain Gran had passed on had worked—or did the Society just really want to oust Olson? But even these victories were dampened by the presence of that damn letter in the rolltop desk. After all, what kind of Agricultural Society president would she be if they lost the farm—or even if they had to sell off part of it?

"I don't need to open it. I know what it is."

She pulled the papers from the already-wrinkled envelope and scanned. She trapped the letter in a closed hand, the Madison Bank and Trust seal visible between her thumb and forefinger, ink smudged under the heat of her hand.

"I can deal with it, if you'd rather," Jack offered kindly.

Alaine shook her head. While the rest of the family was occupied with Delphine's wedding, she knew she couldn't sour the celebration by bringing up overdue mortgage payments and fears over the cherry harvest. Still, every time Mother spent an hour going over the menu for the umpteenth time or fussed over the hem of Emily's dress, Alaine buried a bit more frustration. It only served to remind her that the orchard was her responsibility, and hers alone.

"The money is still on the trees, Jack. We won't have it until harvest—but the apples will cover almost a year of payments on their own."

"A mortgage is a mortgage." Jack took a few steps toward her, then stopped as she shot him a stony glare. He pressed his lips together, the familiar comfort of legalese centering him. "Technically, we are in default. Even if we did manage to make payments on time until the last one."

He was right, of course. How he could parse it out in simple, legal terms, not shot through with a torrent of emotions, she could never understand. Alaine bit her lip before she could say anything. Jack didn't deserve the tongue-lashing she wanted to dole out to someone, anyone.

The money wasn't there. They'd scraped together what they could from Jack's earnings and Mother's savings, but the farm itself was taking greater losses than either of those sources could sustain. Last year's harvest had been bad—bad for everyone in the state, and all the fairy bargains in the world couldn't change a cold spring and a summer drought. The Agricultural Society had been a flurry of emergency meetings and fund drives and pitching in to help one another with harvests so they wouldn't have to hire more workers with money they didn't have. Alaine had pitched that idea—a labor share—and it had saved, she was assured, more than one farm from going into default already.

She had tied their hopes to this year's cherries, but spring had been slow and cold despite successful bargains against late snow-storms. The harvest might be smaller, after too many freezes and thaws through the spring, but Alaine was more concerned that the trees might just drop the unripe fruit altogether—and with it, their mortgage payments—left to rot under the branches.

"I know the apples will have a good year, I just know it," Alaine whispered, heavy desperation flattening her voice. "We'll pay. The money is there—it's just not ripe yet."

"I know that, and you know that, but the law is on the bank's side." Jack sighed. "We could sell off some equipment, maybe, or think about selling off a few acres—"

Alaine flared, heat spreading across her cheeks and fingernails digging into sweating palms. "No. I'm not selling any of Orchard Crest. None of it."

The farm with its orderly rows of trees and grapevines was more than her home; it was her life. Its past was her past, its future was her future. To her, everything about the orchard fit together, seam-lessly, all its intersections of seasons and income and soil and sun and industry. She had learned the whole of it at Papa Horatio's elbow, year after year, season after season, his tutelage affirming a birthright. The thought of someone else pruning her trees or harvesting her grapes pinched her stomach so tightly she thought she might be sick.

Jack hesitated. "I suppose you're right. Besides, we can't sell if we have a lien against the place."

"Optimism, that's what I like about you, Jack Fairborn." Alaine exhaled through her nose, pinched and grudging. "The cherries have to bring in enough money. That's all there is to it." She tapped the paper, eliciting a hollow rattle. "Or we could lose the farm."

"I wish I could do more to handle this, but—"

"Why in the world should you handle it? I know the bank would rather talk to a man, but no. No, the farm is mine." She had planted, pruned, bargained, and bled for those trees, and she would find a way to save the orchard. Alaine pressed her lips together, letting the bank's unyielding seal stare back at her from the paper. She swallowed and remembered she was talking to Jack, not the Madison Bank and Trust.

Jack pulled the paper away from Alaine's stiff fingers, folding it into thirds. "You're right. I know the law, but not the farm—feels like a law degree is a damn waste anywhere but my office."

"Hardly. You've gotten us out of more than one bad contract." Alaine didn't add that she'd known they were bad without the law degree, just by knowing labor and transport and sales. But Jack knew how to ply the language itself to work in their favor. She chewed on her lip. Between the two of them, they had to be able to come up with some solution.

"Maybe we sell Barnaby," Jack said softly. "The Overmayer brothers were asking after him, they need a draft horse for the new ice wagon. They're good folks, I trust them with livestock."

"Jack Fairborn!" Alaine shot up like a spark roused from a smoldering fire, then dropped her voice, remembering Emily asleep in her room. "Absolutely not. Not my Percherons, we won't. Barnaby and Bruno are a team. They're a matched pair. No one but a right fool would split them up—" She leveled her voice as Jack's expression grew stony. "I'm sorry, I don't mean that you're a fool—I can't believe the Overmayers would suggest it, they know horses too well. But either way, the real point is, we need them. Both of them, if we want to get the harvest off the trees and into market."

"There really isn't anything left to sell." Jack's voice slipped to a whisper. "I could ask my parents for a loan. Or Esther."

"Your sister and Fred don't have the money," Alaine countered, ignoring the idea of asking anything from her in-laws. Jack's parents had some money, but not much, and Esther and Fred were only just married, with barely any savings. No, this was her problem, not her in-laws'. She'd find a way to solve it without dragging anyone else into it.

"Alaine..." Jack hesitated. "I know none of the options are good. But you have to consider either letting something go or asking for help. It's only going to get more complicated." Jack pinched his lips together, a look Alaine knew meant he was trying to say something diplomatically and would likely fail. "I've been thinking. With the wedding—and the orchard shares—well, Pierce is technically going to be part owner, too. What with Del having a share."

"That's how Father set it up in his will," Alaine replied, defensive pride in her father flaring. "And how else would it be divided? Mother deserves her widow's portion, and it's not as though Father was going to play favorites between me and Del."

Jack ran a hand through his hair. It was beginning to silver at the temples, just slightly, which Alaine thought suited him. "That's not what I meant— It's that Pierce is a businessman. I don't know what kinds of designs he has on this place, on its operations and productivity. You know how the glassworks runs—all modern, highest efficiency."

"At the expense of anything else, yes, I do." She'd read the editorials in the papers chastising the Grafton Glassworks, among others, for failing to adopt shorter workdays and for lobbying against child labor laws. She didn't know how Pierce Grafton himself felt—he was only one of the Graftons, after all, and his father was head of operations. Besides, he'd never talked business with her, and she doubted he ever would.

Jack watched her carefully. "It's just that I don't know how much profit he wants to squeeze out of his shares. If this place is in default . . . he might be in mind to divest himself."

"Delphine would never—"

"Legally, he might be able to without her, once they're married."

"Well." Alaine thought quickly, around the growing pit in her stomach. Orchard Crest wasn't just a piece in an investment portfolio— it was home. She doubted Pierce saw it that way, and she was sure Jack was right when it came to the law. "Maybe he would be inclined to invest in the operations if he wants to see additional profit."

Jack paused. "That is an angle I hadn't considered." He smiled slowly. "Quite mercenary, here on the eve of your sister's wedding, assessing the leverage of your new alliance—"

Alaine laughed and slapped his arm. "Stop! I'm no robber baron!" She sobered quickly, reality chasing away the brief moment of levity.

"I won't fail the farm." She wouldn't let the orchard falter, even a little, on her watch—not selling land, not selling the horses, and certainly not being beholden to anyone on account of a loan. "The cherries will come ripe within the month, and then we'll have the money."

She could tell that Jack wanted to do more, to offer some comforting platitude or an arm around her shoulders, but she didn't want idle comfort. She wanted action, dirt under her nails, burning muscles that said she'd worked hard and solved a problem. Except this wasn't the sort of problem that elbow grease alone could fix. Lacking that, she could at least walk the rows of trees and reassure herself that they were upholding their end of the bargain just fine.

Bargains. She considered, for a moment, the usual bargains she'd already plied for the harvest, and the success of Gran's silk-and-silver change-of-fortune bargain. Perhaps there was something she could do, even if it was only making herself feel better. She rummaged in a drawer and then slipped out the kitchen door. She inhaled, chest still tight, as she passed from under the eaves of Lavender Cottage to the overhanging boughs of the forest. The cherry orchard lay just over the rise in the hill, but she couldn't bring herself to go inspect the fruit yet again. They would either come ripe or die off. Instead, she veered deeper into the forest, following a path she knew by heart even as the setting sun cast long shadows across it and the light faded pale and purple.

The linden tree. It stood unchanged since the first time Papa Horatio had seen it, all those years ago—unchanged, Alaine thought, for perhaps centuries. Always green, always blooming, even in the middle of winter. Now, at the cresting of summer, it almost blended into the deep green of the forest, except for the perfect circle of velvet green surrounding it. That, and the scent. Ebbing like a tide on the gentle breeze that stirred the linden's leaves, the perfume mingled the ordinary golden florals of linden bloom with strange notes of vanilla and cedar and incense.

Alaine inhaled, more deeply now than she could before, confidence buoyed by the familiar scent of the fairy ring. She dug into her pocket. A silver chain strung with mother-of-pearl buttons. The old bargain for a good harvest, laced with a sprig of the plant she hoped would thrive—cherry leaves, green and waxy. Gran had taught her to leave the bargains in a doorjamb or a window, a garden gate, even wedged into the barn latch, saying that the Fae liked doorways. But Alaine had seen bargains laid here, too, at the roots of the linden tree, other old Prospect Hill families coming right to the door of Fae itself.

Gran had scared her half to death when she was a child with stories of girls who wandered into Fae circles and never returned, or emerged from the woods decades later looking like feral things, or came home and seemed all right, at first, but then went slowly and surely mad. Even so, by the time Alaine was ten, she had discovered the linden tree with its verdant circle of never-fading grass. She was fascinated by the everblooming tree, by the otherworldly scent. Obeying her promise to Grandma Lilabeth, she'd never gone into the ring itself. Now she wondered if the bargains would be more certain, more powerful if she left them here in the fairy circle. Clearly others had done so. And, as far as she knew, no Prospect Hill families harbored cousins gone feral or driven mad from going inside the ring.

No time like the present to try it out.

She felt bolder, after trying the bargain for reversal of fortune and winning the election, less worried that there were shadows in the hidden corners of fairy bargains that she didn't know. She was a Prospect Hill girl, born and raised—she could wield bargains without worrying. Legal matters could stay Jack's domain, and God knew her mother and Delphine were more accomplished in the sphere of decorous femininity than she ever would be. The bargains didn't care if her hair was dressed in the latest fashion or if her skirt hem was crooked. She knew how to bargain, and bargains wouldn't fail her.

She pulled the chain from her pocket and let the silver hang over her fingers, the weight of the buttons sending it into a gentle sway. The buttons swung back and forth, and then, to her surprise, crept out of sync, setting themselves spinning in a circle that tugged, she was sure, toward the tree. She clenched her hand around them, her head beginning to spin, too. Taking a steadying breath, she stepped into the fairy ring.

Nothing happened; maybe the scent grew stronger or the breeze settled, but Alaine couldn't be sure. Everything felt gentle, still, but a strange unspent energy thrummed just under the surface. Alaine whispered the rhyme and nestled the chain and buttons into a mossy nook of the linden's roots as quickly as she could. Then she retreated back toward Lavender Cottage, gooseflesh prickling her arms as she turned her back on the tree.

4

*To prevent fire: Tie a nosegay of roses or other scented flowers with a
white ribband and hang inside the chimney.*
—The Compleat Book of Bargaining Works, by A Lady, 1767

DELPHINE FUSSED WITH the flowers in the parlor of Orchard
Crest, avoiding the mirror over the cold fireplace. She didn't want
to see how nerves had etched new furrows in her face. Tomorrow.
The wedding was tomorrow, and then everything would change.
She told herself she was ready.

"All ready?" Alaine leaned against the doorframe, the stained
walnut catching the last of the late-afternoon light.

Delphine forced a smile. She hadn't eaten more than a few bites of
anything all day, and what Mother had called the "jitters" swirled
her stomach to knots. "As ready as I can be. Everything's been checked
and checked again." Alaine returned her smile, but Delphine could
tell that something was wrong. "Did you forget something, or is
Mother fretting over the cake again?"

"No, nothing like that." Alaine drummed her fingers on the top
of the piano; the anxious staccato made Delphine wince. "I—I hate
to bring up business right before your wedding, but since you own a
third share of the orchard, too, I—"

"In name only, Alaine. I haven't the slightest idea how you run
it." She tried not to sound rude, but there was a bite to the words.

Delphine quashed the impulse to snap at her sister—she *should* hate to bring up business today of all days.

"Well, I just—there's a little trouble making payments on the mortgage. Jack's talking of selling Barnaby—I won't let that happen, but that's how difficult things are."

"I'm sure you'll do whatever you think is best." Delphine had always been on the periphery of the family business, both before and after Father died. She didn't have a good handle on the nuances of the work, the finely tuned schedules and minute adaptations Alaine deployed on the orchard's rows of trees. Now she was leaving, as clear a signal as any that the orchard was solely her sister's domain.

"I didn't realize, at first, how delicate the money situation was," Alaine said as she perched on the arm of the settee next to Delphine. No shaking her now. Delphine sighed, then nodded, encouraging her sister to continue. "The banking crisis back in the nineties did a number on the farm, and between the two of them, Father and Papa Horatio kept us afloat. But it's still eating us."

Despite herself, Delphine was a little intrigued. "What do you mean?"

"We had taken out loans—completely normal, of course!—to expand back in the late eighties. But after the Panic hit in ninety-three, our rates shot up, and we're still a bit behind. Father never told us just how much we owed."

"You had to learn about that as well as how to manage the orchard when he died," Delphine said quietly. "I didn't realize." In the three years since Father had died, Delphine had drifted ever further away from the farm, toward church socials and dances in town and eventually Perrysburg. That was part of dealing with her grief, she accepted now; she didn't want to see the empty spaces in the rows of trees Father used to occupy. And she felt, once Alaine took over managing the farm, that she didn't have a proper place at Orchard Crest. Like she was just in the way, at best an extra pair of hands to assist if Alaine needed it. "I'm sorry, Alaine, that must have been difficult."

"It's not so very bad," Alaine rushed to say. "It's just—there's more debt than I thought. With more interest." She ticked off a few unspoken ciphers on her fingers. "At any rate, our margins are a little tighter than I would have guessed this year, so I'm shoring things up. The fall harvest will bring everything right again," she added, as though it was a forgone conclusion, but Delphine knew better. The lines between her sister's eyes, twin to the furrows Delphine knew spelled worry on own brow, were deep, and Alaine couldn't hold still. She always fidgeted when she was anxious.

"I didn't realize—that is, I suppose I knew that managing the farm was more than timing the pruning and the harvest, but I hadn't considered how difficult the money part might be," Delphine said. "The business side of it."

"It will be all right." Alaine squared her shoulders in a posture Delphine knew was defensive—no one could hurt her, Alaine seemed to think, if she faced them head-on and stood tall. "I've learned the ropes, mostly. I'd gotten through the worst of it, I thought, right after Father died. Everyone expected to deal with Jack, not me. The bank tossed me out once," she said with a hollow laugh.

"No!" Delphine covered an indecorous laugh, imagining her earnest sister, in that shoddy hat with the imitation cherries on it, escorted from the venerable columned façade of the Madison Bank and Trust. "I had no idea, you never told me."

"Yes, they thought my name on the deeds must have been a mistake. You should have seen Jack giving them what for—I wouldn't want to be on the opposing counsel in a trial, that's for sure!" The laugh was real, this time. "And of course Olson is a bear to deal with at the granary—pretends not to see anything that comes from me unless Jack signs it, too." She shrugged, and Delphine knew she was pretending nonchalance. "Most of the other farmers are all right, they know it takes a family to run a farm, and that means the women are invested, too. But not all of them. I sometimes think—" Her voice cracked slightly. "I sometimes think some of them want me to fail, because it bothers them that a woman can do the same job they can."

"I imagine some of them aren't so happy about you being the new president of the Society," Delphine said. Yet another place where Alaine not only belonged, but thrived. Delphine admitted she begrudged her sister that victory a little, but assuaged any mild envy with thoughts of sliding comfortably into the Perrysburg elite.

"I wish—I wish there was more I could do." Delphine caught Alaine's hand in what she hoped was a reassuring grip.

"I know, Del. And I'm sorry to even bring it up, but—well. I thought you ought to know. And—well." Alaine toyed with the edge of the sofa; several threads were coming loose, and Delphine resisted the impulse to stop Alaine from making it worse. "I wondered if maybe you could ask Pierce about investing in the farm. We need the money, Del."

Delphine's brow creased. She didn't have the orchard deep in her blood like Alaine did, but she was, on paper, part owner. Still, asking Pierce—this was untested ground. They had never discussed her role, if any, in her family business, and she had the suspicion that Pierce expected her to fold herself entirely into his affairs. And right before the wedding! She could have been frustrated with Alaine's pragmatic disregard for the timing and lack of romantic instincts, if only her sister didn't look half sick with worry. "Maybe I—I could ask Pierce after the wedding if there's any way we could put a little money into the orchard. Why, it's his business now, too," she added, trying to lessen the tension with a laugh. "Community property laws might as well cut both ways, don't you think?"

Alaine's brow constricted tighter, as though she was torn. Then she softened, forcing a nod. "I'd appreciate that, Del," Alaine admitted. "Don't let it ruin your honeymoon."

"Of course not. I'm sure you've got it well in hand," Delphine reassured her. "And Papa Horatio, of course, too. He knows this place better than anyone."

"He certainly does. And he knows business, even if he doesn't like to admit it. Looking at the numbers now, we're lucky we didn't go under completely during the Panic."

"Plenty of farms did," Delphine said softly, remembering tense conversations over suppers and hushed arguments when their parents had assumed she and Alaine were in bed. "I think Grandma Lilabeth made bargains," she added with a smile.

Alaine laughed. "She must have pulled out every bargain she had—the chickens never laid like that before! And no caterpillars in the orchard, and fair weather every time we needed it."

Now Alaine crafted the small bargains that bought them a little luck when they needed it. Mother had lived steeped in fairy lore since she'd married into the Canner family almost thirty years ago, just as Moore's Ferry was beginning to blossom around the railroad junction. Still, Mother had never learned to bargain like Del and Alaine had, at Lilabeth's knee. Delphine had the impression, though Mother had never said as much, that she felt bargaining was tasteless, a relic of backwoods roots and not seemly for a lady of Prospect Hill. Delphine had wondered the same, herself. It was a question she wouldn't have to worry over now—the veil was certainly closed off in Perrysburg, the Fae world beyond her reach.

"Speaking of," Alaine said. "We should probably take care of tomorrow's bit of good luck, shouldn't we?" The tightly wound nerves in Alaine's gut were beginning to unspool, just a little; asking her sister was the hardest part, no matter what the answer might be. Saying those words—that they needed money, that they could use Pierce's help—felt like admitting failure. The one thing she'd always been confident in was her ability to run the farm, even while she stumbled through every polite gathering she was invited to and Delphine sailed through social functions like a well-spoken butterfly. If Alaine failed now, who was she?

"I've got the coin," Delphine said with a grin. They hurried out the back door together, almost running into Mother in the kitchen hallway.

"The pair of you run around like a couple of schoolgirls! Mind you don't trample the peonies," Mother called after them.

Alaine wasn't sure how anyone could manage to trample Mother's peonies; they were colossal shrubs almost to her shoulder and drooping under the weight of thickly perfumed pink and white blooms. She held her skirt back from the thorns in the rose arbor spanning the opening in the garden fence and shook her sleeve free of a stray climbing rose. "All right, do you remember the words?"

Delphine held up in her hand in mock dismay. "Do I remember

the words? You wound me. 'A penny and sheaf to hold off rain, a dime and bloom bring it back again.' Now where's the greenery?"

Alaine laughed, properly chastised. Delphine might be a Perrysburg socialite after tomorrow, but she was still a Prospect Hill girl, too. "All right, all right. I pulled a fern from the wedding bouquets. I thought it fitting."

"Do the Fae appreciate that kind of poetic creativity?" Delphine laughed.

"I don't know that they care about much of anything besides the gift." Alaine put the penny and the fern in the latch of the garden gate. It stuck; no one used it anyway. She would have to send Jack up to fix it sometime. "I think it's the coin that does the trick, in any case."

"I suppose neither one of us has made a detailed study of fairy culture." Delphine touched the fern lightly.

"A bit disconcerting, isn't it," Alaine murmured as she shut the gate and trapped the penny inside. She repeated the rhyme over the gate. "That we don't know, really, what these trades mean to *them*. I wonder why they like the things they like. There must be some reason for it, don't you think?"

"I suppose." Delphine shrugged. "As long as it works."

"It works. It's worked every time I've done it," Alaine reminded her. "Remember the garden party last summer, when the whole town got a storm and nary a cloudburst here?"

"I know, I know." Del scanned the cloudless sky, lines pulling taut between her eyebrows. "I wish we could do something about the heat—it's bound to be hot tomorrow. And humid—what if Mother's cake frosting beads?"

"Then Mother's cake frosting beads," Alaine replied with a laugh. "I don't have any bargains to keep the frosting from beading. Or the sun from baking the wedding party, either."

"Maybe we should have gotten married in the church," Delphine said.

"Then it would have been stuffy and hot and smelled like too many people's sweat."

"Alaine!"

"It's true." Alaine caught her sister's hand. Delphine had learned painting and piano from their mother, and the fine art of fretting as well. "Del, it's going to be lovely. As lovely as we can make it."

Alaine had her doubts that her encouraging speech had much effect. Delphine circled the garden again, as though taking stock of each blossom. She glanced at the penny wedged in the gate one more time. "I'm sure you're right. As for my part, I'm exhausted, so unless you want the bride falling asleep at the altar, I'm going to bed early."

Alaine watched her sister walk toward the house, the hem of her gored skirt sweeping softly against the grass. She stayed in the garden as the first bats emerged, frantic shadows against the faded dusk. There was more she wanted to say to Delphine, that she would miss her, that she would always have a place on Prospect Hill. That she loved her. The words didn't come when she tried to say them. Maybe it was better that way. Her sister was happy, and she was happy her sister was happy. Already stacks of boxes and a steamer trunk large enough to smuggle a pony waited in Delphine's room, ready to move her sister to Perrysburg, twenty miles away.

Twenty miles was nothing. There was a train station in Perrysburg, just a short walk from the imposing new house Pierce Grafton had built, with the silk-covered walls, and the mural on the ceiling of the parlor, and the ballroom on the third floor. There was a guest room waiting, Delphine had promised—a whole guest suite with a bedroom and a morning room, even a water closet with its own commode. There was nothing but excitement and novelty for Delphine, but for Alaine, there was loss.

"If you watch for fairies, they never show up." Jack stood by a blushing peony bush, arms crossed and a knowing smile spreading wide.

"I know better than to watch for fairies," Alaine retorted. "No one really wants to see a fairy. Tricky creatures. Papa Horatio got lucky." She watched a bat's kinetic swoop and dive. "Just thinking about tomorrow."

"Worried about rain, then."

"Hardly," she said with a laugh.

Jack looped an arm under hers, and she softened in his embrace.

She wanted to melt into his arms—she remembered when she felt as though being held by Jack could fix anything. Now she felt more as though they were fighting, back to back, against the bank and anyone else who threatened them. He lifted her chin and kissed her, but her mind was elsewhere. The farm.

She thought of the trinkets she left in the chicken coop for better layers, in the orchard to keep away worms, of the scarlet silk and cheap silver wedged in the garden gate to secure her the vote for president of the Agricultural Society. Why wasn't there a bargain to keep the farm solvent? She knew bargains for planting and harvest, lame horses and broody chickens and finding lost things. There had to be something she could use, maybe change it, just a little. Maybe, she thought with a dangerous spark, there was. Ribbons and glass beads around a contract was an old bargain for honest dealings. Maybe she could wrap their mortgage agreement in copper wire, or shove silver pins through it, or—

She stopped herself, heart racing. Who knew what that would be asking the Fae to do? Wire might mean some kind of unbreakable binding she didn't want. Stabbing the contract might bring harm to someone—and it wasn't as though the bankers at the Madison Bank and Trust had been intentionally malicious to Orchard Crest. Besides, Grandma Lilabeth had warned a thousand times never to tamper with bargains. It was impossible to know how the Fae would interpret a change in the bits and bobs left for them, what they'd deliver in return.

A new bargain, then. Maybe there was a way to invent a new bargain. And yet even as the thought took form, she recoiled from it. There was a promise she'd made long before she vowed to care for Orchard Crest—she had promised Grandma Lilabeth to never, ever meddle with the unknown when it came to the Fae.

No—she had to count on more prosaic forms of help, even if it meant relying on her glass magnate soon-to-be brother-in-law. She looped an arm through Jack's. "Best get home and rest up for tomorrow," she said with a forced joviality that she could tell Jack saw right through, but had the decency not to mention.

5

With the exception of the singular Compleat Book of Bargaining Works *published anonymously in the eighteenth century, very few fairy bargaining cultures enshrine their bargains in written documents; instead, rhymes and songs serve as devices to commit bargains to memory.*

—*A Ribbon, A Ring, A Rhyme: Cohesion of Folk Poetry Tradition,* doctoral dissertation of Edith L. Showalter

DELPHINE WATCHED THE moon rise over the orchard from her window on the second floor of Orchard Crest, sleep elusive. There was a finality to it, this last night in her old bedroom. She anticipated returning many times, of course, first with Pierce, and later with children—a small circus of them, even. But she would—she was determined on this—return different. She wouldn't be the little sister in Alaine's shadow, or even the perfect imitation of her mother. She would have her own place. And this was her last night before everything would change, the way the shift in seasons changed the whole landscape or the river's floods rewrote the banks. She wanted change, wanted to change—but it meant leaving something she loved behind.

Her reflection in the gilt-flowered mirror across the room looked back at her with the tacit understanding that she was edging closer to making herself cry. She twisted her emerald engagement ring on her finger. Once, twice, thrice. Everything in threes, wasn't that the way Lilabeth had taught her and Alaine to bargain?

Delphine wondered, briefly, what the fairies would trade her for the stone on her left hand.

Probably nothing. The Fae never seemed to value things the same way she would have. A length of red silk thread over a new gown. A scrap of glass over a bottle of perfume. An old key over an automobile—though how they would spirit a motorcar into Fae, she didn't know. That would be some trick.

That silly thought chased away the lump of tears gathering in her throat. Delphine stood and opened the closet door, where the white froth of her wedding gown hung by itself. With the rest of her clothes packed and ready to move to Perrysburg, the effect of the white satin and lace was all the more dramatic. She traced the sleeve, the cuffs fastened with tiny pearl buttons.

Everything was settled. The flowers had been cut and arranged, the luncheon prepared, the silver polished. Right down to the pearl buttons, set in perfect symmetry. And yet, there was still something she could do, should do.

The moonlight spread across the quilt Grandma Lilabeth had made her, the pinks and greens of old cotton scraps lovingly reimagined as interlocking rings. She had thought of asking to take it with her, the way Alaine had taken her quilt from Lilabeth, but she knew it wouldn't fit in the grand Perrysburg house. She'd ordered new coverlets, white work embroidery and lace and crisp cotton, beautiful and expensive and entirely impersonal.

It felt as though Alaine should have been there. Delphine didn't particularly want company tonight, especially her sister with her pragmatic worries about the farm, but she felt the absence, a hollow place where a person would have been, a silence where Alaine's voice should have been. They had shared this room when they were children, and it was full of old secrets whispered in the dark and loud rows when afternoons stretched too long and their patience with each other wore thin.

It was Alaine who never laughed when Delphine said she wanted to paint pictures like the ones they saw in the exhibition at the county fair, or that she wanted to visit Paris and Venice and Cairo one day, or that she wanted to marry this boy or that boy and they would have a big house on a hill. When Delphine fell for the son of one of the field hands they hired one autumn, following him around with a plate of crullers and eyes like saucers, Mother had intervened, making it quite clear that a Prospect Hill girl couldn't be tangling herself up with the hired help. Alaine had held her while she'd sobbed, her sense of tragedy inflated by adolescence, but real shame branding a deep lesson.

There were proper and improper ways of navigating the world. That much Mother had made clear. Delphine twisted her engagement ring again. She wasn't sure if fairy bargains were proper or not, but they could be secret, and they were certainly pragmatic. She opened the trunk at the foot of her bed and lifted the nightdresses and morning jackets out of the way. At the bottom she uncovered several volumes of poetry, a bundle of old letters, and box of photographs. They were mostly from school friends. There was a portrait of Pierce, of course. Emily's baby portrait. Her sister's wedding photograph, a crown of flowers in her fair hair. She put the pictures on top of the stack of hatboxes.

There, underneath the poetry. The things Lilabeth had given her. She opened the repurposed gift box, *Ayres Department Store* trailing in gilt script across the lid. There—thread wound around wooden crosshatches, glass beads in various colors, bits of printed cotton and bright scrap wool, a few feathers and shriveled nuts and pressed flowers, carefully laid between layers of tissue. Wood shavings and flakes of soap. A tiny vial of rainwater.

She sat back on her heels. She could almost hear her grandmother's patient voice showing her how to tie a slipknot with a bit of silk ribbon.

"It's a language," she said, her hands moving confidently as she tied the ribbon, untied it, and passed it to Delphine. "Each piece, each way it's presented, it means something. Like words mean something, and might mean something different depending on how you string them together."

Delphine struggled with the slippery ends, the knot coming out uneven and loose. "Is that why it's got to be the same every time?"

Lilabeth showed her again. "That's right. So the bargain is the same every time. We know these trades; we've learned them. Once a fairy makes a bargain, they can't change it."

"But if we change it, we don't get what we asked for?"

"No, you don't. And it certainly wouldn't be wise. Or safe." Lilabeth untied the ribbon and tied it into a bow. "That's the thing with fairy bargains—you always know, when you make one, exactly what you want to get. So often people ask for what we don't really understand, but you can't do that with a bargain." She handed the ribbon back to Del, who dutifully struggled with the slippery silk. "But it's a good lesson—for any time, not just bargains—to know what you want, really want, before you go asking. There, that's a better knot! We'll put some more ribbons in your box to practice with."

"And the brighter the color, the better?"

"That's right." Lilabeth had stocked her little box with scraps of scarlet and cerulean and emerald-green ribbon.

Delphine had used all of them save one roll of brilliant purple ribbon. That ribbon was meant for one kind of bargain only, one she'd never made before. And, as Lilabeth had said, she knew exactly what she wanted to ask for. The part Lilabeth hadn't explained, but that Delphine and Alaine had learned later, was that the small bits of fairy fortune they could extract from a bargain allowed them to set their luck in motion on a broader scale. Alaine had used the bargain against rain to make sure she had a romantic afternoon with Jack before they started courting. Delphine had used plenty of little bargains to maneuver herself into Pierce's notice. And now she would use one more bargain to ensure that she could establish herself among Perrysburg society before she had any maternal responsibilities.

She lifted the purple ribbon from the box, and then counted twelve silver beads from the carefully folded packet at the bottom of the box. She threaded her needle with silk thread, Lilabeth's instructions echoing in her memory so fresh she could hear her hills-inflected voice. "Like with like—sew cotton with cotton thread and silk with silk." She tacked each bead to the ribbon with three stitches. Once, twice, thrice. When each was in its place, she turned the needle on her own fingertip and produced a single drop of blood. It sank into the center of the ribbon.

The bargain, with the beads tacked in a deliberate row and the uneven stain of scarlet, was strange and familiar, eerie and comforting, tangled together. Under the modern gaslight, it seemed almost foreign, an artifact from another place, another time. Not something that belonged to the new money of Perrysburg, to the fastidiously designed house, to the future. Not something, Delphine thought, as she held this, the last bargain Lilabeth had taught her, that ought to belong to her.

But it did.

Her fingertip grazed the beads, willing the bargain to be true. Placed in freshly turned soil, in the garden, under a new moon, the trinket of silk and silver would be transformed into a request for a certain kind of luck, a certain bend of fate. It would let her put something off until she was ready, giving her time to learn how to be a wife, to navigate the social landscape of Perrysburg, perhaps even to establish herself as a known figure before taking on the work of learning to be a mother. "Not that you shouldn't still be prudent," Lilabeth had cautioned Delphine with a wink. She had wondered then what her mother would think of Lilabeth letting her in on this secret and now, grown and on the eve of her wedding, she knew— Mother would have been appalled. "But far as I can tell, it works every time. Just have to remember to put out a new one every month. Purple ribbon, don't forget."

It had to be placed here, on Prospect Hill. The borders between Fae and Perrysburg were closed, as far as Delphine knew. A new bargain would have to be made every month, so Delphine made several more, identical to the first, each marked with a drop of her blood.

When she finished, she felt calmer, settled. The circus of children, the circus created by only one small baby, was too much to imagine on top of the sea change of marriage and moving to Perrysburg, of learning to be a wife and a Grafton. This much she could control. She closed the box and hid it back in the bottom of the trunk that would stay here at Orchard Crest.

6

Glass for the Fae, bid look around
Something's lost and must be found
—Children's rhyme

THE WEDDING DAY dawned veiled with a humid haze. Alaine watched the sunrise from the bay window of the cottage, pale pinks and golds slowly burning away the silver of the morning. She made a pot of coffee and let the chickens out of their coop, throwing some scratch in the yard for them. Out of habit, she checked their nesting boxes; of course none of them had laid this early. "Lazy birds," she scolded them as she went back indoors.

"Mama!" Emily tore out of her room, her hair and nightgown billowing behind her in a pale blur. The halo of fine curls promised to be murder to comb out, Alaine thought with a sympathetic twitch of a smile. "It's today. It's today! Do I get dressed now?"

"Mercy, no, not until after breakfast," Alaine answered, putting the water on to boil a few eggs. "No use getting butter all over the frills of that new dress, is there?"

"Yes, Mama." Emily's tight lips and downcast eyes had all the trademarks of talking back, but to Alaine's relief, she didn't. "I lost my shoe."

"Your shoe?" Alaine stopped in the middle of buttering a piece of toast. "Your wedding shoes?"

"But I found it." Em grinned. "I used the bargain, all on my own. While you were gone. Aunt Esther doesn't know how, so I just did it myself. Glass on the windowsill."

"Em!" Alaine set down the toast with a hard thump, protective fear sharpening her voice. "I'm very glad you remembered the bargain, but you know you're never to use bargains without my knowledge—never!"

"I'm sorry," Emily replied, chagrined. "I thought...I needed to find the shoe."

"Yes, but—but Emily, any little mistake with a bargain can mean a bigger mistake, a worse problem. Don't ever do them without me, not until I tell you that you may. Is that understood?" Emily mumbled. "Is that understood, young lady?"

"Yes, Mama."

Alaine took a shaky sip of coffee, willing her heart to slow. Of course she wanted Em to learn all her bargains, but under supervision. The Fae were dangerous, and waiting, always, for a mistake, Gran had warned them.

"Where was it, anyway?" Alaine poured a glass of milk for Em. "The shoe?"

"It fell behind the dresser." Em sat on the stool by the window and reached for her milk.

"How in the world did that happen?" Alaine held the milk aloft.

"I don't know! Honest! Maybe I set it there while I was getting everything ready?" Alaine handed her the milk. "But the fairies found it. I could see the toe sticking out, when I woke up. I swear I couldn't last night. I swear!"

"Don't swear, it's not polite," Alaine said automatically. "The glass is gone?" Alaine turned her back to Emily as she sliced more bread for toast so her daughter wouldn't see her smile and think she was making fun. She remembered when she was still enamored by the magic of the Fae, by the scope of possibility in a few fairy stories. She'd lost some of that, the pragmatism of the bargains outweighing the wonder of fairies in the garden. Emily renewed it in her.

"The whole thing! I think I saw fingerprints on the window, too." Em paused. "They're gone now."

Alaine resisted the urge to correct her—might as well let her think she saw some faint trace of magic. To be fair, she wasn't quite sure how the Fae collected their payments. She'd endeavored never to see one.

"If they can find a shoe," Em said, turning her milk cup in a slow circle on the table, "maybe they could find a house closer to Prospect Hill for Aunt Del."

Alaine started, the familiar tightening in her throat amplified twofold—she had failed to recognize until this moment that her loss was shared by her daughter. "I don't think the Fae can do that, Em."

"Why not?"

"Well, for one, it's not bad luck that's taking Aunt Del to Perrysburg. She wants to go. Uncle Pierce"—Alaine forced herself past the sour strangeness of that phrase—"he built a house in Perrysburg, near his business."

"But it's not fair."

"Fae bargains can't make everything fair, Em. I just have a few little tricks I can use to fix a few little problems. I can't do much about the big ones—that's up to us." She steeled herself and continued, "And this isn't really a problem. It's a happy move for Aunt Del. She's excited. We have to do our best to be excited for her."

The morning passed in a flash—helping Mother set out the flowers and the table settings, greeting every Canner and Riley aunt and cousin, Em twirling in her new dress in front of the mirror in Del's room while Del fiddled with the buttons of her filmy white lace gown. Alaine tried to catch the moments in memory, like snapping photographs, one flash after another.

By the time the vows had been said and the recessional played by a Riley cousin with a violin, Alaine wished she had been able to bargain for a cool breeze as well as no rain. She dabbed sweat from her hairline as Emily raced back from the wedding party.

"You did very well not fidgeting," Alaine said, kissing her cheek.

"It wasn't easy," her daughter confided with an honest gravity only the very young can achieve.

"Go say hello to Aunt Imogene." Alaine nudged Em forward. Imogene was Lilabeth's youngest sister, one of three girls. The eldest, Violet, had died when Lilabeth was young, or so Alaine had gathered; the family never spoke much about her. Imogene and Lilabeth, however, had been as tight as two burrs in a wool sock, as Grandma Lilabeth said. Now Imogene was the last of a generation of Prospect Hill old-timers.

"Mercy, girl, you got tall!" Great-Aunt Imogene sat in the shade near the yellow climbing roses, appraising Emily with her knotted ironwood cane. "You'll be seventeen this year, hmm?"

Em giggled. "Seven in the fall!"

"Seven! Not seventeen? Oh dear, then." Imogene chuckled. "Well, you should go 'long and play, then, seeing as you won't be six forever. Seven-year-olds got to be more serious. They'll be sending you on to school."

"I already go to school, Auntie Imogene," Emily said, shaking her head. "Didn't they send you to school when you were six?"

Imogene laughed louder. "Mercy! No, my mama taught us at home, child. We didn't have a school back then, not up here in the hills!" She glanced at some of the Grafton family, gray morning suits tailored in soft drapes and pale gowns sweeping the cropped grass. "Not like some folks." She sucked her lips around her teeth. "Well, run on and play with the cousins, Emily!"

"You look well," Alaine said as Em ran toward a gaggle of children heading for the orchard.

"Can't complain," Imogene replied, watching Mrs. Grafton lift her gown's frothy hem away from the reach of a stray rose vine. "You think Delphine's going to be happy down there in Perrysburg?"

"I'm sure she will be." Alaine forced a blanket of reassurance over hollow words. She couldn't see what drew her sister away from the orchard, or to Perrysburg, but that didn't mean there wasn't something her sister saw there, something she wanted. "You should see the house Pierce had built. It's gorgeous—white limestone, three full stories. Beautiful covered loggia and porches."

"Had built." Imogene sighed. "That's the trouble nowadays. No one puts hand to hammer any longer. Used to be you got to know a place by working it. You know how that is." Imogene turned her sharp eye toward Alaine. "Knowing the place."

"I suppose I do. The pears are coming along in the new section of the orchard," she added.

"You send some my way when they come ripe. Pa always wanted to try for pears and they never took on right. You got a knack for it." She leaned forward, wrapping an arm around her cane. With her iron-gray hair, violet-blue silk dress, and the knotted stick, she looked more than a little like a storybook witch. "Lilabeth always said you were knacky at other things, too."

"She taught me well," Alaine replied. Memory snagged the back of her throat—Gran would have been delighted by Delphine's white lace dress and the way the peonies framed the wedding couple as they said their vows.

"Did she teach you everything, I wonder?" Imogene rocked back. "There's things Lilabeth didn't like to touch."

Alaine began to answer, then stopped. She'd always trusted that Gran's knowledge had been complete, and that she had bequeathed a complete education on her granddaughters. There couldn't be more, could there? Aunt Imogene watched her, dark eyes keen on her hesitance. "She must have taught me every bargain she knew," Alaine said lightly. "It's a wonder I can remember all of them!"

"Ah, of course. *Every* bargain. And not a mite more." Imogene nodded and turned away, the sharp look gone as she watched the cousins weave through the trees. "Them kids will sleep good tonight," She chuckled. Whatever Aunt Imogene was alluding to, she wasn't going to discuss it further.

Mother swept over, her pale blue gown a rustle of silk and rose-scented cologne water. "We're sitting down for luncheon," she prodded. "You want to take Aunt Imogene over to the table, or go chase the children down?"

"I can escort myself, Iris," Imogene said, picking herself up with a hand on her ironwood staff. "Ain't made of glass."

By the time Alaine had rounded up the children, Delphine and Pierce were already seated. She herded the children toward their parents—or, rather, the Canner and Riley families' children, as the Grafton youngsters shadowed their parents with imitations of their reserved courtesy. Alaine wasn't sure if she should feel bad for the boys in stiff collars and girls in spotless white cotton, or embarrassed that her family's progeny had been climbing trees like squirrels with scraped knees and torn stockings. She gravitated toward the former, smiling at a russet-haired Canner cousin with a rogue stocking pooling around his ankle.

Alaine slipped between Jack and Mother, guiding Emily to her seat. Delphine met her eyes over the mounds of roses and hydrangeas decorating the tables and waved. Pierce said something to her, and she turned quickly to him. She looked so happy—her cheeks flushed and her eyes bright, the white net veil and pearl combs in her dark hair. Alaine poked at the chicken fricassee on her plate, her mouth dry.

"Mama, is that Aunt Eula's chicken recipe?" Emily tore into a drumstick with enough fervor for both of them.

"Sure is."

Her aunts had been up since before dawn cooking. The sweets table was piled with pies and sponge cake with fresh berries and Aunt Marline's divinity fudge. She picked at her chicken, feeling her appetite improving with each bite of familiar cooking.

"Can I have seconds, Mama?"

"Of course, let me get some for you." Alaine took Em's plate to the buffet, still loaded with more food than an army could do away with. She chose a drumstick from the plate of chicken, then froze.

"Now, Stella, it's quaint." Mrs. Mark Grafton, Pierce's mother. Alaine stiffened. "They've done the best they can—and I think they rather expected us to enjoy a country luncheon."

"But chicken fricassee? For a wedding luncheon? Are they going to have us dance a reel next?" A woman younger than Mrs. Grafton, but bearing the same sharp dark eyes, tittered quietly.

"I told Pierce they should have a fish course, at least. And a consommé. Of course I knew an aspic would be asking far too much."

"Pierce always did have an independent streak." Stella said this as though it were a blight. "Marrying some country nobody when the Harris girls or Georgia Lawson would have—"

"Not polite to speak of it now, dear," Mrs. Grafton said with a

tone that told Alaine it was only propriety keeping her from joining. Alaine seethed. Delphine wasn't a nobody—she was better than any of these Perrysburg ninnies.

"Pierce has his career to consider, that's all I'm saying. She can't go blundering about, mucking that up. After all, we stand to catch the ill effects of any mistakes she makes."

"I've advised Pierce how to handle himself, and he'll make sure she knows her place. You needn't concern yourself with your brother's affairs." Mrs. Grafton swept away in a wake of heady perfume, but not before Alaine heard her add in a sharp whisper, "He didn't listen to me about marrying the girl, why do you think he'd listen about a fish course?"

Neither Grafton woman had noticed Alaine; they were, Alaine presumed, well practiced in ignoring anything that didn't benefit them specifically. Country nobody, indeed—Del would show them all up before Christmas. Alaine put another piece of fricassee on the plate for herself. If the best chicken in the county wasn't good enough for the Graftons, she would enjoy it double.

"Well, quite a day." Imogene intercepted her on the way back to her table. Mother sat nearby. "Beautiful weather." She winked at Alaine, the bright blue Riley eyes unfaded in her careworn face.

"It is, isn't it?" Mother smiled. "And Delphine—like a painting." It was true. Delphine's thick dark hair seemed made for a white wedding veil and pearls, so unlike Alaine's own fair curls that had fought against her veil and had to be subdued with a wreath of flowers. They hardly looked like sisters, except for the strong blue eyes they had both inherited from their grandmother.

"They make a pretty-looking couple, for certain." Imogene nodded, approving. "They going to have a portrait done?"

"Of course, the photographer will be here just after the cake." Mother sighed, content. Alaine knew that look—her plans had come together in perfect order, like quilt pieces joined in a patchwork.

"They'll make pretty babies, for certain," Imogene continued, still watching the couple. She didn't notice, though Alaine did, how Mother tightened her hand around her napkin. "You suppose they'll start to trying soon? There's ways, you know. Make it happen quicker." She laughed brightly as she turned back to Mother, who had flushed to the same deep pink as the cluster of peonies decorating her table.

"Aunt Imogene, it's hardly a polite topic of conversation!"

"Babies are impolite now?" Imogene's smile sharpened. "You'd have fooled me, I thought everyone adored babies." Several Graftons at the next table glanced over, and Pierce's sister, Stella, leaned to a neighbor and whispered.

"You know quite well I meant the—you know quite well what I mean." As Mother stood, flustered, she knocked her glass over, spilling wine on the pristine white tablecloth. She pinched her lips together, watching the stain spread, unable to fix it. She forced a polite smile. "Perhaps I could show you how the new lilies are doing in the garden."

Imogene winked at Alaine. "Yes, perhaps you could."

7

Beads strung as words, honest and true
On ribbon to bind a contract due
—Traditional bargain

DELPHINE STOOD PERFECTLY still in the parlor of Orchard Crest. The photographer hunched under the canopy of his equipment, making adjustments. The day had flown—from waking before dawn and staring at the window, waiting until the sun rose high enough to gauge whether the clouds outside had any rain in them, to dressing in a flurry of petticoats and lace, to the world suddenly slowing into a framed vignette as they said their vows. Love, honor, and obey—Pierce's firm hands holding her shaking ones—a golden ring for each of them.

She'd barely been able to eat anything, though she did manage a little of Aunt Marline's divinity and a piece of the cake Mother had fussed over for days, teasing each spun-sugar flower and white icing leaf from her recipe books.

"Just one moment more," the photographer said, and Delphine held her breath until the blinding flash released them from stillness, the spell turning them to statues broken.

"You're a vision," Pierce whispered, his breath brushing her ear. She flushed, holding the bouquet of white roses in her hand a little tighter. A thorn she'd missed stripping bit lightly into her palm.

"We should change clothes," Delphine said, rushed. "So we have enough time to drive to Perrysburg before evening."

"We've hours yet! And the motorcar won't give us any trouble covering twenty miles." Pierce glanced out the window. The parlor faced the hills rolling away in orderly rows of apple and cherry and pear trees.

"All the same, I'm going to put on my traveling suit." She checked her hand—the thorn hadn't broken the skin. "I'm terrified of something happening to this dress!"

"It's not as though you'll wear it again!" Pierce's laugh echoed against the wood paneling. "All right, I'll see you in a bit."

She lifted her skirts as she climbed the stairs, the lace spilling between her fingers. Delphine traced the delicate silhouette of lilies in the lace. How could a day be over so quickly? And yet not over—there was still the drive back to Perrysburg, and a wedding night. She didn't like to admit it, even to herself, but she was nervous. She'd insisted on being proper, on waiting. Lilabeth had given her the bargain to avoid mishaps, but part of her worried it might fail, and then what? And part of her wanted to be dignified, terrified of a mistake like a Perrysburg girl would be instead of plying secret bargains like a backwoods slattern. Surely that was what Pierce expected—a reticent, blushing girl.

Alaine waited by her room. Delphine stopped and stiffened slightly. She hadn't expected to see anyone except Mother and maybe Papa Horatio before leaving.

"I thought you'd left," she said, the lace falling from her fingers.

"Jack took Em home. She's exhausted. But I thought you might want help with all those buttons."

"Help? Oh, yes." Her hand flew to the row of neat pearl buttons down the back of her gown. She would have had to call Mother, and perhaps it was easier to talk to Alaine, after all. She opened the door to her room, stripped of most of her pictures and the small trinkets that had made it feel like hers.

"It was a beautiful wedding," Alaine said. Maybe Delphine imagined it, but her voice sounded strained, distant. "I—Em had the nicest time. Thanks for letting her get dressed with you this morning."

"You're welcome. She'll have to come spend the night, some-time." Delphine shrugged the shoulders of the gown away. "When we're settled."

"Delphine, I—" Alaine's fingers stalled on a button. "I'm going to miss you so much."

"Alaine! For pity's sake, it's Perrysburg, not around the world!" She forced a laugh. "We'll see each other all the time, I promise."

Alaine pulled another button from its loop. "It won't be the same. This place won't feel the same without you here."

Delphine bit her tongue. Alaine never wanted more than Orchard Crest, never craved more than the forest and the hills and the fruit coming ripe in its season. That didn't give Alaine a right to pin her down here, too. She relaxed a hand she realized was clenched into her skirt. "I know. But we'll get used to it. Both of us." More than that, Delphine hoped—she harbored a vision of herself as self-assured and confident in her parlor as Alaine was in the orchard. Alaine had grown up into the fullest version of herself, and Delphine wanted that, too.

"I suppose." Alaine moved farther down the row of buttons. "It...it was nice seeing Aunt Imogene."

"I'm surprised she came." The old crone rarely left her little cottage at the base of Prospect Hill's north side.

"I'm glad she did. Em likes her. She seems to like Em. We should try to get over and see her more often, I suppose she might get lonely."

"She embarrassed Mother." Delphine's throat tightened, and she pushed back embarrassment of her own. She had wanted the wedding to show the Graftons just how refined and tasteful their new daughter-in-law was, and Imogene had been a dreadful suggestion that instead, Delphine was just a country nobody, full of bad manners and bad habits.

"Oh, Mother. She should lighten up a bit—Imogene didn't say anything everyone doesn't already think." Delphine held perfectly still as Alaine undid the last button, not trusting herself to say anything measured or kind in response. "She said something funny to me, though."

Delphine couldn't hold back any longer. "Funnier than jokes about making babies?"

"It was meant as a compliment, Del. About how pretty you are. Not making fun of you." Alaine helped Delphine step out of the gown and then took it to the hanger by the closet, draped carefully over one arm. "No, she said Gran didn't teach us everything. That Gran was afraid of some parts of bargaining."

"I wouldn't know," Delphine said. It was her wedding day, for heaven's sake. Gossiping about what old Aunt Imogene had to say about Lilabeth's teaching methods was the last thing she wanted to talk about. Well, not precisely the last. She flushed.

"Do you think there might be more to bargains than Gran showed us? I'd take about any help I could get finagling the finances on the orchard this year and—"

"I really don't know, Alaine." She let her frustration change her voice, make it sharp and jagged. She'd had enough, enough of letting the orchard be more important to Alaine than her wedding, enough of hiding how she felt.

"I'm sorry, Del, I thought it was interesting, was all." Alaine turned. "Are you—are you all right?"

"It's been a long day." She bit her lip. It was dry. "I—never mind."

"What is it? What's wrong?" Alaine left the dress hanging in the closet and sat down on Delphine's bed, rumpling the quilt that Delphine had smoothed just so only that morning. For the last time.

Delphine sat next to her, then leaned against a needlepoint pillow so she didn't quite have to sit face-to-face with her sister. She had dreamed of this day, and had forgotten, in all her plans and hopes, that there would still be room for failure. "Today was perfect. I just—I want to do well in Perrysburg. Like you've done here on Prospect Hill."

"Oh, Del." Alaine sat bolt upright and moved to hug her, but she edged back. Alaine looked hurt.

"No, I just—I don't want Pierce to think I'm not happy. You start in on the hugging and the fussing, and I'll probably cry." The lump was already forming at the back of her throat, tight like it was laced in a too-small corset.

"You'll be a wonder at being a Perrysburg lady." Alaine picked at her nails. "You're so graceful. Perfect. At everything."

"But keeping house in Perrysburg! And hosting dinner parties for his colleagues and choosing the menu. And...and remembering his favorite brand of cologne water and how he stocks his bar and ordering pajamas he likes."

"I think husbands can purchase their own pajamas." Alaine nudged Delphine's foot with her toe. "Every winter, I watch you glide through all the balls and socials and dinners and feel like you were born to live some sophisticated life, like you have practice at it already, somehow. Pierce is the luckiest man in the world."

"I want to be a good wife. I'm afraid I don't...I don't know how."

Alaine was quiet for a moment, then ventured a whisper. "Are you still talking about dinner parties and pajamas?"

"I'm..." Delphine felt her face flush hot. "I'm not, really."

"Oh, Del, I didn't realize." Alaine wrapped her hand around her sister's. "You haven't?" Delphine shook her head, lips pressed mutely together. "It's not complicated. And it's—it's not anything you *do*, exactly—it's that it's you. Pierce is thrilled to be married to you. He'd better be, at any rate! You're the prettiest bride I've ever seen, Del."

"Oh, I am not—I'm sure I was red as a strawberry half the time! I was a wreck of nerves, and then the heat."

"I wish I looked as lovely as you do when I'm a wreck." Alaine playfully tugged her hand, then sobered. "It—you know it might hurt, a little."

"I'm not afraid of that."

"I know! Of course not." Alaine squeezed Del's hand. "But—if it does, he shan't push you into it. He shouldn't make you do anything until you're ready, until you want to. A good man won't push you, and Pierce is a good man. Right?"

Delphine cocked her head at her sister. What a strange question—he was from one of the best families in the county, was heading one of the finest businesses in the state. "He is. Absolutely."

"Good." Alaine let go of her hand. "Then—then there's nothing

to worry about. You trust him, and he is madly in love with you, and that's that."

"Oh! Would you...I mean, they won't work in Perrysburg..." Delphine retrieved the purple ribbon bargains from a hidden corner of her dresser drawer.

"Of course. Once a month. You can leave me more next time you visit." Alaine pulled her off the bed, grabbing her wrists and leaning back as though they were little girls roughhousing in the orchard. "Now let's get you into that traveling suit before he decides to go to Perrysburg without you!"

The suit was displayed like a piece of artwork, framed by the molding of the closet. Alaine took the pale blue whisper-light wool skirt and lace shirtwaist from their hangers, though Delphine didn't need help except for the tiny buttons of the blouse's high neck. It was one last moment of intimacy between sisters who had helped each other button their shoes and tie their aprons and braid their hair before school every morning. Delphine looped a gold watch chain over her waist and assessed herself in the mirror.

"You look like a proper old married lady," Alaine said with a reassuring smile.

Yet, as the touring car rattled down the drive and Orchard Crest disappeared behind rows of trees and the curve of Prospect Hill, Delphine had never felt so small.

8

For a pleasant journey, feathers appeal
Three bound and left in the rut of a wheel
—Traditional bargain

THE DAYS FOLLOWING the wedding were quiet and empty. All the preparations, Mother's fussing, the work filling every spare moment had dissolved into a single day, and now Delphine was gone. Alaine tried not to dwell on it, but she would have given anything to run up to Orchard Crest to see Del for a few minutes. It felt, Alaine was surprised to realize, not entirely unlike the gray and silent weeks after Father had died, when she would forget for a moment and make it halfway out to the orchard shed to tell him something. Once she'd begun to cut an article about pest control out of the paper for him, scissors rounding the corner before she remembered—he was gone.

It was less sharp and didn't gouge her gut as deeply when she remembered that Delphine wasn't up in the parlor at Orchard Crest and she wouldn't be coming to church on Sunday, but it felt like grief, all the same.

And, Alaine decided with pragmatic resolve, there was nothing to do for grief but work. And there was plenty of work to be done. The cherries wouldn't be ready for harvest for weeks, but she watched them like a broody hen with her eggs, checking the progress of the

fruit, willing and bargaining away cold snaps or insects. She found herself, more than once, walking the overgrown path to the linden tree, hovering near its eerily perfect green circle, wondering how she could ply it for bargains. Maybe, she thought with a shiver, if she waited long enough, a Fae would appear and make an offer. Then she shook herself back to sensibility.

Of course, the Agricultural Society demanded her attention, too. There was business she wanted to accomplish within the first few months—bringing in a lecture series from the university's agriculture department, organizing a fall social, pitching a livestock auction as a fundraiser for the Mercy Fund.

She'd picked out her clothes a week in advance for the first meeting after the election, but as she buttoned the jacket of her good wool suit, she wondered if the pale gray was somber enough for the role. She put on and took off two different shirtwaists, her Sunday best lace too soft and delicate to stand up to an Acton Willis or a Howard Olson and their scrutiny of her capability, and a plain cotton blouse too simple. The one she wore now was starched within an inch of its life, and she wondered if she looked like a fool wearing someone else's clothes, like Emily when she played dress-up in her grandmother's worn-out evening slippers.

She checked her hair in the mirror one more time. Best to be as tidy as possible so they couldn't see her as an unkempt madwoman. That was what the suffragettes in the newspaper cartoons looked like—madwomen with tangled hair and warts on their noses, latter-day witches in cheap suits. And what was she, but a step away from a suffragette?

Why had she insisted on running against Howard Olson, anyway? She could have organized the fall picnic and petitioned for improved insurance options and written impassioned letters to the editor as a member in good standing.

But she couldn't, really. Half the members of the Society were women, and yet none of them had ever held office, except Maisie Freeman, who was transcription secretary ten years running, and only because she was the sole person in the chapter with a typewriter.

Alaine sighed and unbuttoned the jacket again to change into the lace blouse.

"You look fine." Jack stood in the doorway, arms crossed, watching her.

"How long have you been there?"

"Three hairpins ago," he replied. "The Agricultural Society won't be assessing your looks."

"That's what you think. Everyone is always assessing a woman's looks." Alaine sighed again. "Do I look respectable? But not fussy?"

"I think I like it without the jacket better, is that respectable?"

"For the kitchen." She smacked his shoulder. "How did we get to this? I just wanted to run the family farm." She said it lightly, but it stuck like a bit of corn between her teeth—it wasn't quite true, even if she hadn't meant to lie.

She wanted more than just running the farm, if she was honest. She wanted the farm to be as successful—more successful, even—than it had been before. She wanted the Orchard Crest name respected. They might not be glass magnates like the Graftons, but no one could look down on Orchard Crest, either. And she wanted to be seen at the helm of that success.

Jack threw up his hands in mock dismay. "I couldn't say. I seem to remember a pretty girl at the Sunday school picnic, and the next thing I knew, here I was."

"This won't make things harder at work, will it?" She smoothed his jacket collar. "The Agricultural Society always makes the papers, even if it's just for the Fourth of July hog roast."

Jack laid his hand over hers. "I say this with complete respect to this farm and to you. The partners at the firm don't care a fig about the Agricultural Society."

Alaine narrowed her eyes, and then laughed. "Well, then, that will teach me to inflate my own sense of self-importance." She turned to the mirror and tucked a wayward strand of hair back in place. "It is only the local chapter of the Agricultural Society, after all."

"Hardly." Jack drew his arms around her and gazed over her head into the mirror. He was stronger, now, than when they'd first been married, hours in the orchard building sinew over a student's slim build. She could cede her weight to his arms. She inhaled the scent of his soap and his shaving tonic, bright and clean like faraway water. "I suppose some folks think the world rolls on no matter what we do, but I think we have to drag it in the right direction. Even in something as local, something as small, as the Agricultural Society."

"But do we have to do the dragging this time?" She lifted her hand, watching it come to rest on his freshly shaved cheek in the mirror in front of them. They looked like a portrait, wrought in speckled glass.

"If we don't, who will? Who in Moore's Ferry? And the county, the state, the whole damn country is made up of Moore's Ferries." The resolute fire in his voice soothed Alaine's nerves—he believed in her, in what she could do. She wrapped herself in his confidence as he kissed her.

With that, she decided on the starched blouse and set off to town.

The Agricultural Society held meetings in the fellowship hall of the Free Methodist Church. Its white clapboard and bronze bell shone in the thick summer light; already a clutch of members loitered outside, chatting under the shade of the oak tree by the entrance.

"And how was the wedding?" Millie Jacobs hurried over to Alaine, shaking her hand and asking a hundred questions at once. "No rain! Quite the bit of luck—and did those sugar flowers your mother was going to make work out? I don't imagine you've heard from Delphine yet—Mrs. Grafton! My goodness, she's Mrs. Grafton now!" Alaine tried not to flinch. "Where were they going to honeymoon? Did your Aunt Eula do her fricassee, or was it too much for her rheumatism?"

Alaine answered as much of the onslaught as patiently as she could, disentangling herself long enough to ask Maisie Freeman if the minutes from last meeting had been posted and check with Lorne Albright about the status of a few outstanding checks. She was feeling fairly pleased with herself, already well on top of the business of running the chapter, when Acton Willis loudly cleared his throat.

"If we've all had enough of the social hour, perhaps we should begin the meeting?" He shrugged his coat against the unrelenting heat of the sun; he and Howard Olson stood far apart from the others, in full sun instead of under the sprawling oak.

Howard Olson led them inside and called the meeting to order, and despite some irrational worry on Alaine's part that he might raise some last-minute objection, formally turned the chair over to her with little more than a frown. She breezed through the old business and guided swift conversations on the new business until Maisie Freeman raised a hand.

"Pardon, but we do need to resolve the...spending issue." She coughed lightly, as though talking about money was indecent, even in the middle of an Agricultural Society chapter meeting of which she was an elected officer. "Last month it was proposed that we might donate some funds to the reelection of Mayor Olson."

Alaine felt her breath tighten. That issue. She'd thought they had firmly voted it down, but no—Maisie was right. They'd ended up tabling the motion. Howard had claimed his brother's friendliness to agriculture meant they had some obligation to keep him in office; Alaine and most of the farmers disagreed, believing political campaigns an inappropriate use of Society funds.

Howard Olson stood up, moustache gleaming with oil, ready to speak. Alaine ignored him. "Thank you, Mrs. Freeman. That motion as tabled—please read it." Maisie complied dutifully, reading off her neatly typed notes. "Is there a motion to bring the tabled motion to a vote?"

"So moved!" Howard glared at her. What did he expect? There were procedures, and she knew full well he would call her on any broken protocol if it served him.

"Second," Acton Willis added lazily from the rear of the room. They hadn't seated themselves near each other, Alaine noticed. Of course—divide and conquer, whispering their opinions to their neighbors.

"Very well, opening the floor to discussion." Fifteen hands shot up, and Alaine withered slightly. This was going to take some time. She carefully called on each farmer and business owner, most objecting to the motion on the grounds that it set bad precedent, and that the money was supposed to be used for direct benefits to the Society and its members.

"I just don't think we ought to go getting involved in political campaigns," Millie Jacobs said, finally circling to her main point. "Why, just imagine—everyone running for office would start coming to us for funds once word got out! And we ought to spend that money for the Society, not on...well." She pursed her lips, finally settling on a polite way to say what she thought. "Political promises are gambles at best."

"Are you claiming my brother is a liar?" Howard Olson shot up out of his chair.

"Mr. Olson," Alaine said firmly. "You have not been recognized. I think we ought to call the vote if—"

"I have more to say!" Olson retorted. He stared at her, daring her to deny him a turn to speak. The room felt electric, all eyes on Alaine. She hadn't wanted this part of leadership, not at all, but now that it was in her lap, she returned Olson's glare, stony and dark.

"Very well, Mr. Olson. Speak."

Her permission deflated him slightly; he'd wanted a fight. "You all go running your yaps about using the funds—but we don't use them! Not really. Bringing in a speaker, maybe, now and again, the Mercy Fund—what good does that do in the long run? No real tangible benefit." Alaine saw some of the farmers' mouths harden into angry lines. Those speakers brought new research and techniques that many of the farms now used. And the Mercy Fund had saved many of them from small calamities time and again. Olson didn't understand how those small calamities could snowball into losing a farm outright. "No real long-term benefit, not like good policy from the mayor's office."

"Yes, Mr. Olson, but you can't buy good policy," Alaine said.

There was a smattering of applause, and she flushed, more nervous at their approval than she had been before. It mattered more now, she realized, having their confidence. What the community thought of her, of her tenure as president, of her management of the orchard—all of it combined to point to the success or failure of the farm. The vote was called, a resounding rejecting of the motion.

"Still. Perhaps you are right, Mr. Olson. There are ways we could consider using our funds to our direct benefit more tangibly." She knew she shouldn't say it, with Acton Willis and Olson already in a stew, but she couldn't help it. "For example, a transportation collective—if we used funds and perhaps pooled donations, we could buy a farm truck that we could all use. Our harvests come ripe at different times, and we all help one another as it is—I know some of your fields as well as I know mine!" She smiled as several members chuckled. Acton Willis glared openly at her—and she knew she'd overplayed her hand, directly threatening his transportation company. "It's only one idea, but I propose—next meeting, we ought to have a discussion about ways to use our excess funds most effectively."

She adjourned the meeting, feeling the icy anger pouring out of Olson and Willis even as she avoided them and subjected herself to another round of wedding questions from Millie Jacobs. As Millie chattered on, Alaine's thoughts turned back to the impending cherry harvest. It had to make enough money to hold the farm secure. Everything she had worked toward depended on the fruit ripening on the trees and what kind of price she could get for it. As she nodded brief answers to Millie's questions, her thoughts bounced between the biting shame of Delphine's promise to ask Pierce for money and the uncanny lure of the fairy ring at the linden tree. She felt danger crackling from both, and wondered which would be necessary.

9

Horseshoe, spike, or unspent ore
Wards the Fae from any door.
—Folk saying

DELPHINE SAT ON the expansive porch of the West Baden Springs Hotel, chasing away the occasional mosquito as she gazed over the formal gardens. A light summer breeze lifted her white cotton dress; nothing else moved. Pierce was in yet another meeting with his Louisville contacts, and her watercolor of the gardens sat half finished on the portable easel in front of her. She considered exploring the grounds, or the stables, or the bicycle track—but Pierce had said bicycling was crass for a woman. She almost laughed, wondering what he would think of Alaine's brief attempt at bicycling—she had the balance of an uncoordinated crab, and abandoned the hobby quickly. Then she sighed, feeling the pinch of loneliness, surrounded by strangers on the crowded veranda.

The height of the season pressed hundreds of tourists into the grounds of the resorts nestled into the hills. Despite the fact that the springs were famous for their laxative properties and most of their fellow guests were there for a healthful regimen of diet, exercise, and the cleansing waters, the hotel and its surroundings were, Delphine admitted, beautiful. The hills rolled and the forests shifted from misted gold-green in the mornings to brilliant hues by afternoon.

And the atrium—well. It wasn't called the Eighth Wonder of the World for nothing. She resolved to move inside with her paints to try to capture the sheer scale of it when an older woman peered over her shoulder.

"My, what lovely work!" The woman, dwarfed by her enormous hat, nodded approvingly. "Such use of color!"

"Thank you," Delphine replied, surprised. "The gardens were so pretty, I thought I'd give it a try."

"Try! You've done more than try, dear. Did you study somewhere near here—or no, you must be from the city. Chicago, maybe?"

"No, no, I'm from—" She stopped herself. Not Moore's Ferry any longer. "Perrysburg. My mother is fairly good with watercolors, she taught me."

"My dear, you ought to get some formal lessons under your belt, too! You could go places." She winked. "Enjoy the gardens!"

Delphine looked over her work with a critical eye. It was hardly the height of artistry; paintings by the impressionist T. C. Steele were displayed in the hotel lobby, and she had pored over the use of color and light, the play of form. When she returned to Perrysburg, she resolved, she would take a class in oils. She wondered, too, what Pierce would think of investing in a few paintings, or sponsoring an exhibit. Patron of the arts—she liked the idea of that title.

Pierce found her on the veranda. "Still painting? Let's see it—flowers, I suppose that's a popular subject to paint, eh?" She gathered her things, wishing he'd noticed the contrast of shadow she'd attempted or the perspective she'd been rather proud of. "Haven't been convinced to try the waters, yet, have you?" He laughed as she wrinkled her nose. Sharing a tiny bathroom was already more disquieting than she had anticipated; laxative waters were beyond the pale.

"Hardly," she replied. "Are your meetings finished for the day?"

"For the week—well, quite nearly. We're having a drink before the fellows head back to Louisville on the five-forty train." He offered his arm. "Stroll around the atrium before I must be charming again?"

"You're always charming," Delphine said with a smile.

"No, my dear, that's your job." He leaned close to her, his voice softer and for her only.

She relished these moments, when she held all his attention. They came more rarely than she had anticipated—in the days between the wedding and their departure, she had expected quiet days at home together, unpacking their things, organizing shelves of cologne and shaving tonic and towels, and deciding which coverlet to put on the bed. Her prosaic imaginings of playing house were quickly upended. Pierce's father and the other glassworks executives commandeered his time, and when he was at home, he was often mired in paperwork or the depths of a newspaper. Even now, on their honeymoon, his attention was on business. He'd seemed disappointed at first, coming very close to complaining about his father on the train trip, but swiftly deployed his charm on the associates from Louisville, Delphine quite forgotten.

"I cannot wait to have you home in Perrysburg—I'll be the envy of every fellow there." Maybe things would settle down once they were home, Delphine acknowledged. Then there would be time to make inroads into the network of acquaintances and neighbors surrounding the Graftons, to find her footing more securely in the society she wanted to move in. She could begin to make a place for herself, to be the center of a small sphere the way that she hadn't been able to be at home.

Pierce laid his hand on her waist, and she flushed warm at the entreaties that hand and her own body voiced silently. The atrium felt suddenly too public, too open. Four stories of balconies looked down on them, dozens of people milled about, and, fighting a deepening blush, she pivoted her thoughts, quickly, to something else.

They landed on Orchard Crest, the memory her sister's worries needling her like a briar caught in her shoe. She'd promised to ask Pierce about money for the farm, and had meant to straightaway after the wedding, but they'd been alone so seldom that it felt like sacrilege to waste those quiet hours on financial woes. It was perhaps even worse to bring it up now, but the nagging thought wouldn't let her be, she was fairly sure, until she voiced it.

"I was wondering—" Delphine began. Her voice grew an echo under the enormous dome, a thin, warped version of itself. She dropped it to a whisper. "I was thinking, that the orchard is struggling a bit, with money. I've a share, of course, and it only makes sense—"

"Talking business on our honeymoon? Why, Delphine, I'm shocked." Pierce laughed, not noticing the hurt on Delphine's face. After all, he'd spent most of the time here tied up in business.

"We don't have to discuss it now, of course."

"We don't need to discuss it at all, dear. I'm not throwing good money after bad—gracious, we don't need that orchard any more than we need a rusty nail."

"Alaine does," Delphine answered automatically, covering her own hurt with protectiveness for her sister. Pierce's dismissiveness came as a shock—not that he wasn't interested in the orchard, exactly, but that he hadn't stopped to consider what it might mean to her or her family.

"Be that as it may, I'm not looking to invest further in agriculture at this point, Del. It's a losing proposition all around. If Jack needs a loan, I've no mind to turn family away, but that's as far as it goes."

"I understand," Delphine said, even though she didn't, not really. The amount of money was tiny compared to what she knew Pierce controlled.

"Del, love, I don't expect you to understand these things!" He tweaked her nose playfully. "Ladies never really do, not about business. But I would ask you not to be so, shall we say, public about these sorts of conversations. It's not seemly for a woman to discuss money like this—imagine if my associates had heard!" There was a warning edge to his voice, a requirement that she steer back toward placid conversation or dutiful silence. She complied with a comment about the gardens, and they spent a pleasant turn around the atrium before the Louisville fellows beckoned and Delphine found herself alone again.

Nothing, she felt with a stab, was going as she'd anticipated, not since the bulb had flashed on the wedding portrait. Pierce distracted by business, the beautiful Perrysburg house quiet and lonely, her honeymoon commandeered for glassworks meetings, and she couldn't even bring her husband's substantive fortune to Alaine's rescue. Would she have to hover at the periphery of other people's lives forever? She wandered outside and down the broad steps into the gardens. The pungent sulfur of the springs hung in the humid air. Foot trails led from the gardens into the hills, and she followed one, leaving the gentle buzz of conversation for the bright calls of birds and faint rustling of leaves. At a bend in the trail, her breath stilled.

A huge oak stood in a circle of dead, gray moss, its branches bare and the bark sloughed from its trunk. It was bone white and looked as though it should have fallen years ago, but not a single branch had fallen or even cracked. Delphine stepped closer, bending to look at the perfect circle of moss, each floret as brittle as though it had been burned. A thin, acrid scent emanated from the center; it settled at the back of Delphine's throat and made it hard to swallow.

"Most folks don't come back this way." Delphine started, almost expecting ghosts in a place like this, but the speaker was a Black woman in the maid's uniform of the hotel. "Sorry, ma'am, but I'd stay away from that tree if I was you."

"Oh, I know, I—" Delphine stopped herself. Pierce probably didn't want her blabbing about her country superstitions, even to a maid. But the woman raised an eyebrow, and she continued anyway. "My family knows a thing or two about bargains and fairy rings. I've never seen the like of this one."

"It's dead and gone." She stood back, thin arms crossed over her pristine uniform. She eyed Delphine cautiously, then seemed to decide to continue. "Been that way for years. But it was strong magic, once, when my mama first started working here."

"It died? I didn't know they could—that is, we have a linden tree at home, and it blooms all the time. It seems more alive than anything else in the forest."

The maid didn't move any closer, but she smiled faintly. "You do know about fairy trees, then. Seldom enough that outside folks do." She let her arms drop to her sides, eyes still on the dead tree, still keeping her distance from Delphine. "That's how this one was, too, when I was a girl. Mama moved us up here from Louisville, and I'd never seen anything like it. All those sprawling branches, fully leafed out all times of the year. And it smelled like—I don't know, cinnamon and cigar smoke, and something I can't even name."

"Our linden is the same," Delphine said. "A ring, and always in bloom. It has a different smell, though—its own smell." She paused. "I don't suppose you left bargains in the doors down at the hotel or in the gates of the garden."

"Mama just always used the tree itself. Leave a trinket, get some kind of good luck in return. She said that was how her mama's family did it, going all the way back to Africa."

"I didn't realize—" Delphine bit the words off in her mouth. Of course Black folks would have bargains, too. She flushed.

"It's all right, ma'am. I wouldn't have thought of it, either, that anybody but my own folks did bargains, if some of the girls from around here didn't know how, too. The rhymes my mama used, half of 'em came from coal mining folks' daughters who came up here to work. They had some real practical trades—could get stains out of the linens with some beads and a song."

"I don't know that one. Seems handy."

"It is."

"When did it die?" Delphine asked. "The tree?"

The woman stepped closer, but still far away from the circle's edge. "It started to fade when the rail line first came in, carved right through the forest to the hotel. They put the tracks too close."

"Iron," Delphine said, and the woman nodded.

"The ring held on, though, until they used all that steel to build the new atrium in the hotel a few years back. That was too much, too close. The bark came off in sheets, and the bargains stopped working."

"Just—stopped?"

The woman stared at the bare tree, her dark eyes unblinking. "At first they just got unreliable, you'd leave your bundle by the trunk and maybe it would still be there the next day and no bargain, maybe it wouldn't and you'd get what you asked for. But then—it changed, somehow. Warped. Leave a chicken feather, and there would be a pile of gizzards when you checked the next day. Leave a scrap of wool, and it would be a tangled little bundle of threads. Little bit of sugar, and it would be maggots by morning. Mama decided it wasn't worth leaving anything there anymore." The woman crossed her arms again, tighter this time, as though wary of the tree and even of talking to Delphine. "And it wasn't worth teaching me what she knew anymore, either."

"I'm sorry," Delphine said, not sure what else she could say. Though the other trees rustled in the summer breeze, even the thinnest twigs of the dead oak stayed stiff and immobile, like the desiccated fingers of a corpse. Delphine looked up at branches reaching ominously toward a brilliant blue sky. She wondered how long until the forest on this side of the veil reclaimed the circle entirely, or if it ever would, leaving the oak a towering grave marker to a dead doorway.

10

Ring of grass or ring of moss
Green as summer field
Do not stay and do not play
For only sorrows yield
　　　—Children's song

ALAINE TOUCHED A cherry tentatively, testing to see if its skin was beginning to pull taut. The trees were as full of them as she could have hoped for given the rocky start to the season, and they hadn't dropped unripe. Now they only had to get through the last weeks of ripening, and they could be plucked and sorted and sent to market.

In her pocket, another bank notice crinkled whenever she moved. Final notice, bold print, all the threatening legalese that, had Jack not translated it into layman's terms, would have sent her into a panicked swoon as swiftly as a dime-romance-novel heroine. Still, the threat was there. The cherries had to bring enough profit to last a summer's worth of mortgage payments. Even though it appeared that the bargain at the linden tree had worked, the harvest as rich and thick as she'd ever seen from her cherries, there was nothing she had learned that would also fetch a good price and a quick payment.

There was nothing she had learned. And staring at that old linden wasn't going to get her anywhere, either; leaving a bargain in its roots instead of the garden gate was one thing, but she certainly

couldn't—and wouldn't—summon a Fae to do her bidding. But what had Aunt Imogene said, back at the wedding? There were things Gran hadn't taught.

The footpath down the ridge toward her great-aunt's house was just past a stand of dark pines on the other side of the cherry orchard. Imogene was one of the only old-timers left who still kept a cabin in the middle of the woods instead of a house within full view of Prospect Street. Sufficiently curious, Alaine ventured down the hill.

"You could come more often, you know." Imogene waited in the doorway. "Saw you traipsin' down the hill like you own the place." She laughed. "You want some tea? Or milk? Just milked Daisy." The ruddy cow cocked her head at them from inside her pen. "Best cow I've had in years for milk."

"That's all right." A thin cloud of woodsmoke blurred the chimney. "Are you doing all right on firewood? You're sure you wouldn't prefer getting fitted out with a coal stove?"

"Mercy, no. Dirty stuff. If you want to send Jack down to chop some more wood, I wouldn't turn it down." She gestured to the bench on the cabin's wide porch. "I don't have quite the heft with the axe as I used to."

"I'll send him when he gets back from the office today."

"The office! Never would have thought I'd see Lilabeth's folks marrying lawyers and such. But we'll forgive him."

"I'd forgive him just about anything, Aunt Imogene."

"Keep it that way," she said with a wry grin. "*Almost* anything."

Imogene sat in her old rocking chair and began to rock, slow and heavy. She waited, patient like the hills themselves, in no mood to rush anything. Alaine perched on the bench, shifting her weight on the hard edges. Imogene had all but invited the conversation at the wedding, but now Alaine found herself faltering under the sharp eyes of the old woman.

"I'm not quite sure how to ask this," Alaine said. "But you said something, at Delphine's wedding."

"I said a lot of things. Apparently your ma didn't like some of 'em."

"Oh! Oh, not that." Alaine hid a laugh behind her hand, and

Imogene reddened. "No, I'm not laughing at you. Mother was so set on impressing the Graftons, she had no sense of humor that day. I actually thought it was rather funny, watching her turn red as a beet for no good reason."

"Your ma's always been a sight too keen on impressing folks. Glad to see it skipped at least part of your generation."

Alaine let the criticism of both Mother and Delphine hang uncontested. Del was, after all, more interested in crafting an impressive Perrysburg life than she was in helping Alaine and her family's orchard. "At any rate, I wondered—you said Gran didn't teach us everything. About bargaining."

"Did I?" She rocked back in her chair. "Mercy, must have been the second glass of that stuff Horatio makes." She winked. "Lilabeth was always a mite nervous about bargaining. Our mama was, too, and Horatio having his run-in made them go straight sour in the stomach when it came to considering anything...stronger. Could have gone much worse, you know."

"I know. Gran always impressed that point on us quite clearly. Papa Horatio got lucky."

"He certainly did. But that's the thing—making a bargain direct with them is different. You can ask for exactly what you want." The pace of her rocking chair slowed. "You figure, every bargain we've got was made first at some point. Once made, it's bound forever to work. But there's got to be a first time."

"Have you?" Alaine breathed. "Have you done that?"

Imogene didn't answer her question. "It's not simple. It's got to be something you really want. And you've got to plan ahead, because there's only one way to find a Fae."

"A circle. Gran said that—that's why you never go inside a Fae circle."

"Right. That old linden tree, for example. You know the one." Imogene waited until Alaine nodded. "Gives me the willies."

Alaine decided not to mention that she'd visited it several times since leaving the bargain at its roots, watching it as though it could give her something. Perhaps part of her wanted a Fae to spring from its branches

and ask her to name her bargain as the Fae had with Papa Horatio, as foolhardy as that was. The rational part of her was grateful nothing had transpired in that corner of the woods. Another part of her, deeper than logic, hoped for some wild and strange magic despite the danger. She felt, waiting for Imogene to speak, that she was on the cusp of it.

Imogene continued, speaking with the same gentle pace of her rocking chair. "Anyhow, you don't use one of theirs. That linden tree, that's one they built. We've got no rights there. You want to broach a new deal, you build a circle of your own—at least, that's how I learned it."

"Build?"

"Well, plant." Imogene stared off toward the edge of her clearing. "Learned it from a lady over on the other side of Lemon Creek. She planted a ring of crocuses, buried a silver ring in the center, and while those flowers bloomed every year, she could bargain."

"But—if I planted crocuses right now, I couldn't expect it to work until next spring."

"That's right. Can't just call 'em up willy-nilly, for just anything. Like I said, it's got to be something you really want. That's been eating you for months, years maybe. Then, well. Then maybe it's worth it. Because the costs? They're not the same. It's not just tokens and coins."

"What did you—"

Imogene shook her head. "Some things ain't seemly to ask, even from my favorite niece." She paused for a long moment, and Alaine hoped the courtesy went both ways—that Imogene wouldn't ask her why she had a sudden and pressing interest in stronger fairy magic than Gran's bargains. She wasn't sure she could shoulder the shame of admitting their financial woes to the last remaining matriarch of the old Prospect Hill Riley family. "But suffice to say, even with bargains, dealings with human folks don't always go according to plan."

Alaine fell silent. The rocking chair treadled on the floorboards on the porch, even and patient. If she could ask for exactly what she wanted—something simple, something she could easily articulate in language the Fae couldn't warp. A record cherry harvest, high prices at the market, quick harvest. A single bargain could solve everything.

But Gran's warnings still echoed in her memory. The Fae weren't in the business of doing charity work, and a wrong step could bring disaster on Orchard Crest.

"Did she see one? That lady by Lemon Creek?" Alaine finally asked.

"Mercy, no. She left the offer in the circle, pinned to a letter. Silver pin, of course." Imogene stopped rocking. "Ink made from ashes, hardwood ashes."

"Does the kind of hardwood matter?" Alaine asked, almost too keen on the answers.

Imogene cocked an eyebrow at how Alaine leaned forward, hands on her knees like she was ready to pounce. "Don't know that it makes any nevermind. Don't know why ashes, either. But Marietta—the lady with the crocuses—she said to use linen paper, or hemp, not the cheap stuff you can buy now. That's how they know you're serious. Shows respect."

Alaine exhaled slowly, her breath hot and her thoughts racing. "Then they read our writing?"

Imogene laughed. "I don't rightly know. Laws, girl, you going to take up a study of fair folk culture down at the university?" She resumed rocking. "They know, however it is that they know it. Maybe they smell what you want on the ink."

"You said it wasn't just trinkets."

Imogene sucked her lips against her teeth, her thin cheeks going hollow. "Depends, I suppose. You want something small, you offer something small. But you want something big, you'd best be ready to give something big."

"But what?" Alaine buried clenched fists in her skirt as though that might bury her frustration. She had hoped Imogene would have a clear answer to her problem, like the pat rhyme at the end of a riddle, but the old lady's responses only created more questions. Maybe Gran had been right to leave this part of bargaining alone. "I don't know what they want, aside from what Gran taught us."

"You take your best guess." Imogene shrugged. "Come, now, you've read enough to know the sort of things they want. Unblemished

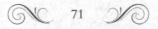

pears or a ring of daisies or the liver of a stillborn calf. Your firstborn child." Alaine swallowed hard. "You make a wager they're going to want what you offer, that it's worth what you're asking."

"What happens if you're wrong?" Alaine asked, fingertips pressed against her palms, going white.

"Nothing." Imogene smiled gently. "Nothing happens. They don't want your bargain, they don't take it. It's just sitting in the ring in the morning, no worse for the wear save some dew. The trouble can come if they take the bargain, but you weren't clear." Imogene looked past Alaine into the forest, eyes clouding. "You don't take chances on that."

11

A pat of butter set out on the sill
Brings a visit of bright goodwill
—Traditional bargain

THERE WASN'T TIME to plant crocus bulbs, Alaine knew that much. There wasn't time to plant much of anything; it would take at least two months for even phlox or Johnny-jump-ups to flower, and Alaine had a suspicion that the blooms might be necessary—or at least some sign of the ring's ability to part the veil. The linden tree was always, faintly, in bloom with whatever strange magic made a permanent fairy circle. She stared into the suds of the after-supper dishwater. The iridescent film shimmered back at her, but didn't offer any answers.

"You're scheming." Jack dried the dishes as Alaine washed them, stacking them carefully in the cupboard. He flicked a shred of green bean from a plate.

"Me?" Alaine pulled half a smile. "Never."

"Always. At any rate, I was thinking. We put the whole of the year into the harvest, but maybe there's some way to make a little extra money. We could raise chickens for sale, or eggs, or maybe even goats. There's a fair craze for goats some places now, new breeds coming over from—"

"That would take years to build up, Jack, not to mention putting

money in for pens or coops." They didn't have years. Or money. She sighed, her breath parting the soap suds.

Jack paused. She knew what was coming next—a chorus of rallying platitudes she didn't need or want to hear. But he surprised her. "Say, why don't you get away for a bit? Go see Del. She'll be back from her honeymoon, and I'm sure she'd like to tell you all about it."

Alaine began to argue, her clenched hands still submerged in dishwater, then stopped, recalling Delphine's last letter, sent just before she and Pierce left on their honeymoon. Delphine had—she stilled her breath—had a garden put in at her new home, the flowers blooming cheerfully along the circle drive and around the piazza.

"Maybe I should," she replied slowly, letting her hands relax into the soap again.

"If you send her a note tomorrow, she'll be able to reply by the end of the week," Jack said, clearly pleased with himself. "Em and I can handle ourselves here for a few days, and if I have to go into the office, she can visit your mother. Or mine."

"All right." Alaine shook off her hands and dried them with refreshed resolve. At any rate, Delphine had promised to talk to Pierce, and she hadn't sent word as to his thoughts. Alaine's hope for that particular solution waned as every day passed without anything from Del in the post. She had to do something other than wait. "I'll write the letter now—you can drop it by the box on the way to the office tomorrow?"

Three days later, Alaine was on the train to Perrysburg. The red velvet seats belied the stiff-coiled springs hidden inside, and by the time the station's green-tiled roof came into view, she had a twin pair of bruises on her backside. She shuffled her valise off the rack above her and scanned the empty platform for Delphine.

She shifted the valise to the other hand and sighed. The train wasn't early. Del must have been caught up at home planning some trifling party with people Alaine didn't want to meet—

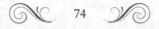

A motorcar honked from the street behind the station. Alaine jumped as the driver waved.

"Over here!"

It was a high-end Waverley electric car—a funny little carriage where the driver sat in the back seat and steered with a bar that looked for all the world to Alaine like a rudder. She'd seen pictures in the monthlies, but no one in Moore's Ferry had one yet.

The driver leaned forward, decked out in a driving coat and a veiled hat. "Alaine, it's me!"

Alaine gaped. Her sister waved again, a veil over her broad hat and driving gloves winking with smart brass buttons on the wrist, just like a proper motorist. Alaine heaved her valise into the front seats—which faced backward like a strangely mobile parlor set—and settled onto the upholstery next to Del, avoiding the steering mechanisms protruding from the floor. "What in the world?"

"Pierce bought it last month! I've been learning to drive as a surprise—I thought I could come out to see you sometime."

"Is it—" Alaine gripped the seat as the car lurched forward. "Is it quite safe?"

"Oh yes! Doesn't go nearly as fast as the gasoline-powered ones, but it's fine for around town or a short trip."

Alaine didn't ask the other question needling her—was it quite proper? But of course Delphine wouldn't do anything that wasn't ladylike, that the other young wives of Perrysburg didn't approve of. And she had to admit that her sister steered with a deft precision and a confidence she hadn't often seen in her. Delphine smiled to herself as she parked and shut off the contraption.

"Well." Delphine shook out her skirts. "What would you like to do this afternoon? I've got you to myself until six, Pierce won't be home 'til then. I've asked the neighbors for dinner—you must meet Mrs. Abbott, she's a delight, and Mr. Abbott keeps Pierce busy talking politics for hours. What shall we start with?"

Alaine hesitated. She should give her sister her full attention, let Del drag her to the tearoom she favored in town, or show off the new piano piece she'd been working up. Even ask after her honeymoon.

But she had to know, before anything else. "Did you speak with Pierce about the farm? Investing in our operations?"

Delphine's face fell behind her sheer veil. "I did. He—he isn't interested in investing, Alaine. I'm sorry, I—"

"No, no, it's all right!" She pasted on a bright smile, covering raw anger at Pierce. What was the money to him, anyway? It felt almost cruel, not only to her, but to Delphine. "I was just curious. Now, that car—it's an interesting design. You know, I've been investigating farm trucks for the Agricultural Society, and they're really remarkable, there are some with conveyor belts built right in and—"

"He said he'd consider a loan," Delphine offered quietly. "You could probably ask him while you're here, if you like."

"No, of course that's not necessary." She swallowed against barbs in her throat that protested it might very well be necessary. But no— she wouldn't be beholden to Pierce Grafton as well as the bank, not if she could help it. She changed the subject as efficiently as Delphine had steered the car around a corner. "I can't wait to see what you've done with your house. Do you think you could explain to me how you fixed up your garden so quickly?"

"My garden!" Delphine laughed. "You've never cared about plants before, unless they grew apples or pears."

"I'd like to put in flower beds at the cottage," she lied easily.

"In that case, you're better asking Mother—almost all of mine are annuals. I'll have to dig the whole thing up in the spring and plant properly."

"Then why did you plant them all in the first place?" Alaine cut herself off before she began to sound like a chiding country aunt.

"Oh, we wanted to start entertaining right away, and all those bare spots were such an eyesore. The greenhouse in town has plants ready to go in the ground, you see, so we filled everything in with those. I'll have the gardener come this fall to draw up a plan for the perennials. We may still fill in with some of the annuals, though..." She trailed off, tilting her narrow chin as she assessed a pink-and-white explosion of impatiens by the fountain.

Alaine couldn't help but look past the profuse blooms to the

limestone house beyond, crisp blue-and-white awnings shading three stories of windows and a sprawling piazza and porticos. Even on Prospect Hill, the nicest neighborhood in Moore's Ferry, no one had a house like this, a veritable mansion that exuded money and taste.

"The begonias were a bit sparse at first, but once they took off, you can see how they filled in that whole bank. And you can't imagine how many colors of impatiens you can get—I had the devil of a time narrowing the color scheme down." Delphine traced a pale pink blossom. "I think pink and white look rather well with the house, don't you?"

"Yes, it's lovely." Alaine found the whole botanical arrangement rather restrained, to tell the truth—far more careful and precise than nature ever provided. She supposed Delphine knew what she was doing. "But you mean you can really get flowers right away, without starting from seeds?" Alaine prompted.

"Yes! It's the loveliest place, too. Like the tropics, all those flowers blooming. The bigger cities all have them now, gardener's nurseries. So you don't have to save seeds or even order from the catalogs if you don't want to."

"Do you think we could go?"

Delphine paused, surprised by Alaine's sudden excitement. "I don't need any more plants now..." She had worried that Alaine wouldn't find anything of interest in her city life, and the indifferent way she'd scanned the house and garden had made her spirits fall. She wanted to share her new house, new acquaintances, new life with Alaine, but she feared her sister wouldn't care—or worse, would dismiss or judge it. Anything Alaine found intriguing, Delphine would twist herself into a figure eight to accommodate. "If you'd like to see it, of course! I suppose I've talked it up a bit now, it's only fair. And we can get tea after!" She tied the net of her driving hat and pulled on her gloves again.

Delphine felt the car spur to life under her hands, and easily maneuvered through the wide avenues of Perrysburg, past the blocks of downtown shops and restaurants and the hotel rising eight stories, turning down a side road toward the gardener's nursery. A strange thing to fixate on, perhaps—but Alaine had always preferred outdoor sorts of activities to taking meals in fine tearooms or going to concerts.

This must be Alaine's way of trying to connect to her life in Perrysburg, Delphine reasoned.

"It's bigger than I expected," Alaine said as they walked into the long, low building.

Delphine slowed and inhaled damp soil and mingled perfume of the flowers. Everything was laid out in orderly rows, each type of flower and ground cover grouped by color, each potted tree and bush neatly labeled. Delphine took off her hat and veil and examined a rosebush in full bloom, the yellow petals fading to pink at the edges.

"That's a new hybrid tea rose we've got in," the shopkeeper said, a bit too eagerly. A mist of sweat shimmered on his balding head. "If you're interested, I'll have stock for fall planting—"

"Oh, not yet, no thank you."

She needed to plan the space, research the root area each would need, determine which spots were sunniest and which the tall oaks on the edge of the yard dappled with shade before she started buying plants. Still, she took a notebook from her pocketbook and wrote down the name and the stock number, just in case.

"Are you finding everything you came in for?"

Delphine sighed—she disliked shopkeepers who couldn't let ladies browse in peace, and of course Alaine wasn't here to shop. She turned.

Alaine had her hands loaded with a collage of petals—yellow calendula and red geraniums clashed with the pink begonias and lavender impatiens. "Yes, I'm quite finished, I think."

"Alaine, what in the world—"

"I figured I'd try a few and see what does well," Alaine said with a shrug, opening her pocketbook.

"We've a buyback policy on the pots," the balding man said.

"It's a rather expensive experiment," Delphine protested. "You must at least know if you need ones that work well in the shade or the sun."

"I suppose I need both." She handed the shopkeeper several crisp bills. Fresh from the bank, or Delphine missed her guess. "We've got both sun and shade aplenty at the cottage."

Delphine sighed as a small shower of dirt clouded Alaine's skirt. "Could you at least give her a crate?"

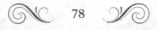

12

The practice of fairy bargaining implies an ability to reorder hierarchies and challenge the institutions of one's culture, even if this ability is entirely imagined.

—*Changelings and Gambler's Chances: Tales of Fairy Mischief*, by William Fitzgerald

BY THE TIME Delphine dressed for dinner, there had been a mishap with a broken calendula pot, potting soil had spilled in the motorcar, and a large muddy stain had appeared on Alaine's shirtwaist. The plants were safely ensconced in the potting shed, and Delphine decided to forget that Alaine was going to make a spectacle of herself carrying them on her lap all the way home on the train.

Delphine smoothed her blue silk dinner dress over her waist, chiffon and charmeuse cascading together from the beaded belt. She'd had it made at the new atelier in town, even though Pierce had insisted he'd be quite willing to send her on a trip to have her wardrobe done. Delphine liked keeping to Perrysburg as much as possible, however; if she was going to be married into one of the wealthiest families in town, to a man that had his eye on politics, she felt she needed to be a sort of local benefactor. The New York and Chicago and Saint Louis ateliers certainly had enough business.

Delphine knocked on the door of the guest suite. Strange—at home they would have both barged into each other's space without

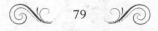

ask or invitation. The newly imposed distance stung, just a little, but also felt like a welcome relief.

"Aren't you ready yet?" Delphine asked as Alaine opened the door. Her hair was dressed, and she'd scrubbed the dirt from her hands and the spot where it had, somehow, streaked her left cheek.

"Not quite," Alaine said, jabbing her thumb at a somewhat creased gown.

"You stuffed that poor dress in your valise, didn't you." Delphine laughed. "Turn the hot water on in the bathroom and see if the steam takes the wrinkles out."

"Good trick," Alaine replied, shuttling yards of dove-gray satin out of the closet. Delphine heard her turn the water on. "Oh! I brought you something!" Alaine rifled through her valise and produced an oddly shaped packet wrapped in a faded cotton handkerchief. "I forgot, before you left."

Delphine took the bundle, and before she shook the handkerchief free, its weight and shape gave it away—an iron horseshoe, old and pitted with faint rust. "Alaine! Why in the world—"

Alaine's eyebrow ticked upward. "Now, you know as well as I do—you want to keep the Fae out of your house, you put an iron horseshoe over the front door."

"If you live on Prospect Hill!" Delphine laughed. "There are no Fae here, Alaine. Maybe Lilabeth would say that the veil holds too firm here. Or maybe it's that we're already hemmed in with iron train tracks and steel automobiles and who knows what all else, horseshoes over the doors or no."

"It's tradition, Del." Alaine smiled faintly, but Delphine knew her sister felt hurt. "I know it's not the same here as it is on Prospect Hill—you'd have been glamouring your dinner parties if it was, and I don't see any straw wreaths on the windows."

"I haven't even tried," Delphine said, though it wasn't true. Even though she'd been quite sure that the veil was closed here, a spark of nostalgia or hope made her try anyway. Their first evening home from the honeymoon, she'd hung a braided wreath of golden straw to catch the light of the setting sun and set a glamour over the table in the breakfast room—to make it special, to bring Pierce's full attention from a stack of contracts to their first meal at home as husband and wife. The wine had seemed lusher to her, the vinaigrette on the salad brighter, the flash and shine of the silver and the creamy porcelain china enchanting. But Pierce had talked about a business meeting and didn't care to have dessert, and the straw circlet had remained the next morning, untouched. Any magic to the shared meal was in Delphine's own mind. There had been no bargain; there would be no bargains here.

"Well, it's a housewarming gift, and I can't return it. Barnaby doesn't want it back." Alaine patted a bit of rouge on her cheeks. "You don't have to hang it up. I know it probably doesn't suit the décor."

Delphine laughed at her sister's joke, but it felt hollow. Alaine was right—the horseshoe didn't have any place in Perrysburg. Delphine was increasingly worried that she didn't, either. Despite gushing entreaties before the wedding to join her for clubs and outings, Pierce's sister Stella hadn't actually called on her once. The dinner guests in their home were business acquaintances whose wives seemed to have full social calendars without room for Delphine. Even at church, no one greeted her except when they passed the peace. The only bright spot was her weekly painting class.

If Delphine admitted it to herself, she was lonely and almost frighteningly unmoored. "I'd like to come to Orchard Crest for a week or so of the cherry harvest," she said. "But I'm not sure Pierce wants me climbing trees."

"You never climbed trees much anyway. Tended to stick to the ladder. And why should he bother about that, anyway?"

Delphine stiffened. "He's been a bit of a bear about appearances. That is, his family is. That is—" She quickly corrected herself, not wanting to give Alaine the impression she was unhappy or that Pierce was unkind. "I only mean that we have to maintain a certain respectability. Pierce has been talking of running for city council, and I suppose he doesn't want it to look as though we're country cousins."

"You are a country cousin," Alaine called from the bathroom.

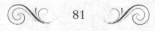

Delphine covered her anger at that idea with a faint sigh of protest. "Oh, I didn't mean it that way—honestly, wouldn't it give him that populist, everyman sort of angle to have a fresh-faced country wife?" She wrestled a hairpin into her lopsided bouffant.

"Then he married the wrong sister," Delphine said, taking the hairpins from Alaine and gently reshaping her fair waves. "I don't think, at any rate, that the populist angle is quite what he's going for." She pulled back, admiring her sister's hair, then swatted her corseted hip. "Hurry up and get dressed!"

Gowned in a mostly de-wrinkled silk dinner dress, Alaine followed Delphine into the dining room, tamping down a gasp at the excess of wood paneling, leaded windows, and velvet curtains surrounding a mahogany table so polished it reflected each crystal facet of the chandelier. She had always been proud of Orchard Crest, with its maple staircase and the pretty marble mantelpiece, but it was a country cottage compared with Delphine's house. And Delphine seemed so at home here! Alaine could see the reflection of her sister's taste in the pale pink silk wallcoverings in the parlor, the stained-glass irises in the stairwell windows, the rosebud china pattern laid out on the table. Who would have believed she and Del had been raised in the same home, had run barefoot in the orchard together, had slept under the same hand-sewn quilts! The realization made her chest tighten with a strange sense of loss.

Pierce stood by the head of the table, conversing with a couple who looked as though they had just stepped from the pages of a society quarterly. Beside them, an angular, bespectacled young woman hung back, quietly observing.

"Alaine, this is Mr. Thomas Abbott and his wife, Edwina Abbott," Delphine said with punctuated grace. "Mr. and Mrs. Abbott, my sister, Alaine Fairborn."

"Fairborn—one of the Perrysburg Fairborns?" Mr. Abbott's graying bottlebrush of a moustache twitched at the prospect of recognition.

"I'm afraid not," Alaine replied. "The Moore's Ferry Fairborns."

"Ah, yes. Picturesque little town."

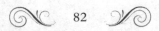

"Alaine and I grew up on Prospect Hill in Moore's Ferry," Delphine supplied. "She lives there and manages the family farm."

"Oh, how quaint!" Mrs. Abbott's round cheeks flushed. "Chickens and cows and the whole bit, then?"

"We do keep chickens," Alaine said. "But we're an orchard, primarily. Apples and cherries, mostly, and we just branched out into pears."

"Branched out!" Mrs. Abbott laughed as though the pun had been intentional, her cloying lilac perfume wafting ever closer. "How delightful. And may I introduce my niece, Ida Carrington?"

"Pleased to meet you," Alaine said, echoed by introductions and pleasantries in a completion of the steps of this particular social dance. Then Mr. Abbott turned swiftly to discuss some matter of exceptional importance regarding coal shares with Pierce, Delphine swept Mrs. Abbott into conversation, and Alaine just as swiftly moved to the other end of the table.

"Sorry." Alaine turned to face the voice at her elbow. Ida hovered, just on the uncomfortable side of closeness, doe-brown eyes wide with curiosity. "I—is it true that you're from the Prospect Hill area?"

"Yes, it is," Alaine said. "I live on Prospect Hill itself, actually."

"Oh! Oh, fascinating. You'll excuse me—are you and your sister from one of the old families?"

Alaine accepted a glass of something faintly pink from a passing servant, and then met this strange girl's eager eyes with guarded indifference. "Yes, we are. On my grandmother's side."

"How ideal. I—I am sorry. I'm a student at the university, you see, and I study ethnomusicology."

"Ethnomusicology?"

"Yes—it's—well, the study of music from cultures not one's own? My particular scholarly interest is in bargaining songs, and to meet someone from an actual bargain-endemic culture, it's just—it's just quite exciting."

"Bargain-endemic, is it?" Alaine sipped the wine, not sure whether to be amused or offended by this young woman who spoke about her as though describing a zoology specimen.

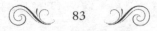

"I am sorry, it's just the term for cultures in which bargaining and Fae lore is accepted. You know, just one of those academic terms, I didn't mean—" She flushed deeply, even her freckles fading into the ruddy hue.

"No, not at all. I am curious," Alaine said, forming her question carefully as she considered the flattened fruit scent of the wine, "how it is that you've never encountered anyone from such a culture before?"

"Oh, I—my family is all from the coast, you know. I'm only here for the university."

"Your aunt and uncle don't associate much with old families, I take it. And neither do the sort of folks one socializes with at the, ah, *university*." She smiled, intentionally piercing. If she was going to be viewed as the country oddity, very well, but it was going to be acknowledged.

Ida paused, chagrined. "I'm afraid we've gotten a rather bad start," she said slowly. "I'm so sorry. I'm forever putting my foot in my mouth and—well, you can see, it's not a small foot." She brandished a sizeable heeled shoe in a fetching blush pink. Alaine hesitated. Ida seemed earnest, if nothing else.

"Then let's say we start over," Alaine said.

"No time now, I'm afraid. Social duty calls." Ida nodded toward silhouettes uniformed in black and white by the doorway as Delphine gestured to the table.

"I believe our first course is ready. Mr. Abbott, you really must try the wine Pierce selected." Delphine beamed at her husband, who inclined his head, accepting her compliment. Alaine shifted uncomfortably. She couldn't tell a French vintage from a backcountry Norton.

Mr. Abbott took an appreciative sip of the pale wine a servant poured for him. "It won't be long before they'll be pricing the stuff too dear for everyday dinners," he said, "if the anti-vice lobbies get their way on the taxation legislation."

"What a dreary subject for dinner," Mrs. Abbott said with a strained smile.

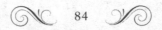

"No, I rather agree with your husband," Pierce said, leaning forward. "Not that I don't sympathize quite wholly with their arguments about the underclass wasting their wages on gin or the scourge of alcoholism among that sort." He laughed politely and the Abbotts followed suit. Alaine bit her lip, feeling closer to the "sort" Pierce denigrated than to the others at the table. She glanced over his head at the silent maid standing by the door. Her face was an impassive mask. "But the imposition of taxes based upon moral valuation is a dangerous road in any case."

"Quite true! There are better ways of alleviating the burden on society affected by the working man's poor choices." Mr. Abbott swirled the wine in his glass. "I say, and that reminds me—what of the bill up for vote in the statehouse?"

"You know my mind." Pierce paused while the soup course was served. Something clear and riddled with tiny green flecks was set in front of Alaine; she dipped her spoon into it and discovered it was nearly tasteless. "You might find the debate interesting, Alaine, given that your husband owns a farm and, I'm sure, employs workers." Alaine bit down on her objection—she hired the workers at harvest and for help pruning and winterizing the orchard. "There is a new bill to include contract workers in some of the legal provisions for—"

"Workers' rights to organize and form unions, yes," she interrupted, a bit too eager. "Oh, it's only that we've been campaigning for adequate protections for farms in that legislation," she explained with a flush.

"I'm sorry?" Pierce said, dredging his bowl with the soup spoon.

"I'm president of our local chapter of the Agricultural Society. We've of course been watching this very closely. There are peculiarities, one could say, to farm labor that need to be considered—the seasonal elements, and of course that we're only employing a very few workers compared to such a large employer as the Grafton Glassworks." Across the table, Delphine's brow furrowed. Alaine smiled politely into her soup, dodging a raised eyebrow from Mr. Abbott and a flustered cough from Pierce. Ida leaned forward, interested, at the first whiff of academic conversation.

"But of course the whole thing is hogwash," Mr. Abbott interjected.

"I'm not so sure—the Agricultural Society is itself a vehicle for organization of non-landowning workers; they can join just like us farm owners do. They've got a stake just like I have." Alaine saw Delphine's wide-eyed stare and stopped herself from continuing. Delphine shook her head slightly. Appearances, then. Alaine fell silent.

Mr. Abbott laughed, not quite a good-natured sound. "Now tell me, Mrs. Fairborn. Do your political aspirations climb higher than the local farmers' aid society? Have you a women's suffrage association in Moore's Ferry, too?"

Beside him, Mrs. Abbott blushed faintly, and dabbed her mouth with her napkin. "I must say, it isn't my preference to discuss politics at dinner at all, but I'm quite sure no one wants to debate women's suffrage before we've even had the main course."

Alaine stared at the filigreed edges of the soup bowl, avoiding Delphine's eyes. This wasn't Orchard Crest, she chided herself, where Papa Horatio enjoyed a rousing conversation over coffee and Jack was happy to hear her opinion. She had a retort ready—that perhaps she should start a chapter of the national suffrage society in Moore's Ferry—and instead swallowed a spoonful of cooling soup and burning humiliation at once. "Perhaps I simply don't understand the impacts of the labor laws on the larger factories," she demurred, the words sour in her mouth.

Ida intervened with earnest enthusiasm. "There are good questions to be investigated in the varied impacts of any—"

"No matter," Pierce replied with a condescending smile. "I find that women are often far more sympathetic to the working class than the businessmen who have to actually wrangle with them." Mr. Abbott responded with an appreciative guffaw. Alaine bristled, watching Delphine for any sign of offense or embarrassment. Her sister kept her eyes on her husband, face delicately neutral. "Makes a good argument why they should stay out of politics, but it's why they do such good charity work, I believe."

"And that is quite necessary," Delphine said hurriedly. "Even here in Perrysburg."

"That is true," Ida said, glancing at Alaine as though she very much wanted to say more. "Why, just last week, you were telling me about the coat collection you've started, Aunt Edwina."

Delphine's eyes turned toward Alaine, pleading for politesse as Mrs. Abbott began to regale them with the successes of a secondhand outerwear drive. Alaine dug her fingers into her napkin, unable to stay her fuming thoughts. Pierce had treated her like an idiot and seemed to have no more regard for Delphine's intelligence—was this how he thought of her, as a pretty addition to his home, just like the mahogany dining table and the crystal chandelier? Delphine was perceptive and creative—any fool, Alaine thought as her fingernails bit into her palms, could glean that from a few minutes talking with her, from seeing her watercolors or her sketches. She stole a glance at Pierce, trying to avoid too obvious a glare. How could a man like this make Del happy? Alaine remained silent as the main course was served and let Mr. Abbott and Pierce Grafton steer the conversation back to the proper interaction between business, politics, and their own substantial influence.

13

To keep something hidden: Tie a ribband into three neat knots and slide a silver pinn through the third knot. Leave in the same room as the hidden objecte, in the furthest corner from it. Do not speak while completing this task.

—The Compleat Book of Bargaining Works, by A Lady, 1767

ALAINE BALANCED THE crate of potted flowers on her lap the entire train ride from Perrysburg to Moore's Ferry. She considered putting them on the floor, but if the train stopped suddenly, as it sometimes had to when there was a deer on the tracks or the Farmers Union had closed the rail crossings to move wagons or livestock, they could spill. There was no time to get more. She could try transplanting wildflowers, but Mother always said that rarely worked, so if she wanted her circle, it needed to be these tame hothouse flowers.

She walked from the station to Orchard Crest, ignoring Mrs. Higgins, who always wanted to chat as she passed her on Currant Street, after dropping her valise at Jack's office so she could manage carrying her unplanted garden. The secretary at the front desk didn't bother asking; Alaine knew she thought that the old Prospect Hill families were strange already.

The long walk up Prospect Hill was even longer with a dozen potted plants in an unwieldy crate, and so Alaine was forced to walk more slowly than her usual brisk clip. The houses had been built in a smattering of styles in no semblance of order as the Hill was settled. The Bradburns' stately Italianate stood next to a Queen Anne now owned by Reverend Clay, freshly painted in a wash of lilacs and yellows and deep gold. The newest build, a brick foursquare with pink geraniums on the porch, occupied an awkwardly small lot between the Fischers' rambling cottage and the Olsons' gloomy Gothic. Alaine smiled. Each of those houses had a story, not unlike hers, of families finding Moore's Ferry for one reason or another and making their mark on the town. At the very top of the hill stood Orchard Crest, her columned porch facing the street, once a rutted dirt path and now paved with brick and dotted with the prettiest new streetlamps the town could afford.

Alaine hauled the box past Orchard Crest toward Lavender Cottage. She set the plants on the porch and peered inside warily. No one was home. She breathed a little easier as she shucked her good dress and changed into an old shirtwaist. Now that she had the flowers, had a plan, she harbored little hesitation, but she didn't want to have to explain to Jack or Emily or, heaven help it, her mother. The nerves cropping up in her stomach were because she was afraid the new ring wouldn't work—at least, that was what she told herself as she dug a pair of gardening gloves out of a kitchen cabinet.

She scanned the yard. She couldn't plant the flowers too close to the chickens; they'd have them eaten before the day was out. And too far away would put them at the edge of the woods. Despite Delphine's clear assumptions, Alaine wasn't completely ignorant—she knew the plants needed some sun. After assessing the space between the house and the forest, she found an unused corner of the yard far enough from the drive that her odd little garden wouldn't be the first thing visitors saw.

She uncovered a rusted trowel from the toolshed and a voluminous apron from the kitchen and began to work. Twelve holes, dug in as perfect of a circle as she could make it, imagining the numbers on a clock or the points of a compass. Too late she wondered if she ought to have oriented the flowers with the cardinal directions, or some other intuitive magic, but they were already in the ground. She didn't want to risk disturbing them again. They had to take, to grow. To live.

She guessed the magic came from the plants being alive, even as she planted the ring in the center of the circle, like a precious barren seed. It was a posy ring Jack had given her, before they were married, embossed with miniature apple blossoms. It stung, piling dirt over it, but she remembered what Imogene had said—this bargain wasn't just tokens and scraps. There was a cost.

She couldn't hover over her bedraggled flowers forever; there was the farrier coming to reshoe Barnaby and Bruno, and errands to run in town, and after all that, an Agricultural Society meeting to chair. She scrubbed the dirt from her hands and changed into a fresh waist.

The fellowship hall of the church was uncomfortably warm, and sweat tickled the back of Alaine's neck. Acton Willis and Howard Olson still watched her like cats ready to pounce on her first misstep, but she found she minded less as she settled into her role. They were fixtures in the fellowship hall, no more unexpected than the lamps or the doors to the church kitchen or the cracked window that no one had bothered to fix in three years. *Fine*, she dared them. *Waste your time glaring at me and hoping I make a mistake. I have more friends here than you do.*

She did, too—that was clear. Olson had struggled to find anyone to chair the Mercy Fund committee or the fundraiser committee; so many members enthusiastically raised their hands to volunteer when she asked that they required an ad hoc election. When she came to the agenda item discussing uses for excess funds, several members had come with already-researched propositions.

"It's much better with you as president," Maisie confided as she passed Alaine copies of the last meeting's minutes. "Howard never gave me time to proofread the minutes before he was asking after them. It takes time, you know." She fussed with the pages, finally relinquishing them.

They'd been in school together; Maisie had been punctual, tactful, and boring as a schoolgirl, and she was punctual, tactful, and boring now. They'd never been close, but Alaine could appreciate Maisie's talents more than when they'd been ten and Maisie had tattled on all of them for smuggling toads into the classroom.

"I hear your cherries are coming along," Willis interrupted them. He leaned in, broad shoulders leveraging space away from Maisie, who stepped away, flustered.

"Yes, everyone's are," Alaine replied, channeling some of Maisie's tact.

"Not everyone's," he said, tone more ominous than the conversation warranted, Alaine thought. "Over across the river, they say they dropped their fruit in most of the orchards."

"Over the river, they get harder weather sometimes."

"Huh. Well. I imagine many of the Society members would appreciate if you let them in on any, shall we call them, tricks of the trade? I thought that was what we were all about here, helping one another. Sharing knowledge and all that."

Alaine stiffened, pausing before she spoke to avoid saying anything she'd regret, however much Willis might deserve a tongue-lashing. "I'm not doing anything differently than anyone following best current techniques."

"The Canners and Fairborns have never held any of their techniques back," Maisie interjected. Lorne Albright stood behind her, turning to listen in on the conversation. "Why, it was Iris Canner who taught me how to grade eggs in half the time, and Horatio gave me his old remedy for aphids."

"And no one can say your family hasn't pitched in to help mine plenty," Lorne added, his bald head sweating slightly at being drawn into something that hinted at confrontation.

"You must be doing something differently," Acton Willis pressed.

"We just have good luck," Alaine replied. The old Prospect Hill families knew what she meant; the newcomers shrugged, as though acknowledging that luck was fickle. Alaine met Acton's eyes and took her meaning one step further, daring him to say anything against her family. "You know that us old-timers are superstitious; I put fairy bargains out, and we wassail the trees every winter. You want to take that as an agricultural method and try it yourself, go right ahead. It's no secret."

Most of the members laughed awkwardly at that, the newcomers having no intention of trying out fairy bargains and the old families knowing full well the newcomers like Acton Willis didn't believe in them. Acton's mouth pinched into a knot. He knew he was cornered.

"Well. We'll need more luck than not before long—you all voted on a use of funds that's a downright gamble." Willis huffed. He elbowed his way toward Olson, muttering that they would be the laughingstock of the county.

Alaine's last thread of patient politesse snapped. "What was that, Mr. Willis?"

It was Howard Olson who answered, eyes narrowed and fixed on Alaine. "He's just saying what everyone outside this little clutch of hens is thinking. That we look like fools for electing some suffragette to office." He spat the word like a curse.

"Here now!" Millie Jacobs flushed red. "Alaine Fairborn is a well-respected farmer, not some . . . some suffragette!"

Alaine closed her eyes. Hardly a resounding endorsement.

"We won't look like fools when we've held a successful livestock auction," she answered instead of arguing the point. Willis and Olson were already halfway to the door and didn't respond. Everyone else remaining shifted uncomfortably. The two businessmen weren't popular, per se, but they did hold a certain amount of grudging respect in town.

"Do you think so, really?" Maisie asked. "I thought that the livestock auction was a good idea—using some of our money to set up a more robust Mercy Fund."

"He's just being a sourpuss, since we rejected donating to his brother's election fund," Alaine said. "It is going to take lot of work, though—and we have to get that permit through for sale of livestock outside the auction houses, and before we can do that, we need to determine a location and a date, and before that—"

"Oh, that should be no problem at all," Millie Jacobs, who had volunteered to chair the auction committee, replied. "None at all. My cousin is on the county board, and I'll get everything squared away." She smiled brightly.

Alaine thanked her and made her escape from the hall, which suddenly felt too hot and too close. She felt faintly sick at having her bargaining called to the floor in front of the members. The truth was, she wasn't being honest with them or anyone else. She told Jack she'd always wanted to try a flower garden and found the plan for this one in *The Ladies' Home Journal* while she was visiting Delphine. He was too kind to argue that no magazine could ever have published such a ragged and ugly garden. Each day as she watered the flowers, she agonized over their drooping fragile forms, hoping fervently that their roots would take, that their leaves would unfurl, and that their blossoms would raise their faces toward the sun again. And while she watched, she thought over the bargain for a profitable cherry harvest, time and again.

"Mama, your garden is funny looking," Emily said one day after school, circling it like a confused hawk.

"Don't—" Alaine's voice pitched higher. She pulled it back toward its natural soft alto. "Don't go inside this garden."

"Mama?"

Even at seven, Em could tease through the kinds of lines that would fool some child raised in Perrysburg or Springfield or Chicago or Saint Louis, somewhere far away from Prospect Hill. Because, even at seven, Emily knew what a fairy circle was.

Alaine swallowed. "I'm trying something. Trying a different place to put bargains. Since I don't know if—since I haven't tried it yet, we should stay away from it."

"You said to stay away from fairy circles," Emily said slowly, still looking at the patchwork garden of mismatched blooms. "You said never to mess with them at all."

"I did. And I still say that."

"Then why—"

"Aunt Imogene said—" No, Alaine stopped herself. There was no pinning this on Aunt Imogene. "You still stay out of them. All of them, even this one. But I might leave a bargain in it, once in a while. To see if—to see if they might work any better."

Alaine could tell that Emily didn't quite believe her, but she left the circle, teasing her steps slowly backward. "Well, the flowers don't look dead anymore," she commented, her voice bearing the sting of being kept outside of both the circle and her mother's secret. Then she went back inside the house without another word.

Regret pinched Alaine's stomach, but Em was too young. Just as Gran had been, she was nervous about this method, uncertain of unbalancing the deft language of bargains. Of loss. Emily was too young to pull her into this particular dance. And yet—and yet she had, Alaine rationed with a firm breath in, then out. Whatever happened, Emily was involved. She was part of Orchard Crest. And that haunting comment of Imogene's—*or your firstborn*—echoed, even though she had no intention of making any such bargain.

The circle was, as Em had noticed, in full bloom and comfortably lush despite being in the ground only a couple of days. *Now or never*, Alaine thought grimly. In response to the sour feeling in her stomach, she added, *It was my own damn idea.*

She still had to figure out the trade. She'd decided, already, to put the same tried and tested silver chain and mother-of-pearl buttons in the ring, along with the sprig of cherry leaves, to communicate what she wanted. But what else could she bargain with? What did a fairy value? The bits of bright ribbon and old buttons and tea-stained paper and rose petals seemed entirely inadequate, and she couldn't discern a pattern of worth to them. Silver coins might be worth less than chicken feathers to the Fae, for all she knew. But she had to offer them something of sufficient value to ensure enough money from this harvest to pay their bills through the fall. She wouldn't take the risk for anything less.

One of the hens edged closer to the flowers, tilting her beady eyes toward a bright calendula blossom. Her bright red comb bobbed as she scratched at something in the gravel. Alaine eyed her, assessing her, ignoring the sick feeling creeping into her gut, and decided.

She waited until after Emily and Jack had gone to bed, guilt needling her over the deception more than the decision itself. She didn't want to raise Jack's hopes, she told herself. But there was more, a sense that doing this made her into someone she hadn't been before, that this changed how she touched the world beyond the veil of blossoming circles.

She wrapped her old wool coat over her nightgown and slipped outside to the chicken coop. She opened one of the side boxes slowly, avoiding the pinching creak of the old hinges, lifted her kerosene lantern, and found the hen she was looking for. Her eyes, like black beads in the darkness, stared back in night-blind confusion. Alaine could stand to lose a chicken, but it had some value to her—and this was her best layer, not a stringy old hen destined for the stewpot. She'd hoped to get a brood of chicks out of her. The silvery-blue feathers and ruddy comb reminded her of the silver beads and silk ribbons she used to entice the Fae into bargains for good weather or diverting beetles and caterpillars from the orchard. Gran had told stories of live animals whisked off to Fae, so it was possible. She didn't stop to think of what use the Fae might have for a hen.

She tucked the chicken under her arm so it couldn't flap its wings, and dragged an old apple crate out of the shed. With a pang of guilt, she shut the chicken inside. Then the bargain. With shaking hands, she took the tin of wood ash she'd saved from a corner of the pie safe, mixed it with water, and thought long before she wrote out her bargain.

A new bargain I would make, the Fae I entreat to take:
Hen for harvest, harvest sold
Cherries that ripen to bountiful gold

14

Make your bargains not in haste, for a bargain, once named, binds all.
—Folk saying

EMILY'S SHRIEKS WOKE Alaine just after dawn the next morning.

She fumbled for her dressing gown and left her slippers on the floor under the bed. Somewhere behind her, Jack's drowsy grunt suggested he might be waking up, too, but she barely registered it as she flung the front door open and ran onto the porch.

Emily stood in the yard in her nightgown, staring at the fairy circle. The white cotton billowed around her like a cloud, but she was as still as a flagpole with its colors rippling in a stiff wind. Alaine ran toward her, and stopped before she could reach the circle.

The hen lay split and flayed on the ground, the grass wet with darkening blood.

"Em, come away," Alaine said, voice rasping. "Don't look at it," she added, even as she continued to stare at the spectacle within the ring of flowers. The chicken—what was left of her—was a shapeless mound of skin and flesh in the center of the circle. The head twisted at a strange angle, the beak pointing nearly straight up toward the sky and the last remaining stars. The feet were gone. There was a thin film of feathers everywhere, the fine down settled into the grass like dust. Alaine swallowed a tremor of fear as she noticed how not even a spatter of blood or a few fine pinfeathers had crossed the border of the circle. Em wavered a moment, then ran to her mother, burying her face in the folds of her thick dressing gown.

"She was my favorite." Em snuffled into the dressing gown. "What happened, Mama?"

Alaine held Emily close as she stared at the fairy circle she had made and the carcass of the hen she'd put inside as a bargain. "I don't know, Em. I'll see if I can tell—you go inside to your father."

"But how did Queenie get out of the coop?" Em protested. "She's my favorite, Mama! She lets me pick her up. I love her!"

"I know, I'm sorry, I—" Alaine caught her breath. "This is what happens sometimes, Em, animals—animals don't live forever and—" She stopped herself. The speech her father had given a six-year-old Alaine when their guard dog, Smokey, had finally succumbed to old age didn't work here. Her daughter's hen was a sacrifice, and Alaine herself had chosen to put her on the altar. "Go inside to your father."

Emily complied, tears streaming down her freckled cheeks, and Alaine forced herself to look back to the circle. At first she didn't dare go inside. Instead, she walked the perimeter, trying to make sense of what had happened, what had rendered the chicken from a living hen to a shapeless mass of meat in the ring. Finally it struck her—the bones were gone.

She caught her breath and forced back the sour sting of bile. The Fae hadn't wanted the whole chicken. They only took the bones. And—she steadied her gaze—the long wing and tail feathers, which appeared to be missing. Gathering her courage, she went inside the ring, half expecting to be spirited away to Fae once she crossed the border into the collage of feathers and chicken blood, but her feet remained rooted firmly on solid earth. She crouched next to the remains and probed them with a stick, stomach knotting as she realized that the heart, liver, gizzard were all gone, too.

Something fluttered beneath the discarded apple crate. She pulled her papers from a pillow of feathers. The pin was gone, but the paper remained. Underneath the words she had written, a thin line of blackest ink twisted and curled into shapes Alaine slowly appreciated were words.

So bargained, so agreed.

She folded the paper carefully, afraid that any smudge or wrinkle would be a sign of disrespect, an invitation to draw Fae ire. Shaking, she found Emily inside, bawling on Jack's lap, his comforting words as hollow as Alaine's had been. By the time Alaine had calmed Em, and convinced her to get dressed and wash the salt stains from her face, she was late for school. Alaine walked her down the hill and slipped a note in her bag for her teacher, vague explanations about Em finding a coyote's work outside the chicken coop, and hoped Em wouldn't go into details about what she'd seen. Her teacher, newly arrived from Chicago, would never believe her anyway.

"What happened out there?" Jack said as she came in through the kitchen door. He sat at the table, an untouched cup of coffee in front of him.

"I thought you'd have gone to the office." She plucked her apron from the hook and began to pull flour and salt from the cabinets, keeping her eyes on the canisters and away from Jack. She couldn't explain to him what she'd done, not now. Not, she admitted to herself, before she knew if it had worked. "It's bread-baking day."

"I thought we needed to talk," he said. "Besides, I needed to clean up that mess on the lawn." She turned to face him with a start; there was dark blood etched under his fingernails. "What happened? Or, more to the point—what did you do?"

"I made a bargain," she said, voice tight. "All there is to it."

She measured the flour by fistfuls, just as Gran always had, and threw salt in by the pinch. Jack stopped her as she reached for the sourdough starter.

"No, that's not all there is to it. I may not be a Prospect Hill old-timer, but I know this isn't ordinary bargaining. This is—" He glanced at his hands, disgusted.

"Aunt Imogene told me how to make a new bargain. A more . . . specific one." Jack waited. The tension in the air stretched and Alaine snapped. "I'm getting us our mortgage payments for the next six months, Jack Fairborn, which is more than you can do!" She regretted it instantly.

He paused a long time, staring at his stained hands. "Maybe I don't make enough money to save the place. I just write up wills and property deeds, and it's not enough to make a bundle in the law business. Maybe that's my fault. And I don't know what you did, exactly. But it's too damn close. That—that thing out there. You called them here. Without asking what I thought."

Alaine wavered between shame and anger, running away from the first by sinking further into the latter. "You're right. You couldn't do anything about this. But I could. I figured out a way. If it doesn't work, you can rail at me then, but nothing matters more to me than saving the orchard. I'll do anything—"

"Nothing? Really, Alaine?" He met her eyes. She turned back toward the bread bowl, tears stinging her eyes. "Em was inconsolable. You'd do that to her? Or worse? God knows, Alaine, God only knows what could be coming through that ring or what they might take."

"It doesn't work that way. Aunt Imogene wouldn't lie to me—" She stopped. She couldn't explain to Jack why she trusted the hearsay and folk stories passed down Prospect Hill so completely, but she did. "What do you want me to say? It's done, and it had damn well better work."

"I want you to say you won't do it again. I won't ask you to apologize for it. But now that we know—" He shuddered. "They took the *bones*, Alaine. Without—without butchering it properly, pieces were just gone. I don't even understand."

She closed her eyes, and a single tear snaked down her cheek. "I know." Her voice scraped past her shame, breaking it. "It was awful. I never want to do it again, Jack."

"Then please, God, Alaine, don't. Dig up that ring."

"I won't use it again," Alaine promised instead, burying her face in Jack's waistcoat and leaving floured handprints on his shoulders.

15

Only a fool looks for gold in a fairy circle.
—Folk saying

DELPHINE DROVE CAREFULLY over the dirt roads between Perrysburg and Moore's Ferry, grateful for her overcoat and her driving goggles as clouds of dust billowed around the motorcar's open sides. Her valise, packed for only four nights, jounced on the seat next to her. Pierce hadn't wanted to let her come; there was opening night at the symphony and a dinner at the Lyndleys'. And truth be told, it was mostly nostalgia with a heavy undercurrent of obligation that goaded Delphine homeward for the harvest. Alaine didn't really need her there; it was one more reminder of how much, in fact, she was unnecessary beside her sister's efficient leadership. Even so, her stubborn Prospect Hill streak had won out, and Delphine had left Pierce deep in a stack of trade newspapers in his study.

Prospect Hill came into view, and Delphine slowed the car and turned away from the broad avenue that led toward the crest of the hill. The white columns of Orchard Crest shone in the morning sunlight at the top of the hill, but she wanted to see Alaine first, not face her mother's interrogation about the safety of motorcars. She was sure, as well, that Mother would want to hear everything about her first weeks as Mrs. Pierce Grafton, and a strange unrest percolated in Delphine's stomach at that thought. She wasn't unhappy, exactly, but her expectations had been so wide off the mark that she didn't know how to feel. Pierce was hardly home, and when he was, he frequently entertained, and she had to deliver a gracious performance for guests. When he was gone, the hours were long and silent in their large house; she hadn't made any friends, and his family all but ignored her. How to explain all that to Mother, who was nothing but delighted at the marriage? She drove instead toward the narrow lane that wound up the east side of the hill. Less used than Prospect Street, and older, replete with more kinks and bends than an excitable snake, Runyon Road let her drive straight to Alaine and Jack's without passing Orchard Crest.

Or would have, if not for a very large, somewhat rusted, exceptionally dirty truck blocking the junction. Delphine stopped her car, waving to flag the truck's driver, who examined the front of the domed hood as though it were painted with hieroglyphics instead of red clay mud.

"Say, are you broken down?" Delphine leaned out of the side of the car, goggles still in place and veil stirring gently in the breeze.

The man started when he saw her, but quickly regained his manners. "That I am, ma'am. I'm not blocking your way, am I?" He stuck his hands deep in overall pockets.

"I'm afraid so. Is there any way she can limp along off the road?"

"Limping would be a miracle at this point. Old piece of—" He cut himself off, but his muddy boot struck the nearest tire with a half-hearted kick. "And I can't push her myself."

"I doubt I'd be much help in that regard," Delphine replied. "Look, my sister lives just up that way. I could give you a lift up there, maybe see if my brother-in-law could take a look?"

"That would be a real help," the man answered. A farmer, probably, though funny that she didn't know him. She knew all the farm families in Moore's Ferry. "Saves me walking my bony rear into town. I'm about ready to leave her here and forget about her."

"Well, come on." Delphine started the car again. He settled into the seat next to her, watching her dubiously as she shifted into gear.

She deftly maneuvered it through a three-point turn, smirking a little at the surprised look on the truck owner's face as she expertly navigated the narrow road.

She steered up the hill and onto the lane where Jack and Alaine's lavender cottage stood at the back of the property. The rambling one and a half stories suited Alaine perfectly, a wide porch curving around two-thirds of the house and crisp white trim festooning the eaves.

Alaine must have been waiting, because she was out the door before the car was off, her stained pinafore over her good tea dress. Delphine peeled off her driving coat and left the goggles on the seat as Alaine nearly bowled her over.

"I've got molasses cake just out of the oven, and we can have a little tea—or chocolate, even, if you want—before we go over to Orchard Crest."

"Hold on," Delphine answered, unwinding the veil from the broad brim of her hat. "Is Jack around? I met this fellow broken down at the bottom of Runyon Road."

"How do you do, ma'am," he said, emerging from the car. "Ronald Fenstermacher."

"Fenstermacher—why, not Fenstermacher Preserves!" Alaine exclaimed. To Delphine's surprise, Alaine's face paled.

"Guilty as charged," he replied. "Out here on business and rather up a crick now, I'd say."

"Alaine Fairborn," she said, clipped. "I'll go get my husband, Jack. He can take some tools and take a look, and if there's nothing doing, he can give you a lift into town." She almost ran toward the barn.

Delphine raised an eyebrow and wandered toward the chicken coop, where a trio of hens scratched in the dirt with dutiful attention. She could hear Alaine and Jack talking inside, the undulations of voices raised and lowered with an urgency incongruous with a stranded motorist on Runyon Road. Jack barely tipped his hat to Delphine as he careened out of the house, working impatient arms into his overcoat sleeves. He was paler than usual, and oddly resolute as he threw a toolbox in the back seat of his motorcar.

"Well." Alaine forced a smile at the back door, hands on her hips, looking like a lithograph of a farmwife with her pinafore and ramshackle crown of braids, prosaic and welcoming except for the furrow between her brows. "Molasses cake?"

"What was that about?" Delphine asked. She unpinned her hat and fluffed her hair lightly before shaking the dust from her coat and veil.

"Oh, nothing, it's—"

"I've only been away from the farm a few weeks, Alaine. I can still smell it when you're shoveling manure at me." Her sister went silent, wavering between laughing and another refutation. But Delphine had her, and she knew it. "Tell me."

Alaine tensed, glancing out in the yard. "Em is with Mother. She'll be waiting for us to go fetch her."

"Then tell me quick." Delphine adjusted the amethyst brooch at her throat. "Honestly, Alaine. You've never been one to go in for land schemes or the like, it's not something like that, is it?"

"No, no, nothing—I'm just worried about strangers on the road, there was a burglary up on Eustace Saunders's place last month."

"Mother wrote me about it," Delphine said, still staring at her sister. "But some fellow with a truck that doesn't run—seems an elaborate scheme for robbing someone."

"Well, who can tell?"

"Besides, you recognized him."

"I knew his name. Lands, he could have been lying!"

"But he wasn't." Delphine waited patiently. Alaine didn't budge. "Is he someone you're in business with? Or aiming to be?"

Alaine threw up her hands. "You caught me. I'm using that poor man's misfortune to my advantage—he owns the biggest jam and jelly company in the Midwest, and I've got a few hundred pounds of cherries I could probably sell to him directly at a better rate than going through a buyer or the auction house."

"Alaine! How mercenary. But it seems that could work out well for everyone, though, doesn't it? If he needs to buy and you need to sell, and after all, you're doing him a favor." She accepted a piece

of her sister's good molasses cake and a cup of tea. "Nothing to be cagey about!"

Alaine shrugged before hurrying Delphine along to go visit Papa Horatio and Mother up at Orchard Crest, but Delphine couldn't help feeling she was holding something back. It stung, but then again, what did she expect? She'd left the farm and its management entirely to Alaine. She couldn't expect to be included in its plans and hopes and decisions any longer.

Jack came back hours later, grease-stained but triumphant, with Fenstermacher following after in the repaired truck.

"Just a loose belt. Glad I learned my way around these old beasts. Alaine, Mr. Fenstermacher wants to speak to you."

Delphine took Emily to the garden to play while her sister and Mr. Fenstermacher holed up in the study. When they emerged a scant fifteen minutes later, shaking hands and smiling, Delphine couldn't help but notice that Alaine looked more relieved than anything else, her eyes darting to the ugly little garden she'd planted with the greenhouse flowers in the front yard. If Delphine didn't know better, she would have thought it looked like a fairy ring.

16

To keep slugs from the garden: Tie a bundle of turnips with tape or ribband
and leave by the gate.

—*The Compleat Book of Bargaining Works*, by A Lady, 1767

"WAS THAT WHAT you expected to happen?" Jack kept his voice low, but Alaine could hear the agitation, churning like old gears in the conveyer belt they used in the orchard at harvest.

"I didn't know what to expect," Alaine said. Her voice sounded strange to her here in the darkness, hollow and void of emotion it should have been brimming with. "But I knew—when he got out of Del's car, said his name, that was it. That was the bargain."

"But how can you tell? Jam magnates break down out on Runyon Road all the time."

The joke was strained. She wished she could see his face, and almost lit the kerosene lamp, but that would be admitting they had something to talk about. She very much wanted to pretend that they didn't.

"It was the bargain. It had to be."

"Maybe. I don't like maybes with this, Alaine."

"Do you think I do?" she snapped, then brought her voice to heel. Emily was sound asleep, but she wasn't sure that Delphine wasn't listening. She'd decided to spend the night at the cottage instead of Orchard Crest, she and Em sitting up cutting out paper dolls by the fireplace until Alaine chased them both to bed.

"This is the last time," Jack said.

Alaine stayed quiet, the silence almost settling the matter. Then she spoke, a whisper in the dark, though she might as well have shouted. "But it worked." They had mortgage payments for months, and a contract to sell directly to Fenstermacher Preserves for the next four years, at better prices than they could get anywhere else.

"It worked," Jack conceded. "It might not next time. And damn it—that chicken. Em's face."

"Do you think she knows?"

"I didn't tell her. But she's a clever kid," Jack said softly. "She knows what a fairy ring is. And she knows exactly what she saw— nothing this side of magic could have deboned a chicken like that."

That sour taste in the back of her throat again. Bitter and sharp. "This is the last time." She couldn't put it into words, but it was an instinct, a knowing deeper than she could explain rationally—she had exposed Em to something toxic, something that could seep over the borders of Fae and poison her. "We saved the farm. And I'm never messing about with Fae rings again."

Alaine was up before sunrise frying crullers and brewing coffee for the field hands and family, who began filtering into the orchard one by one as the sun burned off the morning chill. A thin mist rose around the Montmorency cherry trees, the brilliant scarlet clusters of cherries coated in dew. Stacks of wooden crates and ladders had been staged the day before; a rickety table held coffee cups and dish towels and the swiftly emptying platter of crullers.

She grinned and waved to Art Klinker and his son, who they hired every summer to pick cherries and every fall to pick apples, and the Benning sisters. A few strangers hung back at first, road workers who traveled the river valley looking for day hires. They warmed up to Alaine and her crullers quickly, and soon Art had folded them under his wing, as he always did with the new faces.

Delphine and Emily were already at work on a row of trees at the far end of the orchard. Like a pair of well-tuned automatons swathed in pinafores, they plucked cherries and passed them to a bucket at the base of their ladder. Em climbed into the lower boughs, her slim arms reaching into the crevices the tree's twisting branches created, and Del reached deep into the crown from her perch on the ladder. She handed fruit down to Em in swift succession, chatting merrily as Em joked back. Alaine paused as she ferried an empty platter back to the house to watch the two of them, her sister's cheeks flushed with a brighter glow than she'd seen since the wedding.

By the time they broke for lunch—cold ham and warm bread and all the fresh sweet cherries they could eat—crates were stacked on the wagon, the wide bed offering room for more. Alaine suppressed a shiver that blended pride and nerves. All of them heading for Fenstermacher's Fruit Preserves, all at a choice rate. Barnaby and Bruno waited to haul the fruit off Prospect Hill, hitched to the wagon and accepting offerings of carrots and sugar and nose rubs.

"Think we'll finish this section before supper?" Del called, wiping her hands on her apron. She left a streak of mustard across the starched gathers.

"If you keep at it, sure bet," Alaine replied, directing the Klinkers toward a row of trees. "Need a longer break?"

"Me? Hardly," Delphine said with a laugh. "I've missed working out here. The sun, the yellow jackets, your homemade mustard."

"Some of those are better draws than others," Alaine said, holding the ladder for Delphine. She climbed expertly, narrow feet in buttoned boots finding quick purchase on the rungs. "You're happy to be back, really?"

"Of course! Not that I don't like Perrysburg, but..." She turned her face up toward the sun. "There's nothing like harvest."

"Say, Alaine!" Jack called from the pile of crates by the truck. "You expecting any more workers?" he asked as she joined him. A smart black touring car pulled up the lane.

"Not in a new Studebaker, I wasn't." She squinted. There was no mistaking the car, or the man driving it. "Pierce."

"What in the world?" Jack raised an eyebrow. "Don't tell me he's here to help pick fruit."

"That I doubt very much," Alaine replied, wiping dirty hands on the underside of her pinafore.

Pierce Grafton parked his car at a thoughtless angle next to the half-loaded wagon. He sprang from the driver's seat, face clouded and grim as he squared his hat on his dark hair.

"Pierce, we didn't expect you today," Jack said, striding toward him.

"That's clear enough. I thought I'd drive out to surprise Delphine." Pierce ignored Jack's outstretched hand. "Why is my wife up on a ladder?"

"Just helping," Delphine called with a wave. Her smile was strained, and her fingers on the rung had gone white. She picked her way down the ladder.

"It's been so nice having Del here. Em is doing her best to keep her here forever," Alaine said with a feeble laugh. Pierce looked out of place here, in clothes suited for the office and his impeccably oiled hair, but his stance and flinty eyes belied no discomfort. No, Alaine saw with growing unease, he expected to be deferred to even in the middle of her family orchard.

Pierce kept his eyes trained on Delphine until she was next to him. "Pack your things."

Delphine blanched. "Oh, Pierce, I don't know what you—"

"Now, Delphine. We're leaving." He turned back to Alaine and Jack. Alaine's hand was balled into a fist behind her pinafore and she wanted, for the first time ever, to know what it was like for knuckles to make contact with a nose. "A word, Jack."

"What you have to say to me, you can say to Alaine, too." Jack placed a hand on Alaine's arm, subtly positioning himself toe to toe with Pierce. His voice was level and calm, that of a meticulous lawyer delivering each word with precision.

Pierce swallowed. "It seems indiscreet, but if that's your way of running this place." Alaine reached for Delphine's hand, but Pierce deftly maneuvered his shoulder in front of his wife. Alaine glared at him, white-hot anger burning through any rote civility she had left. "I don't know what kind of judgment you use with the reputation of your family, Jack, but my wife isn't a hired girl to be sent to work in the fields like some immigrant drifter."

Delphine looked ready to cry. "That's hardly fair, I—"

"It's quite a fair assessment. This sort of work is beneath you. God knows it's beneath your sister, too, and your niece, but if they don't appreciate that, there's precious little I can do. My own household, however, is a different matter." He caught Delphine's arm in a firm grip, and she winced.

"Let go of her." Alaine's voice felt like gravel in her throat. "You're hurting her."

For a brief moment, Pierce looked surprised, ashamed, even. Then he regained his indifferent composure. "I'd never hurt my wife. You're only embarrassing her and yourself."

"Don't speak to my wife that way." Unlike her own voice, Jack's was still perfectly, if tersely, controlled. He glanced at Del, who stood wavering in Pierce's shadow, then met Alaine's eyes, shaking his head faintly. "If Del wants to go, of course she can leave."

"Of course I—there is so much to do at home," Delphine said in a quavering voice. "I've been away long enough. Isn't that right, Pierce?"

"I'll help you gather your things," Alaine said, feeling like someone else was speaking. She held her hand out to Delphine again, and this time, Pierce released her.

17

Jack in the pulpit, jack in the green
Fairy ring and tree
Friend in the forest, friend unseen
Makes a bargain with me
　　　　　—Children's rhyme

DELPHINE'S CHEEKS BURNED as Pierce drove the car back to Perrysburg. Jack followed, driving the electric car. Pierce had insisted she was far too shaken to drive herself, and Delphine suspected that he would have been perfectly happy for the car to stay parked in the drive of Orchard Crest indefinitely. Ever-perceptive Jack saw right through it, Delphine thought with the relish of a tiny victory.

Victory—against her own husband? This wasn't how she was supposed to think, to feel. Pierce was acting in her best interest. He didn't understand how things were on Prospect Hill, that her mother and grandmother had both worked in the orchard. She had never talked about work with Pierce—it seemed gauche, somehow, while surrounded by Perrysburg wealth to mention that she hiked up her skirts and climbed the ladders herself. Maybe he was right—those old-fashioned mores were bound to necessity, and she didn't have to help with harvest or pruning or planting. And of course she hadn't thought how it would appear to anyone in Perrysburg, hearing she'd been up a ladder, sticky with cherry juice.

"I—I'm sorry, Pierce." Her voice sounded small against the rumble of the engine that filled the car.

"I don't know what you were thinking. You could have fallen, and what then?"

"I've been climbing ladders with the family since I was a child, Pierce," she reminded him. "It was perfectly safe."

"Your family—putting you to work like that. Tying an apron on you and throwing you out in the orchard with field hands! It's embarrassing."

Delphine smothered the humiliation crawling in her gut. "They didn't mean any harm. Or disrespect."

"They ought to know better." Pierce sighed. "I am sorry if I embarrassed you in front of your family, but they need to learn that there are rules. Ways to behave properly. I can't—" His voice pinched off, pained.

"Yes, Pierce?" She turned and waited for him to resume speaking. His eyes were on the road, avoiding her. She probably deserved that, she thought with the bite of shame.

"I am taking over the glassworks. I've got my eye on politics, too, Del, you know that. I can't have a wife who doesn't follow the rules of polite society."

"I didn't mean to embarrass you," she whispered. "I won't do farmwork anymore."

"It's not only that, it's—you have to understand. You're a lady of some status now, Delphine. Not a farm girl. You have to accept that." He tried for a smile. "Why, embrace it, even! You're a Grafton. That means something. You wouldn't need to spend so much time in the country if you made some friends in Perrysburg—the right sorts of friends."

"I will," she said, resisting voicing the argument that his mother and sister ignored her, and he hadn't helped her make any inroads into societies she realized too late were sealed off nearly completely from newcomers. "I just—I want to do well by you, truly."

"I'm sorry if I was a bit harsh. I forget that this is new to you—I've been steeped in it since I was a boy. You know," he chuckled, "when

I was a kid I was just mad for steam engines and machinery, and announced I was going to be a train engineer one day to a few fellows Father had over from the board. My nanny had a strict talk with me about the whole thing. She made it quite clear that I wasn't going to work for the railroad."

Delphine wasn't sure how to answer him—she didn't think the story was funny, but rather sad. Besides, she didn't know anything but being a farm girl, had spent springtime and summer and autumn in the orchard, had helped butcher chickens and plant gardens and rake up soiled bedding in the horse stalls. That had never been a shameful thing, not on Prospect Hill—they were the height of Moore's Ferry society, even. But Moore's Ferry society didn't climb very high. She sighed and looked out the window, summer's bright greens a smear of color as they drove on.

Jack took the train back to Moore's Ferry after a brief farewell. He looked, to Delphine, more worried than angry. Moments after he'd left, there was a knock at the door.

"No, Mrs. Grafton isn't taking visitors today," she heard the maid say as she stripped off her jacket.

"My apologies, I saw her come home and thought I might drop in." The voice echoed up the stairs. Ida.

"Polly, it's all right. Show Miss Carrington to the sunroom." Delphine glanced in the hall mirror, smoothing hair that had been flattened by her driving hat. She straightened her shoulders and sailed into the sunroom with a convincing smile.

"Miss Carrington! What a surprise." She showed her neighbor to a seat in the sun-drenched corner of the room.

"I am sorry for the presumption, but I saw you arrive home, and it's been so dull with no one about to talk to." Ida perched on the edge of the wicker armchair, leaning forward at an eager angle as though fairly desperate for conversation. "Your family in Moore's Ferry is well?"

"Oh yes, very well." She motioned to Polly to bring—what time was it now, anyway? Late afternoon. Tea, then. "I apologize— I wasn't dressed for visitors." She should have considered that, she thought too late—Pierce would have thought of it. She was still sporting a hard-wearing skirt and shirtwaist from the fields.

"You must tell me where you got that new dress you wore to church last Sunday!" Ida shook her head. "You've the height to pull off that piping and the buttons and then top it off with one of those fashionably gigantic hats. I'd look like a mushroom, I'm afraid. Aunt Edwina says you've already made a name for yourself as one of the more fashionable ladies in Perrysburg."

"Hardly," Delphine said, though she felt warmed by the compliment. *See, Pierce, I'm not a complete rhubarb.* "You should see my mother. She—" Delphine stopped herself, and then, ashamed to hide that her family didn't have their clothes made by couturiers growing up, made herself continue. "She sews all her own clothes and looks like she popped out of *Harper's*."

"Some people have a gift," Ida said. "Your family in Moore's Ferry—were you Episcopalian?"

Delphine set her tea down. An abrupt question, but not unkindly asked. "No, Free Methodist. It was the only church in Moore's Ferry when my papa—my grandfather—settled there just a few years after the Civil War."

"I wondered," Ida said as she accepted a cup of tea, "if it caused any—incongruences with bargaining."

"Incongruences?" Delphine laughed. Ida's interest was strange, but at least she was interested in Delphine at all. "Do you mean to ask if we found it strange to go to church on Sunday and make bargains on Monday?"

"Yes, I suppose that's what I mean to ask." She twitched her nose, adjusting her glasses.

"Not in the slightest. I don't suppose we ever thought there might be some sort of cosmic conflict of interest. No one behaved as though you couldn't believe in both the Holy Trinity and fairies," she added.

"Do you think—" Ida paused. "Do you think I might visit sometime? Your family, that is. I have so many questions about bargaining and the practices locally and—well, if it wouldn't be rude."

"I can't see any reason why it could be rude," Delphine lied. She

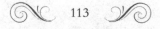

imagined Aunt Imogene on the other end of Ida's fumbling questions. Poor Ida. "Perhaps we could drive out together sometime."

"Oh, perfect! I've a term paper I've got to get together, but after that—a drive to the country and research, how lovely!" She clapped in genuine excitement.

Delphine began to feel a bit sorry for the tongue-lashing Imogene was bound to inflict on Ida, then stopped herself. What would Pierce think, their neighbors hearing all about her family as though they were peculiar anthropological subjects? But he had wanted her to develop relationships with their neighbors and friends—this seemed like a proper way to do so.

Ida was already on to a new train of thought. "I wonder, would you like to go to a lecture down at Glowers Hall with me tomorrow? It's on the musical traditions of coal mining communities in both Britain and the United States, and I would love your thoughts."

"Oh, Miss Carrington—"

"If we're to be friends, I do think that you should call me Ida."

"Very well. Ida. I—I don't know the first thing about any of the things you just said."

"But I don't, either! Isn't that the fun of it?"

"You know more than I do, of course—the theory and whatnot."

"'And whatnot' is precisely right. Do come. It's at four o'clock, we could be quite mad and get ice cream after."

Delphine considered it—a long afternoon at home alone, with nothing to look forward to except dinner with Pierce, or a lecture with Ida and a walk around what the locals called "university town." Pierce might prefer if she stayed home in case of callers, and to oversee dinner preparations, but she found she couldn't quite stomach the thought of a long day at home alone being Mrs. Grafton. She pushed aside anxiety over what that meant and took the escape route Ida offered her. It felt like fresh air, a window opening into a stuffy room.

"I'd be delighted."

18

Good bread and ale will never content one who has tasted of Fae.

—Folk saying

ALAINE FILED COPIES of the Fenstermacher contracts in the cabinet in the study and closed the drawer with a satisfied click. They'd done it—the totals tabulated, the accounts all reconciled. They'd come out so far ahead on the cherry harvest that they could pay the mortgage and all the other bills well past apple season, and moreover, they had established a lucrative partnership with Ronald Fenstermacher. Alaine smiled, thinking of how every time she saw Fenstermacher Fruits cherry preserves and pie fillings on the shelf in Harvey's store downtown, it might have her cherries in it. Already people in town were talking about Orchard Crest differently, mentioning her name in the same breath as the larger business owners in Moore's Ferry.

Outside the window, the fairy ring she'd planted stood staunchly verdant in opposition to the grass browning under summer's worst heat. Jack had asked her to dig it up, but she couldn't quite bring herself to do it. She had no intention of using it again, not really, but the thought had lodged itself like a burr at the back of her mind—it would be useful for emergencies. If she let herself forget the horror of finding Queenie's deboned body, she could almost consider it, simply, *useful*.

A knock at the door interrupted her macabre memories. Millie

Jacobs stood, red-faced and breathing quickly, as though she'd run up Prospect Hill. "I'm so sorry—coming unannounced—but I thought, I felt—"

"Come in, Millie, goodness." Alaine held the door open. "Are you well? Do you need some water, maybe a glass of lemonade?"

"Oh, lemonade would be lovely, thank you! I'm fine, I'm fine, just flustered." She took off her hat, decorated with artificial lilies. She followed Alaine into the kitchen. "I had to come as soon as I heard. Our permit was rejected, Alaine. For the livestock auction, with only a month to go. What do we do now?"

Alaine stopped in the middle of pouring a glass of lemonade. The frost from the icebox clung to the pitcher, making it slick under her fingers. She set it down before she dropped it. "What, Millie? I thought—I thought this was a mere formality!"

"Oh, it is, it is, but wouldn't you know—Olson has a cousin on the board, too." Her broad cheeks went red. "He managed to persuade the board that it was a sanitation issue—sanitation! Of all things! That only the auction houses are properly equipped for live-stock sanitation, and that we couldn't use the fairgrounds."

"There are horse races and a poultry show every year at the fair-grounds!" Alaine half shouted, then remembered that Millie was only the bearer of bad news, not arguing these points herself. "I'm sorry, Millie, I didn't mean to shout."

"I know, I know—but Alaine! What do we do now?"

Millie looked at her, eyes wide and searching. Alaine caught her breath. They were looking to her to solve this, just like she'd solved every petty problem they'd handled so far in meetings. But she couldn't reverse a county board decision or make a permit appear from thin air. And it was too late to change their plans, to move the auction somewhere else or push back the date. People wanted to buy lambs and hogs for fall butchering, and the chickens weren't going to age well over the winter. They'd have to give it up, and that would mean that Alaine and her plans as Agricultural Society president had failed.

She squared her shoulders, forcing confidence into her voice even as her mind raced. "I'll figure something out, Millie. My sister is coming for a visit, but as soon as that's done, I'll find some way to fix it. I'll call next Thursday, all right?"

Millie nodded and sipped her lemonade, chattering about her vegetable garden and her sister's indigestion and all sorts of other things that Alaine only half listened to. She could have just let the plan for a benefit auction go, but she imagined the disappointment of the Society and the gloating look on Acton Willis's face and only felt more resolute that she couldn't. By the time Millie finally left, it was less than an hour before Delphine and her friend from Perrysburg, Miss Carrington, arrived, and Alaine only had time to tidy up and make a fresh batch of lemonade, mind rapidly conjuring and just as promptly rejecting solutions for the Agricultural Society.

Still, as soon as Del's car pulled up the lane, Alaine had more important things on her mind.

She hung back as Delphine gave Miss Ida Carrington a tour of the orchard, the bespectacled young woman peppering Delphine with questions and stopping to inspect various cultivars. Alaine, meanwhile, only wanted to get Delphine alone for a few moments. She couldn't shake how quickly Pierce had cowed Delphine, or how humiliated she looked as he had ushered her, with perfect formality, to their car. Jack had noticed, too, insisting on driving the electric back to Perrysburg even though he confided to Alaine later that he'd been in a nervous sweat the whole time, terrified he didn't know how to drive it well enough and shaken over the confrontation with Pierce. "I've heard of men treating their wives like—" He'd run a hand through his hair, still unnerved. "But bless it, I never thought I'd see it acted out so plainly, in my own family."

Though Alaine wanted to talk to her sister, she wasn't entirely sure what she would say. How could she ask the questions that ignited sparks of anger in her, that balled her hands into fists? *Are you happy?* And worse—when she remembered the iron grip on Delphine's arm, the gray eyes unsympathetic to her sister's wishes. *Is he kind to you? Or does he hurt you?*

But Miss Ida Carrington was occupying all of Delphine's attention at the moment, and that was only fair—she was, after all, a guest.

"Mama! Is Aunt Del here?" Emily called from the lane, her schoolbooks slung under her arm and her pinafore untied. There was a smudge of dirt across the bridge of her nose.

"You look a fright. Did you come across a lion on the way home?" Em shook her head, braids whipping back and forth enthusiastically. "Bear?"

"Mama! There aren't bears in Moore's Ferry anymore!"

"I thought maybe you found the last one." She turned Emily around and tied her pinafore, noticing that it was getting short. "So what adventure did you stumble into?"

"Dottie Fischer said she saw a fairy, and she wanted to chase it, but I said that was a bad idea." Alaine raised an eyebrow, waiting for an explanation of the dirt and rumpled clothes. "She tried to go any-way, so I—pushed her. A little."

"Em. We don't push, shove, hit, kick, or—" She squinted at Em's suspiciously loose braids. "Pull hair. Even if someone does have a very bad idea. The right thing to do is come home and tell me, or Grandmother, or another grown-up." Em nodded. "So. Did she go off chasing fairies?" Alaine wasn't particularly worried; as she was apt to hear at every family gathering, Papa Horatio had been the last to see any of the Fae in decades.

"No, she cried and ran home to tell her mother on me."

"I'll expect a call from Mrs. Fischer later today," Alaine said. "And yes, Aunt Del is here. She brought a friend to call. You can tag along with them as long as you promise not to be a pest."

As Emily ran off to find her aunt, Alaine felt a particular surge of pride in her daughter—her inquisitive eyes, her stubborn streak. Both tried her patience, but she loved even those prickly and less easy facets of her daughter with a fierceness to rival a lioness.

By the time the three of them returned to Lavender Cottage, Emily had thoroughly charmed Miss Carrington and led her straight through the parlor and out the kitchen door for a tour of the chicken coop and the garden.

"She's taken a quick shine to Miss Carrington," Alaine said. Ida had left her coat on the davenport and her hat on the side table, and a slim book on the kitchen counter. "Rather disorganized for a student, isn't she?"

"You should see her room—it looks like a library had a conniption." Delphine gathered the hat and coat. She forgot to add the book to the pile; Alaine was ready to remind her when Del continued. "Ida seems positively enchanted by Emily. Em was telling her fairy stories—something about a little girl at school seeing one?"

"Oh, you told her that was nonsense, didn't you?" Alaine rushed to ask, the book forgotten. "I'll have to explain to her that we don't all belong shut up in the state hospital, seeing fairies in every nook and cranny."

"I don't think she minds whether the stories are true or not," Delphine answered. "Her interest seems to be more who believes what, and why."

"I suppose 'because it's true' didn't cross her mind."

"Aunt Imogene may set her straight on that," Del replied.

Alaine suppressed a laugh at Miss Carrington's expense. Then she turned back to Delphine, hesitant. "Del, I wanted to ask—are you all right? After you left, I—"

"Of course, I'm fine," she replied. Alaine couldn't tell if Del was avoiding her eyes or just absorbed in watching Miss Carrington's reactions to the chickens.

"Because I—I didn't think Pierce spoke very kindly."

"He was upset," Delphine said with a wave of her hand. "He didn't realize that coming out to help with harvest meant—you know, *helping* with harvest. I suppose he expected that I'd be setting up a supper or maybe minding the children, or you'd have me at some pen-and-paper work. It's really my fault for not explaining it better to him."

Alaine bit her tongue—it was hardly Delphine's fault that Pierce had been so buried in his own expectations that he'd thrown a tantrum to rival a child's when they were challenged.

"I just—he may be your husband, but he shouldn't make you feel poorly in front of people like that."

"It was nothing, Alaine. Let it be." She shook her head as though Alaine had invented the whole thing. "Besides, we have more to worry about now—Pierce has decided, officially, to run for city council."

"That's—very exciting." Alaine recovered quickly.

"I think so. I'm hosting a party next week for a few of the local families—just going to feel them out, you know. See what sorts of things he needs to fold into his platform."

Alaine didn't bother to ask if he was planning to ask the workers in his own factory. Seeing that her sister wanted to move on, Alaine did her best to follow suit. "I'll get supper together here if you want to go down and visit Aunt Imogene."

"Yes, we should go soon—Aunt Imogene still goes to bed with the sun, doesn't she?"

Delphine called for Ida, who nearly bubbled over with enthusiasm for the wooded trail down the woods and the old log cabin in the clearing where Aunt Imogene lived.

Delphine and Ida had spent more time together in recent weeks, attending the summer lecture series at the university and picking apart scholarly topics, from the contemporary poetry of Ireland to the religion of ancient Rome, under the awning of the Olympia Candy Shop. Their peppermint ice creams frequently melted to pink puddles as they lost themselves in conversation. She considered Ida perhaps her only friend in Perrysburg, which made this meeting with Imogene all the more nerve-racking. As Delphine rapped on the door, she quashed the tug-of-war of embarrassment on behalf of both Ida and Aunt Imogene. Ida was sure to shove her foot directly into her mouth, but who knew what uncouth things Aunt Imogene might say.

At least, Delphine saw with relief as Imogene answered the door, her aunt was dressed in her good violet afternoon dress instead of overalls or an old Army coat.

"Good afternoon, Del. This your friend you wrote about?" She assessed Ida, lingering over the thick notebook clutched in her hand. "Well, come on in."

She ushered them to her parlor, which held a ramshackle assortment of knickknacks in a curio cabinet and a bearskin rug in front of the stone hearth.

Aunt Imogene leaned back in her rocking chair, her walking stick across her knees. "Well, introduce me to your friend, Del."

"Aunt Imogene, this is Miss Ida Carrington," Delphine said, gently shoving Ida forward with a nudge of her elbow.

"Pleased to make your acquaintance," Imogene said, rocking gently. "Del says you're a student. Quite a thing, ladies going to college. When I was your age, the school didn't even go past the eighth grade here in Moore's Ferry. Well. What was here of it then, anyway."

"That was a long time ago, then," Ida said.

"Thanks for the reminder." Imogene's thin lips pursed into a wry smile as Ida blanched politely. "Now, don't go getting all flustered— one of the only joys left to an old lady is teasing the young folk a little. Del says you've got some questions about bargaining. Come to learn the art?" She paused as Ida fumbled for a reply, then laughed. "My word, you're an easy one to kid! I take it you don't believe in bargaining yourself, then."

"I don't suppose I've ever had the opportunity to believe in it," Ida said slowly, lifting her chin in thought.

"An interesting way to put it," Imogene replied with an approving nod. "I'll answer your questions. But see it like this, girl. You're asking about what's real to me, not some story I tell the kiddies at bedtime. You're asking me about what my ma taught me, just the same as she taught me how to roll out pastry dough and how to butcher a chicken."

"I understand, ma'am."

"Good. Now." Imogene leaned back in her chair and let the easy sway of the rocker take over. "Sit down."

Delphine and Ida obeyed, perching on an overstuffed sofa that Imogene had gotten from Papa Horatio when Mother had redecorated.

Delphine let Ida run rampant on questions she could have recited the answers to her in sleep—how she learned to bargain, what rhymes she knew. Ida bent over her notebook, scribbling furiously. Delphine started when she abruptly changed angles. "And did you happen to learn anything from the Natives?"

"How old you think I am, girl?" Imogene laughed. "They was

long gone before we settled up here. But from what I heard of it, whoever lived here—Potawatomi, I think—didn't hold tow with the hill much. At least, that was what Parson Anderson used to say, and he was a bit of a local historian." Imogene held up a hand as she anticipated Ida's next question. "Dead now, twenty years. But he kept records of who lived on the hill. You could check on that at the library, I suppose. If I recall, before Ebenezer Worthington's folks, seems nobody lived here."

"Whyever not?"

Imogene pursed her lips, considering this. "The way I see it, different folks have different ways when it comes to the Fae. Our way of trading with the Fae is old. Older than I know of, anyway—my ma's people, way back, brought it over with them. But the Natives' way of dealing is old, too, and they found it best to leave well enough alone. Never had a chance to talk about it much, but that Cherokee fella Del's pa used to hire for odd jobs—Hank? Harry?"

Delphine rescued Imogene from her own memory. "Henry. His name was Henry. He was Cherokee."

"That's right. Now, he said they knew of them—called them little people in the hills. Didn't trade none with them. Left them alone, and the little people left them alone. But they had stories. Henry said they protected his people, hid them from time to time. Said they kept some of them safe from the Army when they came to clear them out, back before the Civil War. There was one story—ah, but I'm off on a different goose chase entirely with that one."

"No, please," Ida said, eyes wide behind her glasses. "What was it about?"

"Now, he said there was a boy his grandpa knew—or great-grandpa or further back, I don't rightly know. The kid was sent on one chore or another, maybe gathering kindling in the woods or some such, and a snowstorm blew up. He didn't come home, days and weeks went by and they gave him up for lost, figured he'd frozen to death in the forest or been supper for a panther. At any rate, years after that, the boys' friends were all grown men with sons, and their sons had sons, and they come across this boy in the woods, says that the little folks in the hills took him in one winter day and he stayed a while, did they happen to know his pa?"

"He was still a boy?" Ida interrupted.

"In a manner of speaking. The way Henry told it, he wasn't altogether a boy. Was strange, was...like he hadn't aged much, but he had grown wiser somehow. Different, something in his eyes. He realized that the whole world had gone on without him and he went back into the hills." Imogene shrugged. "What do you suppose he's still there?"

"So if I can clarify," Ida said, scratching more notes in her notebook, "he—did he *become* one of the little people? One of the Fae?"

"The way Henry told it, you could think that, or you could figure he'd gone wrong in the head. My folks didn't have any stories like that. Only bargains and strange doings by fairy rings and such."

"Did it really happen, though?" Ida murmured.

Imogene laughed. "Who can tell? It was one of those kinds of stories, the ones where it happened too long ago and to someone you didn't know well enough to track it down." Her smile faded and the lines settled back into her face. "But Henry told it like he believed it."

19

Former sinkholes, wading areas for bison, and the remains of root systems of large fallen trees are all hypotheses for the existence of so-called "fairy rings."

—*Geographical Oddities of the American Midwest*,
by Gregory Otto Newman

ALAINE DIDN'T FEEL any better about Delphine as her car rattled down the bumpy lane, Ida waving enthusiastic goodbyes from the seat next to her. It wasn't just that she dismissed Pierce's violent reaction as a mere disagreement; she seemed reserved, pulled back. As though her life in Perrysburg was a locked box like the kind they both had as children for their small treasures, only now Delphine didn't to want to open hers for Alaine.

They used to tell each other everything. Silly fears borne out of Grandma Lilabeth's fairy stories. Alaine's hopes of winning the blue ribbon for chickens at the youth fair, Del's of getting a commendation for her watercolors. Alaine had confided all her hopes about Jack, her fears that when he went back to school he'd forget her and start courting some pretty coed instead. And when Del had met Pierce on a trip with her friend Mary Porter, and come home starry-eyed and aching to see him again, Alaine had listened to her soliloquies about his many virtues and helped her devise a plan to see him at the Porters' next party. They had shared everything.

She sighed. Now their worlds drifted apart. Delphine seemed invested only in helping Pierce with his political aspirations, putting on the costume of perfect society wife and running through the pantomimes of dinners and parties to give him a stage. Del, her beautiful sister, fading into a background player in her husband's life. It burned, deep in Alaine's gut. And yet, she was forging ahead in her own life, too, ever further from Del—farming techniques and business machinations and gaining influence in the small-time political sphere that was the Agricultural Society.

The damn Society. She kicked the kitchen chair, and it scuttled across the floor. She couldn't cancel the livestock auction and lose face now. Not only for her own pride, she reasoned, but because everyone in Moore's Ferry—in the county, really—associated her with the orchard, and the orchard needed its good name. The farming community needed the Society strong, capable, trustworthy, not ducking out of its promises at the first sign of resistance.

"Mama?" Emily ducked her head into the kitchen. "What was that?"

"I stubbed my toe, Em, it's nothing." She produced her foot from under her skirt, as though that were proof. "Say, I just baked some plum thumbprints. Want to take some up to Papa Horatio? They're his favorite."

Em agreed eagerly, knowing Papa Horatio would share the cookies with her, and bounded out of the house and up the lane. Alaine funneled her anxiety into tedious action and tidied the kitchen, banging cabinets closed and tossing silverware into the case as though the forks had carried out personal vendettas against her.

As she folded the washrags, she noticed something. The book Ida had left was tucked under some tea towels on the counter. She'd meant to give it back first before Del took her to Aunt Imogene's and then at tea, but was interrupted both times. She'd dismissed the studious, removed understanding of bargains Ida had brought with her, but maybe there could be some hint hidden in her book.

The spine lisped a thin crackle as she opened it. She leafed from a chapter on common household bargains to another on the similarities and differences between various cultures' fairy mythologies—tucking loose paper back in as she went, as Ida had tucked notes with research questions at the end of several chapters—until her hand stilled on a heading entitled "Common Bargains for Social Maneuvers."

There was no way, she scoffed, that a dry academic book could tell her anything she didn't already know. After all, Ida had come here to interview Aunt Imogene, and Alaine knew, at this point, everything Aunt Imogene did. But she was curious. That brilliant ring of flowers she had planted reflected double in the windowpane.

Most bargaining-endemic cultures form ethical boundaries around bargains that involve influencing other people, whether individually or en masse. Alaine narrowed her eyes—influence. That bargain for the election to go her way—had that been influencing others' decisions? She'd seen it as swinging luck her way, pulling for the underdog in a race rigged by inertia and baked-in preference for a male candidate. That was how Gran had taught her to understand that bargain; so much for the theories of academics. *However, most such cultures do still engage in practices where the decisions or actions of others can be understood to be influenced by a bargain. In fact, some cultures engage in what might be considered battles of bribery to ensure fairy influence on decisions. Many of these are recounted as stories of heroes or wise women in folktales . . .*

She skimmed several pages of anecdotes that were, almost certainly, embellished. There were several bargains listed not unlike the ones they used to ensure honesty on contracts, and then Alaine slowed again. *Though most bargains for social influence are rote prescriptive bargains (see appendix 1-C), some direct negotiations are recorded. Eastern European accounts include women entering a trance and communicating directly with fairies; these women most typically claim that they were chosen from childhood as communicators with the fairy realm. Some claim to enter another dimension, others that the communication occurs in a liminal space invisible to those not granted the gift.*

Alaine stopped, found the dictionary, looked up "liminal," and then continued, growing more discouraged. Papa Horatio wasn't blessed with some mysterious gift—he'd just seen a fairy in the woods. This book wasn't describing fairy bargaining; it sounded like

some kind of bizarre ancient ritual, or maybe an unfortunate faint-
ing illness

Still, Alaine read on.

One elderly woman from near Krakow described the ritual in which a
woman, usually identified before puberty as having a sight for fairies, enters
a fairy ring with a mirror. She may mark the mirror with something of hers,
such as a ribbon or scrap of fabric, or even a strand of hair, to tie the subsequent
visions for her eyes only. She then calls the image of a Fae forth into the mir-
ror, communicating with it directly. This is done only rarely, and only when
bargains of traditional nature are not sufficient, most often for maneuvering a
family into better or more exclusive society, such as the procurement of ben-
eficial marriages or business contracts. A lesser version of the ritual involves
speaking a wish or desire into the mirror; some claim that those without fairy
sight must content themselves with this.

Alaine set the book down, marking the page with a trembling
hand. She'd never heard of taking a mirror into a fairy ring, and
everything Gran had taught her emphasized time and again that you
never wanted to see a fairy, let alone negotiate with one. Yet the last
part—it was a strange version of bargaining. What did one offer, she
wondered, in return? Did the mirror work only once?

Was she really considering this? Far up the lane, she heard Emily
and Papa Horatio laughing in the orchard. She swallowed. She
skimmed the rest of the chapter, the appropriate appendices, but
found nothing more about the mirror. The book didn't suggest any
risks—but she knew what Gran would say.

Well. Gran would have said it was a little pushy for a woman to
run for Agricultural Society president, too. And she wouldn't have
approved of the new farm truck the Saunderses had bought, and she
didn't like the new incubators coming out for chicks when she was
still alive, either, and those had all but replaced broody hens among
the poultry farmers Alaine knew. Like Imogene said, Gran was
touchy, nervous. About more than bargaining.

She rifled through the spare room's chest of drawers before finding an old hand mirror with faded roses painted on the back, part of
a long-separated vanity set. She decided against marking it in any

way—the part about speaking a wish into the mirror didn't mention that, and she didn't relish the thought of tying herself, personally, to the Fae any more than she already had.

Still, Alaine crossed the border of the fairy ring with some trepidation. She hadn't been inside since finding Queenie all those weeks ago. Gripping the mirror firmly in one hand, she resolved to finish as quickly as possible, trying not to doubt her decision even as her palms grew sweaty. The permit. That was all she needed.

She hesitated. Was it? Vagaries didn't do when bargaining with the Fae. But she could ask for a bit more, couldn't she? Successful fall harvest, for the pears to take off. A second term as Society president.

No—focus. Any bargain could be misconstrued, turned on its head.

"I need the county to grant the Agricultural Society a permit to use the fairgrounds for the livestock auction scheduled for the last week of September." Her hands shook slightly, and her reflection in the mirror wavered. That covered it. Yet....She couldn't resist. "And for the auction to be a financial success, and well regarded in the community." Enough. What did "well regarded" mean to a Fae, anyway? What if she'd said "discussed widely," and the Fae twisted that into making the auction a disastrous fodder for gossip? She looked deep into the mirror.

There was something behind the glass, behind her reflection and the wash of clouded sky above her. She gazed past the surface, as though she were looking deep into clear water, ignoring the ripples and movements on the surface to search out what lived beneath. A tree, she realized, bending in a faint breeze, draped with purple leaves like streamers. Pure-silver flowers winked and sparkled in the deep foliage, swinging gently like bells, though Alaine couldn't hear anything. She gazed deeper, drinking in the beauty of a silver mist of moss on the ground, of a tangle of pale branches woven into knotwork unnaturally symmetrical, down to thorns bowing deeply to one another in vine-wrought curls.

Something moved in the purple-and-silver forest, a figure, sliding like mist through the boughs. A woman—Alaine started. She was tall and slim, shaped more than anything like a birch tree, with the same silver-pale gleam. Her hair was loose behind her, wound through with purple flowers, painfully bright against her fair waves. She looked up, gazing right at Alaine, almost meeting her eyes—

And then the mirror shattered in her hands.

She yelped, fumbling with the pieces of broken glass, faintly wondering where the blood on the mirror pieces had come from. Pain flared in her left hand, blood pooling on several shallow scratches and one deeper one. Frightened, she threw the pieces on the ground and wrapped her hand in her apron.

Taking a deep breath, Alaine examined her hand. The cut hurt, but it wasn't serious. The mirror was beyond repair, and the shards too small and scattered to collect. She used the toe of her boot to tear up some grass and dirt and buried the pieces. Then she fled the fairy ring.

20

Bone of a rooster or bone of a hen
Brings a lost flock home again
—Traditional bargain

"I DIDN'T EXPECT that Pierce would actually want to come," Jack whispered to Alaine as she hauled their picnic basket from the back of the farm wagon.

"Me, either. Or bring half his family." She watched as Pierce's sister and mother spilled out of the touring car, adjusting their hats. Alaine gave Barnaby and Bruno each a nose bag and a generous ear scratch, making sure that they were comfortably tied in the shade. Impatient, Emily took Papa Horatio by the hand and set off across the lawn to meet Delphine. Alaine kept an eye on the pale blue hair bow bobbing as Emily moved. "Frankly, I didn't think Del would even find it in her to show up."

When Millie had shown up on the porch of Lavender Cottage two days after Alaine had whispered her wishes into the mirror to say that the county had considered their appeal, accompanied by a petition from the local poultry fanciers chapter, and found in their favor, Alaine wasn't surprised, or even shaken. The fairy ring had taken the mirror, she'd decided, the glass as payment for what she'd asked for. In a fit of excitement, she'd written Delphine to invite her and her family to the picnic that would finish the livestock show and auction, and in a fit of regret, arranged to host Pierce, his sister, and his mother on the outing.

"Beautiful day!" Delphine called across the field, waving emphatically. Her pure-white dress almost glowed, all lace and pin tucks. Alaine forced a smile in return. Delphine knew better, once upon a time, than to wear a white concoction to a fairgrounds picnic. She seemed further from the farm than ever.

"Aunt Del! Come see my new chickens!" Emily grabbed Delphine by the hand and pulled her toward the exhibition hall.

"New chickens?" Delphine raised an eyebrow at Alaine.

"We let her get a pair of Sebright bantams," Alaine said. After the loss of Queenie the hen, it hadn't been hard for Emily to talk her parents into a pair of the fancy miniature chickens Josiah Fischer bred, even though they were less than useful as layers and wouldn't have filled a saucepan, let alone a stockpot.

Delphine's mother-in-law arrived at a statelier pace. "Chickens, is it?"

"Our local chapter of the Poultry Fanciers Association set up a display," Alaine explained, wondering if anyone in Perrysburg raised show chickens.

Mother jumped in. "They're not your everyday chickens, of course. All sorts of fancy breeds. Mr. Fischer even brought his Chinese pheasants."

Emily took the lead into the dimly lit hall, barely more than a barn. Alaine saw Stella lift her hem away from the dusty floor. But they all seemed charmed by the birds, with their brilliantly hued plumage.

"These are mine," Emily announced as they came to a small cage with a pair of white birds with black filigree feathers. "Silver Sebrights."

"They are rather pretty," Stella conceded, peering at the pair as Emily beamed. Alaine gave her a smile and a nod. Emily had been diligent about caring for her birds, making sure they had dust baths before crating them for the show and keeping them practiced at being handled. She deserved the praise. Emily straightened, her smile even broader. She was getting so tall, Alaine realized, so confident. "Why, I ought to have brought the children instead of leaving them home with the nursemaid. They might have learned something."

"I didn't realize they came in such striking patterns," the elder Mrs. Grafton said. "Pure white and black!"

"There was a Worth gown I recall seeing once—in a sketch only," Stella amended. "I thought at first it was entirely original, but now I wonder if he was inspired by one of these birds!"

"Hard to believe they scratch for grubs with the others," Pierce said.

"They certainly do," Papa Horatio replied. "And that rooster has no idea how small he is in comparison to the big fellows."

They all laughed, and Alaine let herself feel some optimism—they seemed to be genuinely enjoying themselves. More, the auction had gone off without a hitch yesterday, producing profits that more than doubled their reserves in the Mercy Fund. Everyone had praised Alaine's leadership, and she had been happy to turn it right back around to praise their hard work and innovation. Already they were talking about repeating the event next year.

"Wasn't sure about that Fairborn woman running for office," she overheard gruff Horace Wheeler say as he passed them on the way to the picnic grounds. "But if she hasn't done the best job in decades."

Alaine swelled with pride, suppressing a fool grin.

"How's harvest, Jack?" Pierce settled on the picnic blanket as though it might crease his trousers. Stella and Mrs. Grafton followed Mother's lead, sweeping their long skirts under them and perching like very deliberate, very graceful birds. As though she wanted to emphasize the contrast, Emily toppled Alaine into a laughing pile. Papa Horatio opened the picnic hamper and distributed sandwiches, jam thumbprints, and bright scarlet apples fresh from harvest.

"You'd have to ask Alaine," Jack replied with a laugh. "All I can say is it looks good and tastes better."

"Do you really handle all the operations yourself?" Stella asked. Alaine couldn't tell if the curl of her mouth was curiosity or contempt, but chose to assume the best.

"I do," Alaine replied. "And it's coming off better than I've ever seen. The pears especially."

"My goodness! I can't imagine managing a home and a business." Stella accepted the apple that Pierce offered her, examining it. "I'm afraid I'd let one go in favor of the other."

Delphine met Alaine's eyes. There was a silent request there, willing Alaine not to rise to the bait.

To Delphine's visible relief, Alaine merely smiled. "That's the way of it, isn't it, though? For wives—men go off to the office, and we're set to juggling everything else."

Everyone laughed politely and settled into banal conversations over the jam in the cookies and the chickens in the exhibition.

"She's a real peach," Alaine whispered, catching Delphine's arm as they packed up from the picnic, alone for the moment. Jack had found a work colleague, and Pierce was obdurately torturing both with talk of politics. Papa Horatio had Stella and Mrs. Grafton in stitches over some story, and Mother and Emily had gone back to visit her bantams.

"Oh, don't let her get at you—she's used to being the dainty little coquette with the acerbic wit. I think she rather likes it," Delphine replied. "I never know if I'm just being sensitive, or if Stella means to be cruel. Just last week she said my watercolors were 'just so pastoral' and the dinner menu 'preciously rustic.'"

Alaine shook her head. She couldn't imagine Esther, as prim as her sister-in-law was, saying anything unkind to her without Jack's fierce disapproval. "Doesn't Pierce stand up for you?"

Delphine was taken aback. "Why—I don't think he even really notices it. He's used to his sister saying such things, you know, and—"

"I suppose." Alaine looped her arm through Delphine's. "Well, I don't know the first thing about painting, but if 'pastoral' is a compliment, it's absolutely true, and if not, it's rubbish. You've got a real eye for it, Del. Ever think of doing more? Maybe an exhibition, or teaching?"

Delphine smiled softly. "Truth be told, I've been enjoying going to lectures at the university so much—you remember Ida Carrington?" Alaine nodded. "She and I have been attending public lectures, and well—I've almost considered taking a course in art history."

"Oh, Del, you ought to! You'd enjoy it so."

"What would Delphine enjoy?" Mrs. Grafton had come alongside them with hardly a sound.

"She'd considered—"

"I was just telling Alaine about my watercolors," Delphine interrupted. Alaine gave her a look, but didn't press.

"Oh, yes. You do very pretty work. I always told Pierce a lady needed to have some diversion, beyond home and family. Something small that's her little hobby." Mrs. Grafton smiled. "Of course, there's less time for it once children come along."

Delphine nodded with a terse smile. As Mrs. Grafton drifted back toward Mother and Emily, returning from the exhibition hall, Delphine caught Alaine's hand. "I have more bargains for you to set out. Enough to last through the New Year. You know—the ones for—"

"I know," Alaine said, giving her a sister a curious look. It wasn't her business, of course, but she sensed tension between Grafton expectations and Del's own desires. Worry creased Del's brow. "They work, you know that. No need to fret or second-guess—"

"Oh, I don't second-guess Lilabeth's bargains. I trust everything she ever taught us about them."

Alaine winced. That made one of them, then—ironic that her sister, who had never held much tow with bargains and now lived squarely without them, followed Gran's rules better than Alaine at the moment. She bit her lips together, keenly aware that this entire event, the full Mercy Fund, the shining reputation she was building for herself, were all on account of a bargain Gran would never have approved of. "Then why do you look as jumpy as if you just swallowed a toad?"

Del hesitated. "I shouldn't want to use those bargains anymore, should I? Stella had her first baby within a year of getting married."

"Good for Stella." Alaine snorted.

"Pierce's mother reminds me all the time. And I should want to, shouldn't I? But I—I'm just not ready. Maybe it's selfish, but...I feel as though I haven't had a chance to enjoy the time with Pierce yet. He's always so busy, between the glassworks and starting his political career, and I—" She stopped herself, but Alaine could tell she wanted to say more. She waited, but Delphine didn't continue.

"It's not selfish. Why, if Mother had her way, we'd have seven children in as many years and counting." That made Del smile even as it snagged Alaine's conscience, that small part of it she hadn't quite disentangled from her mother's expectations. "But it's your choice—that was why Gran taught us that bargain, if you get right down to it. To give us some way to make that choice. If you trust Gran's bargains," she said fiercely, catching Del's hand, "trust that. She wanted us to be able to make our own way in this world."

Alaine waved farewell as the Graftons jounced away from the fairgrounds in the touring car. As Papa Horatio and Mother helped Emily load her birds into their crates, Jack stopped Alaine. "Something I wanted to ask you."

Alaine turned to him, bright mood dimming instantly. "Why, what's the matter?"

"Something Millie Jacobs said," he replied. "I didn't realize that the permit on this whole event was denied. And she can't figure out how the decision was overturned, when they were so adamant about the reasons for refusal."

Alaine's pulse quickened. She'd never lied to Jack before, she realized, never even kept something back. But she hadn't told him this. "I don't know. I suppose they realized they were being ludicrous—"

He caught her hand. The scar from the shards of the mirror was still a red welt on her palm. "And I remembered you had your hand bandaged, right at the same time. Alaine, did you do something?"

"No! Well, I cut myself deboning that hen—"

"We butchered that hen the week before."

Alaine stopped, heart pounding. "Does it matter?" she asked quietly. "Does it matter how it happened?"

"Yes." Jack dropped her hand. "Yes, it does. You said we wouldn't

135

fool around with that ring anymore. I'm tearing it out, Alaine, just as soon as I—"

"No! It's not yours to tear up. It's mine." She spoke before she thought what that meant, that she was claiming some part of their shared home, their shared life, that he had no say in, no place in. "I make the bargains, not you. You never have, you never will."

"You don't know what you're playing with, you've said that yourself," Jack whispered. His careful tone was rarely harsh, but it strained against his control now. Alaine shied away; it was hard to make Jack truly angry, and this had done it. "What if—what if something happened to you? Or Emily?"

"Nothing is going to happen! I know what I'm doing," she added, knowing even as she said the words that they weren't quite true. She'd seen into Fae, she hadn't understood the bargain, she'd been lucky. "Besides, I'm only doing this for us."

"Are you?" Alaine felt as though she had been dashed with cold water. "There were other ways. Or you could have taken a hit to your pride." She began to argue, but Jack shook his head. "Your mother is coming back. We'll discuss this later."

Alaine swallowed hard, her heart in her ears. Jack wasn't wrong—she had been lucky. Or maybe not merely lucky—maybe she was bold, and fortune favored her boldness. Still, Aunt Imogene's words rang in her memory—*your firstborn child*. She wouldn't make that mistake, could never make that mistake, but when Jack handed her a spade after Emily was in bed, she agreed silently, and dug up the flowers that had formed the perimeter of the ring. But the verdant grass remained, and she suppressed a shiver at the potential for magic that shone in the brilliant green ring.

21

First the bargain, then the price.
—Folk saying

"MAMA, PAPA HORATIO says he thinks the Smokehouse trees are ripe!" Emily careened through the orchard, a rose-smudged apple in each hand. "But he says you're the judge."

"Well, if Papa Horatio thinks they're ready, they are." She nabbed one apple from Emily and took a generous bite. Sharp and sweet, resistant crunch—perfection. "Here, what do you say, Del?"

Her sister held the apple and took a more delicate taste. "These always were my favorite."

"I'll send a bushel back with you after—" Alaine said, then stopped herself. Delphine wouldn't be coming for the apple harvest. After the scene with Pierce at cherry picking, Alaine hadn't brought it up with Delphine, and Delphine had blithely recited a slate of social events that skated her right through harvest season without a pause for a visit to Moore's Ferry.

"Maybe at Thanksgiving." Delphine handed the apple back. "We'll be so busy through fall. We're hosting the board of directors for a dinner, did I tell you?"

Five times, Alaine thought, annoyed. Of course it would be too much to come for a visit at harvest, let alone help one's family farm, with the high-and-mighty board of directors occupying one's time.

"Yes, you did," she barked, and Delphine started. Alaine softened. Her sister must be nervous, to keep bringing it up. "What are you serving?"

Delphine laughed. "As though you care about the menu!"

"I do! Land sakes, the only thing I could care about dinner with the Grafton Glassworks Board of Directors is the food." Delphine didn't laugh. "You're worrying about the menu? Not sure if they want beef tongue tartare or liver-and-onion consommé or walleye aspic or—"

"Stop!" Delphine finally conceded a laugh.

"What, that's not what Perrysburg's finest is serving? Why, I read an article in *Good Housekeeping* just last month—"

"You did not! You don't even take any magazines."

"I take the *Farm Journal* and *Prairie Farmer*, thank you very much."

"And the walleye aspic, that was in which of these esteemed publications?" Delphine snatched the half-eaten apple back from Alaine. "Yes, I'm nervous. This is Pierce's first social event as the executive officer, and it's very important that I—that we—put on a good show."

"A good show? Sounds like you're hiring cancan dancers." Alaine shook her head. "Del, he's already from the richest family in the county running the biggest company in this part of the state. Who do you need to impress?"

"You'd be surprised," Delphine said quietly. "I—don't tell anyone, Alaine, but I don't think I've made a very good impression. Pierce's mother was supposed to take me on calls with her, but she didn't. Stella was going to introduce me around to her friends, but she's only called once, and it was for Pierce's birthday. No one's asked me to be on the charity committee at church, or to a Ladies Aid meeting, or to garden club. I—" Alaine was surprised to see that Delphine was almost in tears. "The only place I feel like I belong is painting class, but of course those aren't people the Graftons associate with, and it's not as though I could pay any of them social calls."

"I'd tell them—" Alaine bit her tongue. Yes, she would tell her

stuffy mother-in-law to take a hike and her priggish sister-in-law to go eat sand, but Delphine never would. Delphine wanted to belong, Alaine saw, feeling bruised for her poor sister. "I'd tell them they're missing out," she said instead.

"I just— It's not like it was, with Pierce, before. He would watch me sketch, we would take walks and really talk about things—art and music and books we both read. He loves opera, and he wanted to take me to the full season, but he hasn't had the time. And when he does have time, his father squirrels him away to hound him about the business— Yes, I know I've mixed my metaphors just awfully." Alaine didn't know what to say as Delphine forced a laugh. "He hasn't any time for me, and he seems to care more about what his father and mother think he ought to do than anything I can suggest."

"Maybe he's just—" Alaine heaved a sigh. She couldn't excuse him. "He may be nervous or trying to please the almighty Grafton Glassworks, but he oughtn't to ignore you."

"It's all right. I just wish I wasn't so lonesome. Well, at least I have painting class. And I suppose Ida is a friend. I do enjoy going to lectures with her, and do you realize how big the university library is?"

"Do they have a section on agriculture?"

"I'm sure they do," Delphine said. "I never considered how many things there could be to learn in the world. I mean, I did in theory— remember reading Father's *National Geographics*?—but the more you learn, the more you realize you don't know very much."

"That's rather uncomfortable."

"Not at all! It's exciting." She shivered contentedly, and Alaine shrugged and let Emily pull them both into the orchard to inspect the Winesaps and the Ashmead's Kernels.

As Papa Horatio led the procession back to Orchard Crest with a full basket of early apples, Alaine hung back.

The fairy ring she'd dug up was still an uncanny green interruption to the otherwise summer-scorched grass. It had to still have magic in it, despite her digging up the flowers. She circled the ring, feeling suddenly protective of it. Jack had overreacted. What harm did it do to push the bargains further? It had certainly worked in her favor up until now. She ticked the successes off easily. Leaving the bargain in the linden tree's roots made for a bigger cherry harvest, and she'd done the same for the apples, which were bigger and brighter than she'd ever seen. As unsavory as the incident with the chicken had been, it produced a business arrangement that had propelled them to the top of the farms in the area. And all it had taken was a whispered promise in a mirror to get her permit for the Society auction. If she could ask for anything—

Delphine and Emily laughed, far ahead of her in Mother's garden.

Del. If she could ask for anything, she'd ask for something for Del. But she sensed that her sister's troubles weren't as simple to solve as meager harvests or bad prices. That was the difficulty, finding exactly what to ask for. If she could parse that out, she had learned the sort of things the Fae would take—bones and feathers and glass. A farm had plenty of each.

After supper with Mother and Papa Horatio, Alaine left Delphine playing dominoes with Emily and Jack. She snuck a bit of good paper from the rolltop desk, some chicken bones she'd saved from the larder, and a length of red silk ribbon, and retreated to the porch as the last of the sunset leaked purple on the lawn.

She hesitated over the note. The hardwood ash was old soot scraped from the fireplace, but she was sure it would serve. No, it was the words themselves. How to express what Delphine so desperately wanted? She started and stopped several times before penning it in with her thin handwriting.

A new bargain I would make, the Fae I entreat to take:
Ears and voices and eyes shall be
Bound to hear and speak and see
Delphine of Orchard Crest, as new
Exemplar of the social milieu

Feeling very satisfied with herself, she rolled the paper around the bones like a scroll and tied it with the ribbon. Then she tiptoed down the porch steps toward the bright green ring.

"Where are you going?"

Alaine whirled, burying the lumpy scroll in her skirts. Delphine cocked an eyebrow at her and, worse, Emily traipsed behind, already dressed in her white nightgown.

"Just taking the air," she said, trying for nonchalance. She was fairly sure she failed.

"Well, then wait a minute and I'll come, too," Delphine said. "It's a lovely evening."

"That's not fair, I want to go for a walk, too!" Emily pouted.

"It's past your bedtime already," Alaine said.

"It is not, it's still light out."

Alaine shook her head. They'd had this argument fifteen times since summer began, and Emily was not amenable to explanations about the earth's seasonal tilt. "It's very much bedtime. What if Aunt Del tells you a story?" she asked, hopeful to distract two pairs of prying eyes at once.

"No, I want Daddy to read to me tonight."

"Very well," Alaine said, shooing her inside. She skipped up the steps.

Delphine watched her with a soft smile. "She's a good kid, Alaine." Alaine blushed with the deepest sort of pride she ever felt. "She'll take over here someday when we're both old crones on rocking chairs."

"That's the plan." Alaine shifted the bundle to the other hand, the bones feeling suddenly very heavy.

Delphine gave her a curious look. "Say, what are you doing, anyway?"

Alaine froze. "Nothing at all. Just—had some rubbish to throw out." She hastily untied the paper and ribbon, letting them flutter to the ground at her feet, then showed Delphine the handful of chicken bones.

"Alaine!" Delphine wrinkled her nose. "Can't those go in the bin outside? What are you taking them into the woods for?" Her eyes darted to the bright green ring and then back to Alaine. Alaine's

141

pulse quickened. "It's nothing you shouldn't be doing, is it?"

"Don't know what you mean."

Delphine raised an eyebrow. "Because I did want to ask. That awful garden you planted—it's gone now. But—well, any fool could see that the grass is strange here."

Alaine looked away. When she was cornered, she was never good at lying. "Still don't know what you mean."

"You stubborn goat! You know exactly what I'm asking." Del's eyes narrowed. "Is there something funny about that garden you planted? It's a ring now—but it can't be a fairy ring."

"It was just an experiment," Alaine answered, kicking the ribbon farther into the weeds, "to see what would grow, and it turns out, nothing will."

"Hogwash! That grass—" Delphine knelt to feel the velvet green.

"Leave it well enough alone!" Alaine snapped, frustration blazing hot at her sister even though she knew, rationally, that Delphine hadn't done anything wrong.

"So you did try something?" Her sister rose slowly. "Alaine, I—I'd never have believed it. Grandma Lilabeth would never have condoned—"

"I learned it from Aunt Imogene, so lay off the pontificating. It's perfectly safe," she rushed to add.

"People who say something is perfectly safe usually don't know what they're talking about," Delphine retorted. "Now, what are you meddling with any of this for?"

Because it was the only way to save the farm, as though you care, Alaine thought, shoving aside the uncomfortable thought that it had become more than that. Alaine pivoted quickly. "What if you could have anything you wanted, Del? What would it be?"

Delphine grew quiet. "I think you know."

"Well? Think about how badly you want that, and then maybe you can guess why I'd meddle." She gripped the bones so tightly she thought they might crack.

Del's eyes widened. "You've done it already? No, I don't want to know. Alaine, it's not right. Lilabeth taught us better, and—" She

stopped, gazing at the green circle with something like longing, then shook herself. "You should dig it up. Sow it with salt. They hate that, don't they? Salt?"

"Salt and iron," Alaine said quietly. "But it's not hurting anything, Del. It's fine."

"I don't think I want to take that walk after all," Delphine said quietly. "I'm going to go read a story to Emily." The way she emphasized Em's name sunk into Alaine like a thorn. Like Del was admonishing her, reminding her that her daughter mattered more than the meager power of Fae magic. Of course she did, and of course Alaine knew that, she thought with a flash of anger. Delphine simply didn't understand.

"Well, I think I will go for a walk. I need to clear my head." As the screen door cracked against its frame behind Del, Alaine gathered the paper and the ribbon. She had half a mind to throw the whole business out. If Delphine didn't want her help, she didn't have to give it. But she mollified her anger as she wound the ribbon around the bundle, the bright scarlet a little mud stained. Del was just afraid. She'd never been as confident as Alaine with the bargains, and she was likely just as skittish and faltering in Perrysburg. No wonder she was disappointed; fortune favored the bold, Alaine blithely assessed. Why her sister wanted to make a life in Perrysburg, shackled by the expectations of Pierce and the rest of his family, was beyond her, but perhaps Alaine was the only one who could help.

She tied the ribbon in a neat bow. The silk had frayed where she'd stepped on it, and her missive was smudged. That didn't matter, she was confident—the Fae surely wanted the bones, and the message was still, to her eyes, legible. She slid a silver pin through the ribbon, a final touch on a change in fortune for her sister. The evening light was fading, so she dropped the bundle in the middle of the ring and went back inside, rattling the rubbish bin on the way in and letting it lie for her about where the bones had ended up.

She woke while the dawn was still held back by the clouds along the horizon, and slipped outside, feet bare in thick dew. The ring was empty, except for a scrap of paper, more smudged now save that nearly alien handwriting.

So bargained, so agreed.

Alaine carefully folded the paper, a triumphant smile spreading as she went inside to boil the water for breakfast. She could change her sister's fortune as well as her own.

22

Gold is straw, straw is gold
Fae tricks both young and old
                    —Traditional bargain for a glamour

WINTER CAME SLOWLY, a few dustings on the lawn in late November, and a proper squall that kept Alaine and Jack from coming for Thanksgiving. Delphine had always loved the change of the season, fresh snow papering over the frozen mud and bare trees of late autumn. It signaled, this year, a fresh beginning. The fall social season had been draining; though she'd expected a chaotic flurry of dinners and dances and the opera opening, she hadn't expected a sudden onslaught of scrutiny from the Graftons, and even Pierce. It was as though they suddenly noticed her, heard every misspoken word, saw every misstep. Mrs. Grafton seemed to never tire of correcting her, while Stella preferred to ignore her. Worse, she felt she was constantly disappointing her husband.

She would start anew with the Christmas season, she decided. She decorated the house with a relish that made Pierce smile and nod at her efforts, and planned a dinner for all the Perrysburg families the Graftons knew well.

"The red or the gray, do you think?" Delphine said, surveying the two evening gowns hanging side by side.

Pierce barely glanced up from a ledger—he insisted on leaving

work ledgers on the little desk in their room, though there wasn't enough room for them, and Delphine quietly resented their ordered rows of numbers. "Hm? Oh, for tonight?"

"Yes, of course, for— Are you quite all right?"

"Fine, fine. Agitators drumming up discontent at the glassworks again. I need to have these numbers ready for the state inspectors."

"I'm sorry, dear, I—"

"They haven't the slightest idea what they're talking about, either. Child labor—what child labor! We've let off hiring anyone under sixteen for the night shift years ago, and I strictly prohibit hiring anyone under fourteen. And yet here they are, again—they won't be content until we haven't anyone left to run the factory."

"I suppose I—they want them in school instead?" Delphine assayed. "There's a good argument to be made—"

"In school!" Pierce laughed and slammed the book closed with a thump. "What good arithmetic and poetry does them, I can't tell. Truth be told, they want to work. Learn a trade, work their way up the ranks. Half of them are supporting their families."

Delphine bit her tongue—it seemed that fourteen-year-olds supporting families was, perhaps, the problem itself. Instead, she pointed back to the dresses. "Is the red too on the nose? For Christmas?"

"I don't care, Delphine, wear whatever you want."

Stung, Delphine unhooked the closure on the cranberry-red velvet-and-chiffon gown, draped in the layered panels she'd seen in fashion plates, loose over the bust and slim at the hips. The fabrics had seemed cheerful and festive when she'd selected them with the dressmaker, but now the joy had been siphoned off, leaving the gown merely gaudy. Pierce had been short-tempered lately, and nothing she did seemed to cheer him. In fact, she felt herself an annoyance to him more often than not, and that hurt the worst of all.

Pierce had changed his clothes and pasted on a pleasant demeanor by the time the guests began to arrive. The Lyndleys, the Steeles, the Abbotts with Ida in tow, the extended Grafton family. Pierce's sister, Stella, looking as effervescent as champagne bubbles, with her stern, impeccably dressed husband, Lionel, in tow.

"Love, just look at that gown!" Stella swooped on Delphine with a sharp smile. "So *festive*. You nearly look like we could put you on the Christmas tree!"

Delphine swallowed offense. "And you—gray is a lovely color on you."

"I managed to get someone to copy a Callot Soeurs—wouldn't it be something to have an original? The sketches are enough to send me quite mad, but we went to a party in New York last year, and Mrs. Astor was wearing one of their pieces and, oh, my heart— Lionel! Isn't Delphine's gown darling?"

Lionel nodded and went back to discussing something somber and questionably professional for a Christmas party—Delphine heard "glass" and "legality" and "sixteen" floating over the murmur of conversation.

"Oh, lands, Ida Carrington." Stella sighed. "You do think she could last a single party without those spectacles, don't you?"

Delphine bristled. "I'm not sure—my father was nearsighted and couldn't see well enough without."

"For farming?" Stella tittered.

"For anything," Delphine replied.

"What a festive gown, Delphine!" Verna Steele landed next to them like a partridge settling into a branch. "And Stella, simply beautiful. I do love gray in wintertime."

"Good evening, Mrs. Steele," Delphine said, cheeks blazing. Festive, then. Her carefully designed gown was festive. Might as well call it vulgar and cheap, while they were at it.

"I'm sorry, there goes my husband—ruining a perfectly good evening. Have you heard? There's a fuss afoot in the state legislature to ban overnight work by minors." She tut-tutted.

"I don't believe any of our husbands' businesses employ minors overnight?" Delphine said cautiously.

Stella shook her head. "But it's the principle of the thing, Delphine! Industry should be able to choose whom to employ."

"Indeed!" Mrs. Steele tapped her fan on her open palm. "What's next? Requiring certain wages? Making them hire women?" She laughed. "It's all down to folks who have too much time on their

hands and not enough sense, if you ask me. Agitators—who's that woman from the National Council of Jewesses or whatnot, always writing in the paper? Marks, that's it."

"Yes, she specifically pointed to the glassworks, too." Stella raised an eyebrow. "As though the Grafton Glassworks isn't an absolute model of modern industry."

"Isn't she the one who wrote that awful piece on divorce? That the laws should allow for more reasons for it?" Mrs. Steele huffed as though she'd scented something rotten.

"Oh, one of those suffragettes did, I don't recall who." Stella smirked. "It's not worth keeping all their names straight, they spout rubbish. As though there's any good reason for divorce! Why, any woman who would abandon her husband deserves more scorn than she gets."

"You're talking about Lydia Wilde, I just know it." Mrs. Steele leaned forward, eager for fresh gossip.

"Hardly! I would never! But I did think it suspicious that William Thornton called at her parents' last week. To even consider a divorced woman fair game for marriage—well." Stella's eyes were viciously bright.

"I thought her husband had—you know. That it was adultery? That is to say, if it's not a woman's fault—" Delphine began, but Stella laid a hand on her arm.

"A woman can always try harder, to keep a man's attention, to pacify his less temperate natures. Whatever the case may be. You are simply too kindhearted to say what you could." Stella sent Ida Carrington a sideways glance across the room. She was engaged in a lively conversation with Mr. Lyndley's great-uncle. "About anyone and everyone. But you really should consider Pierce's political career, dear. After all, what does it say to constituents if the wife of a city councilman is sympathetic toward radicalism?"

Delphine's mouth went dry. "I didn't say I was—"

"Of course not, ducks." Verna Steele patted her hand. "I ought to see how Mrs. Lyndley is doing, please excuse me."

Ida caught her eye and waved her over.

"I wanted to tell you that I finished my paper, you know, the one with the interview with your aunt?" Delphine flushed, willing Ida to keep her voice down. She didn't need her family's backwoods superstitions becoming a topic of conversation in the midst of a formal Christmas party. "My professor thinks I might expand on the concepts, maybe complete a full ethnography."

"That's lovely," Delphine replied absently. "My family enjoyed your visit."

"Do you think they'd let me come again? I'd like to chat to your grandfather, too—your niece said he saw a fairy? Oh, I'm sure it's just a story, but a story I'd like to hear from him—maybe in the spring, once the roads are better for that little car of yours."

Delphine avoided promising anything, especially now, with both Mrs. Steele and Stella glancing suspiciously at her. "Yes, the car is lovely, but it doesn't handle the roads well in winter," she said instead.

"It's really something that Mr. Grafton bought you the car. Such a—may I say rare?—show of support."

Delphine's stomach dropped. "Support?"

"For women's equity, I mean."

Delphine's mouth fell open, and she swiftly closed it. Could Ida actually be suggesting any such thing, and here and now of all times? Delphine lowered her voice. "He was not trying to make any kind of statement with it. His...politics aren't like that."

"Oh. Aunt Edwina said she wondered if he might be sympathetic to the suffragists after all. Aunt Edwina is somewhat sympathetic." Delphine raised an eyebrow, trying to imagine Mrs. Abbott marching with a banner and sash. "She isn't entirely convinced," Ida added in a rush, "and of course doesn't make any sort of show—oh, you know how it is. But if a Grafton took up women's suffrage, that would be quite the shift here in Perrysburg." She leaned forward, poorly tempering her eagerness.

"Well, Perrysburg is going to have to wait for a different shift," Delphine said. Ida deflated slightly. "And I don't think this is polite conversation for the party, at any rate."

As soon as Ida wandered toward the buffet, Stella drifted back to Delphine's side. She looped her arm through Delphine's with a conspiratorial smirk. "I did mean to ask about your...rapport with Ida Carrington at some point. But now I'm afraid you'll feel picked on." Her pert mouth formed a pout that substituted weakly for apology.

If Stella had any concern for her feeling picked on, she'd leave well enough alone, Delphine thought. "Of course not, Stella."

"Well, it's just that I heard you took her to visit your family." Stella buried a smirk. "To learn about fairies?"

"I took her to see my family farm," Delphine answered, angry heat stoking a blush that began at her collarbone and crept slowly toward her ears. "And my Aunt Imogene."

"Oh, was that the old woman who made tasteless jokes at the wedding?" Stella laughed. "I am sorry, I don't mean to disparage your family."

"You know very well what you're meaning to do," Delphine said, regretting it instantly. Stella merely hiccupped a laugh. "Ida is interested in old stories, and Aunt Imogene knows plenty of old stories."

"I'm sure she does," Stella replied. "Well. There are more... influential friends you could make here in Perrysburg. I could invite you to a few get-togethers once the holidays are over."

If she cared so much, Delphine thought with a blaze of frustration, she could have invited her new sister-in-law along to tea and card parties and drives months ago. No, she'd waited until Delphine had become embarrassing, and now she had to correct the smudge on the family reputation.

"That would be lovely, Stella," Delphine lied, willing the angry blush to go away before it stained her entire face the same crimson as her damnably festive gown. "I'll look forward to it."

The rest of the party was a blur of pleasant conversation and perfectly cooked pheasant and a round of staid, dull charades. When the last guest left, Delphine hastily unhooked the gown with fumbling fingers. Pierce didn't notice.

"Quite a success, I'd say—funny how the harder these unionists and radicals push, the more it strengthens the base for candidates like me. I've got more support now than I did a fortnight ago!" He laughed at his own joke as Delphine's hook snagged delicate chiffon. Tears sprang into her eyes. The whole night, their grand Christmas party, the night she'd looked forward to, just a platform for Pierce. Well, that was what she had signed up for, wasn't it? She wrestled with the hook.

"Pierce, dear, would you—"

"You could do me the favor of spending a bit less time with less... influential members of the neighborhood." He turned, a spark of anger kindled in his eyes. She stopped fiddling with the hook. She knew that look, like a simmering kettle; something had frustrated him, whether it was dinner not to his liking or a mistake on the records or, once, a hat she'd bought that he thought too modish. She prepared herself to mollify him. "I heard from no fewer than three of our friends that Ida was making a spectacle of herself talking about her field trip to see your family."

"Oh?" Delphine's stomach sank. "It's just part of her research, learning more about the old stories and—"

"And here I thought perhaps she'd exaggerated." His voice went to ice and Delphine knew she'd made a mistake.

"You knew I took her to the farm. Perhaps I should have told you more about her aims in going," Delphine rushed to add, "but truly, it isn't so bad as you're making it out. She talked to Imogene and took a few notes and—"

"Imogene!" Pierce replied in a low rumble. "That insane old woman who lives in the woods? Why on God's green earth would you think it prudent to let anyone know you're related to people like that? Didn't it cross your mind to consider that it involves my good name, too?"

"I don't think anyone will—"

"You don't think! Get that idiot dress off, Delphine."

She bit back tears. "It's caught—the hook—I didn't realize—" Faint protestations blended together as Pierce advanced on her and tore the hook free from the delicate chiffon, leaving a tattered shred behind.

"Why can't you think properly?" Pierce threw his jacket across the bureau, scattering Delphine's perfume bottles. "I'm trying to run for city council and I've got a wife whose family is rumored to make voodoo dolls and love potions."

Delphine carefully unhooked the rest of the gown, moving the ripped part aside. Her hand shook, but she didn't cry. If she stayed calm, Pierce's anger usually subsided, too. "Ida was only interested in stories. And even Aunt Imogene doesn't make voodoo dolls," she tried to joke.

Pierce's anger cracked, just slightly. "I know you can't help your family, Del. But please do consider the degree to which we might... minimize how much people here know about them."

Delphine bit her lip, feeling exposed, not only because she was down to her corset and combination. Pierce could split open her life—her childhood home, family, beliefs—and see it all laid out like an anatomy drawing, knowing how each piece would be perceived, how each piece benefitted his aspirations, or not. She wanted him to see her, love her, without dissecting her. "I'm going to bed," she finally said. "Are you coming?"

Pierce glanced at Delphine, as though deciding. He ran a hand through tousled hair, vest unbuttoned and cuff links loose, and she saw a glimpse of the man she'd fallen in love with, the man whose jovial laugh could fill a room. Now the room was filled with only silence. "Go to bed. I'll be in the study for a while."

23

Wassail your trees that they may bear
Many's the apple and many's the pear
—Wassail song

"WELL, JACK, TELL me how the pear trees are doing." Papa Horatio passed Alaine and Jack glasses of the cider he'd made over the winter. It was warm for February; most of the snow had melted from the open spaces, but it clung on in the shade, and Alaine was enjoying the roaring fire in the parlor of Orchard Crest.

"Now, Alaine's the one to ask if you want a good answer," Jack said with a laugh. He sipped his cider. "Good batch this year."

"Thankee." Papa Horatio tipped his head in a mock bow. "And I know Alaine's the expert. That's why I asked you."

"A test, is it!" Alaine laughed. "Well, let's see if you pass third form or not."

"Well, we banked them up well. And they seemed sturdy enough in the fall."

"And?"

"And... they didn't fall down overwinter? I've no idea."

"Well, Alaine, rescue him. No—Emily! Tell me, how are them pears doing?"

He winked at Emily, and she beamed. "They're showing buds," she supplied readily.

"That's right!" Papa Horatio slapped his knee. "Tight as a drum yet, but they'll bud out fair and fresh come spring."

"I think they're well on their way to producing this year," Alaine added. "We'll see. And pears are notorious for dropping unripe fruit, so I'm not counting chickens before they're—ripe?" She laughed.

"Then I'll try my hand at making perry next fall." Papa Horatio took a swig of his cider. "This old dog might learn new tricks yet."

"Tricks like contracts with canning companies? We'd never done any such thing before, but Alaine—I'll say, well done. My word, finding that man on the low road was a godsend," Mother said, setting her cider down.

Alaine had not, and did not, correct the direction her mother sent the credit for their good luck. The knowledge that her daughter had tried the untested magic beyond the simple bargains Grandma Lilabeth wielded would send her into a fit of dyspepsia at best.

"Best harvest in a decade, and we got better prices than ever," Horatio agreed. "I heard that the folks over by Lemon Creek who hired Acton Willis didn't get half their late Northern Spy batch in."

"I think their Ashmeads, too," Jack said. "Must have lost a bundle. And the Saunders are in foreclosure. Their cherries dropped their fruit early, and their apples weren't much." He shared a look with Alaine—that could have been them. They'd be underwater now, if it hadn't been for her bargains.

Was it worth it? Alaine forced the question back. Of course it was. The verdant grass of her fairy ring had lingered as autumn overtook the forest, even seeping bright through the snow until it piled too deep to tell any longer. Now, as it emerged from patches of snowmelt, it was still stained brighter green than it should have been after a long winter.

She wasn't sure, at any rate, that it was still a fairy ring. She had waded through her sister's letters detailing this opera premiere and that formal luncheon, expecting each time to read her sister's social triumphs. Instead, she got bland recitations of dinner menus and theater programs, and a distant tone of sadness that told her that Delphine was no better off than she'd been before.

Either the ring didn't have much magic any longer, or she hadn't left a big enough prize to make more than a little goodwill, or the Fae couldn't wield that kind of power in Perrysburg. No one seemed to notice Del—good riddance to them, Alaine thought.

"Now, where is that toaster?" Alaine stood, turning her back to the fire for a moment to enjoy the warmth. "That's right—we put it in the hall closet."

She fetched the little iron toaster. Even though they had a stove in the kitchen, toasting the bread by the fire was tradition on Candlemas. Papa Horatio saved his best batch of cider for the occasion, and usually Delphine played piano and Mother sang, with a reluctant Alaine providing alto harmonies.

Tonight Delphine's place at the piano was empty. Her short letter blamed the possibility of poor weather for her absence; Alaine blamed Pierce. The train ran in all but the worst weather, and they had both walked up a Prospect Hill coated in ice and snow countless times. No, Pierce Grafton couldn't abide the thought of his wife wassailing the orchard, leaving gifts for the Fae, making a spectacle of herself, even if none of his Perrysburg associates would see it. Alaine seethed when her glance passed the vacant piano.

"Say, Em, know what we called these when I was a boy?" Papa Horatio told the joke every year, and every year they were all good sports and pretended to hear it for the first time. "Toe toaster! Best be careful!"

Jack laughed as he nudged the iron toaster toward the glowing coals with Emily. "How many times did you toast your toes, Horatio?"

"Too many!" He laughed. "There we are, Iris. Good batch of brown bread!"

Mother handed a large platter of thick nut-brown slices to Alaine. "Baked fresh this morning. I did it myself—Susan isn't keen on anything to do with bargains."

"That's what comes of hiring a city girl," Papa Horatio scolded. "Where's she from? Saint Louis? Cincinnati?"

"She's from Maple Ridge," Mother answered with a laugh. "Hardly a city girl."

"Ah, well. The girls have all started to look like city girls, what

155

with the big stores just the trouble of a train ride away, and ordering from the catalogs and whatnot. When I was a pup, you knew where you stood."

"When you were a pup, they hadn't invented the spinning jenny yet," Alaine teased.

"Now, I ain't that old!" He popped a piece of bread into the toaster and flicked the heat from his fingers. Alaine pulled a spool of twine from her pocket and began cutting pieces to length, looping them around her finger and thumb, and snipping with practiced precision. Jack worked a hole through each slice with her sewing awl, then passed the toast to Mother, who tied a piece of the twine in a loop. Emily stacked the finished toast. They worked in familial quiet, no one mentioning the pronounced absence of the piano music.

"I think that's enough," Alaine said as they finished the last batch. Papa Horatio pulled the toaster back from the fire with a satisfied scrape. "Mother, are you coming to the orchard?"

"Not this year," she said. "I've a bit of a scratch in my throat, and it's feeling like rain tonight. Besides, someone has to clean up these crumbs."

Alaine wrapped herself in her heavy overcoat, the weatherworn one she used for chores, and pulled the lanterns from the back of the hall closet. Jack took them without a word and fit candles inside, knowing the pattern, the ritual. He touched a thick sliver of kindling to the coals until it glowed, lit each lantern, and handed one to Alaine and one to Papa Horatio. Alaine balanced the plate of toast and the lantern. Usually Del carried the lantern and she had the toast, and perhaps they should have left one lantern back, but Alaine had pulled all three from the closet, not thinking. Then she reconsidered and handed the lantern to Emily, who accepted it solemnly.

The candle flames punctured the blackness of a moonless night, murky flickering against clouded glass and pinpoints in punched tin. Alaine led the way to the orchard, boots crunching on old snow in the hollows. At the first row of apple trees, she stopped and set the lantern down, the light bleeding into the snow at the roots of the tree.

"Bud well, bear well," she murmured, "all seasons fare well. Take a gift back to Fae, prosper every sprig and spray."

She took a piece of toast and tied it to the bare branches of the tree, and Jack and Papa Horatio did likewise, working down the rows, leaving the trees festooned with their offering, their bargain. An early harvest for the Fae in exchange for a good harvest of their own come fall.

She took her lantern up again when the toast was gone, and recited, "Stand fast root, bear well top, fortune may send us a bright autumn crop."

"Think that works for pears?" Jack asked with a smile.

"We'll find out, I suppose."

The candlelight flickered wan on the snow, sending back glitter and shadow.

"Right well done, girl." Papa Horatio rested his arm on a nearby tree. "When I signed this place over to your pa, I never expected— well." He coughed. "Never figured I'd outlive him, never figured you'd have to take over the farm."

The graveled tones of grief in his voice made Alaine hop over a drift of half-melted snow to hug him. "I know, Papa. I miss him every day."

"Seemed like the best way at the time. He'd take over as owner— he was already managing most of the operations—and you all would be taken care of. It avoided any mess with inheritance, any need to divide shares for a widow's portion—Lilabeth didn't want the orchard split up, anyhow. And here it made a bigger mess, with you and your ma and Del all having shares."

"We've got it figured out, though, Papa—everyone gets a share of the profit after paying out our operating costs."

"And you do all the work and get a third of the cut." Papa shook his head. "You've done better than I ever did, than even your pa did. I just—it doesn't sit right, making you take it on."

"I wouldn't want to be anywhere else."

"Are you sure? By God, Alaine, you're cleverer than most. And Jack, a crack lawyer. You could have made a life anywhere—you

could be in Perrysburg like Del, or even Chicago, and we've tied you here."

"I wouldn't want a life in Perrysburg—and certainly not a big city like Chicago! I promise." She hesitated, then added, "I'm not like Delphine that way. I never wanted to leave."

"And people here—not always as open-minded as they might be. I worried, you know. Worried that boil of a man Olson would chew you up or that all the gossips would henpeck you to frustration." He laughed. "Shouldn't have worried—you seem to have sent Olson and Willis both back home with their tails between their legs."

"It doesn't...it doesn't embarrass you, does it, Papa? Having a woman run the orchard?"

"Embarrass me? Lands, girl, no! You've made me prouder than anything. But I know...this town isn't always friendly when things change, and a woman making her way like you, it's change. Especially folk like Willis, running his mouth like a gristmill."

"I'm not worried about Willis."

"And you shouldn't be! Stuffed shirts like him been keeping things from changing for the better for too long."

"You're going to tell me you're marching for suffrage next."

"Naw, I'll leave that to someone with better knees." He watched Emily's lantern bob in the darkness. "But there's other fights to have, too, and it seems you're fighting them well."

"Can't help it, I suppose. Never could manage to avoid opening my mouth."

Papa Horatio laughed. "Well. I just wanted to make sure that your loyalty to an old man and his dream wasn't holding you back."

"Never," Alaine said, so fiercely that it caught on her throat. "It's my dream, too."

"And you've done a right good job with it. I'm proud of you." He scanned the slope of the hill, the rows of trees, the old gnarled ones and the newer spindles of saplings, watched Jack and Emily as they walked back to the house. "This place will outlive me, and I'm glad of that."

24

Sour milk no Fae abides. Bargain only with the newest cream.

—Folk saying

DELPHINE LET IDA lead the way through the open doors of the Patterson Lecture Hall. Ida was flushed with excitement for the first of their lecture afternoons after the Christmas holidays, which she had spent, from all Delphine could tell, buried in a stack of library books. Delphine had considered refusing the invitation to continue their regular lecture dates after Pierce had chided her for keeping such eccentric company, but the truth was she was lonely. Stella's suggestion of organizing a few outings or parties with more "suitable" Perrysburg acquaintances hadn't materialized, and Delphine didn't have any other friends. The thought of staying home, day and in and day out, even in such an expansive and beautiful house, was stifling.

So she'd agreed to come to the first lecture of the new season when Ida asked, a larger one held in the new building on campus. The wood paneling of the auditorium was so fresh it still smelled faintly of varnish, and curtains in the university's navy and tan swathed a podium flanked by undersized American flags. The hall was crowded—more packed than any of the lectures Ida had brought her to throughout the fall semester.

And the crowd was nearly all women.

Ida picked someone out of the crowd and waved her over. The

stout lady was wearing a pair of sparkling green-and-purple ear-rings that matched a ribbon pinned to her breast. Delphine furtively glanced at the women milling nearby. Several had the suffrag-ist purple and green pinned or sewn to bodices or waistbands. Her stomach clenched faintly. What sort of lecture was this?

"This is my friend, Mrs. Grafton," Ida said, holding Delphine's elbow as though she was worried she might run away.

"Pleased to meet you, Mrs. Grafton. I'm Louise Marks."

Delphine smiled politely—the name sounded familiar, but she couldn't quite place it. "And you're from Perrysburg, then?"

"I was born in Saint Louis, but am a Perrysburg local now, yes. These small industrial cities always cry out with need, don't they?"

"I—suppose they do," Delphine said warily.

Ida laughed. "Delphine, Mrs. Marks is a philanthropist—perhaps you've heard of the National Council of Jewish Women?"

Delphine felt her smile go stiff. Of course—one of the groups that Pierce claimed stoked discontent among the glassworkers.

Mrs. Marks, to her surprise, reached out a plump, compassionate hand. "Oh, ducks, don't fret—I won't judge you on the basis of your husband if you don't judge me for mine."

"I'm sorry, you do have me at quite the disadvantage—you seem to know quite a bit about me, and I know very little about you."

"Not to worry. We've got time to get to know each other—after the meeting, I suppose," Mrs. Marks added, nodding to the front of the hall, where a woman in an impressively sized hat swathed in purple tulle was ascending the stage.

Delphine let Ida hurry them to a pair of seats near the aisle, won-dering if Louise Marks had simply misspoken when she called the lecture a meeting. The woman with the large hat swiftly introduced another woman, hailing from the Chicago Political Equality League.

"She's a regular firebrand," Ida whispered in excited tones next to her. Delphine clasped together palms that were growing damp. The woman situating a set of notes at the podium wore a sash striped green and purple across her shoulder. This was no dry academic lec-ture, Delphine discerned with slowly creeping dread.

The woman was petite and wore unassuming black and gray, but as she spoke, even her pearl earrings trembled with enthusiasm.

"There are no logical impediments to our equality," she claimed, "and yet we are, without recourse, civilly dead. Not only are we barred from voting—that most fundamental function of a democratic society—we are frequently barred from owning property, from bringing suit, from speaking for ourselves and ourselves alone. And if we have the audacity to wish to free ourselves from a marital bond which is not in our favor, we are bound to laws denying even that liberty!"

Delphine swallowed, deep discomfort forming into a ball in her throat. She had never really considered the right to vote a terribly pressing need. And yet, here, this woman laid out the troubles Alaine had faced with the orchard time and again in the same sentence. The suffragists had always seemed like a cadre of fantasists obsessed with an esoteric right—voting. Delphine had never truly appreciated how pragmatic their concerns might be as well. The idea that they might be right, that the women in unapologetic sashes bearing signs might not be wrong after all, gave her an unsettling feeling quite similar to indigestion.

Similar, but with a strange flutter of something like hope.

After the speech, several women shared plans for committee meetings and a gathering in Saint Louis to "voice our sincere beliefs alongside our sisters" at a rally. Delphine hoped no one would ask her to go to such a thing, but the conversation after the meeting broke up was polite and banal, as though everyone knew better than to ask Pierce Grafton's wife what she thought about tagging along on a political march.

"She's quite the speaker, isn't she?" Louise Marks caught Delphine's arm. "When I heard she was going to be on her way south for a convention, I knew we had to convince her to come speak."

"I'm afraid I didn't catch her name," Delphine said.

"Best remember it—McCulloch. Catherine McCulloch." Louise guided her toward a quiet corner. "I must confess my surprise at seeing you here. I had the understanding that the Graftons were not amenable to women's rights."

Delphine briefly considered running away, then composed herself. "If you mean my husband's politics, I don't speak for those."

"So you are in favor of separating a woman's vote from her husband's," Mrs. Marks said with a laugh that told Delphine she needn't answer. "As for the Grafton Glassworks. The conditions, I'm afraid, are—"

"I haven't anything to do with the management of the factory."

"Then you don't have any interest in the welfare of your husband's employees?" Mrs. Marks paused. "I'm sorry, I don't mean to scold. But I can't imagine a lady like you is aware of the number of boys working at your husband's factory, risking a maiming from the hot glass and ensuring they get no education. Fifty hours a week, and no schooling?" She shook her head. "And the glassworks is only one of many such employers we have seen."

"I didn't say—that is, I involve myself in charitable work." She thought of the clothing drive she had helped Mrs. Abbott organize, or the Sunday school picnics they invited the workers' children to. Suddenly her charitable work felt pitifully inadequate.

"I apologize, Mrs. Grafton. I hadn't intended to cause any trouble." Mrs. Marks nodded a farewell to Ida, who disentangled herself from a lively conversation with several women wearing colorful cockades. "I should be going."

Ida offered to take Delphine for an ice cream, but Delphine, confused and more than a little offended at Ida's bold deception, the more she considered the afternoon's events, politely excused herself and walked home alone.

25

Even the name itself is forged from flattery—fairy coming from "fair ones" or "fair folk," one of many euphemistic terms such as "the gentry" or "the good neighbors."
　—*Fairy Lore of Ireland, Scotland, and Wales*, by Alistair Fennimore

DELPHINE MOVED BETWEEN clutches of women in the parlor, their pastel silk afternoon dresses blooming like tulips in neatly ordered beds. The luncheon had gone perfectly, each course planned and executed like culinary clockwork, the conversation steered toward Pierce gently yet effectively. The Howards and the Steeles had promised sizeable donations to a campaign, and of course speaking any more plainly of terms and dollars now would be gauche.

"Mrs. Grafton, what a lovely ensemble." Mrs. Steele stopped her with a flick of her lithe wrist. "That isn't from Lymond's in town, is it?"

"But it is," Delphine said, sweeping the blush-pink hem of her skirt to reveal swaths of deep rose and pale lace inset at the side seam. The design had been in a magazine, and the pert seamstress at Lymond's had taken to sketching a variation on it, making up a version in pink monochrome that exceeded the ingenuity of the original.

"My word! You must bring out the best in them. I haven't even considered going anywhere outside of a city in years."

"Oh, I think our local craftsmen are up to the challenge," Delphine said, rising to the demands of playing politician's wife. "Part of

Pierce's plans for Perrysburg include investing in our local economy. We're more than merely a railroad hub."

"And you, too, my dear?" Mrs. Lyndley was a tall woman, and even the gentle slope of her lace-insert blouse didn't dull her sharp shoulders. She looked down at Delphine through a pair of silver spectacles. "Are you becoming invested in local politics?"

"Pierce is giving me such an opportunity to see the inner workings of government," Delphine said carefully. Always back to Pierce, to his abilities, to his aims. "I had never fully appreciated the extent to which the local tax policies influence business, for instance."

"Ah, well." Mrs. Lyndley smiled, the curve of her lip not entirely pleasant. Delphine ignored a sour feeling in her stomach. "I suppose I was curious if you were interested enough to pursue women's suffrage?"

Delphine's heart skipped a beat. Then she smiled gently. "I am not political myself, Mrs. Lyndley."

"Aren't we all, to some extent. No, I was merely curious, as Helen Howard said she was sure you and Miss Ida Carrington were at some rally to that effect. Just a couple weeks ago, I believe."

"I do go to the occasional lecture with Miss Carrington," Delphine said. She didn't let her smile waver.

"So is Pierce Grafton in favor, then, of women's suffrage?" Mrs. Lyndley's dark eyes drove into her, and Delphine was sure she would burst before Mrs. Steele laughed heartily.

"What an absurd question, Muriel!" She tapped her friend's arm playfully. "Pierce is no rabble-rouser, and besides—what on earth could a city councilman do for suffrage even if he was?" She patted Delphine's hand. "Mrs. Lyndley has been paying too much attention to that lawyer husband of hers—debating people into corners!"

Muriel Lyndley gave Mrs. Steele a pinched patient smile, and Delphine retreated to another group of women, who quizzed her intently on the recipe for the cream of broccoli soup she'd served for lunch.

"I think that went rather well." Delphine found Pierce in his study after the last guests had left. She never felt quite at home in his study, with its bookshelves organized with military precision and the high-backed chair facing the door like a banker's throne. Glass samples from the factory were displayed like insect specimens on the far wall.

"Yes, I think there's quite good support for my candidacy. I'll be able to solicit donations for newspaper advertisements to begin running later this year." He scratched a few notes, barely glancing up. Delphine waited, hoping for some acknowledgement. The luncheon, the perfectly orchestrated conversation, even the cream of broccoli soup.

"That's quite good, then," she said after a long moment had passed, expectation turning to flat disappointment.

"It is." He heaved a sigh and stood, his square hands planted on his desk. "Mr. Lyndley said something to me in confidence which I cannot ignore."

"Oh?" The sour curdle returned to Delphine's stomach. She knew what was next—Pierce was disappointed in her. She'd made some mistake, some misstep. That tone, the steel in his eyes. Someone had noticed her and found her lacking.

"He said he had heard from a reliable source that you've been seen at political meetings."

"No, Pierce, that's a misunderstanding. I go to lectures at the university, sometimes, with Ida Carrington, but—"

"What sorts of lectures? What possible interest do you have for anything they lecture about at the university?" He belted a laugh. "What sorts of lectures, Delphine?"

"Ethnomusicology," she said quietly. "And other topics from scholars there."

Pierce snorted. "You'll be telling me next you want to go back for a degree! Lyndley was convinced this was no music lecture." He waited a mere second. "Tell me!"

"It wasn't a political meeting. It was a lecture on suffrage." Even as she argued, she knew it was no simple lecture.

"By a university professor? They ought to ban such idiocy."

"I don't think she was a professor, no," Delphine hedged. "I didn't know that it was a—that most of the audience would be women in favor of suffrage."

"So you went to a speech on suffrage and were surprised to discover that your fellow attendees were a bunch of political hags ready to shout down the institutions of our nation? Even you aren't that naive, Delphine." He strode out from behind his desk, advancing on her so quickly that she didn't have time to react.

"I would never go to a political meeting on purpose," Delphine insisted. "It's not seemly, it's not polite."

"But you did!" He gripped her wrist. "If this ruins my chances at city council, having my wife gadding about town starting rumors..."

"I didn't mean anything by it, I swear. Pierce, you're hurting my arm."

He didn't let go. "Tell me. Honestly. Why did you go?"

"I swear to God, Pierce, I thought it was just a lecture! I—I like learning about things, I like going with Ida—"

He slapped her across the mouth.

"You stupid little fool." He released her wrist and pushed her away. "I'm leaving early for Chicago. Keep away from any more lectures."

He left Delphine standing in the study by herself. She lifted a tentative hand to her lip. It wasn't bleeding, but her cheek was as hot as the shame growing like coals in her gut. She heard the guttural hiccup and start of the touring car, and the engine gained its voice as Pierce drove away.

She felt strangely detached, as though the world were tripping along without her and had left her stranded in the study by herself. This wasn't right—she knew it wasn't right, that Pierce had been wrong, that striking her violated something basic, something no rational person could ignore. She trembled. She'd blamed herself, tried to be a dutiful wife, but what if she hadn't been the one who was wrong, all along?

And what could she possibly do if that were true?

Her head spun. There were no answers, not right now, but she knew what she needed. Familiarity, warmth, home. She glanced at the mantel clock. She could be in Moore's Ferry well before evening if she left now.

26

Very few folk stories, even the most outlandish, suggest that bargainers ever see the Fae in the flesh. This provides a marked difference from many folk traditions in which contact with the otherworldly is highlighted (see, for example, tales of the Greek underworld).
      —*Flora, Fauna, and Fae: A Study in Cultural Geography,*
      by Leonard Worthington Wilkes

"I COULD KILL him." Alaine's fists balled into her skirt like twin rocks, and her eyes blazed with a fire that Delphine knew all too well.

"But you won't." Delphine smiled faintly, closing her eyes. She'd driven up to Lavender Cottage red-eyed and thin-lipped, and Alaine had promptly sent Jack and Em to his sister's to pay a call. Delphine had told Alaine the whole story, punctuated by outbursts from Alaine that would have reddened the ears of a sailor.

"But I could," Alaine repeated. "You'll stay here, of course. As long as you want. Hell, move back!"

The joke rang hollow. They both knew the impossibility, the shame. Pierce Grafton wasn't going to let his wife disappear. Delphine almost regretted telling Alaine; it made everything more real. Now she couldn't pretend it hadn't happened. If it had crossed her mind, in that fractured moment, would she have stayed home, stayed silent, pretended the incident away?

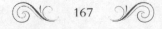

It was too late now, and Delphine would have to fix it, one way or another.

"I shouldn't have gone with Ida. I think I knew, if I thought about it, that it wasn't a good idea, that it wasn't the sort of thing ladies ought to do."

"Going to polite lectures isn't the sort of thing ladies do? And here I thought only climbing trees fell under that particular abjuration. Seems to me, Del, that anything Pierce doesn't fancy, he decides ladies oughtn't to do."

"But it was a suffragette meeting, Alaine. I didn't realize it—I truly thought it was another lecture. It wasn't, it was—it was a sort of a lecture, I suppose. But..."

"It doesn't matter. Why shouldn't a lady consider her political alignment, anyway? Why shouldn't a lady vote? Neither seems unladylike to me."

"Oh, Alaine! You know perfectly well I can't—I couldn't—"

"I know perfectly well that Pierce Grafton couldn't imagine a world where his wife was as intelligent, capable, and endowed with rights as he is. Yes, I know that perfectly well."

Delphine fell quiet. A part of her knew Alaine was right, that it wasn't her fault—but there had to be something she could do to change Pierce's mind, to change how he thought. There was no way out, only forward. Almost one year ago exactly, they had exchanged vows in the garden. What had become of those vows, she thought? She'd done everything she could to love, honor, obey—hadn't she? She felt queasy as the question rose in her mind—did Pierce love her? Had he upheld his vows? She certainly didn't feel cherished or honored.

What did it matter, anyway? The only thing to do was model herself after Mrs. Grafton, after Stella, and try harder to fit into the niche Perrysburg allowed her. But the shame of it all was too much. She pressed her hands against her eyes, willing back tears.

"Alaine, I don't know what to do. I can't face him. He's supposed to be back in two days, and I simply can't face him. Not now, not after this. I—I'm so ashamed. Who knows how many people were laughing at me behind their hands, pretending to compliment my menu while they gossiped about my husband having a suffragette wife?"

"There are worse things they could gossip about regarding him," Alaine snapped.

Delphine started, cheeks flushing hot. She wasn't sure why she rushed to defend him, except that defending him meant defending her choice to marry him, to set her sights on Perrysburg, to believe she could make her way there. "He just needs some time to calm down. And—I can make amends with the Lyndleys and the others if he doesn't come back right away. I can pay a few calls and reassure everyone that it was all an awful misunderstanding—"

Alaine grew very still, waiting for Delphine to meet her eyes, which she finally, reluctantly, did. Alaine's breath caught. Her sister's eyes were red from crying, and deep circles had formed under them. She looked half-crazed and half-haunted, and Alaine wanted to gut Pierce Grafton with the knife she kept for butchering chickens, just for making Delphine look like that.

"How does that solve anything?" Alaine sank next to Delphine and tried to meet eyes that resumed staring at nothing. "A few social calls can't erase what he did. I don't care about the Lyndleys and whoever else—I care about you, making sure you're all right."

Delphine clenched her fists into her skirt. "But there's nothing else to be done. It isn't as though I can hide here forever." She sighed, and Alaine could hear the deep exhaustion in her voice. "I just need some time, Alaine. I don't know how to buy it."

Buy. The word snagged Alaine's thoughts. A bargain. That may be the way out of this.

She could make a bargain, buy Delphine anything she wanted. The pain, the desperation in her sister's eyes—she'd give almost anything to erase that kind of hurt from her sister's face.

Alaine forced a small smile onto her face. "Let's stop fretting on it for a bit. I'll make you some tea. Do you want supper?"

"No, just tea. Maybe some toast, if you don't mind?"

"I'll make you a boiled egg, too. Then you can go lie down."

"All right. And then I'll make myself presentable and go up to Mother's."

"You don't have to," Alaine replied. Mother knew Delphine too well. It wouldn't take long for her to figure out something was wrong.

"I know, but she—she's always a bit hurt when I come here first, let alone if I skip a visit entirely."

That sounded like their mother. "I'll have your tea ready in two shakes. Take that dusty coat off, for pity's sake."

Once Delphine had curled up on the guest bed to take a nap, Alaine quietly closed the door and opened the third drawer next to the stove in the kitchen. The book Ida had left was tucked behind an egg beater, wrapped in a stained towel.

Alaine swallowed and sat down at the kitchen table. She winced as the chair scraped the floor, but no sound came from the guest bedroom. Delphine didn't stir. Alaine waited a moment longer, then began to skim the pages. She steeled herself, reminded of the last time she'd browsed these pages, the dry academic tone pretending to understand something it didn't. But toward the end of the first half, she found a paragraph that made her breath still.

A fairy ring, it stated, *is very much like a doorway, and in several cultures it is perfectly acceptable to knock. Though most American and American-antecedent ethnicities do not practice such summoning, some bargaining cultures did, or do, practice the art.*

Alaine skimmed several paragraphs describing Sicilian stories of joining with fairies to battle witches and the Scottish worship of nature spirits, none of which seemed particularly relevant. She was growing frustrated at the author's apparent disregard for the separation between folktale and true practice when the chapter settled on a long description.

Recent research into English witch trials have revealed a connection between bargaining culture and some occult forms of practice in which fairies are ritualistically summoned. Though some equate the practice with the concept of a "witch's familiar" . . . Here Alaine began to skim again until the author found himself back on track. *Interviewees from several small villages recall stories that those bold enough to enter a fairy ring could summon a fairy by placing a silver pin in the center of the ring, repeating an incantation such as "a pin to mark, a pin to bind, a pin to hail" (additional variants found in Appendix E), and circling the interior of ring three times. It remains, of course, impossible to test the veracity of such stories, but the consistency of the methodology across geographical regions is intriguing, down to the practice of carrying a small bunch or braid of mint into the ring.*

Alaine shut the book on her finger, marking the spot. Impossible to test, indeed. She opened the book again. It began a long ramble detailing various stories of summoning, but Alaine didn't need the repetition to know the method. A short footnote added that *Mint appears to serve in the stories as both attractant and repellant for the fairy creatures, drawing them to the summoner but preventing the summoner from being taken unwilling into Fae, unlike tobacco and various types of sage, which are merely deterrents.*

There was a patch of mint growing in the herb garden outside the kitchen window. Alaine didn't much care for it, the leaves giving off a musty scent when made into tea, but her mother insisted it was good for a sour stomach. Maybe it was good for something else, too. She closed the book and slid it back into the drawer with the tea towels, determined to broker a new bargain.

27

A pin to mark, a pin to bind, a pin to hail
Only the bold may call beyond the veil.

—Folk saying

ALAINE WRAPPED A braid of mint around her wrist, sliding a hairpin through the leaves as a makeshift clasp. The night was soft and unformed around the edges, twilight seeping through the forest in the west, but a sliver of a moon hung angled, beckoning. She closed the door behind her as silently as she could, wincing at the scrape of metal.

She passed the ring of bright green grass in the lawn, slowing to consider it. The flowers were of course long gone, dug up and thrown out, but the grass had remained tinted as though by magic. Still, she didn't know if it was a proper fairy ring or just a relic of one, a shadow remaining after the spell had faded. Besides, it was too close to the house.

Someone might see. And she didn't want anyone to see what she was going to do.

Her white blouse and pale blue skirt seemed entirely impractical now, the clothing like a beacon of light as she slipped through the garden, but she reminded herself—she meant to be found. The scent of roses gave way to the wilder perfume of the woods, its thick notes of damp and green and loam. She took first the wide trail that ran parallel to Prospect Street and the narrow trail, winding through the forest, that only a few people knew well enough to walk at night.

The trail mingled with the shadows, but she was certain of her way. The landmarks, clear as signposts—the ribbon of a creek, the pair of round white beech trees, the stout old fir that looked like a man, or a bear, or something else entirely. Soon she navigated by another sign, the scent of the linden.

The tree was illuminated by the moonlight, as though waiting for her. Alaine took a breath. The tree loomed over her, the grass nearly blazed green in the moonlight, and every bone in her body screamed at her that this was an uncanny danger. She pushed the fear aside; she had to do this, for Delphine. She steeled herself and stepped inside the circle.

In the tangle of roots at the base of the linden, she left a single silver pin. "A pin to mark, a pin to bind, a pin to hail," she murmured, as clearly as her shaking voice would let her. Then she turned, slowly, on her heel, never quite taking her eyes off the tree with its sweet white blossoms, and walked the perimeter of the ring. Once. Twice. Thrice.

She stopped, heart fluttering like a bird against her ribs. But there was nothing. No rustle in the trees, no change in the heady scent of linden, no magic door rending the veil. Her breath left her all at once, rushing in a half sob of disappointment and relief.

"Yes?" The voice pierced the quiet as succinctly as the pin had pierced the moss. Alaine's heart froze. Slowly, she felt her heartbeat resume as a terrified hammer in her chest. She forced herself to turn and found herself facing a woman as silvery pale and thin as her voice. Her stomach dropped and her hopes raced. Was it the woman she had seen in the mirror? She squinted—she couldn't be sure. She took a breath and steadied herself as the Fae woman spoke again. "It has been a long time since we have met someone here."

"I—I think the last person was my grandfather." The words stuck to her throat. *Calm, damn it*, she thought. This was the most important conversation, perhaps, that she would ever have. She couldn't behave like a frightened child. She stood straighter, lifting her chin as though she belonged here in this strange space between their worlds.

The woman's lips parted, briefly, in a flash of memory. She looked almost human for a moment, expression briefly cracking her otherworldly façade. But she wasn't—Alaine saw in each detail, each movement—human. She was too precise, too perfect, an illusion made terribly real. "I see. The Fae he saw was my daughter, not me."

"Oh," said Alaine, not sure how to reply.

Before she could speak, the Fae woman winced. "There is iron here, in this ring. You dare bring iron into a Fae circle, deceitful earthbound creature?"

"No, I didn't—I know better than—" Alaine's hands flew to her waist. Her corset, the steel busk clasping its front closed and its lines of steel bones. "I didn't think, I am sorry."

"You are wearing metal." The Fae woman's eyes narrowed. "Is this a protective charm? Why bear bands of iron on your body?"

"Nothing like that," Alaine replied, imagining corset advertisements emblazoned with slogans promising protection from the Fae. She choked back an entirely inappropriate laugh. "No, it's only—it's the fashion."

"Strange fashion." The woman glanced at the linden tree. "But you cannot stay in the circle, so close to Fae, with your iron gown. See? The tree is dying."

Alaine stepped back with a gasp. The creamy-white blossoms closest to her were fading, the petals dropping around her in a dying snowfall.

"Will you stay to speak with me if I stay outside the circle?"

"If you have come to bargain, certainly." Alaine stepped over the border where the ring of pure green faded into the forest floor. "Now. Your grandfather, he did not summon us, but you have called me. Why?"

She swallowed against a dry throat. "I—I need help."

The woman laughed, a sound like distant bells. "That's not how this works. You can make an offer, and I can accept it. Or not."

"Fine." Alaine thought quickly. "My sister. Her husband is—he's not a good man. He's away now and I—what can I give you to keep him from ever coming back?"

There was something almost like pity in the Fae's face. "That is also not how this works. You make an offer. I take the bargain. Or not."

"Then what's a reasonable offer to keep him away for good?" Alaine bit her tongue—she hadn't meant to imply that she was willing to buy a Fae assassination. And yet, perhaps she was. No one would make her sister feel that kind of shame, that brand of humiliation. She met the Fae woman's eyes, emboldened.

A smile flickered around the Fae woman's eyes. "If you mean you should like me to dispatch this man, however vile he may be, that is outside the bounds of our capabilities."

Alaine spoke quickly, seeing an opportunity. "I thought you were more powerful than that."

The Fae woman laughed again. "Ah, a sweet trick. That sort of thing only works in children's stories. I need not prove my ability to you. But we cannot undo the choices men and women make, and we cannot unbind their lives from the earth."

"Then what can you do?" Alaine almost shouted. She pushed her voice back into her throat. "Can you only keep the milk from going sour and the hail from flattening the corn? Is that the extent of it?"

"Hardly." The Fae's face smoothed into a cool mask, like porcelain. "You wish me to explain to you how you might bargain with me." She shook her head. "I will not help you for free, young one."

Alaine pulled the pincushion from her pocket. "These, then. The whole pincushion. If you explain to me what you can do."

The woman reached out a lithe hand and traced the fluted edges of the strawberry-red pincushion. There were half a dozen pins sunk deep into it. The nearness of her touch made Alaine shiver, but she held her hand steady. "All silver," the Fae breathed. "So bargained, so agreed." She closed her fingers around the pincushion and with a rush of cool air and a scent like snow, it was gone.

Alaine tried not to balk at seeing magic play out in front of her, and mostly succeeded. She took a breath and straightened her shoulders. "Then tell me. What can you do?"

"Eager child." Her smile lifted her pale mask only partially. "You don't want him to come home. I cannot take a life or change his own choices, once made, and eventually he will work his way around whatever deception I can weave. But a train can be late, or a rainstorm can linger over the roads, or a horse can go lame—ah, but you haven't horses any longer. Do you?"

"I do. He doesn't," Alaine answered. "Can you make him kind?" she whispered.

"Can you?" The woman's peal of laughter rustled the leaves in the linden above her. "No, of course we cannot change a man's nature. Or his choice. If those two things are even different from each other. But we can set obstacles in his path, suggestions in his way. Make the unappealing enticing, for a time."

Alaine considered this, carefully. She had hoped for more, but a reprieve—a reprieve was better than nothing. Maybe with some time, some quiet, Delphine would be able to think clearly. Maybe, Alaine thought with a pang, she would just decide to come home.

"He took the touring car. It—it could break."

"It could. It could be difficult to repair, even." She waited, watching Alaine with pale gray eyes. "It could take weeks."

"I—I don't know what to offer." She remembered the last bargain, the flayed chicken, the blood staining the grass. She didn't want to offer that again, but she would, for Delphine. She'd give that and more.

"I see. You should learn to bargain better, youngling, or you might be taken advantage of by a less scrupulous one of my people. You must learn to make offers. You must learn what we want." She became very still, and then, her wintry voice almost like a song, added, "Cherry. I want all of a cherry, from one root. The wood, the blossom, and a stone in the fruit."

"I—you mean you want me to bring you cherries?"

"Is that what I said?" she replied, faintly amused, as though she were watching a child fumble through her chores, tripping over the rake and muddying her shoes with the hoe. "No. I want three things. A cherry with the stone still in it. Some wood. And a blossom. Ah—and I must clarify. From the same tree."

"But—the tree blooms weeks before the fruit comes ripe!"

"That is what I ask." She let the silence open like a gulf between them. "Will you take my bargain?"

Alaine exhaled slowly, thinking. She knew where to find flower, fruit, and branch, but did she know the echoes, the ripples of making this bargain? It seemed too easy, for all of Gran's warnings of Fae cunning. And yet, what choice did she have? Delphine's wide eyes and white knuckles were scorched into her memory, fear incarnate. There was no risk, really, if she delivered on her end of the bargain, or, at least, she could tell herself that lie.

"Yes."

"Leave my price in the roots of the tree, as you did the pin, by moonrise tomorrow." She paused. "And of course, if you do not—"

"I will," Alaine insisted.

"It's not a fair bargain if I do not spell out the terms. Your folk have been so long in simple bargains and so long away from this sort of arrangement, you have no doubt forgotten. Whatever I devise, if your price is unpaid, shall turn around, flip upside down, become its opposite."

"He'd be back sooner."

"And perhaps worse." She did not say no, but Alaine understood that this turn of luck was not entirely automatic, that some creative will of the Fae would take what knowledge Alaine had parted with and devise a punishment for defaulting on the bargain. "I thank you for your bargain."

And she disappeared.

28

Fruits without imperfection appear to be the only agricultural good considered acceptable for trade, and local practitioners insist that Fae refuse all trades tainted with iron or salt.

—*Fairy Lore of Ireland, Scotland, and Wales*, by Alistair Fennimore

ALAINE WALKED HOME in the cooling night. The wind had picked up while she stood in the fairy circle, bearing the cool taste of promised rain from the west. She walked toward the orchard. Tidy rows of cherry and apple and pear and plum stood like sentries along the gentle slope. Pears and apples were months away, but gleaming like jewels in the wan moonlight, the cherries quivered in the wind. She pulled the most perfect fruit she could find from the first tree before the rise of the hill, feeling the weight of it in her palm. Nearly ripe.

She plucked a twig and folded it into her handkerchief. No blossoms remained on any of the branches, not even scattered under the trees. That had never been her plan.

She let herself into the house by the kitchen door, trying to ease the creak and groan of the hinges. She unbuttoned her boots, leaving them by the door, and then tiptoed into the back room that served as study and library and sitting room. On the mantel, next to a marble statue of a deer, there was a copy of *Thornton's New Expanded Dictionary*.

Inside the dictionary were several pieces of folded parchment paper, and inside the paper slid between "Diaphanous" and "Dilate" were a dozen perfectly pressed cherry blossoms. She remembered which tree she'd plucked them from—the knobby one closest to the hill. Alaine peeled one from the paper, pressed and saved with plans for a set of notecards that had never materialized. The rolltop desk in the corner held a stash of linen envelopes; Alaine transferred the cherry, blossom, and twig into the envelope and sealed them inside.

Then, in the pantry, way at the back. An unopened jar of Fenstermacher preserves. They'd been sent a crate of them with a note that their tart Montmorencies made up into the best whole-cherry preserves they'd produced yet. The Fae woman never said that the cherries had to be ripe, or fresh, but in case one or the other was necessary, she'd leave an unripe cherry and a jar of last year's fruit, metal lid left outside the ring, of course.

"Consider it a gift," she murmured.

"What are you doing?" Delphine stood in the half-ajar pocket door, yawning. "It's late."

"I was just looking for a book," Alaine lied. "Something boring to put me to sleep."

"You're still dressed, you loon." Delphine smiled faintly and dropped onto the well-worn settee tucked into a bay window. Her thick braid hung over her shoulder, and in her loose peignoir and bare feet, she looked younger, like the little sister who used to follow Alaine in and out of the orchard.

"Well, why are you up, then?"

"No reason, I suppose." Delphine leaned back, but the carved wooden edges of the settee dug into her shoulders. If she was honest, everything hurt more the past few months, exhaustion and worry seeping into her muscles like some patent medicine tonic in reverse.

"You always had trouble sleeping when you were worried." Alaine set something down on the desk. Not a book, Delphine noted, but an envelope—and was that a jar of cherries? Alaine sprawled next to Delphine. "Heavens, this thing is useless. It's the old one from Father's study. Mother will go on choosing furniture for looks instead of considering if anyone might actually sit on it."

Delphine had to laugh. "Go to bed, you goat."

"Not until you do." Alaine curled against her shoulder, contorting her torso to avoid the hard edges of the settee. "What are we going to do, Del?"

"Nothing, I suppose." She curled her hand around Alaine's shoulder. "I'm hardly the first woman to have a row with her husband— I'll go home and make it right."

"I won't accept that." Alaine drummed impatient fingers on her folded legs. The hem of her skirt had loose dirt on it; Mother would have a conniption if she knew Alaine was dragging mud through the house and onto the furniture. Delphine smiled softly. Her stubborn, mud-stained sister. "I won't accept that it's somehow your responsibility to—to tame him into behaving like a civilized husband. That's not how we were raised, Del."

"We may have to. What option is there—divorce him?" She laughed. It felt caustic in her throat. "I'd lose everything. Including my stake in the orchard."

"That doesn't matter." Delphine could hear the tremor in Alaine's voice, that it mattered very much, but she knew her sister wouldn't admit it.

"It does. I'm sure Pierce would sell it, if he ever thought—" She exhaled. "Even if some judge somewhere would grant me the proceeds, my share would be gone."

"At least he can't sell it now, without your permission."

"I suppose not, not that he has an inkling to." The share in the orchard had been her only contribution to the marital estate, and compared to Pierce's assets, it was nothing. But she knew that to Alaine, the orchard was everything. "Besides, I could never get a divorce. I'd have to prove cruel treatment— No, don't look at me like that." Her hand brushed the bruise on her arm, slowly turning from purple to yellow under her nightgown. "No judge would rule against Pierce. Against a *Grafton*." She sighed. "He'd have to want it, to ask for it. And he never would."

"No way to change his mind?" Alaine looked up, raising an eyebrow. "Take a lover? That burly fellow who was digging the trenches for your fountain's water pipes, now, he seems likely enough—"

Delphine couldn't help laughing. "Alaine, good God!"

"Run away with the circus! Think how shameful that would be, he'd divorce you in a heartbeat. Especially if you did one of those trapeze acts. Scandalous!"

"Alaine, stop." She sobered. Scandalous, indeed—humiliating and utterly mad. Divorce, her sister's silly schemes aside, was not only a foolishly impractical suggestion, it was shameful. "I don't want a divorce. That sort of thing is for..." She stopped. Who were divorces for? "Women whose husbands have run out on them or are adulterous letches or...or women who are unfaithful. Or want to be."

"I don't know that you've got quite the whole of it," Alaine said quietly. She reached out a tentative hand to play with Delphine's hair, like they were children.

Delphine shook her away. "I'd be so ashamed, Alaine. Don't speak of it again."

29

To keep livestocke from escaping: Bury a silver coin or other small item of silver under the fencerow, one every twenty paces.
— The Compleat Book of Bargaining Works, by A Lady, 1767

DELPHINE ARRIVED HOME to a telegram from Pierce. The touring car had lost a belt, and he'd be detained in Chicago for at least another week while the garage he'd limped into found a replacement. She breathed a sigh of relief mixed with guilt. What kind of wife was she, to be afraid of her husband? To prefer the grand house he had built with his money—without him in it?

Still, as she unpacked her valise, she relished the quiet, the lack of expectations. She glanced at the clock: nearly dinnertime, but she had given the cook the day off when she'd left for Moore's Ferry. She peeled off her traveling suit and then, with a furtive glance at the bedroom door as though perhaps Pierce might appear out of the vapor, unhooked her corset and left it on the bed. She put on a cotton wrapper instead of a dinner gown, unpinned her hair, and let it fall around her shoulders. No jewelry, no carmine on her lips. Her shoulders relaxed, and she exhaled, deep and satisfying.

She tiptoed down the stairs, reluctant to mar the quiet even with her own footfalls, and let herself into the kitchen from the butler's pantry off the dining room. There was half a loaf of bread in the bread box, and fresh eggs on the counter. A bottle of milk waited in the icebox. She started the stove and made herself toad-in-the-hole, the egg cracked into the square she'd cut from the thick slice of buttered bread.

She was by herself in the kitchen, savoring crisp bread dunked into runny yolk and a tall glass of cold milk, when the bell rang. She waited a moment, hoping whoever it was would leave, but the bell rang again, persistent. She crossed through the butler's pantry, the dining room, the entryway, hoping that it was only Ida or perhaps a delivery boy she would never see again.

Her mother-in-law waited at the door.

Delphine swallowed mortification and the aftertaste of fresh milk as she opened the door.

"Why, Delphine!" Mrs. Grafton swept inside despite Delphine's most fervent prayer that she would stay on the other side of the threshold. "Are you unwell? Where is the maid?"

"I gave them the day," Delphine replied. "I was visiting my sister."

"Pierce invited me to call this evening before dinner. Why were you in Moore's Ferry?"

Delphine ignored the implied scolding. "I'm so sorry, Pierce was delayed coming back from Chicago. He took the touring car, and it seems a belt broke—"

"The touring car! Why not take the train, those never break." Mrs. Grafton sighed, then took a long look at Delphine in her plain cotton wrapper. "You are sure you're well?"

"Only a bit tired from driving back. I know, I look a fright, I wasn't expecting visitors."

Mrs. Grafton straightened, transformed into an imposing statue in her tailored dress. "Delphine, this is not Moore's Ferry. We must always expect visitors. Especially a woman of your standing. My God, what would you have done if one of Pierce's business associates had come by!" Delphine remained silent. "Well? Would you answer the door in that, or let him stand there?"

Delphine bit back the pert retort that, had they come a half an hour later, she would have been in bed and they could ring the bell until their fingers turned blue. "I suppose I hadn't thought of that," she murmured instead.

"No, you didn't. Oh, come sit down," she commanded, waltzing ahead of Delphine to the formal parlor. "Now. As long as I'm here, I did want to congratulate you."

Something in Mrs. Grafton's voice told Delphine she meant quite the opposite. Her mother-in-law's tone was always precise, carefully controlled, but she slipped ice into it when she wanted to.

"Whatever for?" Delphine pretended she hadn't noticed the flint in Mrs. Grafton's eyes.

"Why, your art debut!" She didn't pause at Delphine's confused interruption. "Your class, at the art school downtown. They've put up a small show of student work. Lovely pieces, really. And yours? So interesting."

Delphine blanched. She'd completed a small still life in oils, her first time experimenting with anything save watercolors, and she was rather proud of it. She'd plied the light just as she'd wanted, illuminating a scatter of ephemera, fraying silk and loose buttons and bits of worn glass. On a whim, she had painted one of her straw glamours, the wreath presiding over the gentle chaos.

"Delightful work, but I didn't realize what it was about until Mrs. Abbott mentioned it."

"About?" Delphine shook her head. "I didn't mean anything by it, it's not—"

"It's a painting of those ridiculous spells your family does! Oh, Mrs. Abbott thought it quite charming, of course, but given her idiosyncrasies, I'm not surprised." Mrs. Grafton sniffed into her lace handkerchief, as though her rose cologne could clear the discomfort of Mrs. Abbott's suffragist and progressive ideas from the room. "She told me all about her niece's publications, as well, and your particular part in them."

Delphine rushed to explain. "She interviewed my great-aunt, for her work on the—on ethnomusicology."

"Ethnomusicology, is it. Your great-aunt. Well, I suppose that's distant enough not to stain." She paused. "Was she the uncouth old woman at the wedding?"

"Aunt Imogene has never been known for keeping her thoughts to herself," Delphine answered, flushing.

"I do hope she didn't say anything too humiliating in Miss Carrington's interview. Only imagine what she might write about you!"

"Imogene only told a few old stories she knows. That's all Ida—Miss Carrington—is interested in. Stories. Not my family, or me."

"Delphine, you are too kind to eccentrics like Ida Carrington. Going to college—I suppose it's a fine enough pursuit, especially given the poor girl's looks. The freckles! And those spectacles, like a little barn owl." She laughed. Delphine didn't join. "But you needn't... involve yourself in it."

"I was only trying to be friendly."

"Yes, I know, but dear—" Mrs. Grafton inhaled through her nose, as though siphoning patience. "Your first responsibility is not to be kind to everyone. It's to maintain your husband's reputation. And yours. To make inroads with people who will benefit his career, to host and charm those who will elevate his standing." She watched Delphine with an expression that looked uncomfortably like pity. "You think of that first. Is this good for Pierce? For the family? For the Grafton Glassworks?"

"I understand," Delphine said. She didn't, exactly. If Mrs. Grafton cared so much about making inroads and cultivating an appropriate set of acquaintances, why hadn't she helped Delphine to do so? It was almost as though she enjoyed seeing her daughter-in-law flounder. Delphine held back a shocked gasp—that was exactly what her mother-in-law and Stella enjoyed. For whatever reason, she was their scapegoat, their ever-available little joke. The country nobody they hadn't kept Pierce from marrying.

"I won't even mention the nonsense about the political rally that girl dragged you to. I'm given to understand Pierce already spoke to you about that."

"Yes, ma'am." She wondered how much Mrs. Grafton knew about exactly how Pierce had spoken to her. The woman's brand of cruelty dabbled more in barbed comments and manipulating the ring of influence around her, not outright violence. But it was what Pierce was raised on—the particular violence of controlling others, of using them as set pieces.

"But let me reiterate. The associates of the Grafton family, those who are of the sort we must care a great deal about, they are not in favor of radicalism in any form, including women's suffrage." She shook her head; the ostrich feathers in her hat trembled. "And your choice of...diversions. That matters, too. I regret even suggesting those classes to Pierce; I hadn't realized your work would be displayed, with your name on it."

Heat rose in Delphine's face. "Was the work so poor, then? That it's embarrassing for the Graftons to be associated with my lack of talent?"

Mrs. Grafton pinched her lips together. "No, it isn't that. It isn't that at all. It's that there's a proper subject for art, and your family peculiarities are not the proper subject."

"Tell me, Mother, what is the proper subject for art?" Delphine looked up, daring her mother-in-law to say it, to say that pretty flowers and tepid landscapes were all anyone ought to paint, that art was nothing more than a parlor pastime. That no one was allowed to say anything or mean anything, that she, in particular, was allowed no views or opinions or, God bless it, preferences for still life subjects outside of what the Graftons wished to cultivate.

"I'm merely asking you to consider your place in this family, in this community. You are your husband's helpmeet, Delphine. You are to support him, first and foremost. Goodness knows his father has had a task of guiding him toward the right path—youth so often has impulses destructive to the proper order of things." Delphine had a sudden, destructive impulse of her own to ask her mother-in-law how she liked being a Grafton helpmeet, whether she was truly happy with the proper order of things, but she refrained. Mrs. Grafton continued. "Especially now that Pierce is running for city council. Do you understand?"

"I do. Very plainly." Delphine held back tears of embarrassment and something else, something like rage and grief mingled together.

"I wonder," Mrs. Grafton said, standing, "how well you do understand. Gadding off on excursions to the country. I told Pierce that car was going to be a poor influence! Don't wear yourself out, dear. There are more important things for a wife to do than ricochet between trips like a rubber ball." She gave Delphine an appraising glance, with a disappointed wavering sigh that told Delphine exactly what kind of duties she was thinking of. Stella had provided pretty grandbabies for Mrs. Grafton to show off; Delphine couldn't even muster that much. She thought again of the flinty anger in Pierce's eyes, of his iron grip on her arm, and she had no regrets that she hadn't complied with that particular expectation.

"Of course," Delphine demurred. "But it is my family. And I suppose, to some extent, my business, too—I've a share in the orchard."

"Oh, that!" Mrs. Grafton laughed lightly. "Hardly worth the trouble, love. I've heard Pierce suggest selling your share, just to have the hassle of it gone. I do think, dear, he'd rather your attentions be on Perrysburg and not Prospect Hill."

Delphine maintained a level face, but her heart fell. Sell her shares of Orchard Crest? Right out from under Mother and Alaine?

Her thoughts raced as Mrs. Grafton sailed out the door and down the steps. Delphine swallowed angry tears and laid her hands against the window frame, the dark wood as cold against her hands as iron bars.

30

The plant found by a fairy ring is twice as potent, whether poison or cure.

—Folk saying

DELPHINE WATCHED AS Alaine carried a tray of lemonade to the porch, the pitcher beading in the hazy July heat. Emily and Mother were busy making ice cream, Papa Horatio and Jack were tacking scarlet-and-white bunting along the pillared porch, and the neighborhood children had begun to line the sidewalk for the annual Fourth of July parade. In the distance, Delphine heard the bells of the fire engines that invariably led the procession.

Delphine waited on the porch, rocking slowly in the shade. It felt like all she could manage to do, rock in the shade, exhausted by the constant pretense that everything in her Perrysburg house was fine. She'd come by herself to Orchard Crest for the holiday weekend, leaving Pierce to address some labor issue at the glass factory. He had slowly warmed after the incident over the lecture with Ida, and Delphine had begun to nurture optimism that, even if her marriage might not be the dream she had idealized, she ought to be able to manage. She just had to change, to adapt to Pierce, she told herself. Considering her husband's ambitions, he had every right to be angry about the rumors she'd caused. Not to strike her, no—but could she expect perfect control from anyone all the time, especially a man tasked with the gargantuan tasks of running both the glassworks and an election campaign? It was her job, she resolved, to make his life easier, not more difficult, as her mother-in-law had said. Any thoughts she'd had to the contrary were, she reassured herself with hollow persistence, selfish and unrealistic. She'd chosen this life, and if it meant taking the thorns with the roses, that was to be expected.

Even if she felt empty.

Alaine set the lemonade down and poured each of them a glass, glancing surreptitiously to make sure no one else was within earshot.

She handed her sister a glass and spoke softly. "Are you— Have you been happy, Del?"

"Why, of course!" Delphine's smile was bright even if she didn't feel anything behind it. "The campaign is going so well that Pierce is quite convinced he's as good as won the seat on the city council already."

"I didn't ask about Pierce," Alaine said softly. "I asked about you."

"Well, is there such a difference? He's so very pleased with how things are progressing, and of course I am, too." She opened her hands as though showing she had nothing to hide, though the look Alaine gave her was clear—she wasn't satisfied with that answer. "I've been taking more art classes, too."

Alaine sat up, interested. "That's grand! How are they? What are you working on?"

"I started working in oils, a bit. And black-and-white pastels, to get a handle on shadow and—well, the teacher says I'm progressing very well. But he's a lovely old duck and says that to everyone, I'm sure." She hesitated, not sure what she wanted to admit, after her mother-in-law had scolded her for it, but Alaine waited eagerly. "He chose a still life I did for an exhibition of student art; mostly it was students who have been working much longer than me, so I was—" She paused. She should have been pleased, to find out her work had been chosen, been honored. Instead, she'd been shamed by the expectations of the Graftons. "I was so surprised."

Alaine clapped. "Well done, Del! What was it of?"

"Oh, bits and bobs, you know how a still life is. I included a straw

glamour, it was such fun to paint." She let her gaze fall away, looking over the summer haze on the lawn. "It's been taken down now, so I brought it for Mother. I thought she might like it for the parlor."

"I'm sure, but—don't you want it? Your debut exhibition piece? Certainly Pierce wants it!"

Delphine feigned a nonchalant shrug, her filmy white blouse turning the gesture into a flagging surrender. Pierce, she wouldn't admit to Alaine, was the reason the piece had been taken down early. He'd tersely explained to Delphine when he brought it home that his father had felt it not becoming of the Graftons to display artwork. But he'd apologized, which was something. At least, she told herself it was something. "Pierce thought Mother would like it. Oh, I was going to say—he's going to New York for a few meetings next month, handling new contracts for the glassworks, and I'll be going along."

At the return to the subject of Pierce and the Grafton Glassworks, Alaine's interest waned. "That will be nice," she said politely as she picked up her mending.

Delphine rocked slowly. Never had her sister felt further from her than she did now. Alaine knew the truth, knew the desperation in her voice when she'd shown up bruised and frightened. And Alaine was honest to her core—Delphine knew she couldn't playact right along that everything was as beautiful and clean as the limestone façade on their fine Perrysburg house. She only hoped she would keep the whole mess quiet, and trust that Delphine had things well in hand now. There was, after all, no path forward save learning to do what the Graftons expected.

But she could, if she was clever about it, meet the Grafton expectations and help her sister at the same time.

"Say, I've been thinking of something." Delphine bit her lip. "I—I don't want to offend you with the suggestion."

"I doubt anything you say could offend me," Alaine replied. "Go ahead."

"It's the orchard. When Father left me a share, I suppose his intention was that we'd both stay here and run it—"

"I don't think he had any plans like that," Alaine rushed to interject. "That is—I don't think he'd be upset that you moved."

"Oh! I—yes, I didn't mean to..." Delphine flushed. "This is why I suppose I worried you'd be upset," she murmured. "I'd like to give you my share."

Alaine fell silent. "Are you sure, Del? It's—it's your stake here. I never—I never imagined you'd want to cut ties, to have nothing holding—"

"It's not like that." Delphine looked at her hands, folded into tight fists. Her knuckles were as white as her lawn skirt, gripping the delicate fabric until it wrinkled. "Alaine, if it's yours, Pierce could never sell it."

Alaine exhaled in a ragged cough, as though she'd been hit in the chest. "Do you really think he would? He must know what it means to you."

"He's moving assets around, and it's—the value isn't much. If he decides he'd make more money on it now than later—I don't know."

"Del." Alaine set her lemonade down. "I don't know what to say."

"Say it's a splendid idea. And pray he agrees. Then it won't ever be something he can hold over me. Or you." Delphine forced a smile. "It should be yours, by all rights. You've poured yourself into this place. And Pierce shouldn't get a cut of the profits just for owning it."

"*You* own it, Del. You could keep the profits, it could be your pin money, like Aunt Imogene calls it—"

Delphine paused. She could, perhaps—having some kind of safety net wasn't a terrible idea. Then she chided herself—she couldn't be the good wife Pierce deserved if she was making plans behind his back, holding back money or secrets. Besides, it was impossible.

"You know I can't. How could I?" Delphine shrugged. "I can't open a bank account and keep the money away from him. Should I stuff it in our mattress?" She caught Alaine's hand. "Let me do this. For both of us."

"All right." Alaine gripped Del's hand tighter. "All right. Do you think he'll agree?" she added in a whisper.

"I hope so. I just have to ask at the right time."

Alaine rolled her lemonade glass between her palms, slowly. "What if...what if I could make a right time?"

"What do you mean?"

"I've a wild idea of an old fairy bargain Gran used to do—"

"I don't remember that one." Her forehead knotted, and Alaine laughed it off before she could dig too much further.

"No, it's—it's a silly idea. But just for old time's sake, let's say you'll ask in three days."

"Well, unless he's in a mood...or there's poor results in the new formula they're running at the factory, or a downturn in the market, or—"

"Let's hope there won't be."

The fire engines turned up Prospect Street with a clang of bells, and Emily shot out of the front door to watch. Alaine leaned her head on Delphine's shoulder. Delphine exhaled, slowly. She could capture this moment like a firefly in one of the jars they made at the Grafton Glassworks, hold it in her hands, claim it as hers. Orchard Crest didn't feel like her own anymore, small and stiff like too-tight shoes, and Perrysburg was aloof and distant, determined never to be hers. But here, sitting next to her sister, watching her niece enchanted by the marching band and a gaudily costumed Lady Liberty, she could claim a small, secret happiness.

It would have to be enough.

31

One, two, three, find a fairy tree
Four, five six, now you're in a fix
—Children's rhyme

THEY SAT ON the front porch of Orchard Crest well into the evening, eating a late supper of fried chicken and Aunt Imogene's strawberry shortcake after the worst of the day's heat fell away. At the
bottom of the hill, someone shot off Roman candles and firecrack-
ers. Alaine waited impatiently for the merriment to fade.

With her husband comfortably installed with his latest Jack
London by the fireplace and Emily tucked into bed, Alaine left the
house through the kitchen door.

The forest, and the linden tree, waited. She inhaled the cool air of
evening and slapped a mosquito. The path, the trees, the last shards
of sunlight through the lowermost branches, all familiar, something
she'd grown so accustomed to they had sunk beneath her skin as per-
sistently as the damn mosquitoes crowding her bare neck and wrists.

She didn't hesitate as much this time, sinking the pin into the moss
and circling the tree. She didn't start when the woman appeared.
To her relief and, she admitted, concern, it was the same woman as
before. She wore a new circlet of silver over her hair, wrought into
leaves as delicate as thread.

"You have summoned me?"

"I did."

She smiled, pale lips dancing over perfect white teeth. "You remembered to leave off your girdle of iron." The Fae woman nodded, approving of Alaine's loose dressing gown of mauve cotton and silk ribbon. "Then you must have a bargain ready."

"You said—before—that you could make the unappealing enticing. So you could influence someone's choice."

"I can suggest and direct, yes. I cannot promise a choice." She tilted her head, and a cascade of hair fell like water over her shoulder. "What sort of choice?"

"I want my brother-in-law to give me his share of the orchard." She paused. "Well, it's more complicated—it's my sister's share, really, but legally he owns it, too, and she wants to give it to me, but he may not be willing—"

The Fae woman held up a hand. "Enough of your laws. The laws of men—flimsy things compared to ours. And complicated! In the end, it is about money, yes? For your sister's espoused."

"Yes."

"Very well. It is easy to entice men when it comes to money. Fortune is fickle, but they always see it as so fixed. Yes, I can put suggestions in his path that will make him amenable to parting with an asset he no longer desires." She waited. "And your offer?"

"Will you take the same as before? All of a cherry?"

She considered. "No. Not quite." Alaine's breath went flat, then the woman spoke again. "I want the same as before, but this time: apples." She cocked her head with a faint smile, as though she knew the impossibility of her request, but had the unbending confidence to ask anyway. "Branch and seed, fruit and flower."

"Branch and seed, fruit and flower." Alaine exhaled slowly. A strange confidence of her own bloomed as she mulled the words. Fruit and flower. The apple blossoms had faded months ago, the fruit only now beginning to form on the boughs. Alaine tilted her head, as though considering the nuance of the bargain, and asked with a lilting challenge she barely recognized, "Need the apple be ripe?"

"Pardon?" The fairy's smile pulled slightly.

"Must the apple be completely ripe?" She raised her voice slightly, buoyed by the diversion. "They're not ripe yet."

"It does not matter, as long as it is fruit with seed." Her eyes shone almost silver. "Some of your cherries were most strange. Yet you did give me fruit, with seed."

"Fruit with seed," Alaine repeated. "You have a bargain."

"Very well." The woman pulled back toward the linden, then stopped. "You could ask anything for yourself. And you ask only for more of what is already yours."

"I don't need anything else."

This was about Pierce Grafton and curtailing his ability to hurt Delphine. She didn't know if the silvery Fae standing in front of her could understand that Delphine mattered far more to her than the orchard. That she had taken certain risks for her own ambition, but that she would bleed herself dry for her sister. The Fae woman's manner and words were cold; was there any warmth in her world?

"Surely there are bargains you could make. A pretty woman like you, young, and ambitious enough to meet me here?" Her metallic laugh at Alaine's surprise rustled the leaves. "And you are clever, as well, yet you do not make your fortune in your cities, either—there are young women who do so, yes?"

"There are," Alaine replied slowly. "I have never wanted to leave Prospect Hill."

"What is there to tie you to Prospect Hill? Save our meeting place," she said with ice in her voice.

"Is that your game? To drive me away so you don't have to make any more bargains with me?"

"Hardly. Believe it or not, I am pleased with the results of our acquaintance thus far." Her pale feet shifted under her filmy skirts. "I simply do not understand your...motivations."

"They're not yours to understand," Alaine snapped.

"Very well." She paused, an expression between pity and interest crossing her face, fleeting. "You know the penalty of an unpaid bargain, yes?"

"I know it."

Her breath caught in her throat as the Fae woman vanished, all at once and yet with no fanfare. She had seen a street magician once, on a corner in Perrysburg, who made a pigeon disappear. His hands were all movement, his voice all passion, and the magic all make-believe. This was real, she thought with a shiver of acknowledgement—magic spun with no fanfare, with no effort, with no thought for the shock of the human witnessing it.

Alaine went to the orchard, letting calm wash over her as her breath grew slower, steadier. The silver eyes, the disarming laugh, the disappearing—the Fae woman had the advantage in intimidation, but Alaine knew her orchard, and her apples. The Smokehouse variety were beginning to ripen in their rows at the far end of the orchard, where the hill sloped more sharply. She pulled one down from the tree; it resisted and the stem snapped off. She pulled another, holding both of the small fruits in one hand. Tinged rose red and washed in gold, and just as bright in flavor, they were among her favorites. She tucked both of the apples in her pocket and returned to the linden tree, stopping just outside the ring.

She pulled her penknife from her pocket, its slim mother-of-pearl handle hiding a wickedly sharp blade, and cut the apple in half, right across its middle. In the center of the two halves was the shape of a perfect five-petaled flower.

Gran had shown her that, years ago, canning applesauce. Alaine turned the crank on the apple peeler, Delphine stirred the pot of simmering apples, and Gran chopped them up. As she swept the piles of apple peel into a bowl—"Won't do to waste, the peels make good jelly," she murmured—Alaine slumped with her elbows on Gran's soapstone counters.

"What's this? Still work time, if we want applesauce this winter!"

"It takes so long," Alaine complained. Sweat beaded on her brow in the hot kitchen, working its way into her thick curly braid.

"Don't you like applesauce? And here I thought it was your favorite."

"It is," Alaine insisted, "but right now it's just work!"

Gran laughed hard at this, and motioned Alaine over. Delphine studiously continued stirring until Gran told her she could stop, too. She took down her big butcher knife, the one with the red paint peeling off the wooden handle, and chopped a fat apple in half, through the middle. She took one half in each hand. "Tell me, what do you see?"

"The seeds," Delphine said astutely.

Gran smiled. "Well, yes. But what do they look like?"

Alaine remembered that she had paused and carefully studied the pattern in the apple. "It's like a little flower."

"That's it exactly. A flower—five petals, just like an apple blossom. Inside every apple is the promise of a whole tree, blooming someday." She gave one half of the apple to Delphine and the other to Alaine. "There's a lot of work between that flower inside the apple and the one in an orchard in springtime. I tend to think it's worth it."

Alaine didn't remember if Gran had let them run out of the kitchen after that and leave the rest of the peeling and simmering and canning to her—she suspected she had. But she had remembered the flower in the apple. And Gran had taught her enough about fairy bargains to know—it was the words that mattered. The Fae had asked for a flower. She was getting one.

32

Though adherents of fairy bargaining would certainly insist that the similarities between cultures' lore indicate the reality of Fae creatures, the explanation is certainly far duller—primitive peoples' limited abilities to comprehend the science of the world around them.
—*A Ribbon, A Ring, A Rhyme: Cohesion of Folk Poetry Tradition*, doctoral dissertation of Edith L. Showalter

AUNT IMOGENE RAPPED three times on the kitchen door, and Alaine rushed to let her in. "What a surprise, Aunt Imogene!"

"I should come up more often. You've got quite the nice setup here, Alaine. Not flashy like your ma's place—just the right size!" Imogene helped herself to an overstuffed chair. "Your ma doing well?"

"Yes, quite—she's hosting the garden club next week and is already in a tizzy, but aside from that—"

"Ha! Of course she is. And Horatio?"

"He's fine, a little quiet since Del moved away, I suppose."

"Figures." Imogene rapped her stick on her palm. "He always liked having a crowd around. Must be a mite lonely up there with just him and your ma. He and your pa used to talk up a storm over a dram or two. 'Spose sometimes a fellow just needs a young buck around to remind him what he used to be like."

"I should send Jack up?"

"If you need somewhere to send Jack, I need some help reshingling

the shed." Imogene rocked back in her chair. "But yes, you ought to think on looking in on old Horatio more."

"And how have you been, Aunt Imogene?"

"Well enough. Do you know, I've had a visitor down at my place more often since summer's come on."

"Who might that be?"

"Ha! Figured you didn't know. Em comes down some afternoons. Didn't figure you minded, so I let her hang about."

"Oh, Aunt Imogene, I'm sorry, I hope she's no bother—"

"Now, didn't I just say us old folk like having someone around who reminds us what being young was like?" She laughed. "And she's much like I was. Muddy hems and stained face and all. Wild like a bird's wild—knows the woods, knows her own way to fly."

"I do hope she's no trouble."

"No, Em is a charmer. She helps around the house and would you believe it, but I think she actually likes all my old stories."

Alaine paused. "What sorts of stories?"

"Well, that's rather what I wanted to talk to you about. She's gotten in mind to asking stories about fairy circles." Imogene leaned forward, eyes suddenly bright. "You want her knowing more than you're teaching? Or maybe you've been teaching without your knowing?"

"I don't think I know what you mean."

"I don't know as I believe her. But she says she watched you one night, go off into the woods toward that old linden tree. Says you weren't dressed proper for a stroll."

Alaine forced her expression to remain calm even as she tamped down nerves. "It's silly, I know, but sometimes I go for a little walk after I've gotten into my dressing gown. I shouldn't, the neighbors might see—"

"Only if they're trespassing, all the way back here!" Imogene cackled. "Not that old Tom Porter didn't try, back a few decades. I told Em there was no reason you'd be going to the linden tree, except passing by it. And of course that she's to stay away from it."

"Thank you for that."

"But you tell me. Why are you messing with that ring?"

Alaine's mouth fell open in silent shock.

"Oh, girlie, you were never a good liar, and that face of yours tells everything you won't say out loud. Besides, you let that ring you planted last summer go fallow."

"It was annuals, it would have had to be replanted." In the fullness of summer, the ring looked nearly the same lush green as the lawn around it.

"Ah. But the truth of it is, you don't need it no more."

Alaine's face flushed, and she squared her shoulders. "That's right. I don't need it any longer."

Imogene watched her for a long moment, rocking back and forth, reading every line of her face. "Alaine, you tell me. What's got you so worried you're messing with the old linden tree?"

Alaine swallowed. "It's Del. Pierce is—he's been—" She met Imogene's eyes.

"He's been a right bastard." Imogene shook her head. "Knew he was trouble the minute I saw him. That sort thinks he owns the world by right."

"Don't tell Mother."

"Judas priest, I wouldn't tell your mother for all the tea in China. Your mother wouldn't know the first thing to do, she'd just fret. We never had that kind of trouble in our family. Well, the Porters did, I suppose, but—" She glanced up with a hint of a smile. "Bess Porter told me what Walt done, and I told my pa, and he and the others, they set Walt straight. Never laid hands on her again. But folks like the Graftons—ain't no one there to set them straight."

"No, there isn't." Alaine sighed. No one, not even Jack or Papa Horatio, who both would have been listened to here in Moore's Ferry.

"Never has been, never will be, I suppose." Imogene shrugged. "But there's nothing to be gained fooling with Fae magic over it."

"What if there was, Aunt Imogene?" Alaine asked, impulsive. "What would you do, if you could?"

Imogene's rocking stilled. "Child, if I could and what I can are two very different things. And you've got Em to consider. She knows you're up to something. If she decides her mama's messing about with a fairy ring, she might take mind to mess with it, too."

"I know." Alaine sighed. "I'll—I'll talk to her."

"You do more than talk. You stay away from that thing." Imogene resumed rocking with unrestrained ferocity. "Trust me. You'll lose more than you bargain for."

"Aunt Imogene, I—you talk like you know."

"Of course I know!" She threw her hands in the air, exasperated, and then gripped the arms of the chair as though worn out by the effort. "Of course I know, and you know, too. How many stories Lilabeth tell you?"

"Plenty."

"She tell you about our Great-Aunt Sarah? Back in Wales?" She rocked back and forth, waiting. " 'Course not, that story was too damned sad. Lilabeth didn't tell you the real sad ones. The ones that were too close. The ones she knew were real."

"She taught me plenty," Alaine repeated, defensive. Gran had been gentle in ways Imogene wasn't, quiet but firm.

"Great-Aunt Sarah," Imogene continued, ignoring Alaine's argument, "knew her husband wanted a son. We've got the bargain to keep it from happening, and the bargain to hurry it along, but we don't have nothing for picking boys or girls." Imogene's wry smile twisted into the deep creases lining her lips. "Maybe there's good reason for that, menfolk being how they are about their boys. We'd have more boys than girls afore long."

"She made a bargain?"

"I don't know what the bargain was, so don't ask. And it seemed to work, at first—the boy was born, and born in the caul, fortunate-like. But I think that was them claiming him as theirs. Great-Aunt Sarah must have defaulted on the deal, somehow. Don't know how. Or maybe she misunderstood from the beginning and was only getting the boy on loan."

Alaine sat motionless, holding the chill lapping at her at bay. "They took him?" she whispered.

"Boy disappeared. Went out to milk the cow the day before he

201

turned ten, just as the sun went down. Sky was awful red, she said. Red like paint, red like blood. And he didn't come back. There was the cow, milked, and the bucket of milk next to the barn. And no trace of him."

"He could have run away, or been kidnapped or—"

"The caul was gone, too." Aunt Imogene slowed the rhythm of the rocking chair. "The caul, that he'd been born in, that was good luck, that Great-Aunt Sarah kept wrapped in good linen at the bottom of her trunk. No one could have taken it without upending the whole damn thing. And the linen was still there, folded nice and squared up on top of a stack of wool blankets."

"That's awful," Alaine said softly.

"It's damned awful, and I'm telling you to warn you. You don't know what you're getting into, Alaine. None of us really does—they're tricky, the Fae. They sell a bargain only they understand." She sucked in her lips. "It's awful about Del, but land sake, Alaine. You're married to a lawyer, your folks have money. There's other ways out of this than holding tow with the Fae."

"I—I'm afraid there might not be, Aunt Imogene."

Her great-aunt softened. "Well, I suppose it's not always easier nowadays. Why, in my day we'd have just moved home."

"I did suggest that."

"You can't fix your sister's beliefs on what's right and what's proper with a fairy bargain, Alaine. You just can't."

Alaine sighed. It was more than that—Delphine wasn't wrong that the social standing of the Graftons stood in her way, and that the law put her in a corner.

"Shame is a funny thing, I suppose," she finally said. "It keeps people bound up in far worse things than it is itself."

Aunt Imogene nodded sadly. "And you can't undo that, not with fairy bargains or anything else I know of. Just be careful."

33

Some believe in the Papal See
And some rely on the Trinity
But the only trick
I've found to stick
Is found at a fairy tree

—Folk song

PIERCE HAD COME home in a good mood, fueled by a favorable opinion piece on his candidacy platform in the newspaper, and it presided over the table through dinner. Delphine took a steady breath. Three days, Alaine had said—it had been three days, and she had to hold up her side of the agreement. Even if the thought of derailing Pierce's pleasant mood put a sour taste in her mouth.

"I want to give my sister a gift." Delphine exhaled a thin breath, lace collar almost painfully tight against the pulse in her throat.

"A gift? Why not?" Pierce smiled indulgently. He did have a charming smile, bent around the faint dimple set into his left cheek, when he was in a good mood. "What were you thinking of? Books? New dress?"

"Alaine isn't much for fashion," Delphine said with a wry laugh. "I was thinking of something somewhat bigger." She took a breath—now or never. "My stake in the orchard."

"Your share in the orchard—why, I certainly didn't expect this!"

She had a list of reasons that might appeal to Pierce ready. "Yes, but we certainly don't need the income, and I've no interest in learning horticulture." She laughed, hoping it sounded dismissive of the notion of taking up managing the trees, not full of nerves.

"Not like your sister." His smile twisted into a mocking grin. "Damned embarrassing—the Lady Baroness of the Apples, is it? Head of their little agricultural club?"

Delphine pushed back anger. Her ambitious, driven sister—reduced to the punch line of a joke in Pierce's eyes. And for no reason; the orchard was thriving, the Agricultural Society doing quite a bit of good in Moore's Ferry, Alaine well respected. She'd watched her sister reach for and grasp her ambitions over the past year, and here Delphine was, still feeling left behind. She tried to convince herself she had found some success—after all, she was managing one of the most fashionable homes in the county, supporting her husband's run for office. Then why did she feel hollow, like a footnote in a story someone else was writing?

"Goodness, Del. You look like you'd swallowed a bee!" Pierce laughed, not cruelly. He was in a jovial mood, or maybe it was just the port. "Perhaps it would be better to divest ourselves of that kind of attention."

"Perhaps," Delphine said, recovering. "I—I certainly wouldn't want anyone to think you're involved."

"I doubt they would—it isn't as though Moore's Ferry agricultural news makes the gossip pages here." He leaned back in his chair, pondering the ruby port in his glass. "Do you know, I only just read an article in the newspaper today about the declining value in agricultural land, after the big fallout in the nineties. And a small operation like your family's will almost certainly be hard-pressed to keep pace with the larger farms, the ones with capital for machinery."

"You know more about that than I do," Delphine said cautiously.

"That fellow writing the article was an economist out of Chicago. He highly advised divesting investments in agricultural real estate—though of course we wouldn't be taking on any risk at all keeping the land in the portfolio."

Delphine swallowed. Her home, her family's livelihood, an entry in a portfolio. "Even if the orchard takes a loss, I suppose you're right overall."

"It could take a loss." Pierce set his glass down. "By gum, Del, you're right. I just spoke with Perkins at the office about his family's old lumber mill—he's having to throw good money after bad just to keep her afloat. We're owners in that orchard, we're liable for losses, as well. Jack could sue for our share."

"Oh, I'm sure Jack wouldn't—" Delphine stopped herself. Wherever Pierce was getting these mad worries from, it was only helping her case.

"This is business, Delphine, not family. No, I think it's a fine idea, in the end. Still. You seem to have changed your mind since last year." He leveled his cool gaze at Delphine, and she felt herself shrink into her silk. "I suppose this means you don't see a need to invest yourself in the day-to-day operations of the orchard any longer."

Delphine had expected this step in the dance, and though she hated to give it up—the joy of harvest time, the cozy tradition of wassail—she knew what she had to do. The bargain was laid clearly before her. She took it.

"I suppose there isn't a need. Alaine has things well in hand."

"I'm sure she does," Pierce replied. For a long moment Delphine was sure he'd refuse. But then he set his glass down abruptly. "Well, I'll have Lyndley draw up the papers this week. I have to leave on business again in a fortnight, I suppose you'll pass the time at your sister's."

"How long this time?" Delphine asked.

"Shouldn't be more than a few days, but I'm going to meet a new supplier and if it looks as though a deal is going through, I may just stay."

"Of course," Delphine murmured, wild hope rising in her chest that this time he'd be gone longer. The touring car breaking—that had been a lucky accident, but maybe he'd be detained again. She felt a sudden crushing guilt for hoping. She had resolved to be a good wife, and this was hardly the sort of wish she should be harboring.

"Don't look so down, dove," he said, mistaking her guilt for disappointment. "I say, next time you'll come with me. I've a mind to go to New York before the end of the year, we'll see the sights, take in a show."

"I've never been to New York." He wasn't a bad man; if she only tried harder, perhaps.

"I know. My country wife." He laughed. "Mayor Haverford and his wife would like to come to dinner this week. I told him that Thursday would be best."

"Of course," Delphine said swiftly. "He likes lamb, doesn't he?"

"And this is why I married you," Pierce said with a pleased smile. "You remember these things that I never would." He slid closer to her so she could smell the cedar and citrus of the cologne he wore. "You are the loveliest creature, Delphine."

He wrapped her hand in his and drew it to his lips, grazing her knuckles. Once, that would have made her feel intimately cherished, brimming over into desire. It ebbed in shadows, in the fringes of memory, but his kiss on her hand now couldn't erase the back of his hand on her cheek or the vise grip on her arm. She let a gray blankness roll over her as he drew her close.

34

Purple silk, row of beads
Stills and stops the wayward seeds
—Traditional bargain

ALAINE HELD THE telegram from Delphine with nervous fingers. They'd smudged the ink and wrinkled the corners already, and now they roved the paper for something else to mangle. COMING TOMORROW. IMPORTANT. How could a message be both insistent and direct and yet say so little? The pit of worry in her stomach expanded as she filled it with more guesses at what Delphine had decided was IMPORTANT.

As the touring car rumbled up the drive, it was clear that she hadn't deemed the fact that Pierce was coming vital enough to tell her. She smoothed her hair and tossed her apron on the hook, wishing she'd dressed for visitors instead of her sister, wishing she'd asked Jack to stay home from the office, wishing Mother and her endless supply of polite conversation were here. That could be arranged, she thought, later. She'd send Emily over to fetch her after school—yes.

"Hello, Alaine!" Pierce's deep voice echoed from the car. He raised a hand in greeting, almost pleasant. She returned a tentative wave. Pierce had never seemed so happy to be on Prospect Hill before.

"I'm so sorry for the last-minute visit!" Delphine rushed to her before Pierce could cross the yard. "He said yes, pretend to be surprised!"

"Del—"

"He wanted to come tell you himself, but if he thinks it's not his idea—"

"Of course," Alaine said, finally understanding. The stake in the orchard—Pierce was giving it up. "I made pound cake, and there's a jar of last fall's apple butter waiting!" she called loudly.

Seated at the dining room table, the best tablecloth quickly procured from the cupboard and the pound cake cut, Alaine finally slowed her breath. "Apple butter, Pierce?"

He spooned a large portion next to his pound cake, not quite touching. "Grafton glass, too!" He proudly tapped the emblem on the front of the jar.

"It's all we use," Alaine lied.

"We're going to try a new design in the fall—a wider-mouthed jar. I think women will like it for preserving whole fruit." Pierce cut a large forkful of cake. "Of course, that's just what I'm told by the design people!" He laughed heartily.

"How is business?" Alaine asked politely.

"Oh, the same, the same. State passed a measure on overnight labor restrictions, but of course we weren't hiring women or children overnight anyway." He considered the cake on his fork. "Excellent apple butter, Alaine."

"Thank you. And Perrysburg? Did you get that big storm last week?"

"And how! Yes, the river's about over the banks down by the park." He sipped his coffee. "I suppose you appreciate the rain out here, though!"

"We were a bit dry—the orchard was looking a little wilted." Alaine wondered at Pierce's easy conversation. Was he always like this when he was with his Perrysburg associates? Or only when he was in a good mood? She'd always wondered what Delphine had seen in him—perhaps this was a glimpse. He could be charming, after all.

"Well. That is what I wanted to talk about." He set his fork down with a decisive clank. "Delphine and I were talking, and it occurred to me that our share in the orchard is—well, it's really in name only, isn't it?"

"Now, I wouldn't—"

"No, no, I'm not offended. Neither Del nor I have any interest in the operations of the place, and it does feel a bit like we're skimming profits without doing any work." He caught Delphine's hand. "Doesn't it, Del?"

"Yes, it's—you're really the rightful owner of the place." Delphine shared a smile with Pierce.

"So, we talked it over, and we've decided to sign our share over to you and Jack. The papers are already filed with my lawyer."

"Oh, I never—I didn't at all expect—"

"Now, don't worry about it. It's what we want to do." Pierce cut himself another slice of cake. "There's copies for you and Jack in the car, and I'll send finalized paperwork once I get it back."

"Thank you, Pierce." Alaine forced deference into her voice even though talking around that kind of insincerity felt thick and gummy.

"I say—we ought to celebrate," Delphine said. "What if we got Mother and Papa Horatio over here for dinner? Something simple, of course, we've sprung this on you."

"An excellent idea! When does Jack get home from the office?"

"Early today—he promised to pick Em up on the way home, too, so we'll have a nice little party." Alaine was grateful to be able to retreat into the kitchen to plan dinner, with Delphine on her heels.

"Sorry, Alaine, he insisted on being the one to tell you," she whispered.

"It's perfectly fine. I'm just a little surprised, is all. Let's see—will you check the icebox and see if there's enough ham in there for all of us?"

By the time Jack and Emily came home, Alaine had an early dinner well in hand. She sent everyone up to Orchard Crest to fetch Mother and Papa Horatio, Pierce happily strolling away from Lavender Cottage bellowing something about the importance of family businesses. Delphine stayed behind, ripping the woody stalks out of early chard.

"Can you do me a favor, Alaine?"

"Of course." Alaine set down the potato she was peeling.

"I've another batch of bargains. You know…"

"Yes, I do." She toyed with the potato, hesitating, but said it anyway. "It's wise, I think, to put off starting a family. I know Pierce has been…better, of late, but if anything changes, you may decide to—"

"Leave off that talk!" Delphine's hands went still over the chard. "It was one time, it won't happen again. I just have to learn to—to accept him. As he is."

"No, you don't, Del. Not if—"

"Especially if. I made mistakes, I've learned from them. He won't again, I'm sure."

Alaine searched for the right words, finding them all incomplete. "It's not what he did, Del. It's that he…that he felt the right to do it."

"Please. Stop talking about it."

Alaine pinched her mouth shut. Maybe her sister was right, and Pierce's outburst was a single aberrant loss of temper. He seemed pleasant enough today. Still, she couldn't trust him. He moved through the world as though he owned it, parlayed what others had into what he wanted. She saw him just outside the garden, talking with—no, rather, at—Papa Horatio, his stance broad and commandeering. Delphine had left for Perrysburg brimming with enthusiasm and optimism, and every time Alaine had seen her since then, she had diminished and faded into a shadow of herself.

"All right," Alaine said, resuming peeling her potato. "And after all, I—well, you said before harvest time last year that you felt you hadn't quite—broken in, I suppose? With the society folks over there?" She had been disappointed in her bargain for Del, convinced the Fae had taken the bones and given nothing in return. "I suppose you feel you're still establishing yourself."

Delphine picked up a potato and scrutinized it as though it held deep and mystifying secrets. Alaine waited. "I can't make heads or tails of them most of the time, Alaine. I just—I only wanted them to notice me, and it seems that, every time they do, they see the worst in me."

Alaine's hands went cold and she set the knife down. She'd asked for Del to be noticed, to be seen as exceptional—but noticed wasn't always good, and exceptional could mean exceptionally bad. She suppressed a groan. She'd only asked the snobs of Perrysburg to notice her sister, not to change their horrid, stupid opinions. She'd asked the Fae woman to make Pierce kind, and she'd laughed—surely the same applied to the wretched mess of them.

She had to confess. "Delphine, I—I should have told you. I tried to make a bargain for you, for them to notice you—"

"Oh, it doesn't matter, Alaine. I know you were fiddling with that fairy ring last year, I'm not surprised it didn't work." She forced a smile and picked up the knife to begin peeling the potato herself.

"No, Del—what if it did work? You said—you said they did notice you. What if—what if they did?"

Delphine blanched and set the knife down. "Last fall. It was worse last fall after I visited—oh, Alaine! I said it wasn't safe, didn't I? That Gran would never—" Delphine dropped her voice. "And without asking me."

"You wouldn't have agreed!"

"With good reason, apparently!" She threw the potato in the sink. "I don't suppose you can undo it."

"I can try, I could ask for—"

"Don't. You might only make it worse."

"But—"

"You ignored my wishes the first time, don't do it again!"

"Besides, Del," Alaine said quietly. "It's them, not the bargain." They had noticed her, just like the bargain had specified. What kind of wretched people wouldn't see only beauty and elegance and artistry and kindness in Del?

"Don't try to slough off the blame! You always were like that, when we were children, it was never your fault, you always had to point blame somewhere else—" She took a steadying breath, and Alaine kept her mouth shut as Delphine continued. "Don't try to help me again. Stay out of it. These bargains are obviously beyond your understanding."

Alaine tempered her anger. Beyond her understanding—when she'd saved the farm, when she'd succeeded beyond her grandest hopes. She picked up the abused potato. "I won't. Don't worry. Why don't you put your own bargain out now, while the potatoes boil? It's a new moon tonight."

"Fine." Delphine swept out of the kitchen in unusually visible anger to the garden, purple silk in hand. Alaine sighed. She wasn't just sloughing off blame—the problem was Perrysburg. Always had been, always, she was afraid, would be.

Mother arrived with a pie in hand, and Papa Horatio settled himself on the porch with Pierce, conversing with seeming ease about the weather and the new automobiles Studebaker was putting out. Emily pulled Delphine to the orchard, with Jack and Mother trailing behind. Alaine finished dinner, pleasantly surprised at the quiet bustle that settled around the house with the whole family here. Could it be like this, she wondered? Could they settle into a pleasant family rapport, forgetting how Pierce had treated Delphine?

Everyone tumbled back into the house and settled around the table. Alaine set it with her wedding china, sprays of gray flowers on white, and Emily brought in newly blossomed roses from Mother's garden.

"How lovely," Papa Horatio said with a satisfied smile. "You know, the view out of this window is the same Lilabeth and I had in that old cabin. But the view inside? Much improved!" He laughed.

"Did you really live in a cabin at first?" Pierce clapped his hands. "American ingenuity, there you have it!"

"We did. A two-room place, with a cheap stove that didn't heat the whole house well enough. We made enough after those early years to build Orchard Crest, but I'll admit—this side of the hill always had the better view."

"I feel badly we didn't just move into the cabin," confided Alaine.

"Whyever for?" Pierce laughed.

"Because Papa Horatio built it," Alaine replied, failing to keep the edge from her voice.

The Fairy Bargains of Prospect Hill

"I suppose, I suppose," Pierce conceded. "I don't imagine you'll stay here forever, either."

"Then you don't know Alaine very well," Mother said with a smile.

Papa Horatio nodded. "And Jack ain't interested in moving, as far as I can tell. Prospect Hill's bit him, and he's stuck."

"I only mean—this house is small, I assumed at some point you'd want a larger place. For entertaining, especially as Jack advances his career."

"They can have Orchard Crest anytime," Mother said confidently, though Alaine knew that wasn't quite true. They could have Orchard Crest when Mother had grown too old and arthritic for her gardens.

"And I don't need a grand home for my sort of career," Jack added. "To be honest, I like leaving my work at the office."

"I suppose that is one kind of ambition," Pierce said swiftly. The table fell silent.

"There's plenty of other work to be done here." Papa Horatio gave Alaine a long look and then added, "Right good work, too." Alaine knew he meant more than he said.

Pierce coughed. "Of course. Well. A toast—to the orchard, and to the creation of a controlling share."

He raised his glass, and Alaine joined him in the toast, any celebratory spirit muted by his loud laughter.

35

The brighter the silk, the stronger the spell.

—Folk saying

AFTER EMILY HAD given Pierce a tour of the garden and chicken coop and Delphine had helped Alaine with the dishes, they set out for home. Pierce was in a quiet mood as he drove, which surprised Delphine after his charming conversation over dinner and his pleasant laughter on the porch.

In fact, he barely spoke, and by the time they arrived home, a dark mood seemed to be brewing like a summer storm. Delphine took off her duster and veil, and when she went to their bedroom, Pierce was already there.

He carried something she recognized instantly.

Pierce held the purple ribbon with its neat row of beads between two fingers as though presenting her with a dead thing. The ribbon was stained with dirt along one edge and was crumpled where Pierce had grabbed it, but the beads were intact, her precise stitching holding firm. "What is this?"

"It's nothing," Delphine whispered. "Just an old superstition."

"Why are you burying old superstitions in your sister's garden like so many corpses?"

"I—we always did, back home."

"You set out your fool charms for reason. I know that much about

that nonsense your family believes." He dropped his voice and leaned forward. "What is this for?"

"It's for...women's things," Delphine said, the incomplete truth gumming her words as effectively as a pure lie.

"Tell me the damn truth, Delphine! What is this? Is this some kind of curse?"

Delphine almost laughed at the absurdity of it. "No, of course not."

"Of course not!" he yelled. "How in the hell am I supposed to know what this kind of thing is? If it's some kind of spell meant to— what? Is it meant to harm someone? Me?"

Delphine's stomach dropped. "I would never harm you!"

"You certainly wouldn't with this foolishness! It's make-believe, Del, but you putting it out there, meaning to do something to me, to our life—"

"It's to keep from getting pregnant," she interrupted, her voice barely a breath.

Pierce was very still, and at first Delphine thought he understood. Then his hands met her shoulders, and he slammed her against the wall. She cracked her head against the wainscoting and blinked back stars and betrayal.

"Meant to keep from giving me children?" His face was close to hers, too close, and she tried to turn away, but he kept his eyes centered with hers. "What else are you doing, what other ways are you cheating me?"

"I'm not trying to cheat you! I thought—I thought I should learn to be a good wife, first, before—"

"Wives obey. Love, honor, and obey." Pierce released her shoulders with a disgusted shove. "There's nothing to learn."

"I'm sorry, I should have—I should have never done it. I should have asked you when you wanted children, I should have—" She struggled to bring her breath under control. Each breath pressed against the bones of her corset and left stale air in her lungs. "I'm sorry, throw it in the dustbin, the Fae won't want it then."

"The Fae aren't real!" Pierce roared, pitching the ribbon across the room. "It's not real. Good God, Delphine, you think you've upset me because this was *actually* preventing anything?" The ribbon lay next to the open window. Delphine swallowed, eyeing the glint of the beads in the last of the evening sunlight. "You sound like a lunatic. I could have you committed."

Even as Pierce turned away from her, Delphine was confident that he could. Not only that he could make laws and regulations bend to his desires, but that he would if she kept making these embarrassing errors, if she was too eccentric with talk of fairy bargains among the Perrysburg families. She edged away from the wall, beginning to shake, and sank onto the bed.

"I will be spending the evening away. Clean that mess up."

He ran a hand through his disheveled hair and paused in front of the mirror to comb it back into place. Delphine watched, silent, as he dabbed pomade on his comb and straightened his collar. He left without a word. She didn't move until she heard the door shut behind him, then lay down on their bed, numb, waiting for something she couldn't imagine yet.

She must have fallen asleep, because when she woke, moonlight streamed into the room. Pierce still wasn't back. She sat up, eyes drawn to the swath of moonlight, where the ribbon lay on the polished floorboards.

She couldn't stay here.

36

But the girl could not go back to the human world, having tasted of the Fae's foods, though they were but three ink-black berries.
—"Fairy Ring of the Forest," *The Collected Stories of the Pyrenees,*
by Robert C. Mulvaney

ALAINE DIDN'T REMEMBER collecting her silver pins or leaving the house, didn't notice when the evening shadows bled together into night. She didn't think about what she would offer or what she would ask, only that something had to be done to stop Pierce Grafton from ever hurting her sister again. She certainly didn't pause to ask Delphine if she approved. She didn't care; she'd help her sister one way or the other.

The Fae couldn't unbind his life from the earth, as the Fae woman had put it, but Alaine was certain there was some way to unbind Delphine from him. As Del had sobbed into Alaine's shoulder, Alaine had gently asked. Would Del come home for good? If she could, would she leave? Would she let Prospect Hill fold her back into its embrace, let her sister help her? Delphine had only held her closer.

That was enough for Alaine. Against all Delphine's protests, they'd told Mother just enough to explain why Delphine was home, brushing it off as a quarrel. They could explain more later, or Mother would figure it out. Then, mother and daughter sat silently on the porch, watching Emily chase fireflies as Alaine plunged into the forest bent on one thing and one thing only.

A bargain.

She placed the pin in the moss and circled the tree. Her hands flew to her waist, remembering the steel hidden in her corset, and stepped back, outside the ring. She waited, stone-faced, until the Fae woman appeared.

Alaine wasted no time with greetings. "I want my sister to come back to Prospect Hill. I want her free of her husband." Alaine could barely believe she'd said the words out loud. But there they were, the request waiting, the unspoken desire made real.

The Fae woman smiled faintly, perhaps taken aback by Alaine's forthright demands. "You cannot do this. It is undoing a contract that cannot be undone, except by the person who made the bargain to begin with." The Fae woman raised a pale hand. The moonlight caught thin silver rings on her fingers. "Your sister must make this bargain."

"She won't bargain with you." The Fae woman raised her eyebrow, a question unspoken. "She won't."

"Then I don't think I can help you."

"What is it you want?" Alaine shouted, voice rasping desperation. "These trinkets, what do they matter?"

The Fae woman hesitated, standing on the border of refusal. "I don't have to tell you anything without payment."

"No. And I don't need to know." Alaine clenched her fists, breathing ragged and gasping, as though she'd run a mile. She hedged her bets and took her gamble. "I don't need to know, and you and I don't need to bargain any longer."

The Fae woman's smile was thin and pained. "We can twist the fate of your world and bind its luck up with our will, but we cannot make anything of our own."

"Make?"

"In Fae, nothing grows. There is no ore hidden beneath our barren soil. We must ply whatever we would use from what we are given in trade. Some things—silk, silver, bone—we can work better than others." Her pale fingers moved against her hair; a sheer filament of silver wove a plait of her mist-colored hair from one temple to another. "This was spun from one of your pins."

Alaine leaned forward, looking closer. Wrought into the thread of metal were flowers and leaves, their minute veins and even dustings of pollen worked in silver. "Everything that you have is remade from our world?"

"Yes." She let the breeze stir her hair and her gown, and Alaine wondered what scrap of silk ribbon had been stretched and unspooled to a thin shadow of itself to produce the diaphanous cloud of pale blue surrounding the Fae woman, the wonder of it almost enough to make her forget the reason she had summoned the Fae. "Some blows in through the doorways. Some wanders in of its own accord. And some we take in trade."

"The apple, then. The cherry."

"I wished to grow my own orchard." Alaine couldn't be sure, but she thought she saw a faint glimmer of hope in those cold gray eyes. "The apple . . . it did not work. Your trick with the blossom hidden in the fruit, it was clever, and it foiled me."

Alaine began to protest that she had never meant to thwart the Fae woman's plans, but then stopped. If the fairy saw her as a masterful negotiator, perhaps that was better. Or perhaps worse. But she was speaking again before Alaine could decide. "I could not make it grow. But I made more apples." She drew an apple from the folds of her gown. Alaine gasped. It was translucent, with a blush like blood on ice in its thin skin. "Try it."

The Fae woman held the apple to Alaine, who took a step back, all of Gran's warnings and fears flooding into her at once.

"I know better than to eat Fae food."

The woman smiled a sharp grin. "Of course you do. This wouldn't harm or bind you. It is offered freely, and offered in your world, not ours. But—as you will." She split the apple in two with her lithe fingers as she stepped near the edge of the ring. The fruit snapped like dry bread, drops of silvery juice falling on the grass like dew. "What food is shared cannot bind," she intoned solemnly, and held the slice of fruit to Alaine with a steady hand.

Tentatively, Alaine took half the apple. Her teeth sank into it as though she were biting into water, and the pale starlight flesh yielded and dissipated in her mouth. The sensation was unsettling and deeply unsatisfying, but the taste—the flavor of the fairy apple was newly unfurled blossoms under sunlight and tart fresh cider and, faintly, the smoke of applewood.

She felt she understood the woman better, saw her bargaining as more desperate now.

"I still don't understand why you won't take a bargain with me for my sister. You've done it twice now. Is it the undoing of a marriage bond that you object to? Divorce, separation, all that is outside the bounds of Fae magic?"

"Ah, you do not comprehend me. It is not that I will not make a bargain. It is that I cannot make it with you. Your sister made the bargain for her marriage. Only she can bargain to undo it."

Alaine felt the air leave her lungs, then rush back in, her corset meeting her ribs reminding her of the here and now. "She bargained for the marriage?"

The Fae nodded. "A good bargain, too."

"But there is no bargain for making someone fall in love with you, making someone marry you!" Alaine thought she knew every bargain Gran had taught them better than Delphine.

"There are bargains that clear the way, that set the stage, in our particular language. This language we have written together." Another glint of silver in the moonlight, another whisper of silk. "And you know as well as I, as well as she, that you can maneuver a small bargain into more. Into marriage, if you wish it."

"I bargained for good weather," Alaine said, slowly understanding what the Fae woman meant. "So the Sunday school picnic would go on as scheduled, when everyone said it would be canceled on account of rain. Because it was the last time I'd see Jack before he left for school."

"Yes."

"And so my marriage is a Fae contract?"

"Of a sort, yes. Did you wish to break your contract, too?"

"No, but I certainly didn't think..." She took a breath. "I never considered that meant our marriages were contracts with the Fae."

"A bargain is a bargain and a contract is a contract," the Fae woman said with a smile. "You make what you will out of what you are given. You made a marriage out of a bargain. So did your sister. And she must unmake it herself."

37

A bargain wrought can't render what's bought
If changing the heart of another is sought.

—Folk saying

DELPHINE LEANED INTO the scent of roses in Mother's garden. On the other side of the boxwood hedge, Emily played in the
grass, her light voice telling snatches of a story to herself and laughing brightly at something Delphine couldn't see. Mother and Alaine
had both insisted that she let them do the washing up, and shooed
her outside, and she had obeyed with a frightening pliability. She
wondered if this was what an asylum was like, being quiet in the garden and letting others do the work and just barely hearing the talk
and laughter of the real world outside the walls.

Her throat constricted and gripped her breath tightly.

"First off, Jack says he can't just sign you into an asylum." Delphine jumped at Alaine's voice. "There are, in fact, laws, even if a
Grafton thinks they don't apply."

"For a Grafton," Delphine said softly, "they often don't." She lifted
a rose blossom closer and inhaled. "I know Jack knows his business,
but he's forgetting that Pierce has influence. He'll be a city councilman by fall, and there's no shortage of favors he can bargain with."

"Bargains." Alaine shook her head. "I tend to think the Fae have
a better way of thinking of bargains."

"Silly little trades," Delphine murmured. "If I had left that behind, maybe there would be no reason for Pierce to be so angry."

"He had no reason as it stands," Alaine replied, a flint edge cutting the soft rose-scented evening. "What if you did have a child by him, Del? Think of that."

"Maybe he would be happy with me then, perhaps—"

Alaine pulled back, horrified. "Del! It's not your fault he's an absolute snake." She heaved a sigh that was half growl. "If you had a child by him, he'd have rights over you there, too. You think he'd let that go? Damn it all, Del, you'd be stuck forever. But you're not—all because of a silly bargain."

"Just a bargain, just silk and beads." Delphine twitched her fingers over the edge of her peplum on her dinner dress. It, too, was just beads and silk, far more of either than she'd ever left for the Fae, and she wore it for an ordinary dinner at home. She swallowed. "You're right. Of course you're right." It felt like a relief to say it aloud. "He's made it impossible, hasn't he? I wanted to be a good wife—you remember? I said, last year, after the wedding, in our old bedroom. That was all I wanted, I—"

"You deserved better, Del." Alaine's voice was quiet.

"But what can I do? There's no way out, Alaine."

"Yes, there is, Del. It's not what you want, I know, but—" Alaine reached for her hand, but Delphine pulled back. "Come on, Del. Think. What other option do you have?"

Delphine clenched the skirts of her dinner dress in her lap, wrinkling the delicate blue crepe. She had the answer that was expected of her by everyone—everyone other than Alaine—memorized. Go home and try to do better. Love, honor, obey. Mollify his bad moods and mold herself to his expectations. Take her due when she failed. What she had done for the past year, since he had wrenched her from the cherry harvest and dragged her home in disgrace.

She found she couldn't. Not now, not ever again. And yet. "You don't understand," she finally choked out.

"What don't I understand? That Pierce Grafton is a cruel man, and his family are wretched for treating you as they have, and—"

"You don't understand why I left Prospect Hill."

Alaine fell silent.

"I left because you belong here, and I don't." Delphine raised her hand, stopping Alaine's immediate protests. "You don't just run the orchard—at this point, you *are* the orchard. Maybe I could have stayed, but I always felt like I could only have a tiny corner, something you were kind enough to carve off for me. I thought I could be somebody, married to Pierce. That I could be someone in Perrysburg, making my own way, be respected and well known and—well, like you."

Alaine took a long time to answer. "I had no idea, Del, I—I never meant for you to feel that way here, I—"

"I know you didn't. And you didn't make me feel that way. I just did. I still do, I suppose. I realize now I—I asked for something I didn't really understand, and I got something I didn't really want." Lilabeth had been right, all those years ago—never ask for something unless you understand yourself first. "Divorcing him means admitting I made a mistake."

Alaine flared. "This is entirely his fault, you can't blame yourself for him behaving as he did!"

"I don't blame myself for what he did." Delphine inhaled slowly—she found, for the first time, that she didn't. "That was entirely Pierce's fault. But marrying him was a mistake. It would have been a mistake even if he had been a kind man."

"You weren't wrong to want more, Del. To want to have your own place in this world."

"I know." Delphine reached for her sister's hand. "I went about it the wrong way. It was illusion and façade, not really what I wanted. But I—I don't know how. The laws—"

"Let Jack worry about the law. He's very useful that way." Alaine gave her hand a squeeze. "We'll find a way. Somehow." Her eyes gazed over Delphine's head, out toward the forest.

"I feel like I already have found my way." Delphine pulled Alaine closer. "I've been lost this year, but I didn't know it. I thought if I just kept on, I'd eventually get somewhere. But if you choose the wrong

path, you're not going to end up where you wanted to go by charg-
ing on ahead, are you? You have to stop and turn around sometime,
even if it's not easy. I—I think I'm ready to turn around."

Alaine nodded. "I wish we could just use that bargain for not getting lost on a journey," she said, a strange hitch in her voice. "Three
feathers tied with string."

"More fairy bargains!" Del forced a laugh. "How much do you
think they'd need to get me out of this jam?"

"Well." Alaine sank onto the ground next to the bench. "How
much did it take to get you into it?"

"What?"

"Surely you bargained," she suggested, testing her sister's reaction. "I did, for Jack."

"Lilabeth said it didn't work that way!"

"I don't mean directly. But I got sunshine that day of the picnic,
before Jack left for school. That was the last time we saw each other, and
I knew—" She paused. "I knew if I didn't see him then, that I might not
have another chance, before some university girl caught his eye."

"He only ever had eyes for you, Alaine. Since we were kids."

"That's not true, Del. At least—we talked when he came back
at Christmas. There were other girls, Del, I know there were. But
we'd been writing already, see, and he asked if I was quite serious.
A fellow doesn't ask that unless he's making a decision. So I know,
if I hadn't talked to him that afternoon on Getty Lake and said we
should write, he'd have been tied up with another girl by the time he
came home again."

"I didn't realize," Delphine said slowly. She let herself drift back
in memory, casting loose on what were now painful recollections.
"I—I found his lost book."

"What?"

"That was the first thing. Remember, I went to Finney Woods
with the Porters for the week that summer, and he was there, visiting. He lost a book he was reading, and I—I bargained to find it. A
little scrap of glass, you know. So we had a reason to talk, and he
knew who I was. I suppose there were others after that. The good

luck to get him on my dance card for the waltz at the New Year's ball." That had been a silver coin tied in a scrap of silk. Orange silk, she remembered, like a flame.

"That was the year of the big snowstorm on New Year's Eve." Alaine clapped her hands to her mouth. "You! You're the reason it didn't hammer us like everyone else!"

"Yes—oh, I almost forgot!" Delphine laughed. "Shut down rail traffic from every other station to Perrysburg except ours. I got the last train through. Mother was furious! She thought I'd be trapped in Perrysburg the rest of the month, imposing on the Porters." She sobered. If she hadn't made the train, if she hadn't had the waltz with Pierce, would he have forgotten her? Would he have started calling on some other girl, married the daughter of some Perrysburg associate? She had nurtured a sweet nostalgia of that dance under the dimmed chandeliers with Pierce, her lavender gown rustling on the tiles as his strong arms maneuvered them in the ring of dancers, the snow settling on his black overcoat and catching in her eyelashes when he walked her to the station the next morning with a promise to come calling. Now the memories were fetid, lilies left to fester. "And of course I glamoured the parlor when he came to call," she finally said.

"Del, there may be a way to bargain you out of this."

"How? I don't think a divorce would depend on good weather or finding a lost book."

Alaine looked up at her with her eyes large and solemn. "You have to promise not to get angry with me."

"How could I ever be angry with you?" She caught her sister's hand. "I mean truly angry, not ready to box your ears for ruining one of my blouses."

"You might be." Alaine hesitated, turning to face Delphine as though being called to recitation. "You were angry before. About bargaining with the Fae. I've been using different ways. I've...I've been using them for you."

"Alaine?" Delphine heard how frightened and small her voice was. Beyond the boxwood hedge, Emily was quiet.

Alaine pulled her sister away from the hedge toward a bench in the center of the garden. "I—oh, hang it, there's no way to explain it except to say I meet with a Fae woman and we make bargains for exactly what I want."

"Good lord!" Delphine shot upright from the bench, leaving several delicate strands of silk tangled in the rose vines. "You've done what?"

Alaine swallowed and repeated herself, calmly. "I've gone to the fairy circle around the linden tree. A woman comes when I summon her. We make bargains."

"You summon her." Delphine's focus reeled, looping from one impossible sentence to another. "But Lilabeth said—that's dangerous! You know it's dangerous! I, for the love of God, know it's dangerous."

"If you're not careful, I—" She stopped. "I know I wasn't careful before. I realized my mistake, I can't count on changing people's minds. That only works some of the time—the Fae would say humans are wrongheaded and fickle." Delphine couldn't argue with that; Pierce and Mrs. Grafton and Stella were each cruel in their own ways, no Fae interference required. "I bargained for the time you got away from Pierce, when his car broke. And I bargained for him to give us your share of the orchard."

"You said—" Delphine paused. Alaine had seemed cagey about the request, insisting on her three days to lay an old bargain of Lilabeth's. But it wasn't an old bargain at all. She'd negotiated with some Fae creature for a new arrangement. Delphine's stomach lurched. It had worked—she'd never expected Pierce to yield so easily. "What did you give her?"

"She's wanted things from the orchard. I—I suppose I tricked her, the second time."

"You tricked her! That can't be good."

"Perhaps not, but she didn't do anything to hurt me. They need the bargains, Del. I didn't realize—maybe no one did—they can't grow or make anything that doesn't come from us."

"That doesn't mean you should tamper with their magic."

"It doesn't mean I shouldn't," Alaine retorted. "And we can use what I've learned now, to get you a bargain. The last one we'll ever need, maybe."

"No, Alaine. I won't let you do that for me. Not again."

"Funny thing about that," Alaine said with a soft smile. "I can't. You made the bargains that resulted in you getting married. So, in essence, you made a bargain for Pierce and you're the only one who can bargain to get out of it."

"You asked already!"

"I had to." Alaine stood to face her, defiant chin jutted out. "He hurt you. He's lucky I haven't figured out how to put strychnine in his fancy port."

"Don't say that, Alaine, and don't even think of—"

"I won't. And don't worry, the Fae can't kill him off, either. They have rules about that, apparently."

"Don't tell me you asked about that, too."

"No, that was one of the few pieces of information the Fae woman offered." She sighed. "You could bargain with them, Del. All we need to know is what to ask for. Exactly what to ask for."

Delphine clamped down on the bitterness coursing through her, but the gall came out anyway. "They can't just undo the whole marriage? Make it like it never happened."

"No, but they can affect other things. Whatever you decide to do—file for divorce or leave or—whatever you need, we can bargain for a little...nudge."

"A little nudge!" Delphine sat back down on the bench with a heavy thump and a loud laugh. "A little nudge! You're meeting a Fae creature in a fairy ring and selling God knows what for a little nudge!"

"But it works." Alaine bunched her skirts into Delphine's as she sat close on the bench. "What is it that we'd need? What has to change to get you out of this?"

Delphine considered the question carefully, slowly. "If I were to file—" She paused. Saying the word made it real, she felt, and it was heavy and ugly in her mouth. "If I were to file for divorce, I

would have to prove cruel treatment. A judge would have to rule that there's cause, and they won't rule against a Grafton."

"Maybe...maybe with a bargain they would."

Delphine shook her head. "I will have one chance, Alaine. And then—you and Jack might say he can't have me committed, but you don't know the reach the Graftons have. Who they know. He could simply have me sent away."

"Over my dead body. Or his."

"Alaine!"

"What? So help me, Del, I would if I could. He hurt you. So if you're squeamish about murder, I'm afraid fairy bargains are the only way to go." She shot Delphine an impish grin. "A judge won't rule against a Grafton. Unless we have a bargain assuring us he will."

38

The laws of Fae won't break the laws of Man, but the laws of Man may bend to Fae.

—Folk saying

"DIVORCE LAWS ARE actually fairly complex, and vary by state," Jack said. Alaine hovered beside her husband, peering over his shoulder at his book. Alaine really believed this would work, Delphine thought. She hunched into the back of her chair even though slumping made her corset bite her hips. Jack wore a pair of silver spectacles when he read, giving him a studious intensity Delphine hadn't seen in him before. Of course, she hadn't ever seen him practicing his profession, either. She'd never had a reason. "In fact, in some states, you're still required to prove adultery or abandonment of the marriage to obtain a divorce. This is interesting reading—some Midwestern states were among the earliest to offer divorce for cruel treatment."

"But you still have to *prove* that." Delphine squinted at the tight black-and-white print of Jack's book, the legalese hiding the plain truth: There was no way out for her, not if she had to prove her case in a court.

"Did you know," Jack said, flipping through pages that smelled of old cellar, "that until the legislation tightened on proof of residence requirement in the 1870s, Indiana was considered a divorce mill? The courthouse in Hammond, for example—"

"Jack." Alaine laid a hand on the rapidly turning pages. "It's not 1870. And we're not in Hammond."

"No, I suppose not. Fortunately, we also are not in New York, where adultery is still the only grounds for divorce. There's a whole scam in New York where couples desiring divorce spoof a tryst in a hotel—" Delphine heaved a sigh, and Jack quickly redirected his wandering focus. "The point is—divorce hinges entirely on the legal reasons for the claim. If you don't have to prove adultery, that changes the question entirely. The claim here is most certainly for cruel treatment."

"Yes, but I'd still have to prove that. Somehow." Delphine felt her voice go flat.

"You have witnesses who saw him speaking harshly to you, and who have seen the..." Alaine caught herself. "The bruises. Any rational judge would—"

"Rational, yes. But no judge would believe it of a Grafton, or even if he did..."

"That's where the bargain comes in." Alaine chewed on her lip. Delphine knew that look, the plotting, deciphering look, her calculating how-many-barrels-of-cider-to-reserve or how-many-rows-of-pears-to-plant look. They hadn't told Jack about that part of their plan, only that Alaine was going to ply some of their backwoods luck where it would be most useful, swearing Delphine to secrecy. Alaine didn't want Jack knowing she'd summoned and bargained directly— she said he'd worry. Damn right to worry, Delphine thought, vaguely uncomfortable keeping secrets from Jack.

"Case first, bargain second," Jack said. "The paperwork is fairly easy to draw up, but of course I want to have everything squared away and airtight. I haven't done many divorces—ah, I didn't mean it to sound like that, Del. Just that I'll have Collins look over it—"

"No!" Delphine sat bolt upright, surprised at the force of her reaction. "No, I don't want anyone to know, I don't—" She heaved a sigh that strained against her ribs.

"Del." Alaine dropped next to Delphine's chair, catching her hand. "There's no way to avoid people knowing, one way or another.

Eventually." She tried for a smile. "It doesn't really matter, in the end, no one—"

"That's easy for you to say." Delphine shook her hand free. "You never cared much what people thought—you didn't mind being mud stained from the orchard when Mother had people for tea, or saying exactly what you thought in Sunday school." She clamped her words closed in her mouth. Alaine never cared if she made people gossip, so long as she was doing what she thought was right. It was as though she'd never felt the sting of shame. "But I care."

Jack cleared his throat awkwardly, taking off his glasses and folding them carefully next to his book. "The trouble is, Del, there's no way to help you with complete and total discretion. None of us is going to go about town posting signs, but it is a matter of public record. When you leave your hus—Pierce's—house for good, of course people will know what's happened."

"I know," Del said softly. "But I don't want the gossip, the— Mother will be furious," she deflected.

"Mother should be furious," Alaine interjected. "About Pierce Grafton."

"Now, Alaine." Jack restrained her sister's tongue with a gentle hand on her shoulder. Delphine laughed, silent and bittersweet, at the two of them. Here they were, proof that marriage didn't have to be a dismal venture, that it could even take two people and temper them into better versions of themselves. "Be that as it may. For me, professionally, this is a simple matter of filing the correct paperwork and producing the correct affidavits and presenting them in the right places. But for the parties involved—" He cleared his throat again. "For all of us, as a family, it's personal and understandably emotional, and not in pleasant ways. But it is, I think, necessary."

Delphine fidgeted with the buttons down the side of her dress. Buttercup-yellow lawn, made up in a style she'd pulled from a magazine last year. She'd imagined wearing it entertaining guests on the piazza, or on a stroll with Pierce on the trip to New York he'd promised. Now she saw it at home in Orchard Crest, going to church on Sundays or hosting the garden club with Mother. She didn't think she fit in either place anymore. "All right. Do what you need to do."

"And if you can make up your papers, we'll make our bargain," Alaine said confidently. She clapped Delphine on the shoulder.

At that moment, a car rumbled up the lane.

"What in the world?" Jack pushed aside the curtain, but Delphine didn't need to know who was there. She recognized the timbre of the engines. Pierce's Studebaker.

"No. He can get the hell off my property." Alaine stalked to the front door, and Delphine was sure that if Jack's hunting rifle had been handy, she would have it cocked and pointed down the driveway.

"Alaine," Jack said, quiet but firm. "I'll handle it. Why don't you take Del up to Orchard Crest—"

"No." Delphine stood up. "I'm staying."

Jack hovered by the window, clearly unwilling to accept this, but there wasn't time to argue. Pierce was already knocking on the door. Jack gently cut Alaine off from the doorknob and opened it.

"Pierce. You've come a long way this afternoon." Jack held out a cordial hand.

"Let's dispense with the pleasantries, Jack. I'm here for my wife."

Next to each other, Pierce and Jack were nearly the same height, but Pierce's broad shoulders and barrel chest dwarfed Jack. Still, Jack stood straight and resolute, refusing to let Pierce pass.

"I'm afraid I'm not in the business of serving people up like packages for delivery," Jack said. "If she wanted to go with you, she'd be free to. But she's of a mind to stay here a while."

"She's coming back with me. I'm sure you understand, Jack, a man can't have his wife absent from his house too long, or people start to talk. There's plenty of vicious minds for gossip in Perrysburg, and I've no intention of being on the receiving end of it."

"I think you ought to have thought of that sooner," Alaine said.

Delphine shook her head, silently willing everyone to stop talking, to just go away, to disappear.

Pierce glowered at Alaine, but recovered quickly. "Well, what do you say, Del? Come on back with me, we'll worry about your car later."

233

The world narrowed in focus, pinpoints of light on Jack's resolute stance and Alaine's reddening ears, on her own ragged breath, on Pierce already beginning to push the door open to lead her outside, back to Perrysburg, back to a life she was only pretending was hers. Delphine met his eyes.

"No."

"What's that, Del?" Pierce forced a laugh. It was too loud, garish and uncomfortable in the silence. "Come on along to the car."

"No," she said again, stronger this time. Her palms sweat into her skirts, and her heartbeat was in her throat, but she managed to continue, "I'm not leaving with you. I'm not coming back at all."

"What! Why, Del, that's nonsense. We've had a misunderstanding, but—"

"It isn't a misunderstanding, Pierce." Jack shifted slightly, blocking Delphine from Pierce with his shoulder.

Delphine shivered as Pierce's eyes darkened. "I don't know what she's been telling you," he said. He may have been speaking to Jack, but he looked straight at her. "I don't think she's been quite right lately, a bit nervous, perhaps. The things she was saying about those silly trinkets her family leaves out for fairies, as though she thought they worked. I don't know but a bit of a time in a rest home wouldn't be the best thing for her."

Jack caught Alaine's arm as she lurched forward. Delphine was sure that, given the opportunity, Alaine might actually bite Pierce with those bared teeth. "You're not sending her off to some asylum, you wretched—"

"Alaine!" Jack interrupted.

Pierce only laughed. "Why, I never said any such thing. Did I?" He met Delphine's eyes, his own now schooled into an overcast gray, and her stomach dropped. He'd said all that and more. Come home now, dutifully, obediently. Or there would be consequences to being inconvenient.

"I'm terribly sorry," Jack was saying, "that you came all this way for nothing. But I'm afraid Del is simply not going back with you."

Pierce wavered at the door. Delphine wondered when the last time someone other than his father had told him no was—certainly she hadn't. Anger vied with something else in his face—confusion, perhaps, dismay that the world was not acquiescing to his demands as it usually did. That Delphine was not slotting comfortably into place in the life he had orchestrated for her. He stalled a moment, and then decided, abruptly. "Well. I won't be made a fool of any longer standing here. I'll be back, Delphine."

"The hell you will," Alaine muttered as the door closed behind him. "Oh, Del, I'm sorry. I should have—if I'd only—"

"No, Alaine. There's nothing you could have done." She sighed. "He's not a bad person." She cut Alaine off as she began to argue. "No, he's not, not really—before we were married he was kind—compassionate, even. I suppose always tied up in his own interests, but—" She paused. "He's weak."

Alaine's eyebrows shot up. "Weak? Del, you may be being—"

"No, he is. Being a Grafton has broken him, and he thinks he should break me, too, to keep the world turning as he thinks it ought, to pacify his parents and the board and the constituents and—" She shook her head. She couldn't explain it to Alaine, especially not now, while Alaine's cheeks were still flushed with unspent anger. She believed there was a better man buried, broken, warped out of shape within him. She had to. But she couldn't unbury and mend him, not without tearing herself apart in the process, subsuming herself further and further into the role he wanted her to play. Delphine inhaled, her chest opening with the breath for the first time in months. "File the paperwork, Jack. I don't care who knows anymore."

39

Sparrow and swallow, fly away home
The bats are abroad and the Fae do roam
We've morning and evening and all through the day
But night is for the roving Fae
                    —Children's rhyme

DELPHINE WAITED OUTSIDE the ring.

She was not a stranger to the fairy tree on Prospect Hill, and Grandma Lilabeth had taught her well: *Stay away from the old linden that never fades. Don't step on the vibrant circle of green. Don't speak to anyone you find in the forest.* Now Alaine had given her instructions that prescribed precisely the opposite. She had left her hairpins and her corset at home, divesting herself of steel and iron. She carried a silver pin in her pocket, threaded through a scrap of wool. With a breath that shored up her resolve, she stepped across the threshold into the vestibule of the Fae. As Alaine had told her to, she sunk the pin into the moss at the tree's roots and repeated the rhyme.

"A pin to mark, a pin to bind, a pin to hail," she intoned carefully, wondering if the words themselves had power or if it was only the custom, the action. She circled the tree—once, twice, three times. And then she waited.

"You are not the one who I have bargained with before." The voice was pale and cold, like winter's wan sunlight stretched thin.

Delphine shook as she turned, but the woman was not the terrible creature wrought of beauty and fear she had expected. She was more woman than nightmare, but a woman rendered ethereal and immortal under an artist's brush. More metaphor than reality, more illusion than human.

"No," Delphine said softly. "I am her sister."

"Ah. Then I know the bargain you have come to reverse." She smiled, cold and glittering against the warmth of the late-summer woods, and Delphine felt a chill pass through her. She saw something of the nightmare now.

"Yes."

"And how have you decided to do it? Your laws are labyrinthine things, and a woman seeking her freedom could get lost in them."

"Unless," Delphine said, "there is some escape hatch in the maze."

"You must be more specific. So muddy and brackish, your people's laws. So many ways to flick fortune here or there and change the course of your existences." She waited, like a queen presiding over a court of supplicants.

"I have to go before a judge." Delphine and Alaine had discussed every angle. Could they ask for a favorable judge, or simply sympathy for one day from whoever sat on the bench? They had settled on what seemed the surest option. "It must be someone who is not tied to this place. Someone who doesn't know or care about the social repercussions of his judgments."

"An outsider?"

"That would be best, yes. And he must rule in my favor."

"Bring some stranger to hear your case. And make him hear it true, hear it as the proper recipient of his clement judgment." She smiled faintly. "Fate can be warped in such ways, yes."

"Then you can do it?"

"Oh, I can do it, fair one."

"How?"

"How!" The Fae woman laughed, bright bells cutting the evening. "How? Can you explain how a seed bursts from its shell and the tenderness inside grows tough? Can you tell me from whence the

gold in your mines came? You do not know the magic of your own world. How can I explain the magic of mine?"

"But I have to know that you can do it. That this will work."

"It will. The influences are many. Many ways to pluck a man from his intended course and set him awry, many ways to manipulate the rivulets of your thoughts. Many moments to trick the eye or ear. It will be done."

"I'm sorry, it's only—this is strange for me."

"Not so strange. You have never doubted our bargains before, have you? That the glass brought back a lost book? That the pat of butter brought a visitor? You have never doubted how some silk and some beads could stay your husband's seed within you?" Her lips curled upward in a smile, and Delphine tasted the hints of bitter cruelty there.

"No," she answered quietly. "I suppose I haven't."

"We must discuss price."

"My sister told me that you are building an orchard. We have pears."

"Pears—the golden fruit with the thin skins." She smiled softly. "Yes, pears are lovely things. But I want more. This is a greater bargain than what I have made with your sister. It requires a price to match it."

"What do you want?" Delphine's mouth went dry. Alaine had been so sure she would accept the pears—all of the pear, blossom, fruit, and seed. Just as she had with the cherries and apples.

"There is a magic in first fruits, did you know that?" The Fae woman began to move, deftly, bare feet leaving faint marks on the soft grass. "I want the first fruits of your sister's grove."

"The first harvest? Of the year?"

"The first *fruits*, fair one." She moved past Delphine's vision, forcing her to turn in a tight circle. The Fae woman's robe trailed behind her, a billowing cloud that shifted with every breath. "Do you agree? The first fruits of your sister's grove."

Delphine bit the inside of her lip. "How do we know what to leave, how much, or—"

"We will not take more than our due. The magic is there whether we take a bushel or a single piece. I shall only ever take the single fruit. And we can gather first fruits ourselves. No need to leave them here. That is part of the magic, as long as it has been bargained and agreed."

"Is it only this year, or—"

"The first fruits. That is every turning, every type that bears its own fruit. But only the first. We know which one it is, even, if the whole tree blossoms and fruits at once, even if there is naught but a wizened nut."

"The first fruits, for my freedom."

"Yes."

Delphine felt dizzy, the diaphanous robes of the Fae woman circling her and the bargain ringing, over and again, as she considered it. There was nothing wrong with the loss of a few apples, a few pears. Even if the Fae woman took them every year, from now until—

She stopped herself, seeing the trick. "What if it's no longer my sister's land? What happens if the land passes from my family?"

"If the land passes from your family? And the orchard of Prospect Hill goes to another?" Delphine nodded. "Then I have gathered all the fruits from its orchards that I may gather," the Fae woman replied with a shrug, "for I will take only what fruit your sister has yielded." Her silvery hair rustled like taffeta. "But the rewards of the bargain you have wrought will remain." She turned and examined Delphine's reaction with a face so still it might have been made of glass. "We shall gather when the moon comes full on ripened fruit."

Delphine inhaled, trepidation mingling with the heady scent of linden. "Very well. I make this bargain. The first fruits of my sister's grove are yours."

"So bargained," the Fae woman said with a new, velveted ferocity. "So agreed."

40

DELPHINE DROPPED A lump of sugar into her tea with a shaking hand. "I can't believe it's over. How did you do that more than once?" She sipped gently, both hands gripping the cup.

"Desperation, I suppose," Alaine deflected. It wasn't, at first—those early forays fed her ambition. But she wouldn't hold that against herself if it led to this. Del would be free, and all the Fae had asked was fruit. "It doesn't seem like much at all to ask in trade," Alaine said, brow forming a twin pair of furrows.

"The bargain?"

"Yes. It seems a small thing, and you say that the Fae woman claims this was a greater bargain than before," Alaine said. "Yet this seems a smaller price. Or perhaps it only seems that way to us."

"You said they value things differently."

"And I suppose . . . it is every year, in perpetuity."

"The way you've hung onto the orchard, it will be." Delphine set her tea down. "We didn't tell Mother, did we?"

"Heavens, no." Alaine laughed. "She's going to take to her bed for a week when you file for divorce."

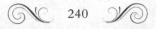

She suppressed a sigh. Delphine was far better at managing Mother's moods than she was, but she supposed this one would be up to her. Hardly fair, she chided herself, to dump Mother's conniption over the divorce in Delphine's lap.

"Don't remind me." Delphine almost laughed, but then her face clouded. "I—I shouldn't be afraid to do it now, should I? After what I just did?"

"Del, of course it's not easy. You can come back here, of course. You can live with us. Or—why, Jack was just saying that the apartment above his office is going to go up for rent, if you wanted a place of your own—"

A flash of hope brightened Del's eyes—then wavered. "That would take money I don't have," she reminded Alaine.

"Well, maybe someday. Gosh, Del. What do you want to do? I mean, after all this is over and done."

"I haven't the slightest."

She toyed with the handle of her teacup, and Alaine wondered if she was being honest. Her sister had always wanted more than she did—the excitement of city life, the promise of being somebody in the influential circles in town. And in smaller ways, too, to master piano and watercolors, not just as a means to an end like Mother, but because she could see beauty in a blank sheet of paper or an unplayed score and want to capture it. She wondered where else she wanted to go, what kind of wanderlust abided in her sister's soul.

"You could go to the university," Alaine said abruptly. "Art history, or language, or—"

"What?"

"Like your friend. You could—if you wanted to study something, that is."

"I suppose I could," Delphine said slowly. "I had thought taking a course in art history would be interesting—maybe someday, if I keep working on my own techniques and study, I could teach." Alaine thrilled at the spark that lit her sister's eyes. "Well, carts and horses and all that. One thing at a time."

Alaine nodded. "Jack will arrange everything. Don't worry about that. He'll file the paperwork and get you your appointment with the judge and—" Delphine shrank back, shoulders rounding. Alaine paused. She was barreling ahead with her plans, forgetting that the real concern was her sister. "I'm sorry, Del. I can only make this easier by taking care of the practical bits, but I wish—"

"I know." Delphine smiled weakly. "I appreciate all that. And... perhaps you wouldn't mind telling Mother?"

Alaine traipsed up to Orchard Crest shortly after breakfast the next day, Emily in tow. Em ran off with Papa Horatio down Prospect Hill to run errands in town as soon as they arrived, leaving Alaine with no audience, but also no reinforcements for the conversation she dreaded with her mother.

"Coffee?" Mother passed the milk to Alaine without needing to ask. "Emily is going to need new dresses for fall, she's grown out of nearly everything."

"She certainly has—legs like a grasshopper."

"I'll make up something, if you like. Maybe I could take Emily to look at fabric sometime."

"I'm sure she'd like that. Mother, I—"

"She really does need a bit more... structure, I think. Start to learn to rein herself in. Piano can be an excellent way to learn self-control, and—"

"Mother, I'm not here to talk about Emily." Alaine tamped down any frustration she had at Mother's criticisms. Now wasn't the time.

"I only mean—"

"I know. But it's important, Mother, please." She took a breath so deep that it strained against her corset. "Delphine is staying with us down at Lavender Cottage."

"Oh, how nice—how long? I could—"

"Mother, no. She's staying for a while. She's filing for divorce."

Mother blanched, hand falling away from her coffee cup. "Divorce? Why, Alaine, it—"

"He's been wretched to her. Jack says there should be no issue proving cruel treatment, open and shut. She's not trying to ask anything for herself out of community property—she already signed over her share of the orchard to me—"

"You're thinking of the orchard at a time like this?" Mother's ears reddened, blooming around pearl drops. "Alaine, this is inconceivable. She needs to go home to her husband right away. I can't believe you would encourage this in her."

"Me?" Alaine swallowed. She'd expected Mother to take the news poorly, but anticipated hysterics or anxiety, not blame thrown her way.

"Yes, you. You've always been jealous of Delphine, ever since she was born." Mother stood and paced, her white summer dress swirling into a blur. "And marrying into society, and that beautiful big house, and—all your scraping and fussing over your little fiefdom here doesn't hide it."

"Mother." Stillness washed over Alaine, numbing her as the shock of Mother's accusations settled. "I never—I'm not jealous of Del. When we were young, maybe, but only because—" She found she couldn't say it. Because Mother had seemed to care so much more for Del, that she seemed constantly frustrated with Alaine. But she had left that behind, chosen to let her sister have one role while she took on another, more necessary one. She wasn't jealous of Del. If anything, she was sometimes sorry for Del, that Del didn't seem to have a direction for her ambition in the same way the orchard gave Alaine a purpose.

None of that was helpful now, not while Mother was fuming.

"Mother, he hit her. More than once."

"Oh." Mother stilled, then roused herself. "I'm sure it was a misunderstanding, there's no way a man like that—"

"It wasn't a misunderstanding. It's been happening for months, over a year. And it's precisely because he's a man like that." Alaine waited for her mother to absorb this, silently. "Del wanted to be just like you, I think," she added. "Building a lovely home and raising a family and—making her house a place that was beautiful, for other people, always for other people. She can't do that with someone like Pierce."

"But now she can't do that at all," Mother whispered. "Who will marry a divorced woman? What place can she possibly have in the world, aside from a spinster aunt living in someone else's house—" Mother choked on her own words, and Alaine resisted the urge to argue. Divorce wouldn't make Delphine's life easy, but it would be her life. Not the pale shadow she'd become living in Perrysburg.

"Maybe we can trust Del to find her own way," Alaine said quietly.

Mother finally sat down again. The flush of anger was scoured from her cheeks into a still, pale mask. She folded her hands, orienting herself back to the pragmatic present. "Well. If he really is as awful as all that, she can stay here as long as she likes. Should someone go to collect her things?"

"I hadn't even considered—yes, of course." She thought of Pierce, intruding on their home, demanding her sister's return. There was no way Delphine should have to face him, and sourness curdled her stomach considering going herself, or even sending Jack. "I'll arrange it."

"Mama!" Emily dashed into the parlor, dropping a kiss on her grandmother's cheek and a paper sack into Alaine's lap. "We bought coconut creams—Aunt Del's favorite!"

Papa Horatio met Alaine's eyes over Emily's head. "Sounded like Aunt Del could use some cheering up."

"I take it next time we have family news, I ought to send Emily instead of coming up myself," Alaine said with a rueful laugh.

She went to the linden tree right away, leaving Emily and Del browsing the pages of the *Harper's Bazaar* that Papa Horatio had brought home. The steps of calling the Fae were familiar now. Alaine surprised herself as she acknowledged the ease of calling across the veil. For all she knew of bargains and rings, she didn't understand the silvery woman who appeared at her behest, or what manner of plans and power she had constructed in her own world. A year ago that uncertainty would have cowed her, sent her running from the edges of the fairy circle into familiar forest. Not anymore.

She didn't have to know the nuances of the Fae to know that the woman wanted what was in her bundle, and that Alaine could buy what she wanted in return.

The Fae woman appeared with a breath of soft air and a scent like rain. "I confess I am surprised to see you so soon," the woman said with bland indifference that suggested no emotion, least of all surprise. Alaine had never called her in broad daylight before, but she was no less ethereal in the afternoon light.

"I have a bargain to offer."

"Indeed." She smiled faintly. "What this time?"

Something had shifted in the woman's manner, in her urgency. She put Alaine in mind of a rooster after it had won its spurs against the others, the pecking order decided, the dominance assured. It was almost enough to make her forgo the bargain entirely. She didn't need it, not really—she and Jack could go and gather Delphine's clothes and pack a trunk themselves, even with Pierce guarding his home like an angry bear. But it was easier, much easier, if he could be away and Delphine could direct them. And Alaine felt that Delphine deserved the chance to say goodbye to the parts of that life she'd been fond of.

"You've kept my sister's husband from home before. I need you to do it again. Make sure he's not home a week from today." She opened her bundle. "In return, I offer—all of the tree."

The bundle held a pear blossom, preserved and pale, as well as a stone-hard fruit, and a twig.

"It's pear. I saved the flower, and the fruit is still a little ways from ripe. But it's all there." She considered the cotton napkin in her hand. "You can keep the cloth," she added.

The woman didn't answer, but she reached for the bundle. "Shall I break his car again?"

"I suppose that would be fine."

"Very well." She nodded, and the curious look she gave Alaine before vanishing wrapped her heart in ice.

41

Many's the fool pleased to make a bargain and woeful to pay it.

—Folk saying

THE FULL MOON rose low and yellow over the orchard. Delphine sat on the porch of Lavender Cottage, a glass of last year's apple wine in her hand, the divorce paperwork filed. She still wore the dark brown suit she'd carefully picked to go to the judge's office— newly appointed in interim after Judge Dalton had retired abruptly following what Jack's colleagues said was a mild stroke. Delphine felt a stab of guilt—had the Fae caused that? Was this the manipulation, the slight redirection of currents that the Fae woman spoke of? Or had the appointment of the soft-spoken man with mouse-brown hair from Saint Charles been the only bit of Fae coercion, an outsider as they had requested?

Pierce hadn't come. His lawyer, Lyndley, blustered that this was all a sham, that Mr. Grafton wouldn't concede to show his face at such an abuse of the justice system, that it would have wasted his client's time to appear in person, as the judge had no intention of granting the petition anyway. Delphine could have sworn she sensed a crackle in the air, a faint scent of far-off snow; the very words that would have driven a local man, deep in the Graftons' confidence, into denying her petition, seemed to kindle a bit of fire under the mousy fellow from Saint Charles, and he cut Lyndley off halfway through his speech with a crisp knock of his gavel and granted the divorce with no further conversation.

"Penny for your thoughts," Alaine said, closing the screen door softly behind her.

"Why pay for them when you must already know?" Delphine said with a quiet smile. She set her glass of apple wine down on the side table. "No going back now."

"Well, technically—"

"Technically I could retract the paperwork or—or something, I'm sure." She leaned into the porch swing. It creaked gently in rhythm with her movement. "But Pierce will know by now that the petition was granted."

"I don't envy that Lyndley fellow the job," Alaine replied. "But yes. That is—that is what you wanted?"

"Yes," Delphine said quietly, then louder. "Yes. It is. I—I was a fool, too old to be thinking like a child. No matter how kind Pierce was when I met him, I ought to have thought of it—what becoming Pierce Grafton the glass magnate, Pierce Grafton the councilman would do to him. What marrying into that meant. Should have considered his family, their influence." She thought, briefly, Mrs. Grafton, and couldn't help but feel faint sympathy for the woman who was so wedded to her life of misery she couldn't see any rational choice but to shackle Delphine, too. Mr. Grafton, who she rarely saw but whose beliefs guided and goaded his son like a lash.

"He was the fool, not you." Alaine crossed her arms and stared at the moon as though it could stand in for Pierce Grafton and take a tongue-lashing. "He's never stopped to consider what he has, what it's worth, not really. He doesn't with his money and his influence, and he didn't with you. He's a wasteful idiot of a man."

"Well. It's over. Thank God—" Delphine stopped herself. Thank God the bargains worked, that there was no child wrapped up in her mistakes and Pierce's cruelty and the great ugly mess it made. "I can bear the shame of it, you know. I can hold my head up in church and make polite conversation at the garden club even while I know what people are saying about me. They'll stop eventually, or they won't, or I'll stop caring, or I won't. But if there was a child, I—I couldn't have done it."

"Oh, Del." Alaine held her sister's hand tightly. "Have you been worried?"

"The last fight we had. I didn't tell you why. It was—he found the bargain. The ribbon and beads."

"Good God, Del."

"I was afraid maybe he'd found others, maybe we—" She brought her breath under control. "But no. I don't know why he cared. He didn't believe in it anyway."

"Alaine," Jack called from the hall. Delphine's chest tightened. Something was wrong. His voice was too high, too strained. "Alaine!" He stumbled into the parlor. "Emily is gone."

"Gone?" Alaine shot up from the porch swing, toppling the side table and the half-drunk glass of wine. It shattered on the wooden boards.

"Careful, it's—" He righted the table and picked up the largest piece of glass. "I'm sure she's just hiding somewhere or went outdoors to play or—"

"She knows better than to go outside after bedtime," Alaine said, voice low. "And Del's been here since I tucked her in."

Slowly, Delphine looked at the rising moon, full and brightening to a pure white over the orchard. The branches of the trees hung heavy, coming ripe with apples.

First fruits. The full moon. The Fae were collecting their bargain.

"Get Imogene," Delphine said. Her voice was weak and distant, a tinny echo of someone else speaking. "Get Aunt Imogene," she repeated, stronger this time.

"Imogene?" Jack shook his head. "Why in the world—"

"Trust me, just get Imogene!" Panic rose, dizzying, as Delphine told herself she was overreacting, that the uncanny glimmer of the moon on the trees was only a trick of the light and not Fae magic, that Emily was probably just hiding in her closet or under the bed.

Jack set off at a run toward Imogene's cabin while Alaine searched every corner of the house. A cold terror sinking into the pit of her stomach, Delphine made her way into the orchard. Nothing was different—fruit still hung blushing and ripe on the boughs, the moonlight still wove through pruned branches, crickets still sang in the grass. But the dew shone an almost painful silver, and the faint scent of linden hung hazy everywhere Delphine went.

She returned to the house, the lights blazing and Imogene waiting. Her great-aunt listened, stone-faced and silent, as they detailed the bargains, one after the other. Jack paced the room, eyes always on the windows. Looking. Hoping.

"Oh, you pair of prize fools." Imogene sat motionless when Alaine finished, face as grave and still as a granite statue. "Couple of idiots."

"How could we have known?" Delphine said. Her mouth was dry as cotton, so dry she could barely speak. "We had only discussed the orchard. I was sure it was the orchard. Oh God, Alaine, I'm so sorry!"

She almost choked on the tears as they streamed down her face. Jack barely glanced at her, his face drawn into a gray mask of horror. And Alaine—Alaine looked like a ghost, barely registering any reaction at all.

"No, it isn't your fault." Alaine forced the only emotion she could feel right now, white-hot anger, back into the hollowness at her center. "I sent you. I told you what to do. I would have agreed, too." She faltered. Would she have agreed? She wasn't sure. The Fae woman gave hints, suggestions—she was not impossible to read. Or, perhaps, Alaine had read her wrong the entire time.

Imogene stamped her cane on the floor. "It's both your faults. You messed with the ring. You called her. This is why we don't meddle with them! The set bargains are safe, but look at how they turn a word. I told you, Alaine. They sell you on a bargain only they understand."

"But how?" Delphine wiped away her tears with the cuff of her blouse. "We never even spoke of children, let alone about Em."

Imogene leaned forward. "Ask your university friend. Ask her what first fruits are. Lands, I know enough old stories to put it all together. Either of you ever bother to read your Bibles?"

Alaine flared, the thin thread of control she'd managed to hold onto snapping. "This isn't the time for a lecture on saintly behavior, Imogene—"

"No, the *words*! The words themselves. They even show up there. The first fruits. The firstborn. That's in the law of Moses, for pity's sake—old as dirt, first fruits are the acceptable offering. And here you two don't know what you were bargaining away."

"How were we supposed to know that?" Delphine's voice wavered.

"You were supposed to stay away from that damn tree!" Imogene trembled. "I told you not to. I told you why. And you still didn't listen."

She fell silent, out of breath. Alaine had never seen Aunt Imogene angry, but she felt, if it was possible, even worse as a single tear formed in the corner of each of her great-aunt's clouded eyes.

"You didn't tell us everything, did you." Alaine spoke with perfect diction, every word clipped and precise. "There was more. That tree. Something happened here, didn't it?"

Imogene stared at a worn spot on the rug. "I haven't spoken of her in decades. We all agreed we wouldn't. Violet. My oldest sister."

Delphine's brow creased. "I thought Lilabeth—"

"No. Lilabeth was in the middle. Violet, then the boys, then Lilabeth, then me. Violet was much older. She was born afore Ma was married, and the fellow run off without so much as a farewell. Folks didn't say as much about that then, 'round here, as they do now, but we all still knew. Everyone knew. Pa married Ma anyway, was head over heels for her regardless."

"But how—"

"Del, for God's sake, I'm getting there. It was my fault. Well. In a manner of speaking. Ma lost a baby between Lilabeth and me, and was real broke up about it. Violet thought she could help. I don't know what she did, what she said, but she went to that tree, and she made a bargain that Ma could have another one even though Doc Gideon said it weren't possible."

Imogene sighed and closed her eyes. "The day I was born, Violet disappeared. She'd traded herself. Lilabeth told Pa after she was gone that Violet bargained at the tree for another baby. But it was too late—she was gone, and I'm here."

Jack was the first to speak. "Why would she do that? Trade herself, I mean."

Imogene shook her head. She was still staring at the spot on the floor, not looking at any of them. "I can't imagine she knew that's what she was doing. Lilabeth thought maybe she did. That maybe she was tired of the talk, of people saying she was a bastard—but I don't think so. They turn their words, they get the bargain they want."

"That's why you told me about making my own ring," Alaine said quietly. "You thought that was safer."

"I thought so. I realized my mistake, that you started with the ring you made and then kept right on going. That tree is a damned curse."

"It doesn't matter." Alaine's voice was as heavy as lead. "It doesn't matter. Emily is gone. What do we do now?"

"I haven't the faintest idea." Imogene hefted a sigh. "You've made a mess of it, you have. And I don't know how to fix it save haul yourselves into Fae and get her back—and how that's done, I haven't the faintest. My folks didn't know when Violet disappeared, and I sure as hell don't know now."

"I'll go." Alaine snapped to attention at her sister's words. Delphine's voice was thin and strained, but she had a new confidence in her shoulders and the resolute line of her jaw. "I made the bargain, I have to go undo it."

"How?" Alaine caught her arm, the white-hot anger returning, mingling now with the terror of losing her sister as well as her daughter.

"March to the tree and demand it, I suppose. Drive as many pins into the roots as I need to. Bang my fists bloody on the trunk—I don't know."

"That's right, you don't know." Jack ran a hand through disheveled hair. "None of us do, and I don't think we know where to find out. But that friend of yours, Del. The student. Maybe she's got something."

"Ida." Delphine considered this. "I can't tell her. I—oh, God, we can't tell anyone!"

"You're right." Jack pinched his lips together. "We report this, there's an investigation, and what do you imagine they'd suspect? The authorities won't be looking for Fae interference. They're looking for a lost child, or a kidnapping, or a murder. I've seen enough cases in my journals to know that parents are not above suspicion."

Alaine went suddenly lightheaded and sat down on the sofa with a ragged breath.

"Judas priest, Jack, you know how to make a bad situation even uglier," Imogene said.

Jack paced toward the fireplace and stared into its black grate. "And from what you say, Delphine is the only one who can go undo this. She made the bargain, only she can renegotiate. Right?" Alaine nodded silently. "And if there's a murder investigation on, it may well be she won't be allowed on the property."

"He's right," Delphine interrupted Alaine's protests. "He's right. I'll go to Perrysburg and talk to Ida—I don't know how, I'll figure it out. As soon as I can figure out how to get into Fae and what I have to do once I'm there, I'll come back right away." She met Alaine's eyes with determined hope. "And I'll go after Emily."

42

A bit of leather and an antler tip
Makes good on a hunting trip
        —Traditional bargain

DELPHINE HAD HOPED no one would see her as she drove to her neighbors' house—well, she amended, the Abbotts would be her former neighbors, now. Between the rumors that were bound to start when the divorce filings were public and the very real threat of legal investigation into Em's disappearance, she wanted, for perhaps the first time, to be invisible to the fine families of Perrysburg. She didn't want to talk to anyone, see anyone, encounter the slightest curiosity or notice, and to her relief, the Abbotts were out, and only Ida received her in the parlor. After stilted pleasantries and the torture of waiting for tea, Delphine finally found a crack in the conversation that didn't seem too strange a place to wedge her questions.

"I wondered—well, I was curious if that interview with my aunt was helpful at all?"

"Oh, of course! That's been ages ago now. I'm refining this paper to submit it—it might do to plan a follow-up interview at some point."

"Yes, of course," Delphine said, confident that such an interview would never happen. "My niece is doing a school project and had a funny question."

"Oh? What sort of question?" Ida's eyebrows lifted and her back straightened like a retriever upon hearing a gunshot.

"She was wondering if there are any stories about people going into Fae. You see, they're supposed to tell a family story or a story their families tell, and then find one in a book, and you know we tell that silly story about how the family got Orchard Crest—"

"Yes, that your grandfather spoke to a Fae woman. Absolutely fascinating concurrent themes with several stories I've encountered."

"Right, that one. Well, she wondered—if the Fae can visit us, can people visit the Fae?"

"There are of course stories of people stumbling into the Fae realm—you know, the Rip Van Winkle sorts of things. And that story your aunt told. And of course changelings—"

"Of course," Delphine rushed to cut her off before she talked about stolen children anymore. "But she wondered more about going on purpose."

"On purpose. The way the Fae seem to visit humans."

"Right." She paused, mouth dry. The question was foolish, idiotic, even, whether one believed in the Fae or not. She asked anyway. "How does one knock on the door of Fae?"

"Well, that is an idea. I've got reams of research on what varying bargaining cultures do on this side of, ah, shall we refer to it as the veil?" Ida laughed. Delphine's stomach twisted. This was almost a joke for Ida, a rabbit trail of research in an amusing warren of questions she didn't believe had any bearing on reality. "But there are a few I recall." She plucked her glasses from the nest of her hair and scanned her bookshelf.

Delphine fought to sit still as Ida leafed through first one book, then another. Each bore the university stamp on its spine, as did most of the books lining Ida's shelves. Strange, that a seat of learning could stock so many books on something they knew so little about. That professors could pontificate on the commonalities of bargaining rhymes and the differences in fairy ring myths and never know the terror of a missing child.

"Ah, here we are—the Aziza of West Africa are noted as mainly beneficent but timid, and live deep in the forests. Hunters must seek them for—oh, but they never mention actually leaving the mortal realm, only going deep into the forests. Not what we were thinking of, I suppose."

"How do they find them?" Delphine leaned forward, trying not to sound as interested as she was. Perhaps the forest depths were, themselves, Fae.

"They leave an offering and follow— Well, this is confusing. Some sources say that the Aziza leave a trail of hairs to follow, but that seems improbable, likely an error in translation."

"And?"

"Well, that's it. It doesn't say anything beyond that."

Delphine controlled her breath. One disappointment. One dead end.

"Honestly, Delphine, I wish I knew why you looked like you've got a case of dyspepsia. Are you unwell?"

"I'm fine." She pasted on a smile, her best hostess smile, the one that covered headaches and exhaustion and frustration with Pierce's most belligerent colleagues. "It's been a busy week. What with—" Her thoughts reeled, landing always on the truth, the hollow terror of the moment she realized that she'd bargained her niece away. She recovered her smile. "What with the election coming up."

"That's right! My uncle says Pierce stands the best chance of anyone at that seat on the council. Says he's got a good head for navigating the more dangerous ideas rolling about—I suppose he means mostly economic regulation and all that. I haven't the slightest clue, myself. What will he do then, do you think?"

"Pardon?" Delphine's thoughts had run back to the fairy ring when Ida had mentioned Pierce.

"Well, is he planning to continue on in politics? Once he's been on city council, it seems a rational move to consider, oh, a commissioner's seat, or even mayor. Maybe think about state representative."

Delphine's smile faded. "I don't know." Who knew what the end of Pierce's ambition was, after all? It wasn't hers. Soon enough all of Perrysburg would know that.

"I'm sorry, I'm prying." Ida turned back to her books and selected one with a spine emblazoned in smudged gilt, *Adventure Stories of the Otherworld: Collected in the British Isles* by Albert C. Frye. "Well, there is this. An old Irish story—it seems rather silly, but then again, most stories are, when you get down to it."

Delphine's heart increased to a nearly painful staccato as she leaned forward, resisting snatching the book out of Ida's hands. "Yes?"

"It assumes that there's a ring, to begin with."

"That's fairly common—in stories, I mean." Delphine swallowed. "But we can't go through—that is, the stories always have the Fae coming through them to us," she amended swiftly.

"Well, this story—it's part of a longer story, you know how Irish stories are, practically like magazine serials with the ins and outs— anyway, a hero is on some sort of longer quest and he manages to get on the bad side of a local ogre..." Delphine's hopes began to fade again as Ida turned the page. This was just a story, an old amusement for firesides and long evenings, not a story with real magic wrapped in its core like Aunt Imogene's. "He finds a fairy ring, and he knows, of course"—Ida laughed—"that the fairies come through it and he figures, well, why not go the other way?"

"Why not?" Delphine laughed weakly.

"So—this is the interesting part—he draws a door on the rock in the middle of the ring, and he jumps through."

Delphine stared at Ida for a long moment that she realized belatedly was uncomfortably serious for what Ida thought was an after-noon diversion, a silly story for Emily. "Jumps through it," she finally repeated.

"Yes, it's a fascinating story, academically speaking, because typi-cally in these stories any incantation or, well, 'spell' if we want to call them that, involving fairy bargains are spoken, but this is written."

"It's a door."

"Well, it's a door, but—it says in the story pretty precisely what he drew. And here in the footnotes"—Ida handed the book to Delphine, who took it with shaking hands and a smile that tried to cover any reaction save idle curiosity—"there are some sketches of several Irish rings with what might be considered doors on rocks and trees and such."

It was more than a door.

A simple arch, the shape of a cathedral's grand entrance or the gate to a garden. But it was what was inside the arch, which Delphine quickly dismissed as a mere frame, that told her it was a bargain, an agreement. Three rings, interlocking, in a line. They were drawn thick, almost smudged. A note in thin italics beneath the image specified that, in the story, the hero had drawn the doorway with blood from his left thumb, and used a braid of his own hair as a handle.

"Ida?" Delphine whispered.

"Hmm?" Ida looked up from another book. "Sorry, this is fascinating stuff on Chinese legend, but nothing that's helpful, I'm afraid."

"Do you think I could borrow the book?" She swallowed. "For Emily?"

"Oh, sure! It's a library copy, but I've got it on loan for ages yet. She's a good kid, I'm sure she wouldn't lose it."

"Of course! I won't even give it to her, in fact." Delphine gathered her things, the book carefully nestled in her arms. Ida would never know, could never know, the real world hidden inside her dusty books, and Delphine wished she never had to find out. Too late for second guesses or regrets—she would brave Fae and more for her niece. "But I'll show Emily what I've learned."

43

The presence of "everblooming trees" or other seemingly magical phe-
nomona are likely due to the presence of hot springs or, even likelier,
exaggeration.

—*Geographical Oddities of the American Midwest,*
by Gregory Otto Newman

DELPHINE DIDN'T TELL anyone in Perrysburg she was leaving. If she disappeared forever, she considered with frightening
pragmatism, she wondered how long it would take anyone to notice,
who would realize first that she was silently absent. Perhaps someone would file a report that she'd gone missing. If anyone realized
Ida was the last person to talk to her, Ida would detail their discussion with her scholarly detachment, would recall that she was bor-
rowing a book to take to that sweet niece she'd met once, in Moore's
Ferry. And that would be that.

She didn't bother with a message for Pierce, but she did do him
the courtesy of leaving the car at the house so he wouldn't have to
come to Moore's Ferry for it. Technically, he owned it, and she supposed he'd claim it if the worst happened. If the worst happened.
Strange term, Delphine thought as the train jostled to life and the
Perrysburg station fell away behind her. *If the worst happened*, and yet
she had no idea what the worst might be.

She walked from the train station in Moore's Ferry up the broad avenue of Prospect Hill, waving politely back at people she knew, keeping her face obscured by the broad brim of her hat so no one could see how sick and terrified she knew she must look. "I knew something was wrong," they'd say, Delphine imagined. Or "I knew marrying into Perrysburg money was a bad idea." And yet only a few might guess, might have any inkling as to the truth. The old families, the ones with their own paths into the forest.

She forced herself to stop and visit with Mother and Papa Horatio. "You look tired, dear," Mother said. "Alaine told me about—well. That you'd filed the paperwork."

"I knew you'd be disappointed," Delphine said quietly.

"Disappointed!" Papa Horatio snorted. "Ashamed to all hell that a man like that got anywhere near our family."

Delphine's eyes flooded with tears. She blinked them back. She didn't deserve support or pity right now—and both of them would know that soon enough if she couldn't get Em back right away. They'd agreed not to tell Mother and Papa until absolutely necessary.

"No, dear, I'm not upset. Well." Mother sighed. "I'm upset, but not with you. That it came to this. Now, is there anything particular you want me to say, when people ask? I don't want to be unseemly, but—"

"No, Mother. I—you can say it wasn't a good match." She would stop short of spreading rumors about Pierce Grafton that she didn't want to defend in court. "You can say I missed Prospect Hill so much I came home to crawl into it."

Mother laughed lightly, but Papa Horatio looked at her strangely. She finally extricated herself from Mother's questions and made her way to Lavender Cottage as the moon rose over the tangled branches at the edge of the forest. Jack met her at the door with a tighter hug than he'd ever given her before. Alaine waited as Delphine checked a few things in the satchel she carried, and then, wordlessly, they took hands and walked toward the linden tree.

Alaine slowed as they reached the border where the mani-cured orchard gave way to wild bracken. The clouds shifted, and the moonlight drew shadows across the mask of her face. Delphine shivered, even though the night was warm. Bats darted against the pale clouds, and Alaine looked up, watching their rise and fall.

"Are you sure?" Alaine whispered, still looking at the sky.

The clouds shifted again and the stars of the summer triangle emerged. Alaine used to know all the constellations, when they were children. Perhaps she still did, Delphine wondered. Perhaps she could map the seasons on the sky.

"Yes, I'm sure. If this even works. It's only a story from an old book—"

"I think it's going to work," Alaine answered. "That's what I'm afraid of." Her face crumpled and she sat down hard on the moss. "I've lost my daughter. And now I might lose my sister. I—if you don't want to go, Del, I—I don't want you to go, either."

"But you do." Del gathered Alaine's shaking hands in her own. Both of them had cold fingers, and gripping each other's hands didn't warm them.

"But I do." Alaine took a trembling breath. "Oh God, Del. I've never been angrier at anyone in my life. I—I hated you, that moment we knew she was gone. But that was only because I hate myself. I did this. Not you. I did it."

"No. We both did. I—we should have listened to Imogene."

"We! Imogene never even talked to you about all this. It was me. From the beginning. I thought I could outwit them. Every little bargain I made, I thought I was winning. The orchard was thriving, because of me. The Agricultural Society was going so well. I thought it was so important, that I was important, that I'd found a secret I could use for my own gain. Now?" Tears spilled fresh from her eyes. "Now I think that Fae woman was playing a game all along, to lure us to this point."

"Maybe," Delphine said. "Maybe not. Who knows how they think, how they work? Who knows why they want our children to begin with?"

"You're far kinder than I am, worrying about what they want. I want to stab that Fae woman clean through her silver face."

"I'm not worrying about them," Delphine said softly. "If I know what they want, maybe I can understand how to outbargain them. How to give them what they want to get Em back."

"Don't eat their food," Alaine said, almost automatically.

"I know." Delphine had considered how this limited the length of time she could spend wandering Fae, how long she could barter for Em.

"And they don't like salt. They won't even let iron in the ring, but salt, I don't know. And things to bargain with, you should—"

"I have a jar of canning salt in my bag. And some other things." She opened her knitting bag—the largest bag she had short of a suitcase—and showed Alaine the lengths of fabric, the silver, the bones she'd cleaned from the kitchen scrap pile. "I tried to think of the most common things the bargains used. The metals, the fabric— I figured it couldn't hurt."

"That's brilliant thinking, Del." Alaine wiped her face with the back her hand. "Delphine. The book didn't say how to get back from Fae."

"Ida figured it was the same way you get in," Delphine lied smoothly. "Something about the mirror actions of parallel worlds or some academic jargon like that." Delphine closed her knitting bag and stood as tall as she could. "It's time."

"I'm coming with you to the tree," Alaine said, rising to her feet. "It's the least I can do. I—I should come with you, but—"

"But that might violate some bargain or some way of making the deal. It has to be me, by myself. And no. Go home. Go back to Jack and wait. I don't think you should be anywhere near that tree." She paused. "Promise me you won't go near that tree."

Delphine watched Alaine waver between arguing and acquiescing, and breathed a sigh of relief as she landed on agreement. Alaine gathered her sister in a hug, and Delphine bit back tears as Alaine whispered, "Good luck," in her ear. When her sister turned back toward Lavender Cottage, Delphine picked up the path through the woods toward the linden tree.

She'd walked this path hundreds of times as a child, but this was only the second in a year. The first had ended in disaster. And this might end no better.

Delphine had already considered what she would do if the bargain she was offered was to stay behind in Emily's place. She would do it. Without hesitation. When the thought first crossed her mind, moments after realizing that she might be able to enter Fae, she knew in a bright blaze of certainty she would stay if it meant Em could go home to Alaine and Jack. Then, darker, macabre, that staying in Fae forever would mean she could escape the failure of her marriage, shuck all the residual shame. There might even be an investigation. Scandal. A blot on the Grafton good name.

She clamped down on the fantasies that bent toward revenge. What if simply hoping, in Fae, had the power to render reality? What if fairy magic could use her curdled thoughts against her?

There was no way of knowing. And there was the linden tree, its boughs thick with blossoms, and the scent in the air almost dizzying.

Delphine stepped into the ring and strode to the tree, facing it with shoulders back as though it represented all of Fae and she could intimidate it into submission. Yet under the moonlight it looked like an ordinary tree, dim foliage and pale flowers and deeply wrinkled bark shifting in shadow and light as clouds skimmed above it. She pulled the pincushion from her knitting bag, kitted out with silver pins, and drove one into her thumb before she could think about how much it would hurt. Blood welled in a fat droplet, and she drew the three interlocking rings on the trunk of the tree.

She didn't bother drawing a door. That was, she was sure, an affectation, a way of explaining the story. The blood was the bargain. The blood, and the ring of her own hair that she pulled from her bag next. Dark waves, bound tight in a braid and tied with thick cotton thread. She took a deep breath, her thoughts reeling. What did it mean, offering her own hair and blood to the Fae for entrance? What was she selling?

Delphine stopped the stream of questions and clenched the braid in her hand, digging her fingers into her palm. Used the hair as a door handle, the book had said. Well. A handle goes on a door. She arranged the hair carefully in her hand, a perfect circle on her palm, and then slammed it against the rings of blood on the bark of the tree.

The world went slack around her. The tree seemed to blaze in the soft white of its blossoms, the green of the grass rose up to meet her like a cloud, and a faint humming grew louder and louder until it drove into her temples, as piercing and sharp as one of her silver pins. She tasted bile and iron and dank, thick fog. With a choked gasp, she collapsed against the tree, hand still pressing the braid to the blood, fighting for consciousness as blackness washed in waves against her eyes.

44

Ring round, marks the ground
One, two, jump!
Scatter salt, Fae will halt
Three, four, jump!
　　　　—Children's rhyme

DELPHINE'S FINGERS BRUSHED rough bark, and her head
leaned against the same thick trunk. She gripped the solid wood for a
moment, regaining her footing, and blinked her eyes. The heady linden scent soaked into her senses, and her stomach dropped. She was
still here, still next to the linden tree, and the invocation of blood
and hair hadn't worked. She dug her fingertips into the bark, willing
something to change, but the thick scent and the rough bark didn't
move, didn't part in a brilliant flash of magic.

She was so dizzy. She blinked again, eyes grainy and her mouth
thick as though stuffed with cotton wool. She leaned against the
tree, its solid trunk holding her limp torso upright, squeezed her eyes
shut, then forced them open.

A strange landscape stared back at her. Delphine gasped and let
the tree support her weight as she slowly took in the sight of the forest drawn tight around the ring of moss surrounding the linden. The
trees were skeletal and pale as bone, branches gnarled and twining
in complicated knotwork that might have been intentionally woven

or might have been the wild striving of trees reaching for the sky. There were no leaves, but a thick hoarfrost of silver coated every branch, every twig, every barren bud. Bracken grew tangled at the roots of the trees; it, too, was layered in sparkling pale beauty.

The ground was covered in the same thick silver, which Delphine slowly appreciated was not cold at all, but still as fragile and sharp as frost. No grass grew on the ground, only a thick carpet of the same moss surrounding the tree. The silver didn't pass through the circle, fading to a film near the green encircling the linden tree. She stepped toward it, her hand leaving the trunk of the tree with a pang of fear. Could the intricate frost, so clearly magic, harm her? What else lay beyond the safety of the circle? Safety. She breathed a laugh. To think she would ever have thought of a fairy ring as safe. The cloying linden perfume beckoned her to stay, rest. Think.

She blinked and inhaled sharply, forcing herself to take another step forward. Em was out there somewhere, perhaps hidden in that beautiful barren waste. She had to leave whatever semblance of protection the linden and its ring offered her. She swallowed against a dry throat and stepped into the silver.

Nothing happened.

Delphine exhaled relief. There was a thin path through the trees, uneven and often nearly invisible, as though the brambles themselves had held the saplings back from choking it out completely. As there was no other suggestion of which way to go, she picked her way through the undergrowth toward it.

"I saw you come from the tree."

Delphine bit her scream back and turned. The pale voice belonged to an equally pale girl, with wan gray eyes and a faint smile. A girl—no, a Fae. A Fae woman who was, Delphine reminded herself, dangerous. Even if she looked no older than fifteen and seemed as though a strong wind could wrap her around the nearest tree trunk, she was dangerous.

The girl waited. "I will tell you my name if you tell me yours."

Names. "Not quite yet," Delphine said. She knew that much— names always held power in fairy stories. She'd keep hers safe by keeping it to herself.

The girl smiled. "I would not have told you, in any case. You are wise, then. You did not simply stumble into my forest. You know of bargains, yes?"

"I know of bargains."

"Very good! It has been many years—so many years—since someone who knew of bargains came through the circle." The girl glanced at the ring, the moss green almost garish against the pale Fae wood. "Usually they slip through and do naught but fall asleep. And even that—it has been many years. Before my time, even."

"Most of my folk know better."

"Most of mine, as well." She wore a strange cloak, opaque but vaguely iridescent, like the long wing feathers of a bird angled in the sunlight. "And yet. I know of your world. It is a rich place."

Delphine nodded. "You have me at a disadvantage, then. I don't know your world at all."

"Well." The girl smiled faintly. "You know of bargains. Perhaps you wish a guide."

"Do you know your way through these woods?"

"Of course," the girl scoffed.

"And you know...you know the others who live here?"

"The others all live close to the Court."

"I see," Delphine said slowly. This girl lived in the wilds, then, and the Fae woman she sought would be in the Court. Like a city, Delphine wondered, or like a fortress? Like a castle or a maze or a trap? Perhaps all these and more. "Do you know the way to the Court?"

The girl paused. "I know the way. I cannot accompany you within the Court."

"Then to accompany me to the Court, as my guide, and back again. What is your price?"

"That is not the way of it. The earthbound names the price." She was trying, Delphine saw, very hard not to seem too eager, but there was hunger behind her pale eyes, and her hands dug into the edges of her cloak, growing even whiter at their thin knuckles. Delphine looked at the cloak again. It was not of one solid piece, as she had first thought, but fronds overlapping one another sometimes incompletely, leaving gaps when she moved. It was a feather—a feather stretched and remade.

"I will give you a length of wool one yard long." Delphine opened her pack and drew the fine broadcloth from its folds, the scarlet blinding against the winter-pale forest.

The girl's eyes grew wide. "The full ell?"

"Yes." Delphine unfolded the wool. "The whole...ell. The whole length, rather. But you must guide me true. You will ensure my safety on the journey, both from your own kind and...whatever else lives here. If I must rest, you will wait with me. If I must eat or drink, you will not allow me to eat or drink anything that will cause me harm. You will not deceive me or trick me." She paused. "And when I am ready to return to the linden tree, you will show me the way."

"I will be a true guide," the girl said. "The bargain is struck."

"And one more thing."

"The bargain is not struck?" The girl looked almost wounded.

"You will answer all my questions honestly."

"Of course. That as well. The bargain is struck?"

Delphine handed her the length of wool. "The bargain is struck."

The girl gathered the wool in her arms and clutched it like a swaddled baby.

"My first question."

"Yes?" The girl didn't look up from the wool, testing the edge with lithe fingers, running her thumb up and down the grain.

"How do I go back through the door?"

"You are not going now, are you?"

"No. But I wish to know now." Delphine watched her carefully. The girl folded the fabric precisely and then glanced over her shoulder at the tree.

"We can go through just by asking."

"Can I go through by asking?" Delphine rushed to ask.

"I don't know. But I could ask for you."

"For another bargain."

"I did not say that. I will answer all your questions about how to

go back when you wish to return, and if your mortal lips cannot ask correctly, I will ask for you." She stood as imperiously as her skinny knees and elbows allowed her. "I will include this as a part of our bargain, as your guide."

"Very well." Delphine nodded. She seemed honest enough—or at least, willing enough to answer questions. "Show me the way to the Court."

45

One of the most egregious examples of stealing from Old World stories is that of Washington Irving's "Rip Van Winkle," which mirrors precisely the narrative of time-altered disappearance and reemergence of a traveler into Fae.

—*Fairy Lore of Ireland, Scotland, and Wales*, by Alistair Fennimore

IT WAS CLEAR to Delphine within minutes that she would have been hopelessly lost without the Fae girl's lithe figure ahead of her on the path. More than once the bracken spilled its silver filigree across the trail, obscuring it completely, but the girl deftly picked her way through the least snarled corners and rediscovered the path in the worn moss. Then the trail split, and split again, curling off into the forest on either side. The girl did not slow.

But Delphine did, more than once. A riot of transparent blue flowers grew up the side of a tree, reaching its highest branches and sending tendrils of milky blue to nearby trees. A net made of tiny lilac-hued blossoms crawled over the moss, snaking into the patterns of the bark. And overhanging the path, where two branches came close to touching each other, a canopy that looked as though it must have been made of downy feathers, if feathers could be diluted into something like a cloud. It was eerily strange, yet so beautiful.

"Who made this?" she murmured, tracing a blossom of syrup

gold suspended by a streamer from something not unlike a willow tree. "Did you?"

"No one made it," the girl answered. "It is just—this place. It takes what it is given from your world and uses it."

"The whole world—the world does this magic?"

"What is magic?" The girl lifted her finger and beckoned Delphine. She pulled a thread from the red broadcloth. "Where did this come from?"

"It's wool, the fibers from a sheep. It's cut off, and spun, and woven, and—"

"Sheep. Where did 'sheep' come from?"

Delphine paused. "I—I suppose from some wild animal, domesticated many years ago."

"Ah. A wild animal. A creature, begot from—what? Its dam and sire?" She shook her head. "Now that is magic. And your plants—they sprout, from seeds in the ground? That, too, is magic." She tested the thread between her fingers, rolling it—no, Delphine saw with wonder, stretching it. It became thin under her fingers, flat like a ribbon, and lengthened, the color washing from scarlet to pink to palest apple blossom as the single thread became two yards long and the girl wrapped it around the crown of her head, binding her wheat-sheaf hair.

"And that is what we call magic."

"It is but your castoffs, reimagined. Remade." The girl tightened her hair ribbon. "You may not be able to tell, but night nears."

Delphine glanced up. The wan light had grown thinner, gray seeping into it from the edges of the forest. "And we cannot walk all night?"

"We could. You would not tire—at least, not unbearably so. And I would not tire. But it is not wise."

"Not wise?"

"Things roam the woods at night. They will not dare molest Fae, but you are not Fae." The girl nodded toward a copse of trees like straight birches, festooned in gauzy pale pink in their uppermost branches that Delphine realized as she drew closer smelled like rose petals left to dry too long. "You may take your rest here. Have you salt?" Delphine nodded. "Scatter a bit of salt beside you, you will be left alone."

"You knew?" Delphine's hand rested on her satchel.

"I can feel it. It prickles, a little. We all can. Do not believe that you could trick anyone by hiding it. Of course," the girl said with a sly smile, "only a great fool would venture into Fae without."

"What of you?"

"I will keep my distance from your poison salt. Do not scatter it too wide, for it will bleach the earth you scatter it upon, and it will be many of your years before it is purged of the poison." She glanced at Delphine's hand over her bag and shivered. "Ugly stuff."

"Uglier than the things you say roam the forest?"

The girl gave her a true smile. "In truth, yes." She slipped between the trees and disappeared into the silvered bracken.

Delphine was sure she would never sleep, even as she sprinkled salt in a thin ring around her, conserving it more for concern she would run out than concern for minimizing the effect of poison on the Fae world. The silver on the moss nearest the salt shrank back and shriveled. Delphine touched it; it dissolved to dust under her fingertips. She lay with her head resting on her arm and her coat tucked around her. The air wasn't cold; it wasn't warm, either. It didn't feel damp or dry. It wasn't really anything, Delphine thought as she closed her eyes, except breathlessly still. She was not hungry, or thirsty, despite the long walk. And she didn't feel tired at all, though sleep began to beckon. She let herself sink into it.

She woke with a start sometime in the night. It was not nearly as dark as at home, and no stars punctured the haze of gray above her. Instead, a thick gloom hung over the forest as though someone had drawn heavy curtains. The pale world was strange, muffled. And then she knew why she had woken so suddenly. A wail broke through the silence.

Delphine sat bolt upright, her heart pounding in her ears. The sound was close, but no shadows stalked the copse of trees, and she didn't hear footfalls. The sound tore through the forest again, something not entirely unlike a peacock, but a strange lower pitch. Delphine didn't move. The sound was farther away. She felt her breath release, slowly, tentatively. From very far away, other calls joined the first. They bantered with the silence for the rest of the night.

Delphine sat awake until the light lifted. As the gray shifted subtly toward the Fae morning, she stood, the salt around her undisturbed. She had no sooner stepped outside the barren ring she'd made than the girl returned.

"What was that?" Delphine asked, shaking out the crumpled hem of her skirt.

"What was what?"

"Those awful cries. In the night."

"There were many," the girl answered, looking weary and a little sad. "There are many every night. Rushes and timbles and ryls and knooks. All devilish in their own way, getting into rows as soon as the shadows overtake the wood. Come. It's safe to venture again."

Delphine gathered her pack and followed the girl silently for some time, but curiosity overtook caution. "Why do you live here, alone?"

"That is not a proper question for a human woman to ask."

"I am sorry."

"You could not be expected to understand our transgressions or our laws." She paused. "Remember that. In the Court. There are rules to everything. I would be a poor guide not to warn you."

"What sorts of—"

"Everything. To explain would be impossible. But this—every bargain, once made, is bound forever." She met Delphine's eyes, her pale gaze unwavering. Delphine's breath caught. She was not so unlike a human girl in that moment, innocent, vulnerable. Delphine fought the impulse to take her in hand and sweep her home to a hot bath and a warm bed. But there was something wild and distant there, too. Not human. Purely Fae. "That will do you well to remember. We are not so far from the Court now."

"Who is . . . in charge? In the Court?"

"No one," the girl replied, confused. "And everyone. Each is their own master in the Court. The bargains one has made give one status."

"There is no queen? In our stories," Delphine explained, "there is often a fairy queen."

"That is silly earthbound talk," the girl replied. "But also flavored with some truth. For the greatest of the Fae is the Fae who has bargained best. That is the status, conferred by the magic. One might make oneself into a queen by bargains. But it is never permanent. There is always another bargain to be made, always another to take your place." She paused. "And for you? Your business will be with the one you bargained with alone, none other."

Delphine nodded even though she was still confused. An oligarchy of equals, then, each outpacing the others in turn, status undulating with each new bargain.

As they drew nearer to the Court, the path widened and the wood grew less wild, more orderly.

"These were made by Fae," the girl offered suddenly, pointing to a silver cascade of flowers like bells that whispered soprano tones in an invisible wind. "You seemed to want to know which things were made by a someone instead of made by the wilds themselves."

"Yes, I—were they made from things that blew in?"

"No," the girl answered. "These were made from something bargained. I do not know what."

"Have you made many bargains?"

The girl looked at her sharply. "That is also an improper question for a human woman to ask. To ask of making bargains is—it is not seemly."

Delphine flushed. "Rather like asking humans about making babies," she murmured.

"Is that indecent, then?"

"Some would say so," Delphine answered with a wry smile, remembering Aunt Imogene and her shocked mother-in-law.

"Then I will refrain from asking you." She nodded, trying to look wise and perceptive, just like a human girl overhearing things far beyond her comprehension. Just like Emily. Delphine bit back a laugh. "What is it? Did I say something wrong?"

"No, you didn't say anything wrong. You reminded me of someone, that's all."

"I see. The Court is near. That is the Spire," she added, pointing off the path at a spiral of darkest wood, polished like glass, taller than Delphine's fine three-story Perrysburg home.

"What is it?"

"The Spire," the girl replied slowly, as though wondering if this particular human woman was a dullard.

"Yes, but—what *is* it? What does it do?" Delphine gaped at it, the wood twining like cords in a complex braid.

"It marks that the Court is near." The girl cocked her head and watched her for a moment. "You have not told me your name." The girl watched her with large unyielding eyes.

Delphine crossed her arms, as though she could pull her ignorance close and hide it. "I was given to understand that doing so in Fae is unwise. That names have power."

"Names do have power. But only for the Fae themselves. I suppose your own name has its power where you are from, but it is worthless here." Delphine thought of the name Grafton, of its particular power. The name Grafton meant nothing here, was less valuable than dust. She smiled. "You need not trust me with your name if you prefer it thus." The girl cast her luminous eyes back to the Spire.

Delphine hesitated, but the girl had sworn to be honest. No—to answer questions honestly. There might be a trick hidden in that turn of a phrase. "So, knowing my name gains you nothing, and loses me nothing?"

"That is correct. Except, I suppose, knowing you the better. But that sort of binding is not Fae magic."

"I am called Delphine."

"That is pretty. Del. Feen." She nodded as she tested out the sound. "One more thing you should know. There is a law. Old, firm. If you know the name of a Fae, you may gain your bargain in trade for nothing."

"I don't follow."

"You may ask anything you want, within a Fae's ability to give it, and it is yours. The price is waived, because you know the name. Do you understand?" Delphine nodded slowly, appreciating what this

Fae girl was telling her. "One bargain. Only one. It is called the favor, and it is not taken lightly."

"I see," Delphine said.

"Perhaps, perhaps not. For—to have one's name known is a great shame, in the Court, save by those to whom one is bound. It's almost enough to get you banished." She sighed, a wistful sound like wind in unseen rafters. "I cannot go past the Spire. You go on alone, down this path. I—I will wait here." Lest Delphine let herself believe she had made something akin to a friend, the girl added swiftly, "In case there are more bargains we might make."

"I consider our first bargain binding until I return through the tree."

"Of course. But you may require more." She glanced at Delphine's satchel with open longing. "I will wait. Here, near the Spire."

Delphine nodded, a blend of agreement and farewell, and turned back to the widening path.

46

To bring a woman's pains when due
A single egg of perfect blue
—Traditional bargain

THE SNAKING TRAIL through the Fae woods turned into a proper road within a few hundred yards of the Spire, paved in something pale white that seemed smooth but crunched faintly with each step Delphine took. Just as in the wood, all was still, calm, unmoving. When she heard voices and rustling near the road, she strangled back a scream, but it was only a pair of birds, chained to a vine of soft silver with lapis-colored links. They preened and squawked and eyed her with a not entirely inhuman wisdom buried in jet-black eyes.

"Did you...speak?" she asked, but the birds only looked back at her with mild disinterest. One tossed its storm-colored tail, and the other chittered out a sound that matched a woman's distant laugh with uncanny precision. Like parrots, perhaps, Delphine realized, sound mimics. One lifted its foot, each toe tipped with a terrible crystalline claw, and flapped itself to a higher branch.

Faintly rattled, Delphine rounded a curve in the path and found herself at the edge of a clearing, the trees pulling back from a carpet of verdigris grass. They gave up the wildness of the wood here, tamed into symmetrically intertwined branches whose openings revealed more pale paths into the forest. The diffuse light of the forest concentrated here, as though emanating from hidden gas lamps. Delphine toed the boundary of what she now saw was an enormous fairy ring.

A structure of pure white rose from the center of the ring, the beams arching like the bones of a cathedral, the space between filled with delicate filigree of brittle white. Windows like translucent dragonfly wings shone under cornices carved like birds and flowers and trailing vines. A castle, Delphine thought, or a church—all the same emphasis and gravitas translated here, and something stranger and deeper.

At first Delphine saw no Fae, and she regretted not asking more questions of the Fae girl. Then she saw movement behind the irides-cent windows of the pale cathedral. She steeled herself and entered the circle.

The grass seemed to pull back from her, flattening around her feet as she stepped, and the silence of the Court intensified. Faint timbres of bells and birdsong echoed from deeper within the forest, but no one spoke behind the still windows. It was as though they already knew she was here. For the first time since she had tumbled head-long into Fae, she felt deep, cold terror.

There was no door at the entrance, only an open archway of the same delicate white as everything else, embossed with flowering vines and covered in leaves the color of silver and winking with flowers like stained glass. The hush inside seemed to swell until it thrummed against her ears, and then, suddenly, gentle music shattered the silence, a rainstorm finally giving way against an oppressive summer day.

She stepped inside a vestibule with a silver bowl of pure, clear water set on a pedestal made of what Delphine could only assume was a very large, very sturdy zinnia. Was she supposed to wash in it, or was she firmly barred from touching it? She glanced in its shallow depth, and it began to pulse and swirl with pale light. She stepped away quickly. A filmy veil of light separated the interior; she held out a tentative finger, and the light brushed it like organza and separated for her. She stepped through into the Court, sprawling and open to the sky above, yet bound by the pale walls on all sides.

Inside, the Court looked back at her.

Dozens of Fae, gathered in twos and threes, beneath trees of gold and silver and around pools of deep azure blue, inside pavilions made of sheer flower petals and on carpets that must have been woven bird feathers. They all watched her, silently, unmoving. Each was almost painful to look at, beautiful and yet sharp and cold. All of them were arrayed in the spoils of their bargains, with sheer gowns of watercolor silk and robes of pliable silver, elaborate braids adorned with finely wrought metal and tautly bound silk, and even, on a few, wings and horns and talons refashioned from wood and bone and glass. Delphine was terrified of them, and yet also drawn to them. A great and terrible power hummed among them, just below the surface, a nearly tangible potential for change, for creation, for more than anything the world on her own side of the veil could offer.

She shook herself free of the fascination blooming within her and scanned the crowd, looking for the Fae woman. Looking, with a rush of panic, for Emily.

A Fae man with golden eyes shining in his coal-dark countenance rose. "Who do you seek, earthbound woman?" His voice was soft and impeccably polite, and yet it terrified Delphine.

Her mouth had gone dry. She swallowed hard as a woman with faint lilac cheeks interjected from beside the still waters of the reflecting pool, "What is the name of the one you seek? Or do you not know?" Several laughed, cruel detachment and arrogance clear behind their hands.

They were not so different from the Perrysburg wives in her drawing room or gathered on her loggia, bedecked in pastel silk and sniping at the weakest among them with gossip and barbed jokes. Delphine lifted her chin and smoothed her face into the mask she'd worn many times, the mask of Mrs. Grafton. "You know that I do not know her name," she replied, surprised by the strength in her voice. "I seek a woman who has bargained with both my sister and me."

"We bargain with many," the man boasted.

"Not as many as you once did," Delphine retorted, horrified she had been too brash until the uncomfortable hush around her confirmed her guess. "And so you have good reason to deal fairly with me, if you will keep bargaining with us on our side of the veil at all."

"Enough." The voice, like faint bells, like wind in winter treetops. Delphine knew it though she'd only spoken with the Fae woman once. She stood from behind a copse of pale gold beeches with peeling pearlescent bark. Absently, she picked at some of the fallen bark, examining it carefully. Delphine bit her tongue with impatience. "You are bold to seek me here, instead of calling for me."

Delphine had not thought through how she would proceed once she and the Fae woman were in the same place, what she would say, what she would ask for. She hadn't anticipated, at all, the rush of blinding rage and its companion courage that overcame her. "Where is my niece?" she demanded.

The woman regarded her with distant silver eyes. The rest of the Court remained silent, but less malicious than before. No, they were watching with intent attention, the way men betting on horses watch the race. She blinked, and dropped the bark with intentional disinterest. "She is in my dwelling. Would you like to see her?"

Delphine's vision whirled. "Yes, I—of course!" She clamped her mouth shut. Was this a bargain, a trick? Caution, she admonished herself. Caution above all else. "I wish to see that she is safe."

"But of course you would," the woman said, sliding through the pale gold trees and stepping down several steps carved into the slope of the hill. "She is safe, and well."

"I can see her now?"

"I suppose. The hunt is beginning soon, at the crest of the day." She turned to the man with the golden eyes. He inclined his head. "But it will wait for me to return from this errand. Follow me."

47

To prevent visitors (as when there is sicknesse): Set out onions, garlic, or leeks a fair distance from the house. Knock each on the door thrice before using.

—The Compleat Book of Bargaining Works, by A Lady, 1767

ALAINE STARED OUT the window, while Jack paced the floorboards. It was strange, just how little a body could feel at once. It was her back against the settee, yet she didn't feel its hard ridges. It was her face angled into the sunlight, yet she didn't feel its warmth. Her own nails dug into her palm, but she felt neither pain nor pressure. The yawning gulf inside her swallowed all of it.

"You've got to eat something," Imogene pressed. Alaine shook her head, declining for the eighth time or the eightieth, she wasn't sure. The aroma of Aunt Imogene's chicken and noodles wafted from the kitchen, but the familiar scent turned Alaine's stomach.

"It's been three days already," she whispered through cracked lips.

"Time's like as not to run different there, you know that." Imogene sighed and sat next to Alaine with a creak and a wince. "All the old stories have that. Folks gone for weeks, years even. Then pop back in looking same as afore."

"That isn't exactly helpful, Aunt Imogene," Jack said.

"Sorry if the truth ain't palatable," she retorted. "Judas priest, why the two of you concocted such a fool scheme to begin with."

"Not again, Imogene." Alaine's argument had no force behind it, but Imogene didn't press. "They're not coming back at all. We should accept it now, stop fighting—"

"Never." Imogene sat bolt upright, and if her cane had been in reach, Alaine was sure she would have felt its sting—actually felt it, despite the numbness creeping through her. As it was, the fierce admonition stirred something in her.

"I think we've a visitor," Jack said, low. Alaine's heart plummeted right back to despair as she saw who it was—Marvin Trowbridge, driving his old farm cart and plow horse. Trowbridge, the family Emily's new teacher from Chicago boarded with. The floor seemed to drop out from under Alaine.

"What do we say?" Alaine said, pulse thrumming. Fear drove some feeling back into her.

"Well, we can't tell the truth, I suppose," Jack said, squaring his jaw. "I don't like it, lying to Trow—"

"Now, you leave it to me," Imogene said. "I knew him when he was a pup and don't reckon but he's still a mite afraid of me."

"Don't—don't say anything we can't follow through on," Alaine pleaded. "That could make it worse, if—if they don't—"

"But they will. Now, you think I'd spout falsehoods if I doubted that?"

Alaine didn't answer, but she let Imogene push her into Emily's bedroom, and Jack followed. She glanced at the drawn curtain on the window, nodded her satisfaction, and then shot Alaine a look that she recognized as pure warning.

Footsteps in the parlor, then by the front door. The creak as it opened. And Aunt Imogene's voice, impossibly steady. "Hello there, Mr. Trowbridge."

"Awful sorry to trouble you up here, Miss Riley." Marvin had the resonant voice of a church choir baritone and it echoed through the empty front hallway of Lavender Cottage. "Miss Renfew sent me up here. She's Emily's teacher down at the school, you know?" Imogene murmured her assent with patient reserve. "She said they hadn't seen Em this week and thought I should check in. She'd come up herself, but she ain't any good driving the horses, you know."

"They've had some kind of fever up here the past few days. You know how it goes—I suppose we ought to have said something to the school."

"Ah, I see. Well, I'll pass a message to Miss Renfew—unless you'd rather?"

"No, no, you go right on ahead." A long pause. Alaine's pulse quickened in her throat. It was a relief to feel anything, even fear. She almost hoped Trowbridge would see through them, would insist on seeing Emily or searching the place, would find only Alaine and Jack in Emily's room, find her guilt-stricken face, and call the law to haul her away. She deserved it. She had doomed Em as surely as if she had murdered her. A sob caught in her throat. She tried to muffle it, but the tears broke past her defenses.

"Well, thank you, Miss Riley. And you be careful—wouldn't do to get ill, too, you know."

"Me? Oh, I've had all of 'em already." Imogene laughed— How could she manage it? Alaine choked on the sobs that racked her frame, bent her back. Jack laid a hand on her shoulder, but she didn't want comfort. She wanted justice meted out painfully and swiftly, entirely on her.

The front door closed and Imogene's footsteps returned.

"I'm setting out some onions," Imogene announced.

"No more bargains," Alaine said, the thought of even a minor trade with the Fae sending her reeling into panic. "Who knows what it might do?"

"Marvin's buffaloed for now, but what if this takes time? What if someone gets suspicious? That new sheriff they elected last year—he's bored as a tomcat locked in the barn, itching for some real work to do. Who knows what he might do if he finds out Em's really missing? Especially after I heaped a passel of lies on Mr. Trowbridge about her being sick?" Imogene rapped her cane on the baseboards. "I trust your sister to fetch her back, fool as both of you may be. But I want insurance you're not going be in the penitentiary when that happens."

"Onions?" Jack unfolded his arms stiffly, winced, then folded them again. "What about onions?"

"Trade onions for keeping folks out. Set out a perimeter of 'em, and nobody comes sniffing around, curious-like. Won't keep out anyone with a real mind to be here, but it should discourage most idle busy-bodies." Imogene jabbed a thumb at Alaine. "You keep her inside. She's got a look like she'd run to that fairy circle and throw herself in."

Alaine sank back onto the bed. "I should. Maybe they'd take me in trade. Maybe—"

"Fool girl," Imogene said. Frustration melted from her voice, leaving only well-worn affection. "You know they wouldn't. Might take you, too, along with her."

"Isn't that better?" Alaine seized the idea, as wild and frayed at the edges as it was. "If she can't come back, shouldn't I be there, too?"

Imogene sighed. "I can't—I don't know if it works like that, Alaine, you'd like as not—"

"Don't." Jack dropped a single syllable that stopped Imogene's protests and Alaine's racing thoughts at once. "Don't. My child is gone. Maybe forever. Don't take my wife, too."

"But, Jack," Alaine whispered, but he cut her off.

"I can't lose you. I wouldn't survive it, Alaine. Not both of you. God! You want me to stand here quietly and let you rail and rant and I can, I can be strong for you. But you can't lay that on my head and expect me to stand." He slowly unclenched his fists. "Besides. They'd say I did it. They'd say I'd murdered both of you. And then my family, ruined, too, my parents and Esther. Don't you see how this spreads? It stops here."

"I can't go on, Jack. I can't go on without her." Without both of them.

"Yes, you can. People do. All the time. When the diphtheria went through those years ago, you think those mothers didn't grieve and wish themselves dead for a while? You think they still don't feel the loss?"

"This is different, it's my fault—"

"And you don't think plenty of parents say the same? 'It's my

fault'?" His voice rose, only a little, but enough for Alaine to sense the raw pain behind his control. "There's no easy way out. The only way out of this is through. And if we're fortunate, we'll have our daughter and Delphine back. Both of them."

"And if we're not so fortunate?"

"Then we're no different than anyone else!" Jack's voice broke. "You'll have to live with it. Carry it. But God, Alaine. Don't make me carry it all alone."

Imogene edged out of the room as Alaine collapsed into Jack's waiting arms.

48

Some have suggested that the preponderance of trickster stories in folk-
lore ranging from the Norse Loki to the Coyote of the New World may
have in their origins stories of bargains gone awry, though the opposite
may be as likely to be true—that stories of human pride's comeuppance
are a commonplace theme.
> —*Changelings and Gambler's Chances: Tales of Fairy Mischief,*
> by William Fitzgerald

THE PATHS FROM the ring led back into the forest, and Delphine surmised quickly that they were walkways to homes of the Fae who were now occupied at Court. The Fae woman strode in front of her, her pale purple gown billowing behind her. It was soft and gauzy and striped in faint lines; Delphine realized the skirts were violet petals, stretched and draped with Fae magic.

"What do you want with my niece?" Delphine asked, modulating her voice to a low murmur.

"The same we always desire of earthbound." The Fae woman slowed and paused, toying with a single soft pink flower blooming by the path. She stretched it, turned it, flicked it into a cascade of tiny blossoms. "You know more than most human folk, to come here, to make the bargains you make. But have you not surmised why we desire—no, need—human children?"

Delphine went still. "You can't have children of your own."

"No." The woman turned to face her. "We cannot. We can only make them from your children. Once? Once there were many of your children who came to us. Do you know this, too?"

"Why can't you steal them as you once did, then?"

"Steal them?" The woman rose up to her full height, still slighter than Delphine, but imposing in her fierceness. "We never steal anything. Your changeling stories, they are earthbound blasphemy. They were all bargained. We never sent any back in their places. Some of them came willingly of their own accord. Some were given in trade by their families. All our children were bargained for, fairly."

"Except my niece, then."

"Your niece was bargained for fairly." The woman shot her a sharp look. "If you sign a contract in your own world and choose not to read it or do not know what the words mean, you are still bound."

"That is not how I see this bargain."

"It doesn't matter how you see it. It is fair, in the law of the Fae. If it were not so, she would have been rejected by Fae itself. And yet, that has not occurred. Your niece is beginning to become one of us already. She will become more and more so, in time."

Cold fear dashed against Delphine. She had anticipated the difficulty of bargaining Emily back, but what did the Fae woman mean? Becoming one of them—a dark realization seized her. "Then—all of you were once human?"

"Yes. We are not born, we become." She watched Delphine studiously, belying no emotion at the understanding passing between them, that she had once been human. She had been warm and feeling once, with blood and passion and affection once coursing through veins that, as far as Delphine could tell, now pulsed with ice. "This is my dwelling."

A bower bloomed in a crook of the forest path, silvery branches blended together into the walls and roof of a shelter, knit together with swaths of pale white and purple flowers. Where the tree trunks bent and curved, pale glass filled the space, staining the light streaming through them yellow and pink and blue. Cornices of silver wound around the joins of branches. A woven curtain of silk served in place of a door, and the Fae woman held it aside for Delphine. The colors—purple in the same shade as the ribbons she had traded—thinned like paint.

The Fae woman laughed at her recognition. "Thank you for my new doorway. It serves me well."

"The glass," Delphine said. "And the silver. It's from my family."

"Yes." She motioned inside. "Come in."

Delphine had a moment of panic that entering a fairy house was somehow forbidden or dangerous, but decided against caution. After all, she was already in Fae. And Emily was inside.

Emily. She took a breath, the still, thin air of Fae strangely unsatisfying, and stepped past the silk threshold. The interior was hung with silk and carpeted with what she guessed might be feathers, and Emily sat in the center, couched like the most precious gem in a jewel box. She was absorbed with a pile of glittering chips and didn't notice Delphine at first. She built with them like blocks, their edges clinging together as she added leaves to a silver and copper tree.

"Hello there," Delphine whispered, afraid she wouldn't be recognized, afraid of what would happen when she was. Would Emily panic, or cry, or—the fear gripped her—ask her to leave? Had she already become?

But her niece simply looked up and smiled. "Aunt Del! I'm glad you came to visit. Come see my tree?"

Speechless, Delphine sat down beside her. Emily handed her aunt a chip of metal—flattened and stretched, Delphine was sure, from some trade. "It's almost like magic!" She took a chip in her own palm, and touched the edge. It curved, slightly, under Emily's fingers, and slowly she coaxed it in to the shape of a birch leaf. Delphine gaped as Em added thin veins with her fingernail.

"You try!" Em said as she pasted the leaf onto her tree with a swipe of her fingertip.

"I—I don't think I can," Delphine said.

"No, you cannot. Not yet. If you stayed, you could." The Fae woman crossed the room and took a pitcher from a recessed alcove. She poured a delicate sapphire cup of water and knelt beside Emily, handing it to her with a caress of her braids that made Delphine want to smack her away. "That is the way of it." She collected a handful of chips, and then let them spill through her fingers as a brief metallic waterfall. They landed on the carpet in new shapes. "We teach our children with these—they are already made malleable by many years in Fae and many hands remaking them."

"Emily," Delphine said softly, quiet so the Fae woman couldn't hear her. Her niece looked up at her with willing eyes. "We've missed you. At home."

"Home? Oh." Em's brow furrowed. "I didn't think they'd notice yet."

"Notice?"

"That I'd been gone. It's not been long, has it?" She turned back to her tree, smoothing a bit of sculpted bark. Delphine began to try to explain how many days, how long—and realized she didn't know. One night in Fae, but the time felt as though it passed strangely here, thin and yet slow, tumbling unmeasured like a stream over rocks instead of ticking by like the hands on a clock.

The Fae woman met Delphine's eyes over Emily's head. She smiled, faintly, and laid her lithe hand on Emily's shoulder. "I must go with the hunt now, my love. Would you like to come with me and see the hunt?"

"Oh, yes!" She jumped up and clapped her hands.

"If we are very lucky, I shall capture a ryl for you. A little one, one that can be put in the menagerie. Or a baringbird, and it shall learn to sing for you, any song you teach it."

Delphine swallowed against a bitter tightness in her throat. She was being foolish—but she felt the rejection in Emily's excitement keenly. The Fae woman met her eyes again, and she saw victory in the smile. She was *becoming*. She was choosing Fae over family.

But no—what child wouldn't be distracted by the prospect of a fairy hunt, riding alongside the beautiful creatures into an enchanted wood full of magical beasts? That was all this was. Very well. Delphine straightened her shoulders. "I would like to go, too."

"Yes, can Aunt Del come, too?" Emily grabbed her hand, and

Delphine felt a surge of hope as the warm, solid fingers wrapped around hers.

"But of course. You must go on foot, though, not ride."

"I don't imagine that I know how to ride whatever you keep here," Delphine answered, deftly avoiding the fact that she hadn't ridden anything but a farm horse, when she was much younger.

The Fae woman nodded. "Our mounts are lovely things, but nothing like yours. My own mount was a kitten, once." She smiled. "But I shall not ride today, either. We shall all go on foot."

Delphine hid disappointment that she wouldn't have time with Emily alone. Instead she thanked the Fae woman.

The Fae woman turned back to Emily. "Are you hungry, my love? I shall fix something for you." She plucked a handful of cherries from the rafters, growing in the mass of branches tangled overhead. Delphine was suddenly hungry, a strange sensation after the time spent in the forest where she neither hungered nor thirsted. But now, faced with the rosy orbs, she wanted them, wanted to taste the juices, wanted to break thin skin and tear into dark flesh.

She stopped herself. Fae food. She wasn't really hungry, she chided herself, she was only bewitched by the food itself. "Wait, I don't think—"

"It is too late for that," the woman replied smoothly. She handed Emily the fruit and moved next to Delphine, speaking low in her ear. "And it doesn't matter in any case. She was bargained. Partaking of our fruits will not change that."

"And if someone who wasn't bargained ate them?"

The woman waved a hand. Silver glimmered along each finger, limning each fingernail in filigree. "You know from your tales, yes? Time is lost completely, the earthbound world abandoned, the human creature never wishing to leave." She snorted. "Did it ever occur to any of you that perhaps humans who stumble into our lands do not wish to leave in any case?"

"Then the fruit is not enchanted?" Delphine replied. "It certainly seems so."

"It is Fae fruit." The woman shrugged. "Even in your world,

it would be near perfection, though dimmed by your soil and air. Here, it is the ideal, the beautiful. Is that enchantment? Or is the spell only your own desire?" She pulled the silver band from her hair and rewound it, binding her long braid to her head. "It is time. The hunt begins."

49

Though there may be rhymes, there is little reason to what materials are considered acceptable offerings for Fae bargains.
—*A Ribbon, A Ring, A Rhyme: Cohesion of Folk Poetry Tradition,*
doctoral dissertation of Edith L. Showalter

EMILY TRAIPSED AFTER the Fae woman, her steps skipping and light as they walked back toward the Court. She caught Delphine's hand and the Fae woman's in turn, chattering about the flowers and the trees and telling Delphine about her bed in the bower, which she said was made of cobwebs and rose petals. She didn't ask about home once.

As they entered the clearing, the Fae woman strode ahead. Before they could come in sight of the rest of the Fae, Delphine stopped Emily and knelt beside her. "Em, do you—do you miss your mama?"

"Mama? You mean—" Her face clouded. "Do you mean her?" She pointed at the Fae woman's back.

Delphine bit back rising panic. "No, Em, I mean—I mean back home. Your mama. My sister."

"Oh! Oh, yes. Mama. And my chickens and the roses at Grandmother's house." She smiled brightly. "There are roses here, too, but some of them are made of different things. Like silver, or dew."

Delphine rose on shaking legs. "Maybe you can show me some of your favorite flowers here, sometime."

"Yes! I like the purple ones, by my bed. Those are flowers, though, just regular flowers. There are different sorts in the Court. I haven't been inside the Court yet. I'm not ready."

"I see." She took Emily by the hand and they walked toward the Court. "What is it made of, I wonder?"

"Bones." Emily tugged her hand. "See? It's bones."

Delphine fought disgust as she realized that the pale spires and arches and twining filigree walls were a great, transformed skeleton. More than one, probably. "You can make almost anything of bone," Em continued. "It's very ... mally able."

"Malleable," Delphine corrected automatically, even though it didn't matter.

"Some things are ... malleable." Emily tried the word out. "Some aren't. And some are bad."

"Bad?"

"Salt and iron, mostly. I learned that right away. No salt, no iron." Her eyes narrowed. "I wonder—do you know that salt is bad?"

"I know that the Fae folk don't like it," Delphine answered carefully.

"Because I think you have salt with you. I taste it, I think." She pinched up her mouth and sniffed. "Yes. It's sharp and it bites. It's ugly."

"I am allowed," Delphine answered, fighting terror of what it meant that her niece could scent salt. "It is for protection."

"From what?" And there was Em again—all curiosity and innocence.

"There are things in the forest that can hurt you. If you're alone. I had to come here alone."

"That's right. You came from ... where I came from." Her eyes grew distant, and she blinked.

"Do you—do you want to come home with me, Em?"

"Maybe," she said slowly. "I miss Mama tucking me in at night. She sang to me. But—but maybe not until after the hunt?" She looked up at Delphine with excitement flooding her face. "I want to see the hunt."

"Of course." Delphine forced a smile as they rounded the bone castle and gasped at the scene that met them.

Only a dozen or so of the Fae who had been gathered in the Court

when she arrived waited on the green. Most held the reins of creatures so incredible that even Delphine, subsumed with sick fear about Emily, was momentarily transfixed. The Fae man with the golden eyes stood next to a salamander on legs like tree trunks, its ink-black body spotted with brilliant yellow. It opened its maw for a treat from the man, revealing a row of terrifying gilded teeth. A woman with dark blue eyes and a faint blue tinge to her complexion absently stroked the head of a white chicken whose comb bloomed with crystalline roses and whose dark red talons raked the earth. A dark-haired Fae woman with sinewy arms and strong shoulders bare had turned a black-and-white goat into a unicorn by twining its horns into a single ivory-hued spiral, as well as giving it a generous increase in size.

Emily clapped her hands in delight.

"Would you like to pat one, love?" the Fae woman asked, guiding her toward a bronze-furred creature that Delphine slowly appreciated had once been a squirrel, its size now outstripping a large dog. "That one cannot be ridden, but he is as good a scent hound as any earthbound canine."

"Where did they come from?" Delphine gaped.

She didn't expect a reply, but the man with the salamander laughed. "The same place you do. They wander in, rarely. When the door is opened, whether we mean it to be or not. Occasionally, they are bargained. But mostly they are just strays." She opened her mouth to ask how, and he cut her off with an abrupt wave of his hand. "We do not know how it works or why the doors open of their own accord any better than you, and we wish they would not."

"Why, when they become wonders like these?" She reached tentatively toward the squirrel, who butted her hand with his enormous velvet head.

A slight man in a tailored suit of dark pink, the most brilliant color Delphine had yet seen in Fae, slid closer to her to reply. "That is only when we intercept them quickly, and even then, it is long and difficult work. One mistake, and a monster is born. Most creatures we are given in trade, we do not even attempt the taming and take only what we can use easily—bones, feathers. Livers." He unslung a silver bow from his shoulder and tested the string. It thrummed and echoed even after he stopped touching it. "If we do not capture them quickly, they are changed. They meld with one another, and with wild things in the wood, and with the thoughts of the wood, and become chimeras we can never tame."

"And these chimeras, we hunt. Some we trap for the menagerie," the Fae woman added. "And some we can only wound, and the wood takes them back, but they do not stray so close again for a long time."

Delphine was surprised. The girl in the wood had seemed unafraid of the creatures that roamed the wood. "They can harm you?"

"They can. Only rarely do they succeed, for we stay in the Court, and they roam the wilds. But we must drive back the wood, constantly, or it would subsume us, too."

A bronze-antlered woman in a gown made of stretched and overlapped leaves sounded a horn. It ricocheted brightly through the forest, and the mounts pawed at the ground in anticipation.

"The hunt begins," the Fae woman said to Emily. "Stay close to us, my love. Do not wander from the paths." She did not bother with a second look at Delphine as the horn sounded again and the mounted hunters rode for the wood.

The man in pink and several others walked with them, and Delphine surmised quickly that they were tracking, seeking signs of chimeras as they moved deeper into the forest. The squirrel nosed his way ahead of the woman with the hunting horn. Something caught his attention, and he sat upright on his hind legs with a melodic alto squeak. The woman lifted her horn and blew three sharp blasts, then released him with a flick of her hand. He dove into the forest, and the hunt was off.

The mounted hunters surged ahead, and those on foot, save the woman with the antlers, who had taken off at a sprint, could only follow their calls and laughter and the sounds of feet and tails and talons tearing through the forest. The Fae woman pulled Emily ahead.

"You are a pretty maid," the man in deep pink said, standing closer than Delphine preferred. "I thought as much when you came into the Court. If you stayed, you would make a lovely addition to our Court."

"I have no intention to stay. I made my purpose clear."

"Yes, you made your purpose clear. You are on a fool's errand, my dove. No bargain such as *she* has made will be undone." He sighed as though honestly sorry. "But you might stay, too. You might stay with your young kinswoman. Such is allowed."

"Allowed?"

"To come of one's own will. *He* did." The man in pink nodded toward the man with golden eyes and the inky complexion, who had just ridden back into sight on his salamander. "Once, long ago. I was already in the Court when he came and asked to stay. I have no idea how he got in." He laughed and pulled a huge handkerchief from a hidden pocket, the pale pink and soft sheen like a rose petal. "But he learned very quickly, how to ply the magic, how to bargain. Here, one becomes whatever one can. You could learn as quickly."

"I don't want to learn," Delphine answered bluntly.

"Oh! Oh, but you *do*," he said. "I can see that in you. You want *more*. Perhaps you always have, my dove, but it is most certainly why you are here now. You bargained for *more*. Didn't you?" The argument formed before he'd finished speaking; she hadn't pushed the boundaries of bargains the way her sister had. But she had, she acknowledged silently, made her own sorts of bargains, reaching for Perrysburg in pursuit of more.

"Not in the way you might imagine," she replied, curt.

"But you do want more. To see more, make more, do more—be more." He watched her with eyes as clear as glass. "Oh, and there is much to see here. This is not but the vestibule of Fae, what you have seen. There are places where the earth is rent by brooks of azure flame, and places where mountains rise shining like crystal. Night falling on the underside of a ceaseless ocean, stars borne forever on the waves—"

"I don't want to see any of that," Delphine snapped, and the man in pink turned away, miffed. And yet, it wasn't quite true. To paint that nightfall ocean or—she shivered—to paint *with* it, to change and bend the world around her the way the Fae did.

She shook herself. That was no way to think, not when she had

come here for one reason alone. Emily walked ahead with the Fae woman, and Delphine quickened her pace to catch up. The hunt circled and constricted around something thrashing in the bushes, which rattled and twinkled and made a riotous noise like cymbals in turn. Delphine gasped when she saw it, and in horror covered Emily's eyes.

The creature was the size of a large cat, and perhaps, had it fur or whiskers or ears, might have looked like one. Instead, its bare skin was white as wax and pulsed with each breath over jagged ribs and a hollow belly. Scarlet-red mouth and slits where ears should have been punctuated its face, and it screamed shrill and furious.

"Aunt Del!" Emily shoved her aunt's hand from her face with a child's refined indignation. "I want to see, too."

Before Delphine could protest, could explain to her niece that she really didn't want to see the living nightmare pinned to the forest floor with spear tips and tracked by arrows, Emily pushed her way forward.

"What shall we do with it, my love?" The Fae woman slid next to Emily, who had become very thoughtful as she gazed down at the creature. Delphine felt nearly sick looking at it, but Emily was unfazed. "It is a knook, they are not so rare as to be a valuable addition to the menagerie. But we will do as you wish."

"It is an ugly thing. And it does not smell of magic." Emily tilted her head. Her voice was cold, distant. Delphine's heart raced. "It should be blooded."

"Very well," the Fae woman purred. She nodded to the woman with the antlers, who held the spear to the knook's flank. Emily watched, silent and imperious, over the trembling creature. Delphine wanted to shove the Fae woman aside and pull her niece away, but it was too late. Nearly gentle in her movement, the antlered woman drove her spear down into the creature's flesh. The knook emitted a shriek like the grinding of a train engine's wheels.

Delphine's hands flew to her ears, the echoes of the creature's scream vibrating even her teeth. The knook's eyes rolled, independent of each other, like a picture of a chameleon she'd once seen.

She'd thought it was funny. This creature wasn't funny at all; it was a nightmare incarnate. None of the Fae moved. Emily didn't even blink.

The woman pulled her spear from the knook's side. The wound gushed dark red. "It has been blooded."

Emily nodded sagely. "Then it may go."

Delphine watched her niece, dismayed. This was not her Em, who cried when chicks didn't survive hatching, who made valentine cards with doilies and paste for her teacher at school, who asked her mother to take extra cookies to church picnics so if anyone didn't have dessert, they could share. Emily couldn't be cruel to a worm— she moved worms off the path after rainstorms—but she smiled faintly as the knook scrambled into the underbrush, trailing dark blood.

50

To keep a child from straying into Fae: Spin thread with wool soaked in mint or tobacco and tie around the wrist.

—*The Compleat Book of Bargaining Works,*
by A Lady, 1767

NIGHT CAME ON Fae in gentle shadows and slowly dimming light. The hunting party made its way back through the forest paths, laughing and jubilant at their success. One, the man in pink, sang something very like the old ballads Imogene and Papa Horatio sang, the ones she couldn't find written down anywhere when she wanted to play them on piano. He could pitch his voice higher and deeper, in turns, than any human.

Delphine clutched Emily's hand in her own, growing more desperate as Emily bounced from flower to flower along the path, plucking a few and making a pretty little posy like the ones she used to bring home for Alaine. She was still there, the sweet human girl with her childlike wonder and her funny laugh. Delphine had to take her home. If the Fae woman couldn't be bargained with, why not just take her? The path back to the tree was clear, and the girl would be waiting in the woods to help her.

It had to be tonight. The hunting party was jovial and distracted. Emily was still herself, but who knew how long until she changed, *became*? Yes, the woods were full of chimeras, but Delphine had her salt. She slowed Emily's steps beside hers, letting the hunting party spill into the clearing ahead of them.

"Em, sweetheart." She knelt beside her niece. "Do you miss your mama, Em? Do you want to go home and see her?"

Emily's eyes clouded, and her smooth brow wrinkled. It tore into Delphine's gut, seeing the twin furrows appear between Em's eyes, but she had to push forward. She had to make her hurt, make her ache to go home so she would come with her.

"There is still so much here to see," she said.

"Yes, but love—there is more to see in our world, too! We don't really belong here—it's nice to visit, but we—we can't stay, can we?" She didn't let Emily think long on that. "But if we wait too long to go home, I—the door might close, you see?"

"You don't want to stay longer." Emily watched her carefully.

"No, sweetheart, I don't. It's very pretty, but I want to go home. Don't you want to go home?" She hesitated, then pulled the last arrow left in her arsenal. "Your mama and dad might be worried. I'm sure they will be worried before long. What if we can't get back?"

Emily's eyes filled with clarity and a sudden brilliance of tears. "I miss my mama," she whispered. "I want to go home."

"All right." Delphine stood again, gripping Em's hand firmly as she swallowed against the now very real prospect of danger. "Stay close. There is a friend in the woods who will help us."

"They told me not to go in the woods," Em said. She inched closer to Delphine.

"They were right—you shouldn't go alone," Delphine confirmed. "But you're with me, so it's all right. I promise, it's all right," she said, to herself as much as to Em. She picked her way along the tree line, finding the path she had come into the Court on. The wagon-wheel spokes looked similar to one another, but here it was—with the pair of strange birds cooing at each other as they took their roosts for the evening. Their long tail feathers glowed dim gold. Emily watched them with gentle amusement while Delphine pushed back faint horror.

The Spire rose ahead of them, this time a warning that the wilds of the woods were coming rather than a marker of the Court. Leaving,

rather than arriving. Delphine shifted Emily closer to her, an arm wrapped over her shoulder rather than only holding her hand. The bracken beside the path pulsed with shadows, tricks of the faded light, and every one sent Delphine's heart into her throat.

The path narrowed. Surely the Fae girl was nearby—she said she would stay near the Spire. She thought to call her, but they were still so close to the Court. Silence was more important—and speed. Silence and speed. If they didn't have a guide, they could still find the tree. Delphine quickened their pace, and she felt Emily stiffen beside her.

"Why are you afraid, Aunt Del?" she asked in a whisper, as though she'd sensed the need for quiet.

"I don't want to meet one of those knooks," she half lied.

"Maybe we should get the others," Emily said.

"Perhaps you should." A voice like the roaring of a river in flood swept over them. Delphine's heart fell as she turned. The Fae man with the gilded eyes. "It is not safe alone."

"I'm not alone," Emily said defiantly. "I'm with my aunt."

"So you are." He smiled, not entirely kindly. "But now you both must come back with me."

For a moment Delphine considered running. But he was all piercing eyes and broad muscles, and the way he stood in the path, powerful and sure, made her reconsider. They couldn't evade him—not even if they hadn't been in a Fae forest Delphine barely understood.

"Wise girl," he said as Emily filed past him. "Both wise girls," he added as Delphine followed. He caught her arm at the wrist. "Run ahead, youngling. Run and play in the clearing. Nothing will harm you here."

Emily complied happily, and Delphine felt the thickest despair she had known since coming. Em's brief clarity, her homesickness for her mama, forgotten in an instant. She wanted to sit down in the path and sob, but the Fae man's hand was tight on her wrist, and she refused to give him the satisfaction of making her cry.

He slowed their pace and spoke in a low voice. "She is not going to deal honestly with you. Nor will she tell you what she is willing to bargain."

Delphine pulled back. He released her wrist. "And you will?"

He laughed, revealing canine teeth tipped in gold. "If it benefits me."

"Very well." Delphine watched the man's reaction or, rather, his impassive face bereft of emotion. "What is she willing to bargain?"

"Nothing." His mouth curled in amused detachment. "She will not let the girl go."

Delphine swallowed hot anger and pushed herself into the mold she'd made of Mrs. Grafton. She drew herself up, trying to look dispassionate and imperious. "Then I will have to find another option, won't I?"

"Do you know what would have happened, if you had managed to find your way back to the tree?"

"How do you know—I wasn't going to the tree." Delphine flushed.

He laughed. "Where else would you have been going? You might have succeeded if I hadn't stopped you. You must not know the whole of it if you tried to take her to the tree."

"So I tried to take her home. What else do you think I came for?" Anger flared again, and she pressed it back. "I'll try again."

"To your woe, you would succeed. Yes, the girl could go with you. But she will simply be brought back again, and again."

Delphine stopped, her stomach clenching, imagining the mistake she had almost made. Emily, stolen again. Alaine, reunited and then grieving her daughter all over again. She shuddered. "Then there is nothing I can do."

"But I have just told you that you can, though you may not wish to. You can take her, again and again if you must." He shrugged, sinews of muscle propelling even that simple action.

"That does not help me."

"You are quite sure? Imagine the frustration of coming to fetch her, time and again. It is not—how would you understand it?—free to cross the veil, to carry things over. Especially living things." He flicked a leaf from an overhanging branch. "Perhaps she would tire of the game. Perhaps she would soften herself to your offers."

"And if she didn't?" Delphine watched as Emily chased a silver dragonfly down the path and into the clearing. "What would happen to my niece?"

The man's jaw strained and then softened. "Most of them go mad, eventually, coming and going too often. They doubt what is real, and the forest claims them."

Delphine's breath left her all at once, appalled by the casual cruelty of the man's dismissal. "That would matter very much to me."

"But it would matter to her, as well."

They emerged into the Court clearing. The hunting party lounged in a circle of violets newly bloomed around them. His cool gaze fell on the Fae woman, fingers working through her long plait of pale hair.

"You could be lying to me."

"So very trusting, human creatures are!" He laughed again. That sound, rich and resonant, was beginning to grate on Delphine. "Yes, I could be. Test me if you would like. Take her back through the wood, pull her through the veil, watch as she disappears again. Then you'll know truly I did not lie."

Delphine felt as though knowledge was a cage, closing in around her. "What happens to her—to her mind? If the bargain is undone, and she comes back with me for good?"

"It will not be undone." He raised his dark eyebrow. "But. If a bargain is undone, and one is taken back to your side of the veil, one will forget this place. In time."

"How long?"

"I cannot say, I have never done it." He flashed the cruel gilded smile again. "The longer she is here, the longer it will take. They say the ones who return keep this place as dreams and fancies. That they are your artists and your poets. But they say, too, that those who tarry too long here cannot lose this place completely. That they are driven mad by its absence," he said with deft detachment and a sweep of his powerful hand.

"How long?"

"What?"

"How long would a person have? Before they've been in Fae too long?"

"I haven't any idea." He watched the hunting party laugh over some jest the man in pink had made. He didn't meet her eyes, and she wondered if he was truly ignorant on that point, or choosing not to answer.

Delphine decided not to dwell on the question of how long she had before Emily went mad. It couldn't—or wouldn't—be answered now, and it didn't change her plans. She would get Emily home as quickly as possible. Her niece ran toward the gathering of Fae, who welcomed her with languid amusement. Impulsively, Delphine cut the Fae man off and stood in front of him. "Why does she want a child, anyway?"

"We all do, at some time or another." He glanced at the Fae woman, who tilted her bow toward the sky and plucked the string for Emily. It sang out a clear tone like a harp. "But she, more than others. Her first daughter was banished."

"I—how sad." Silently, she planned her questions even as she smoothed a dull mask over her thoughts. "What does that mean, banished?"

He raised a dismissive brow. "Do you not have the word in the earthbound vocabulary? Cast out, sent away. Not allowed to return. One who is banished from Court must live in the wood, alone or with others who are cast out."

"I see. That is—that is a loss, then, as losing a child is?" She measured her words carefully, but her thoughts raced.

"Yes, but you miss my point. We make our rank here. For one's daughter to be banished?" He smirked. "She spent years regaining her status."

Delphine sensed a rivalry, deep and old. She had begun to see the way the Fae deferred to one another, or asserted themselves. The man in pink—he gave way on the path to the woman with the unicorn. And the woman with the burnished antlers—she had waited for Emily's word at the request of the Fae woman. This Fae man had seemed closest to her equal, facing her in the Court. And now she knew, a little, why he might be giving her loose pieces of information, bits and bobs of knowledge that could be ammunition in a war of wits. He wanted to see the Fae woman fail again.

"It must not be so uncommon," she said carefully, "to be banished?"

"Terribly uncommon. And it takes many years to return. There is only one in the wilds from *our* Court," he said, with a boasting tone that made her wonder what gossip raged between Courts. The girl in the wood, then—she must be the Fae woman's adopted daughter.

"I see." Delphine wrinkled her brow in mock confusion and asked a question she knew was an easy barb. "And you don't want her to regain her status?"

"My wishes are my own," he replied sharply. "But you should know. She may toy with you, but she will not let that girl go."

Delphine nodded as though simply accepting this information. She remembered the Fae girl in the woods and her unwillingness to explain herself, and asked with feigned innocence, "What did her daughter do?"

"Ah, a good question." The gold smile flashed again, a face as dark as night briefly illuminated. "And well asked, for *she* would not tell you. The girl made a poor bargain. A very poor bargain. We cannot make unequal bargains. They are a bad precedent. Once made, the precedent stands, for any other. And this girl, this little fool? A wretched bargain, indeed. One that granted rich land and heavy harvests, that gave generations of prosperity for the cost of a scrap of fabric."

Delphine fell silent as her eyes went wide. A scrap of fabric for land. She remembered herself, pulled the mask of Mrs. Grafton back on firmly, but the gilded Fae man hadn't noticed her.

"She was not even supposed to be on the other side of the veil. None but those esteemed by the Court may venture thus." He shrugged. "Ah, well. You have time to learn, do you not?"

"Hardly." Delphine met the man's gilded stare boldly. "We both know what I am here for and what I want."

The Fae man shook his head, a curious fascination blooming in his gold eyes.

51

Fae knows not name or face
Only blood may Fae folk trace.
                              —Folk saying

ALAINE HOVERED ON a precipice, moment by moment, between feeling she could go on just a little longer and collapsing in on herself, giving up completely. All the long week since Delphine had gone into Fae she had balanced the minutes against hope—how long until they would be back? How many hours was her daughter alone, afraid, a captive to that cruel Fae woman? How long would Delphine wander whatever strange world the Fae inhabited, searching? She imagined her sister lost, cold, and hungry, and clamped down on her thoughts before they bore her into utter despondency.

By the time a week had passed, she could no longer ignore the work waiting for her. The first waves of the apple harvest were well underway, and they could only pretend to be ill for so long before someone grew suspicious. She kept everyone far from the house, and directed Art Klinker and the Benning sisters to take charge of the other hired workers. She drove Bruno and Barnaby silently through the fields, hoping everyone would take her haunted expression for worry over the daughter she said was still sick in bed.

The lies had been said, the stories invented, and a short reprieve assured from curiosity on this side of the veil. The school had been told that Emily was slowly recovering but would not return anytime soon. Imogene had taken the worst upon herself and told Mother and Papa Horatio the truth. Either she had told them to leave Jack and Alaine alone, or they were too disgusted with Alaine to come down to Lavender Cottage.

Alaine assumed the latter, given that she was thoroughly disgusted with herself. Every warning in every story and every rhyme and every lecture Lilabeth had ever doled out, and she still had run headlong into believing she was better, smarter, more capable. She wasn't. She accepted this now, that the shrewd bargaining she gave herself credit for was as likely as not the Fae woman maneuvering her ever deeper into a trap. She hadn't been in control at all. All her success, all her pride—it was nothing.

She found that caring for the Percherons was the only task she didn't dread, their stoic stance and patient eyes saying nothing as she sobbed through their grooming. She couldn't wait for the cold to overtake her completely and choke out that hope until it didn't revive itself. She had to do something. She had promised Jack, and Imogene, and herself—no more bargains. Anything she tried to trade or do might counteract what Delphine was doing—God, what was taking Delphine so long! Still—wasn't there something? Anything?

As she left the barn, eyes red and smarting and bones as weary as dust, she spied the green velvet of the ring in her yard. As summer had faded, carrying the color of the rest of the grass and leaves with it, the ring had remained brilliant green. To her despair. To her hope.

Whatever she had made, it was permanent. She stepped tentatively toward it, wondering. Was it a ring like the linden? Could she call a bargain here? She was ready to call a truce with the winter-pale Fae woman and offer anything, everything, for her daughter and sister. The farm, the Percherons, herself. Anything.

She stepped into the ring for the first time since last year, when she had broken a mirror and cut her hand, and a strange buzzing filled her ears. She blinked—the sun seemed brighter, heavier. She forced herself to look down, away from the sun's painful brilliance, and nearly fainted. The grass under her feet faded, and an undulating pool like shimmering glass appeared instead. She sank to her knees, disoriented and shocked. Beneath her, through the glass, she made out trees and shivering plants. Purple and silver—she had seen this before. Last year, in her mirror. The same filigree vines, the same silver tree, the same purple blossoms.

She could see into Fae.

Alaine's heart raced. She pressed her hands against the ground, willing the mirror to part, to let her fall through like Alice tumbling into Wonderland, but it didn't yield. She hit the glass, and it rippled but didn't crack or break. She clenched her fists and beat them against the glass, accomplishing nothing except bloodying her knuckles when they glanced off the glass and scraped rock. She pulled back, forcing herself to think.

Of course it wouldn't break. It wasn't real, not like a proper window. She'd sowed the broken pieces of her mirror here, and this magic grew in its place, like a scrying glass from a fairy tale, like Snow White. Maybe it would work like that mirror—she slowly sat back on her heels and found her voice.

"Show me Emily," she said in a hoarse whisper. Then, louder, "Show me my daughter!"

The mirror didn't change. Alaine's heart sank, the baseless hope she'd felt flare in her chest fading quickly. "Please. Show her to me. I want to see her. I want to see that she's safe." Her bloodied fingers brushed the glass, leaving a smear on the surface.

The mirror flared under her hand. She leaned forward as it shivered and shifted, and the scene washed away, replaced with another. An open field of perfectly green grass, with a purple-and-white carpet—no, violets. Violet blooming thick in a circle, and in that circle, Fae. They could only be Fae. They glinted with a strange gleam in the mirror, as though partly made of stars or crystals, just beneath their skin. She didn't care about them, didn't linger on their perfect features or their impossible clothing, because she saw what she was looking for, in their midst.

Emily.

She was plucking the hunting bow held by one of them—the

Fae woman, Alaine realized, the same woman she had bargained with. The Fae woman's smile glinted silver as Emily laughed—oh, God. Alaine could hear it through the silence of the glass in her own memory. She looked well, she admitted. She wasn't lost, hungry, or cold. Instead, it looked as though she was at a party, celebrating a holiday. Her clothes were crisp and clean, the white nightgown she'd been wearing refashioned into a fanciful party dress festooned with blue ribbons. The Fae woman fussed with Em's braids, weaving a bit of silver into them. No, Emily wasn't being mistreated.

Whatever this was, it was somehow worse.

At that moment, another figure entered the violet circle. The drab skirt and shirtwaist were strange among the riot of color, but her sister's bearing and confidence weren't out of place at all. Delphine. She asserted herself next to Emily, and relief flooded Alaine as Emily's attention shifted to her sister, caught her hand, pulled her toward something outside the ring.

Del was with Emily. Del would save her, she had to believe that. She would find a way to bring Emily back, and until then, Emily had her aunt to keep her safe. She let her hand rest on the mirror, fingers framing her daughter and sister as though she could hold them close.

"What are you doing?" Jack. His voice sounded faraway and faint, but when she glanced up, he was at the edge of the ring.

"Jack! They're here!"

"Alaine, what are you talking about? Get out of there, it's—"

"No, come see! I can see Emily, Jack! Del is with her, they're safe, they're—" Jack was beside her before she could say another word, kneeling next to her, breath hitching. "See! Del is with her, there are others, but she's taking care of Emily—oh, they're leaving the others now, good!"

"Alaine." Jack's voice was a strangled whisper. "Alaine, there's nothing there."

"Jack, can't you see it? Can't you see Emily? It's a magic mirror, I must have made it last year, with my old mirror that broke, I—" She looked up at Jack. His face was contorted into a mask deliberately devoid of expression. "You can't see it?"

"You've had a hard time of it, Alaine. You're—you're not yourself. Come on out now, and we'll go to bed."

"No! Jack, I'm not going anywhere. I can see Emily. I see her right now—she's talking with Delphine— Oh God, Jack." Her eyes spilled tears down her cheeks. "Her dimple, and her freckles. I thought I'd never see them again."

"Alaine, please." His voice cracked. "I can't leave you out here all night."

"You really can't see." She whispered the words, realizing she must sound like a madwoman, ranting over unseen worlds. "It must be because it was my blood, with the mirror." She looked up at Jack. "Maybe if you bled on the mirror, you could see, too. But maybe not—I buried blood with the mirror pieces last year."

"There is no mirror. It's just grass, Alaine."

She traced Emily's image in the mirror, one more time. "No, Jack. It's hope."

52

Come now while the fairies play
The moon, she shines as bright as day
Come with a song and come with a call
Come to stay or not at all

> —Children's rhyme

EMILY SLEPT SOUNDLY in the Fae woman's bower, a canopy of blossoms draped over the bed of moss. Delphine inhaled, steeled herself. She had to try to negotiate with the Fae woman once more. She could see no other way forward—if the gilded man was right, there was no way she could simply take Emily away. She had thought of other things, other bargains. None were pleasant. But they had to be tried.

Delphine covered Emily, fussing over the blankets, though her niece didn't need them for warmth. Her face was softened in sleep, and she could almost forget Emily wasn't in her bed at home with one of Grandma Lilabeth's quilts tucked around her, she looked so peaceful.

"You are not enjoying the fine things the Court has to offer." The Fae woman stood in the doorway, its shimmering arch framing her like a warped stained glass window of a saint. "There is song and merriment there now."

"I have come for her." Delphine stood squarely in front of the Fae woman. "I'm not here for your distractions."

"I will not bargain." A thin smile played around the Fae woman's lips, steeped in confidence. Delphine knew she was little more than one of the knooks or baringbirds that flitted too close to the Court, a petty annoyance to the Fae woman.

Delphine pressed on anyway. "There must be something I could give."

"You could give even yourself in trade for her, and I would not accept." The Fae woman barely blinked as she spoke, and Delphine tried to match her rigid resolve. "There is nothing you can offer me that replaces a child."

"I could take her. I know the way back to the linden. I marked it in my memory so I could take her."

The Fae woman whirled on her. "She would be back in my arms before the next sunset of your world." But there was fear in her voice, a tremor Delphine wouldn't have noticed if she hadn't already heard so much of her perfectly silvered speech. So it was true, what the gilded man had told her. Taking Emily could harm her. And in a bizarre and yet comforting twist for Delphine's negotiations, neither of them wanted Emily to come to harm. She met Delphine's eyes, calmly unflinching. "I will not let her go."

Delphine decided to test the Fae woman. "Especially as your first child was banished."

The Fae woman's nostrils flared, and her silver-filigreed nails bit into her skirts. The confidence of the thin smile cracked. "What do you know of such loss? Arrogant earthbound creature."

"I know a little of loss," Delphine answered. "My sister knows more, knows the loss of a child. You would inflict that on another?"

She exhaled, regaining control and holding deathly still. "I inflict nothing. You made the bargain."

"But now you know its price, too. I am telling you its price. A sobbing mother, a grieving father. You'd keep the bargain?"

"They can have another." She leaned forward, the intensity of a cat who has a mouse cornered. "It seems pitifully easy for most of you. Why, you bargain with me every pass of the moon to ensure it won't come upon you. If children are so dear to the earthbound, why do this?"

Rowenna Miller

Delphine remembered, in a flash, Pierce's iron grip on her arm, his hand leaving marks on her face. "You couldn't understand."

"So I do not understand you and your kind. Just as you do not understand me and mine. The child is mine now. She stays."

Delphine steeled herself, and then said the words she dreaded, in a rush. "What if I found you another?" Wild thoughts coursed Delphine's mind, orphans and the boys who worked at the glassworks, schemes of dubious legality and certain immorality. "Another child. A girl, if you want. Or a boy. Two. I could bring you two children for her, I—"

"You can do none of those things." The Fae woman waved her away with a flick of her filigreed fingernail, then she looked again at Delphine and saw, perhaps, the fierce recklessness that Delphine felt. She raised an eyebrow. "Or, perhaps you can. It matters little. I am uninterested. You remember—we named the child in the bargain."

"We did not *name* her," Delphine insisted.

"We named her. She is the first fruits. Your family had claim on her, on her guardianship. You name no child in this bargain you propose, for you have no claim on any child." She shook her head, pale hair shaking free of a binding of glass-beaded net. "I will not yield. You can stay, or you may go home. Consider which your sister would grieve more," she added, ice in her voice.

The sentence was intended to wound, and it did. Delphine bit back tears. Perhaps her sister would prefer that she disappear. She had caused this—she had made the wretched bargain. But before, it was her marriage to Pierce that forced the issue of bargaining in the first place. Her selfish wanting, as the Fae man in pink had discerned with painful precision, *more*.

That was all bargaining was, a bid for more. A gamble that magic could yield what laws and work and plain luck could not. She gathered a ragged breath and pushed that plain luck further than she was sure it would hold. "You just said—we had a claim to Emily. To her *guardianship*. She didn't belong to my sister, not like an object or like livestock. Humans can never belong to one another that way—"

"Your history begs to differ."

"But it's wrong to do so. And—" She stopped, watched the shifting expressions in the Fae woman's face. "Emily doesn't *belong* to you, either."

"She belongs to me as much as a child belongs to her mother on your side of the veil."

"Not entirely." Delphine licked dry lips. "You mistake our laws if you think so. The child belongs to herself, and you are her sole custodian." The Fae woman trembled slightly, and then smoothed her countenance. "I explain it correctly?"

"Yes. But your children—they are bound to earth and flesh as surely as you are. She is bound to Fae."

"Let me see if I understand. My niece belongs to herself, as an individual free person, but is bound to Fae by the bargain you struck with me. And you have claim on her guardianship, per that bargain."

"As the negotiator of the bargain, I claim guardianship," the Fae woman replied smoothly.

Delphine chose the next question carefully. "So another could claim guardianship?"

"You cannot challenge my guardianship," the Fae woman replied, "for you are not of Fae. You are bound to earth."

But perhaps another could. What would the process be? And would another, once granted the custodianship, give it up freely? Delphine decided to press it, to see how the Fae woman would react. "But a Fae could."

"No one would dare!" The Fae woman lunged forward. She stopped short of striking Delphine, who stood straight and unmoving, heart echoing in her ears. "No one," she repeated in a malicious whisper, "would dare challenge me. That is—you do not understand what you are suggesting. The kinds of power at play."

"I think I understand power," Delphine said quietly. "And I think I know what it takes to challenge it." She remembered the crowd of women in the auditorium pulsing with the energy of change. "It doesn't take a guarantee you'll win. It takes a conviction you have to try."

The Fae woman didn't react, but Delphine hadn't entirely expected her to. She was thinking about something else—her position, her status, and who might be angling to challenge it. Delphine knew better than to press further. She knew that fear—a kind of fear only the powerful have, at seeing the order they had meticulously, perhaps cruelly, built threatened by a stray idea, a new voice, someone who wasn't willing to stay conveniently silent. She had watched it gnaw at the Graftons and their ilk, watched how they'd reacted in fear veiled in scorn at the activists like Louise Marks, at the academics like Ida, even at her sister, daring to share her opinion at dinner with the Abbotts. She saw it working its claws into the Fae woman now.

She turned and left the Fae woman quietly fuming in her bower built from the bargained scraps of Prospect Hill. The woods were all shadow now, but she turned down the path anyway, toward the Court. She had salt in her pocket and desperation wound into every nerve.

53

Many local tall tales relate doorways or "thin veils" through which locals have seen fairyland. Most can be accounted for with the phenomenon of heat hazes or other such common mirages.

—Geographical Oddities of the American Midwest,
by Gregory Otto Newman

ALAINE WAITED UNTIL Jack turned down the long lane away from Lavender Cottage, then was out the door in a flash, just as she had done every day since discovering her scrying glass. She often had only an hour alone, between Jack's hours at the office and Aunt Imogene coming to check in, and she wouldn't waste it. Sometimes Emily was sleeping, other times she was playing by herself in a wide green lawn, and once she and Delphine had been walking together—but Alaine had discerned that time, as Aunt Imogene had insisted, must run differently in Fae. She was comforted, at least to some degree, to confirm this. The days that passed on her side of the veil might be minutes in Fae; Delphine hadn't been gone over a week but, perhaps, days or even hours. She knelt in the brilliant green as it dissolved into clear glass beneath her and drove a pin into her thumb. A drop of blood fell into the center of the ring.

"Emily," she whispered.

The mirror shivered under her touch, as though it was growing to know her, to learn to obey her quickly. It settled on Emily's face, in

firm concentration. Alaine hiccupped a smile—she knew that look. It was Emily at her arithmetic, or Emily cutting out paper dolls. But Emily wasn't wielding scissors or pencil. She held something in her hand, smooth pebbles—no, Alaine looked closer. Metal. Little disks of various metals.

Emily picked one and pressed it into her palm. To Alaine's amazement, it flattened under her hand, spreading until it nearly covered the tips of her fingers. Emily curled the edges, twisting the metal as though it were taffy. She set it down and did the same with another, gathering a pile of what Alaine slowly realized were flower petals. She fashioned them into a wobbly rose, turning the flower she'd made in her hand, admiring it. Then she began to disassemble it.

Someone knelt beside Emily—not Delphine, Alaine saw quickly, the diaphanous robes of the Fae woman pooling pale around her feet. She regarded the new flower Emily was crafting from the metal pieces with approval. Disgust hitched in Alaine's throat—this Fae creature coddling her daughter, encouraging her, teaching her—

Magic.

Alaine's breath arrested in her chest. Emily was doing magic, crafting pieces of metal into new shapes, manipulating the material in a way no one should have been able to do with hands alone. What did that mean? What did it mean that her daughter could do magic, could wield whatever strange power inhabited Fae?

"No," Alaine whispered, for she had just seen it.

A faint shimmer beneath Emily's skin, mimicking the brilliant gleam she saw in the Fae woman next to her. Fae magic, or essence, or whatever it was, imbuing her daughter with its poisonous glamour. She clutched the smooth surface of the mirror. "No, no! Emily, don't!"

"Alaine."

This time, Alaine didn't wait for Jack to come to the circle, to come inside and confirm he couldn't see anything. She looked up. "I will tell you what I see, if you promise to stay calm this time."

"This isn't the time to stay calm." Jack half ran across the lawn, hesitant as he reached her, as though she might lash out or collapse into gibbering nonsense. "You're talking about things that aren't there."

"When have I ever lied to you about fairy bargains? And Fae magic?" Alaine sat back on her heels, leaving one hand firmly planted next to the image of her daughter. "This is important, Jack. I can see Emily."

"I don't know if I want to believe you or not." He held out a hand to her. Reluctantly, she took it and let him pull her from the ring. "If you are seeing things that aren't there, that's certainly a problem. But even if this is real—what good does it do you to keep seeing Emily? You'll drive yourself mad that way."

"No, I won't. I've got something I can do, some thread I can hold on to." She gripped Jack's arm. "I can at least keep an eye on what's happening. Please believe me."

The strained look he gave her told her he didn't. "I think you should go inside and rest. No—even better, let's go up to Orchard Crest."

Alaine didn't want to see Mother or Papa Horatio, but she conceded to being herded down the lane. "I suppose you're not too concerned that I need rest, with a pace like that," she said. "Why did you come back home, anyway?"

"Forgot some papers." Jack kept his eyes trained forward.

When they reached the broad porch of Orchard Crest, Jack maneuvered her into the parlor while he caught Mother's arm and whispered in low tones with her and Papa Horatio in the hallway. She heaved a sigh. They'd set him straight, certainly.

Instead, Mother came stiffly into the parlor while Papa Horatio went back out with Jack. "Now don't argue," she said quietly to Alaine. "We all think it's best if that patch of grass is torn up."

"Mother!" Alaine bolted out of her chair. "No—I know Jack doesn't believe me, but you must know it's possible. After all this time on Prospect Hill."

"I've never heard the like of it, but what's more, I've never seen Jack worried like that, not about you." Mother laid her hand on Alaine's, and though Alaine wanted to, she didn't pull back. "And what good does it do?"

"What good?" Alaine shook her head. "Mother, if I were gone, whisked away to another place, wouldn't you want to be able to see me? To know I was all right? To know if I wasn't, even?"

"I suppose, but this isn't like that, it's—"

"It's exactly like that. I can see Emily. I know no one else can, but I can. And Del, too. And oh, God, Mother, it gives me some hope. Something to hold on to." And something to fear, too, the Fae shimmer beginning to take hold of Emily. But even that particular horror, even if she couldn't stop it—she wanted to know. She craved it.

A shadow of doubt crossed Mother's face. "They won't be convinced otherwise, Alaine. It's for the best. Tampering with Fae magic like this—" She inhaled sharply, and her face hardened. "It's not wise. We know that. We knew that. Lilabeth—"

"I know," Alaine whispered, miserable. "Lilabeth taught me better. I know."

She wanted to argue her case, but there wasn't anything left to stand on. Either she was mad, or she was meddling with unknown Fae magic, and either way, her family would keep her from it to protect her. Alaine knew she wasn't mad, because she could see their logic clearly. In their shoes, she would have done the same thing.

But they didn't understand. Sit and wait—she couldn't. It was her deepest and worst fear, to be useless, to be unable to do something, anything. Handing the task over to Delphine was the hardest thing she had ever done. The mirror let her lie to herself, a sweet lie that kept her from going mad—that she wasn't completely helpless.

It was late in the day when Jack took her home, past a muddy patch where the fairy ring had been, verdant green blotted out.

"Did you dig up the mirror pieces?" Alaine asked quietly.

"Mirror pieces? No, I didn't see any."

"Oh." The Fae must have taken them, Alaine thought, then a slender stalk of hope began to grow. If the Fae had taken the mirror pieces in exchange for creating the scrying glass, maybe it didn't matter if the fairy ring stayed green and blooming or not. It wasn't a fairy circle anymore. It had been made into something else

After Jack left the next day, she tiptoed carefully through the sod to the center of the ring. The familiar faint buzzing, the brilliance of the sky weighing down on her—and at her feet, the mirror opened. She pricked her finger and whispered her command. "Emily."

54

Set the table, china fine
Acorn cup and dewdrop wine
Crumbs of cake, berries wild
High tea for Fae beguiled
　　　　—Children's rhyme

THE ARCHES OF bone stretched over her, and Delphine felt small and dull, a sparrow set among parrots as she moved among the Fae. She had to observe them, learn how they jostled for power, and quickly— it might be the only way to get Emily home.

They gathered in the center of the Court as evening deepened the gloom of the forest. Tables covered with Fae delicacies rose from the moss itself and parted the waters of the brook. Delphine had not imagined that temptation could wield such strength. There was no hunger, only desire; she had not felt hunger, or thirst, or any other mundane discomfort since she crossed through the linden. But the fruits and breads and crystalline ices and even those things far stranger—clouds encapsulated by thin leaves, braided blossoms that shimmered with uncanny glaze, lacework wafers like the finest marzipan—all of it beckoned her, begged her to taste, to try. Their scents were faint but heady, rosewater and citrus and pungent herbs and the air after the rain. They promised more—savor, yes, but deeper, thicker draughts of pleasure, joy, knowledge.

She shuddered as she pulled back, realizing too late that someone stood behind her. With a light laugh, the antlered woman made space for her. Her leaf-gown was replaced with an organza-like cascade bound at her waist and undulating at her feet. "Are you lost, doeling?" Her voice was low and honey sweet.

"No, I—" Delphine squared her shoulders, pretending, as if it might help, that she was wearing the new evening gown that hung in her closet at home, sapphire silk to stand against Fae artifice. "I am where I mean to be."

"Ah. The woman who came for the child. It's like a pretty story." She slid a hand past Delphine—the nearness of her made Delphine's skin prickle—and selected one of the pieces of lacework. The beguiling scent of oranges and violets percolated into the space between them as she bit into it. "She will not give that girl up."

"So I've been told. In very certain terms."

The antlered woman laughed. "So you should have guessed! By the veil, the arrogance of the earthbound." She studied Delphine's face with an intensity and depth that the cold eyes of the others had lacked. "Perhaps not arrogance alone. For love requires arrogance, and ignorance, too, does it not?" Her eyes were so dark as to be almost black, but blue shimmered in them. The perfect planes of her face softened as she met Delphine's eyes.

"What do the Fae know of love?" Delphine whispered.

"More than you would guess." She caught Delphine's arm and led her away from the center of the Court, to one of the sunken gardens. "Of pleasure we know much. Of binding and bargains and seduction and artifice, and even the earthbound mistake these for love from time to time. Yet these are not that of which love is made." She settled herself into the curve of the ground. "Sit with me, doeling."

Hesitant, Delphine sat, and the moss beneath repositioned itself to hold her. She looked down, and gasped—her hard-wearing skirt and blouse were rearranged, changed, now cast a deep midnight blue like her best evening gown. In the moonlight, the fabric shone like silk.

The antlered woman smiled. "So you see, you wield magic, too."

"You did this," Delphine accused.

"How could I? I do not know what conceits you hold in your mind to best suit yourself. But they are," she said, lower, sweeter, "very lovely conceits."

Delphine felt the stir of desire again, but this time not for food. Not for this woman, either, exactly, but something deeper and fuller. As though the Fae woman's lips could ply sweeter things than kisses, her body could produce keener things than pleasure. As though Fae itself might ask for her and she might yield, and in yielding, gain potential she'd never dreamed. She bit the inside of her lip. *No—this is real*, she reminded herself. *Pain and blood, not Fae illusion.* She winced and sat up straighter.

The antlered woman leaned back with gentle control in her smile. "You do not trust me." Not a question, and not angry. Still, Delphine resisted the impulse to argue. "It is better not to trust, not here. I suppose that is why you do not believe we could know much of love. But we see this—to love truly, one must trust completely."

Delphine's breath caught in her throat. The woman looked straight through her, saw her too thoroughly.

"And the earthbound, I suppose, are not so dissimilar to us. That it is difficult to yield completely." She pulled her eyes from Delphine. "Do you want something? You look hungry."

"I know better than to eat Fae food," Delphine countered quickly.

"Hungry for more, I would wager, than mere food." A faint smile played on her face. Delphine flushed, feeling exposed, naked despite the brilliant blue gown. "But even that diversion, it won't harm you, not really."

Delphine retreated to what she knew by heart, the familiarity of folktales and Lilabeth's admonitions. "I know the old stories. If I eat your food, I'll want to stay here forever."

"And you do not already wish, at least some part of you, to stay here forever? No, none who comes to us is ever prohibited, truly, from leaving."

"Then why don't they just leave?" The words were flat against the thick sweetness of the Fae woman's. But they had power. Delphine heard their weight—they hung in the air and demanded answers. She liked this, this feeling she could break spells and shatter illusions.

The woman smiled. "We do not make that easy, do we? They are beguiled by magic, they are enchanted with rare beauty. They eat of our food and taste our waters, and the foods of earth are like ash by comparison. But they are free, always."

"It doesn't sound like freedom to me."

The woman laughed, a sound like low, sweet thunder. "No? What is freedom like in your world, earthbound creature? Is it without costs? Is it simple?"

Delphine cast her eyes downward.

"You came here to seek something. Perhaps a bargain could be struck." She studied her perfect hands, each nail bearing a copper crescent moon. "I would be willing to negotiate with you."

"No, I—I know the rules." Delphine flicked her skirts, the deep blue folds rippling disconcertingly.

She laughed again, intoxicating and warm. "Which rules?"

"Only the one who makes a bargain can undo it."

"That is between the earthbound and the Fae! Not what we may do with one another. Doeling, have you never heard of politics? He does a courtesy, so she is owed another. I have done some service for her, and he is owed something by me, so she provides his satisfaction."

Delphine swallowed bitter memories of glassworks and petitions and workers strikes, of caustic comments exchanged in parlors and dining rooms. "Yes, I know something of politics. But I also know that my niece belongs to Fae, and that the Fae woman who bargained for her is her sole guardian."

"If you think that's the end of it, you don't know politics as well as you think. I might be able to wrest that earthbound child free of Fae, if you are willing to grant something to me." She didn't wait for Delphine to ask her price. She leaned forward and whispered, sweet and thick, "I would like you."

A hot blaze of anger and something painfully similar to desire lanced through the cold in Delphine's core. "But you can't undo her bargain," she insisted. She wouldn't be misled. The antlered woman's manner was gentler than the Fae woman's silver cold, but that didn't mean she was safe, or trustworthy. Still, Delphine waited for her answer.

"Not precisely, no. But you see, guardianship is not governed solely by bargains. We can contest the guardianship. We do not, often. It requires a great stock of political capital spent all at once, to so disrupt the balance of power."

"You would agree to bring this contest of guardianship, then? If I—" Delphine's breath hitched. Was she truly going to consider this negotiation? Continue it, even? She'd promised herself that she would, if it came to it. But it felt almost too easy.

"Yes. If you stay in Fae, I will bring a contestation to the Court. And oh, but she would be furious." A coy smile played on the woman's lips. "Her first daughter, banished, and another, sent back?"

"You don't seem to care much for her."

The antlered woman inclined her head, the curves of the antlers taking on a conspiratorial tilt. "I do not, particularly." She smiled. "It doesn't matter if I like her or not. She has held sway too long in Court. There are many who would see her status reduced."

Delphine thought of the man in the brilliant pink suit, of the gilded man, both slipping her tantalizing bits of information. She remembered how the antlered woman had waited for a signal, for permission to blood the knook. Now she saw the indignant reserve in the antlered woman's stayed hand.

"So, my doeling?" The antlered woman slipped closer, gown like fog creeping over the moss. "You could stay with me. I would care for you, and teach you." She laid a hand, surprisingly warm, over Delphine's. "I could teach you many things."

And suddenly, Delphine wanted to stay. She wanted it more than she had ever wanted anything—the desire for the Fae food paling compared to a promise of more. The Fae woman's beauty, it could be her own. Her power, too, could be gained. She didn't want the food, or the caresses, or the wine, not really—she wanted what they had coursing beneath them, the silver-bright magic. She wanted to *become*.

She pulled back, gasping for air.

The antlered woman raised an arched brow. "Do you deny you are intrigued by this possibility? Of staying? Of learning?"

"You said the bargain—" Delphine forced herself to be calm, to consider every angle of this bargain. Divorced from her own desires, her own fears. "You would contest Emily's guardianship. But what would happen next?"

The antlered woman shrugged. "We will spell it out, then. If she is granted to me, I will free her back to her earthbound mother. I would dissolve all bargains affiliated with her. There. So bargained?"

"You said if." Delphine paused. "*If* she is granted to you."

She threw her hands in the air as though the whole thing was a lark, but Delphine sensed a flare of frustration behind her flippant laugh.

"Well, of course *if*. I cannot control the decision of the Court. There are those who still would not go against *her*."

"Then you lied."

"No lie. We cannot lie in the process of bargaining, or the bargain is invalid." The antlered woman reached for Delphine's skirt, for the chiffon trim on the silk, and toyed with it. Just close enough to fluster Delphine. "It is still the best chance you have to free that girl child."

"There must be some other way—some way of at least making a guaranteed trade."

"There is none. None other would even bargain with you, or I miss my guess. No. I have told you nothing but the truth, doeling. And yet you do not trust it." She met Delphine's eyes, unblinking. "The truth of yourself, perhaps, you do not trust. For you know you want to stay with me."

"You may be telling the truth," Delphine admitted. "But there's a stronger truth, isn't there? This place—it—" She couldn't explain it, except she felt as though she could touch power itself, wrap it around her like a coat, wield it how she wished. She could change—herself, the world. Anything.

The woman laid a gentle hand over Delphine's. "And yet you fight it? The human child, she does not fight it."

That was the Fae's mistake. Delphine broke free of the woman and stood. "She does not know she must," she retorted. "She does not realize that this world is emptiness lacquered over with lies."

"So you will not negotiate with me?"

"No. There must be another way."

"Very well. For now. You do not have much time until she is too far changed to return to your side of the veil. Unless you wish to take her back a wasted husk, a girl with mind gone. You may come to think differently." She smiled. "And if you do, I will bargain with you again."

55

Warnings to children to beware fairy mischief of course conceal caution
for real dangers—wolves in the wood and strangers on the road.
—*Flora, Fauna, and Fae: A Study in Cultural Geography,*
by Leonard Worthington Wilkes

DELPHINE FOUND SHE could not sleep. Fae's eventide shadows shifted eerily in the gray gloom, and she couldn't shake the feeling that there could be any number of things lurking in them. She thought of the wax-white knook and shivered as she brushed against a pale pink tree branch. Was nothing the proper color here? Even the greens were more brilliant, more like paint than nature, the kinds of outlandish color she usually tried to temper in her own artwork.

If she stayed, she thought absently, she could paint with the trees themselves, learn to sculpt petals and dew, hone even an animal into an ideal she created for it. She could craft beauty more rare and arresting than she ever could with watercolor and oil. She'd craved more of the world on the other side of the veil, wanted to taste the kind of success and belonging Alaine had, wanted recognition for her talents. Perhaps she could make that for herself here. Perrysburg, Pierce— those had been poor illusions blurring what she really wanted.

It would not be all pain, would it? Trading herself for Emily? All the places she had ever wanted to go, all the things she had ever wanted to see, all the art she had ever wanted to create—didn't this

place outstrip anything in her own world for beauty and discovery? She wouldn't have to face gossip or disgrace, and she didn't deny that the power intrigued her. The bald desire of the antlered woman, the churning reply her own soul gave.

But it was a gamble. Pure and simple, it wasn't a guarantee, and she would settle for nothing less than Emily returned to her parents. She wanted to scream.

Instead, she circled the Court, circled the wide ring that surrounded it. The old incantation at the linden tree had required she circle that ring three times—was there any way to make someone, something appear to her here? Appear and tell her the next step, the way to get Emily back?

She clenched her fists, angry. Angrier than she had been since— she couldn't remember the last time she'd felt true anger. That she'd allowed herself, she amended, to feel anger. When Mrs. Grafton or Stella had sniped at her, anger was subsumed by humiliation. When Pierce struck her, anger was smothered by shame. And when Emily disappeared, the anger she had felt had turned against herself only, in deep guilt. But no—she was angry at these beautiful creatures and their impossible politics and their inscrutable rules. She had come all the way here—she had gotten into Fae, as ludicrous as that seemed— and she had to play their games to save her niece.

There were only two ways forward. One, learn the name of a Fae and leverage it for the favor. That seemed, she was fairly sure, impossible. No Fae would divulge their own name, not if she understood the girl in the woods correctly. Two, bargain with the antlered woman and stay in Fae in Emily's place. If she even trusted that it would work. How would the laws of Fae yield custody of one of its own to another? She imagined a judge in a powdered wig presiding over the bone cathedral of the Court and stifled an irrational laugh, then sobered immediately. If it came to it, that was her only recourse. She would bargain. And she would stay in Fae forever.

She took a shaky breath and kept walking. Purple blossoms rustled as she passed, with the faint scent of cinnamon. The silver woods broke into a tangled cascade of trees, but in their midst, she saw something else. A glint of sharp light, like a pool, or a mirror. She picked her way through the pale bracken, knowing that straying from the path, even this close to the Court, was probably unwise. It was a pool—if a pool rippled in its depths, instead of on the surface. Or perhaps it was a mirror—if a mirror shifted and pulsed.

Delphine drew back. What kind of Fae magic was this? And what did it do? She took a breath. Maybe it could do something. She rifled through the catalog of Lilabeth's stories, remembering nothing about magic pools or Fae mirrors.

Mirrors—they weren't Fae stories, but fairy tales had magic mirrors. She dismissed the idea as absurd, then remembered that she was in Fae, and it was unlikely that anything was as absurd as she first judged it. She stepped closer, careful not to touch the shimmering silver. She peered into it.

The surface clouded and roiled. Delphine's heart went into her throat. This was magic, and she realized she had no idea what it might do to her, but she pressed on, looking deeper past the turmoil on the pool's surface. And in its depths she saw—

"Lavender Cottage?" she whispered.

It was nighttime, and the stars were spread bright behind the familiar eaves and gingerbread trim of her sister's home. Delphine's chest tightened in lonely homesickness, seeing the stars. She hadn't ever considered them, their constancy, until the gray wash of sky in Fae. Now they meant home, familiar safety. A single light illuminated a window in the cottage. An oil lamp, in Emily's room. Behind it, a silhouette she knew instantly as her sister, slight movement of the shadow on the wall.

She burst into tears.

Alaine was waiting for her, holding on to hope that her daughter was safe, keeping a single light burning through the night. Why did the pool choose to show this to her? She had no idea, but she knew what it meant to her. She couldn't give up so easily on going back home. There had to be a way to get Emily back without staying behind. Fae offered her rebirth, creativity, reinvention—but not without rendering her as good as dead to her sister, and her sister lost to her.

The shadows of Fae were lightening as Delphine tiptoed back into the Court circle. Another morning—how many was it now? She shook her head. It didn't matter. Who knew how time was running back home? She realized with a start that the little plum tree in front of Lavender Cottage had looked sparse in the moonlight—it was losing its leaves. Fall had still been a promise on the breeze when she'd come into Fae. Had it been weeks already?

Her heart plunged. Alaine, waiting, not realizing that mere hours were passing for Delphine while days flew by on Prospect Hill. She rushed back to the Fae woman's bower.

The Fae woman was gone, but Emily was already awake. Her white dress was changed for a blue gossamer gown, and she was playing with a scatter of forest flowers.

"Why, Emily! You're up early!" Delphine forced her voice to a pleasant timbre that wouldn't reveal the renewed panic she felt.

"I wanted to see if I could make myself a dress!" She held up the blossoms. "She made me this dress yesterday, from a ribbon. Isn't it pretty?"

"It's lovely, Em." Delphine recoiled at the thought of the Fae woman dressing Emily in Fae magic, outfitting her like a doll. "But we can't make things from ribbons and flowers like they can, Em."

"But I already did." Delphine's stomach lurched. Emily lifted a pale purple length of stretched, warped petals. They overlapped like scales, transparent and shot through with crooked veins. "Well, I tried. I don't really know how to make a dress."

Delphine watched as Emily played with the petal fabric, looping it over her arms and draping it over her shoulders. Her eyes were distant, but not in a vacant way. No, she was focused, looking right past the reality that Delphine held firm to.

"It's very pretty, Emily." Delphine couldn't keep the tremor out of her voice now. "But don't you think—that is—" She had to explain it to Emily somehow, to convince her she had to hold on. "Emily. Do you miss your mama?"

"No?" she said, still stretching a bit of a pink leaf between her fingers. Not looking up. "I don't know what you mean."

Delphine bit back horror. "Your mama, Emily. Emily! Look at me." Emily looked up, finally. Her eyes were lit from within with the metallic gleam of Fae. "Emily."

Her niece stared at her a long time, then seemed to shake herself. "Aunt Del?"

"You still know me."

She giggled. "Of course, Aunt Del! You're here visiting."

"And—Emily. Your mama. And your house. And your chickens— your bantams, Em! Remember those?"

She paused. "My pretty birds. Yes. And Mama helped me feed them."

"Yes! Yes, Emily. If you—this is very hard, now, Em, please listen, but don't be scared—if you want to see them again, you have to try not to do Fae things. You can't use their magic, you can't let it get into you. Do you understand?"

"Not really, Aunt Del. You're not making any sense. I'm not doing anything strange, am I?" She lifted the leaf again and began to smooth its thick creases under her fingers, rendering it smooth as silk. "I don't want you to be sad, Aunt Del."

Delphine let out a shaking breath. There wasn't much time before Emily was too changed, too much a part of Fae to ever leave, no matter what bargains she made. "No, love. Not strange at all."

56

Plantain for rashes, comfrey for teeth, yarrow for fever, tansy for fleas
Neglect you not to offer a sprig, right at the root of the fairy's trees

—Traditional bargain

THE FAE GIRL was where Delphine had hoped to find her, near the Spire, just on the other side of the line it marked between the Court and the wildwood. "Are you leaving?" she asked, unfolding herself from the crook of a sprawling pale pink willow tree's roots.

"Not yet. I'm not finished."

"I saw you try to leave with the girl child." She bit her lip. "I wanted to help, to come talk to you, but I saw *him* behind you."

"So I trust he isn't here now?"

"No. None of the others, either." She pulled a frond of willow spray from the swirl around her and absently bent it into a comb and tore tines into it. It hardened into a translucent green beneath her fingers.

"I need to know something. And you're bound to tell me the truth. As my guide."

"That was our bargain."

"There is a woman. In the Court. She is willing to bargain."

"And?"

"And I want to know if she is truthful."

The Fae girl laughed. "I can't tell you that!" She rushed to explain

as Delphine began to argue. "I cannot—it is not that I will not. I would, willingly. But I cannot know if another lies."

"Can you tell me if the bargain she suggests is possible?"

"Perhaps. It depends on what she is capable of doing. And that, I am afraid, is also beyond my knowing."

"She says she can free Emily if I agree to stay."

The Fae girl sat bolt upright. "Oh. Oh my."

"She says she'll bring a—a sort of legal case, to have my niece's guardianship transferred to her. Can she do it?"

"She can certainly bring a case as such. Any of them could."

"Would she succeed? Would the Court—"

"I have no idea. But I see why she would want to, why many of them would. That is a bargain that would undo *her* plans quite wretchedly."

"That is what they want, isn't it? To undermine *her*."

"Yes. They chafe and grumble when one is too powerful, in the Court. They never want the balance too uneven, unless of course it is uneven in their own favor."

"Tell me about your mother."

"Mother?" She drew her new-made comb through her tangles. "I have no mother. I mean, I'm sure the woman who birthed me across the veil is long dead." Her brow wrinkled briefly, as though remembering something important. "And I don't recall much about her, in any case."

"No, your mother here. The woman who bargained for you."

"She didn't bargain for me, exactly." The Fae girl unpicked a snarl with her willow comb. "That is—I wasn't bargained away by someone else. I did it myself." A glimmer of tears in her eyes, and Delphine wasn't sure if they were from the tangles in her hair or the memory. "But she found me and brought me to the Court, and so I was her ward."

"She is very powerful here."

The girl's eyes widened, and she lowered her comb. "Yes. I was—I was an embarrassment, you might say. But she has grown more powerful since I was banished."

"I understand how power works in my world. But here—how does one become powerful?"

"The powerful are the ones who have made the keenest bargains," the girl answered easily. "And those who are allied with others who do, too. Isn't that how it works in your world, too?"

Delphine considered this a moment before answering. "Yes. The terms are different, but it's the same idea. But *she*—she is not well-liked here?"

"Are powerful people liked where you come from?" She laughed. "She protected me well, and she is not cruel or dishonest with the other Fae. But she does not share her power, and she is...distant with her affections."

"Affection?"

The girl blushed. "I don't know if it's seemly to talk about. Where you are from. But that is one way of cementing the bonds between us here. You may form an alliance with another by virtue of guardianship, or by...affection."

Now Delphine flushed. "I understand." The Fae woman who walked by herself, then—making her power and sharing it with no one, elevating herself and refusing to broker that distance with relationships. "In my world," she began, uncertain, "sometimes, when someone is very powerful but also very much disliked, people... well, they do things to take their power away. Is it like that here?"

The Fae girl studied her comb, thrumming the tines with a finger. They hummed a dissonant melody. "Yes, but I don't know the way of it. I know they each have ebbed and flowed in status here, over many long years. Ageless centuries of gaining and losing power. A new one comes, the order is changed. Or"—she smiled ruefully as she gestured to herself—"unchanged after all."

"Could you ever go back?" Delphine asked impulsively. "To the Court?"

"If someone took me in, as their ward once more. But that is unlikely." She smiled a thin smile that covered humiliation and shame. "Or, over time, as I build and grow and create here—it is not easy, if one is not of the Court, for one cannot claim the bargains of the earthbound in the same way—I may earn enough status to reenter the Court."

"I—if I could do something to help, I—"

"You have done much already, by bargaining with me. There is little enough else can be done. And you have other things to worry about. You haven't gotten the girl back yet. How will you do it, I wonder?"

"I don't know yet." Warm tears flooded her eyes, and she let them spill. "I don't—I don't know at all. And I'm afraid, do you know why?"

The Fae girl shook her head.

"I'm afraid she's forgetting us. That she will forget her mama, and her little house in the woods, and her grandmother, and her stupid chickens, and—me. Even if I'm here, that she'll forget who I am. That she'll forget how to love any of us."

"I remember a little," the Fae girl said. There was a strange reticence in her voice, as though she was on the brink of a decision. A very big, very important decision. Delphine waited. "I remember a little house on a hill, and my mama. I loved her very much. And my sister. My little sister." She closed her eyes. "I was too much trouble, I was sure of it—I wasn't keen to get married, and no one was much keen to marry me, either." She wrinkled her brow and met Delphine's widening eyes. "I remember why, now—I didn't know my father. That mattered, there. It matters still?"

Slowly, Delphine nodded. The girl continued. "But I remember how much I loved my mama. I loved her so much that I made a bargain. She lost something she wanted very much, and I hated to see her cry." She sighed, ragged and full of unshed tears. "She had big blue eyes that crinkled up when she laughed. And she had red hands from laundry and washing up. She sang all the time, songs she'd learned from her mama, and I still remember the songs. The man in pink, he sings some of them, and it makes me sad, in a strange, lovely way. She had a horn comb like this one that she used to braid my hair." She pressed the willow-frond comb into Delphine's hand.

The Fae girl looked up. "So you see? I remember. And if I remember, I'm sure the girl child does, too."

"Thank you," Delphine breathed, knowing who this girl had once been. Imogene's sister, her great-aunt. Violet. Whoever she was now, whatever name the Fae had given her along with her other-worldly gleam and her deft magic, she had once been family. When she looked at the Fae girl's eyes again, she recognized the bright Riley blue, her own eyes reflected in the uncanny face.

57

ALAINE CROUCHED IN the mud of the scrying glass, her hem heavy and black. Rain had mired the mirror in thick sludge, but she didn't care. Through the glass, Emily played with a pile of pink blossoms, making a crown out of them. She watched in mixed horror and amazement as Em plied the stems longer and flatter, braiding them easily. She'd always liked making daisy chains, but was frustrated when the recalcitrant stems broke or frayed.

"I guess you solved that problem, didn't you, love?" she whispered into the mirror.

Of course Emily didn't look up. The silvery wash of Fae was stronger on her now, and sometimes when Alaine could see her eyes, she saw Fae glittering there, too. She spent more and more time at the mirror, torn between the need to see her daughter and the terror of what she would find.

A sharp rap at the door brought her back to her senses. She stood up quickly, mud coating her bare feet and spackling her dress. What if it was Emily's teacher, or Mr. Trowbridge? *God*, she thought with sickening panic, *what if someone had sent the sheriff up?*

But it was only Papa Horatio.

She picked her way out of the circle. "I'm here, Papa Horatio." She didn't bother to lie about what she'd been doing. The evidence was there on her skirts, in the dirt caked under her fingernails, in the stricken look on her face. She didn't even manage to say a word before she started crying.

"Ah, dear, that's all right. All right." He held her arm as she wiped salt streaks from her face. "Thought you and I might go for a walk. Get your mind clear, maybe?"

"It really does work, Papa." She pushed back fresh tears. "I know no one believes me. But it does."

Papa Horatio shook his head. "I don't rightly know what to believe when it comes to the Fae. But Jack was worried, and rightly so. Look at you."

Alaine glanced down. "I'm a wreck."

"I didn't want to say so, but you do look like you've gone a few rounds. It don't matter to me how it works, but you're seeing things that ain't right, that ain't good. It's bound to crack you one way or another, sooner or later."

"I hate it, Papa Horatio," she whispered. "I hate not being able to do anything. All I can do is watch, and wait. I see Emily, I see her slipping away, and Del can't do anything, or at least I can't tell what she's doing, and—"

"You don't like sitting by helpless. You never did." Papa Horatio sighed. "You was always one to do something, to fix everything. I remember when you was—oh, ten or so, maybe. That old cow took sick and you were down there rubbing its back and trying every kind of liniment you could get your hands on. I think Lilabeth drew the line when you tried to bring it a hot water bottle."

"I remember," Alaine replied. "I took the hot water bottle out to the barn anyway."

"I don't think you can fix this with liniment or hot water bottles or sitting up all night or anything else," Papa Horatio said. "And that's the hardest damned thing in the world for you."

"I don't know if I can do it, Papa Horatio."

His brow creased. "I don't think there's anything but to soldier on through it, Alaine. It's—" He paused. "I didn't come here to scold, you know."

"Aunt Imogene has handled that well enough already," Alaine said. "Not that—not that we didn't deserve it."

"You and your sister." Papa Horatio sighed. "I'm surprised at it, that's all. Del—well, she listened to Lilabeth like a right dutiful granddaughter, but I never thought she was as interested as all that in Fae things. And I can't think what possessed the two of you to mess with it."

"It's not what you think." Alaine straightened. It wasn't, was it? She had been blaming herself for the bad bargain, but after all—they were only trying to help Del. "It was Pierce Grafton. He—he was cruel to her." Papa Horatio waited patiently. "And she wasn't sure we'd get a judge to grant the divorce. Because he's... well. A Grafton. And he threatened to have her committed, even."

"And the Graftons have pull." Papa Horatio's mouth twisted like he'd tasted something sour. "Man like that has everything—money, prestige, a future. And he can't bring himself to treat his own wife well."

"She was ashamed."

"Ain't no reason for Del to be ashamed. None." Horatio slowed his pace. "Was reading just the other day about divorce—funny how once a thing matters to you, you see it all over the place. Some states wanting to add clauses to the laws to let judges grant for any cause they see fit." He coughed. "That article in the paper—well, fella was real fired up about it. How it would be an easy out for divorces. For women, especially. What did he call them? Yes, immoral, wanton women." He snorted. "Sounds to me like we all know full well Del ain't the only woman tied to a cruel man."

"What are you saying?"

"Just thinking, is all. You and Del go running to Fae to solve your problems, to fix something you see as your trouble. But it ain't just your trouble, is it?"

"I suppose not." She considered the other bargains of the past

year, scraping and wheedling to make headway in the Agricultural Society, maneuvering to be taken seriously as a business owner. She'd seen them as her problems alone, but they weren't, not really—how many other women felt as she did, struggled with what she fought?

"Just saying, think of the bargains you might have made instead. The ones that would have taken a crack at the mess for everyone."

"It's not worth my daughter." Alaine flared with defensive anger.

"I'm certainly not saying it is! Nor that you should think so. Lands, no."

"It would be very nice," Alaine said through a tight jaw, "if we could effect some change in this world without selling our children to another."

Papa Horatio slowed and turned to her. "Whatever we do, we're bargaining with our children. We make laws, we invent things, we build a future—it's our children who get the dividends. Good or bad. Just turned out a little more literal in this case."

They rounded a bend in the path where the linden tree stood.

Alaine shrank back. "I hate that tree. I'd have it cut down if—"

"It is not your tree to cut."

Alaine nearly came out of her skin. The voice was unfamiliar, but lilted with the uncanny echo of the Fae. A girl stepped out from behind the tree into the green ring around the linden. It wasn't the woman Alaine knew—this Fae creature was younger, with fair hair in a braided crown and a red cloak clasped at her throat. She looked almost human, a faint blush coloring her cheeks, but there was a silvered distance in her eyes.

"You?" Another shock—it was Papa Horatio who spoke, with recognition blooming in his eyes. "You don't look any different than—than fifty years ago!"

"Well met, friend." The Fae girl was lithe and straight as a birch tree, and vaguely silver white like a birch tree, too. "May I call you friend?"

"I suppose," Horatio said slowly. "Our bargain served me well. Seems others—not so much."

"I know." She toed the edge of the vibrant green circle. "I know of those dealings."

"Then you know how dirty the bargain was," Alaine interjected.

The Fae girl cocked her head. "Dirty? I am not sure I understand that. Oh! I remember—yes. You say it when you mean unfair. Or unlawful." She smiled, a faint, pretty smile that made Alaine feel queasy, as though she were looking at a schoolgirl and not a treacherous Fae creature. "I assure you, the bargain was lawful, or it could not have proceeded."

"It was still," Alaine said, "dirty."

"I will remember that way of saying it. Dirty. Yes." She turned back to Horatio. "It is your kin, too, who was brought to Fae?"

"It was my kin." He straightened. "We bargained once. Would you bargain with me again? To get her back?"

"Papa, no," Alaine hissed. "We can't—if De—" She stopped herself. Names—names had power. She wouldn't say any names. She glanced at the innocent face staring back at them from the fairy ring. "They can't be trusted."

"It was my bargain, child." Papa Horatio looked tired. "I'd give back what you gave me."

Alaine's breath stilled. Orchard Crest for Emily. The family farm she had cultivated and maintained, that she hoped would someday be Em's. Yes. She'd see it razed to the ground if it got Emily back. In a heartbeat.

"No," the Fae girl replied. "For one, the kerchief you gave me is long gone, changed. Too far altered to give back. That is how it is done, to undo a trade—it is the original bargain reversed. And for another, your fifty acres is changed, altered as well. It was fifty acres of forest and wilds and you have made it something else, no?" She spoke of the bargain almost proudly, as though she had something to do with the transformation, as though she was connected to it. "To get your girl child back would be another bargain entirely. And I don't want to make one." She paused. "You don't, either."

Alaine lurched forward. "Does that mean that—that my sister is close? To undoing the bargain?"

"No. *She* will not bargain." The way the Fae girl spoke of the silvery woman made Alaine think she trusted her, liked her, even, no more than Alaine did.

"A new bargain, then?"

"Not exactly. But there are other ways. You must stay clear."

Cold seeped back into Alaine's core. "Why should we trust you?"

"You need not trust me if you do not want to. It matters little."

That was true enough. Whatever bargain Del was striking, whatever machinations were turning behind the veil, it didn't matter what Alaine thought or did or believed. It could only matter what she said—if she bargained. And that wouldn't happen, couldn't happen. She was powerless to help her own daughter, even standing here with one of the Fae an arm's reach away. "Even if I can't trust you— is she all right?" Alaine whispered. She had a hundred questions, and a thousand worries that hadn't been answered or assuaged by the images in the mirror.

"She is safe, and cared for with greatest kindness."

"I'm not sure I trust Fae kindness," Alaine answered. Her daughter, reflected in her mirror, never seemed unhappy or badly treated. But the gifts—clothes fashioned of flowers, trinkets of silver, the playthings for practicing magic—they all made her shiver.

"And well you shouldn't," the girl replied with a wan laugh. "But she is not badly treated, nor is she harmed."

"Is she afraid? Does she miss home too terribly?"

The Fae girl halted, a flash of pain like light across her pale eyes. Then she shook her head. "She is of course homesick for her mother, by turns, but the diversions of Fae are many. And time runs in a different pattern. She does not realize how long it has been—she does not feel it the same way you do."

Papa Horatio laid a hand on Alaine's trembling arm. "She's all right, then. Doesn't matter what else happens, if she's all right."

"I only came to warn you, though I had forgotten how the Fae cannot be trusted," the girl said with a faint smile. "But trust me now. Do not meddle. Do not bargain. The song is carefully written, and one wrong note will throw it into disharmony. I have arranged the notes myself, and those far more powerful than I am will conduct them. Do you understand?"

"I think I do," Papa Horatio said, cutting off the stream of protests that rose in Alaine's throat. "I think I do. I should thank you, for what you did for me fifty years ago. But—I have to know. Why?"

"Why did I bargain with you?" The girl smiled then, a real smile, warm and true, and Alaine could have forgotten who she was entirely, believing her to be a strangely dressed girl, lost in the woods. "Because I could." She hesitated, and looked at Alaine with that uncanny weight in her eyes. "Or why do I come now? Because I can. And because I knew, once, about sisters."

With that, she laid a gentle hand on the linden, and disappeared.

58

What's the difference between a fairy and a recruiting sergeant? Both will steal you away, but the fairy food is better.

—Folk saying

DELPHINE ENTERED THE Court silently, keeping to the lacework edges of the bone cathedral. Low fires of dim purple light glowed here and there, and crystal lanterns held dancing flames of brilliant blue and orange. Couples and sometimes trios nestled into the soft moss and inside bowers, their shadows dancing along with the flames. The contortions of some of the dances made Delphine flush, though she didn't look away.

The antlered woman sprawled under the swaying boughs of a weeping cherry tree, blossoms singing like faint chimes. Delphine flushed deeper—the woman was entirely naked, and she was caught firmly in the embrace of the golden-eyed Fae man. Her face shone with a strange ecstasy that merged pleasure with power. In every cheap dime novel Delphine had ever read, the heroines surrendered to kisses. There was no surrender here.

Delphine slipped back, out of the play of lantern light and into shadow, but the woman saw her. She untwined her leg from the gilded man's, who did not look as perturbed as Delphine imagined he might have been. Instead, a joyful hunger played on his face. The antlered woman greeted her. "My doeling, you are returned! From the wildwood, if the scent serves me."

"I had questions, but they can wait," she replied. The antlered woman and her paramour shared a glance. The Fae man smiled.

"Questions—yes, those can always wait," the antlered woman said, her honey-thick laugh softening every word. "But you need not leave. Join us. Our embrace is large."

Delphine glanced at the Fae man, whose smile grew broader. "I will not hurt you, earthborn."

"I," the antlered woman said, standing, her body shining in the lantern light, "make no such promise. But the hurt is sweet in our bower."

They were quite serious, Delphine realized with mingled horror and longing. The woman traced her cheek with a gentle finger, then tilted her chin back so she looked her full in the eyes. She grazed her lips with her own, and Delphine trembled. She tasted power and lush, sweet danger, and she wanted it.

"Oh, my doeling," the antlered woman whispered. "You are a lovely thing, indeed." She glanced back at the Fae man, who rose to his knees behind them. "So lovely that I find I cannot share you with another."

She drew the man to his feet with a sweep of her arm and kissed him fiercely, their heights matched nearly perfectly and her muscles strong enough to equal his broad shoulders and chest. For a moment Delphine wasn't sure if she was watching a passionate kiss or a struggle for control, but it was over before she could decide. The Fae man strode lightly past her, appraising her again with a smile.

The antlered woman resumed her place, supine beneath the tree. Delphine sat nearby, legs crossed perhaps too primly to be conversing with a nude Fae creature. "And you, doeling. I fear you are uninterested in such things as kisses, despite the beauty of this night."

Delphine leaned forward. "The Fae woman who has my niece. What would you do, to see her cast down?"

The woman laughed, delighted. "You are forward! Far less timid a doeling than I thought. Oh, you would do well here." She leaned forward, her eyes dancing. "I have played and planned at far greater schemes than you could imagine to see her diminished."

"I suppose I wouldn't understand them."

"You could, you know. If you stayed." She sat straight, matching Delphine's prim posture. "Have you given consideration to my bargain?"

Delphine hesitated. "I have given it consideration. But I wonder if there is not a better way. I've heard of the favor."

At this, the antlered woman laughed loudly enough to attract the attention of nearby clusters of Fae. "The favor!" she whispered when she'd regained control. "Do not tell me you have learned one of our names already! Clever thing."

Delphine didn't answer directly, instead turning the antlered woman's attention back to the Fae she clearly despised. "Does anyone know *her* name?"

"*Her* name?" She laughed so deeply her antlers trembled. "No one knows *her* name, doeling. And even if I did, I could not tell you. It is forbidden to tell a name outright."

"Even your own?" Delphine rushed the question, and the antlered woman tasted the desperation, she was sure.

"Even your own. A name must be guessed, or it must be earned. That is the rule. There are ways of earning the knowledge of another's name. You would have to stay a very long time for many of them, though the learning..." She moved close, long arm entangled with Delphine's. "The learning is a joy and a pleasure." There was perfume in her movements, roses and sandalwood. "Or so I have been told."

"Be that as it may," Delphine replied, edging back, "how else does anyone learn a name?"

"Some guess it." She narrowed her eyes as though making a playful wager. "Do you want to play at guessing mine? That is not nearly as enjoyable as other ways of finding a name, but I would play such a game with one as pretty as you."

"It could be anything." Delphine sighed.

The woman opened her mouth, then closed it again. She smiled, a playful lilt to her perfect face.

"Or not?" Delphine's brows constricted. "What rules bind your names?"

"It is simple. Our names are as they were, once. We keep them."

"When you become Fae, you keep your human name." She understood, slowly and with growing appreciation for what the Fae girl had done for her. She had been given the key to guessing a name—not a very powerful name, but the favor didn't require that. She brought her expressions under control, so as not to betray the very great knowledge she now realized she had.

The antlered woman nodded. "We keep the earthbound name even as we become Fae. It is...a souvenir. A memory."

"And do you remember?" Delphine asked abruptly. "Your before?"

"I remember a shack of a cabin, before iron bound your world up so tightly."

"Before the railroads."

"Before them, and before much else besides. I remember that dirty shack echoing with screaming, with my mother in childbed time and again, with hungry children given no supper time and again, and my father in his cups. Time and again. I remember a dark night when he caught me coming home—from fucking the soldiers at the fort, he said." The words fell from her mouth like clods of mud. "I had slept with no one. I had been at the mission, with the priests, learning to read."

"You wanted more," Delphine whispered.

"Oh, yes. I wanted more. I tasted those books—and the priests only had lives of the saints and a battered old Bible—but they were doors to other worlds, places, yes, worlds of mind and spirit, too. And I wanted all of them." Her blue-black eyes shone. "My mother knew of bargaining. She taught me to say the rhymes and leave the trinkets dangling in the tangles of a holly tree, always bright with berries. Red, like blood. I pricked my fingers on the holly and willed a door into the tree, and it opened."

"I—I have never heard of that bargain."

She laughed, less cloying than before, but still rich as amber honey. "It is a deeper magic that bids desperately and is willing to barter life itself. It needs no rhyme or sigil. You have known something of this bargain, or you would not be here."

Delphine wondered, uncomfortably, if the marks she had drawn on the linden and the braid of hair had mattered at all, or if the bargain was borne on something simpler. On desperation and blood alone.

"All of them—the others? Did they will themselves here, too?"

"I do not know. He—" She gestured at the man still wearing the immaculately tailored bright pink suit. "He came of his own accord, after my time. He came with iron around his neck and a brand on his cheek. He wanted the chains off for good, but if you look very closely, there is still a mark kissing his face where the brand once was." She looked at him, thoughtfully. "He could will it away, and yet he does not. Perhaps he wanted to remember something, after all." She turned back to Delphine, eyes soft. "But you? I think there is much you might like to forget."

Delphine's breath caught in her throat. The woman laughed. "Doeling, it shows in your eyes, in your footsteps, in that dainty voice of yours. Fear has a ring to it, a tinny little vibrato—you would learn to hear it, in time." She inclined her head. "You made bargains in your world, too, for *more*. The bargain was bad?"

"I married a cruel man," Delphine said.

"There are other kinds of men?" She laughed again. "No, don't defend the earthbound. They are all either fools or cruel."

"That isn't—"

"But isn't it? Which were you?"

"I would like to believe," Delphine said softly, "that a person can be wise without being cruel."

"Even if one can"—she waved the question aside—"why do you still refuse my bargain? What do you have to return to? A cruel man—no, a world of cruel men?"

And Delphine found she had nothing to argue. "What happens," she said instead, "to someone whose name has been guessed?"

The Fae woman shrugged. "It is a great loss of prestige, or can be. Now, to earn a name—that is different. That is an alliance born of stronger stuff than bargains, even."

"Do you know his name?" Delphine asked, nodding toward the broad-shouldered shadow at the edge of the bone cathedral.

The woman hesitated. "No," she said, "not yet. And nor does he know mine. In time." She narrowed her eyes. "I will convince you to stay, one way or another, and then we shall all three know one another's names. And none could counter us. But for now, he awaits me."

Delphine curled into the moss, mind racing, as the antlered woman swept away.

59

The thistle and the rose both serve for different bargains.

—Folk saying

ALAINE WAS KNEADING bread dough with detached, rote precision when a motorcar roared up the driveway. She should have been afraid, after all the predictions of investigations and sheriffs and arrests, but instead she merely felt a bone-deep exhaustion. She had almost grown used to the numb cold that lived in her gut, except that hope was a more tenacious thing than she had given it credit for. A creak at the door, the flash of a movement at the window, rustling in the brush at the edge of the forest—anything that meant Emily might be back, and it surged to life, burning away the ice of grief for a short moment, only to fade into slumber again. And the painful cold resumed.

There was neither relief nor more fear when she saw who the car belonged to—Pierce Grafton. She sighed and picked sticky bread dough from under her fingernails.

Pierce pounded a rapid demand on the front door. "She's been gone for three weeks," he said by way of greeting. "And I assume you know where she is."

"Pierce, please—we've been ill and I—"

"No excuses, please. I know you've been hiding her, or helping her in some way. She didn't take any money, and didn't withdraw anything from my accounts since. So she's either here or you gave her money."

"Interesting deduction," Alaine said softly. She stood in the hallway, blocking his entry but not his line of sight. His eyes narrowed at the disarray behind her, the unswept floor and the teacups scattered on the tables. "Please, Pierce, it isn't a good time."

"You're damned right it isn't!" He ripped off his hat and clenched it between whitening fingers. "Surely you know that the election is approaching. The social season in full swing. And I'm making excuses for an absent wife. I gave it a week, then two. But my patience is worn out."

"Your patience?" Alaine raised an eyebrow. "Fine, Pierce, come in if you've a mind." She swept her arm toward her cluttered parlor. "Where do you think she went?"

"How should I know! She runs here every time we quarrel." His fingers twitched at the edges of his hat. "She filed for divorce. Did you know that?"

"Yes, I did."

"I didn't think she was serious. I thought it was a fit of pique—that she'd never follow through on it, actually stand before a judge."

"She did. And she got that divorce granted, didn't she?"

"Yes. But now she's gone, and I've had a call from Perrysburg police—"

"Oh, dear." Alaine's lips parted in surprise. "They think you've gone and done something rash, is that it? And you need to produce a living, breathing wife?"

Pierce glowered at her, but there was a lost, confused pain behind the anger, like a child who had been punished and didn't understand why. "She was coming here, last she was seen. She didn't take the car. Ida Carrington was the last person to see her before she left Perrysburg, except the ticket agent at the station—he knows her well enough." He sighed. "Ida's no help at all. Kept babbling about a book Delphine wanted to show your daughter, as though it mattered."

"I'm sure Miss Carrington is trying to be helpful," Alaine answered, measured. "A book from her studies, I assume."

"Of course. Fairy nonsense." Pierce paced toward the window, glanced at a yellowing potted fern, and paced back. "Please, Alaine. Tell me where she is."

If he wasn't such an awful pustule of a man, Alaine could have felt sorry for him. As it was, she felt only a slight, bitter satisfaction that the rippling effects of her own personal nightmare were at least unpleasant for Pierce Grafton.

"I wish I could." She stared at her hands as Pierce paced back and cursed the windowpane. "But I don't know, Pierce. I don't know how to follow her this time."

"She tells you everything."

Alaine hesitated. "She does," she finally said, steadying her voice. "Tell me, Pierce, why do you think she left?"

"Why do—" He turned on her, his face a strange battle of anger and grief. "I don't know."

"I think you do." She stood, her height no match for his, but she pretended that it did. "You hit her, Pierce."

He was shamed into silence.

"And more than that. My sister is intelligent, and compassionate, and talented. And you—you squandered those things about her. You told her, in action if not words, that she was *less* than the Perrysburg Graftons until she learned to be like them. You fool—she was *more*. She is the best person I have ever known, and I hope she stays far away from you."

Alaine caught her breath, her heart racing. Pierce only stared at her, anger boiling behind his eyes. "I only ever wanted to help her."

"Help her!" Alaine bit back laughter that was too close to hysterical. "Help her do what, Pierce? The only thing you wanted was for her to help you. To be a perfect Perrysburg Grafton, arranging your parties and making you look good. Well, she's worth more than that. I hope she—" She bit off the last words—*that she never comes back.* For a moment, Alaine forgot herself, forgot that she knew exactly where Delphine was. But in a rush, she realized that she would rather have seen her sister happy in Fae than forced back into Pierce Grafton's conniving hands. Instead, she whispered, "I hope she knows that. I hope she knows how much she's worth."

He stared at her in silence for a long, terrible minute. "You really don't know where she is," Pierce finally said.

"I don't. But," she said, hesitating only a little before pressing on, "I am beginning to wonder if you do. So I would advise going back to Perrysburg as soon as possible before I decide the sheriff ought to come have a word."

As the car rumbled over the dirt road, Alaine sank into a chair, head in her hands. She didn't hear the back door open, but startled as it closed with a crack against the frame. "Did well getting rid of him." Imogene leaned against her cane in the parlor doorway.

"How much did you hear?"

"Enough to know he's scared for the first time in his damn life."

Alaine hiccupped something like a laugh. "Yes, that's about it. Thank God he left when he did—what if he'd started asking about Em? Or—or anything, really. He's no fool, Imogene, for everything else he is. He'd find out eventually that Del came here before..." She inhaled once, and exhaled slowly. *Before she went into Fae*, something she could never say outside of Orchard Crest. "I thought you put onions out."

"Ain't no warding bargain I know of to keep a man like that out. Works mostly for strangers with no real business poking about." She sighed. "Say what you like about the Fae, at least they don't go where they ain't wanted."

She knew Imogene hadn't meant anything by it, but the words sank into her like a barbed hook. *They don't go where they're not wanted.* She had asked the Fae here from the beginning—well, no more. She would ring the house in iron, stake the orchard with it, cut down the linden tree, and salt the ground where its roots lay.

"What are you thinking, child?" Imogene said, and Alaine came to her senses, her hands balled into fists in her lap.

She thought of saying what she'd been thinking, all malice and iron, but instead, she whispered, "This can't go on much longer, can it?"

"Wish I knew. You realize, I don't know of any story, real or folktale, where someone went into Fae like your sister done." She coughed. "We're not much good at patience, we Rileys. At waiting. But now that's about all we can do." She shot Alaine a curious look. "Wait and *watch*, if what Papa Horatio said's true."

"It is, Imogene. I can't explain it, but I can see into Fae."

"If that don't beat all. Well. You're not out there now."

"No. I—I promised Papa Horatio I wouldn't spend too much time watching it." She paused. It had become too painful, some days, to see her Emily grown silvery and distant. "Besides, we needed bread."

"That's the way of it, girl. Times go to utter shit and a family still needs the bread baked. Animals still need fed and watered, house needs caring for. Life presses on, and you press on it with it."

Alaine's stomach clenched. "I know, I just—I don't know if I can."

"I think you can, and I think you will."

60

No one may tell me for no one knows
The names of the Fae, the names that they chose
                    —Children's rhyme

"OH, IT'S PRETTY!" Emily clapped her hands. "My I pet it?"

The Fae woman lowered her arm, and the emerald-and-gold bird perched on her wrist bobbed as it righted its balance. "It is yours, my dove. A summer baringbird, one of the rarest colors."

Delphine watched as Emily tentatively ran a finger over the brilliant plumage. The bird cooed, its voice unearthly and nothing like any bird Delphine had ever heard. It hopped to the ground, bound to the Fae woman by a thin gold chain, and displayed its wings in a sweeping gesture for Emily, not unlike a ballerina's curtsy.

"Delphine's throat tightened. What could she possibly offer to pull Emily away from Fae? Even Emily's beloved Sebright bantam chickens at home, with their striking black-on-white plumage, couldn't compare with the creature emitting a melodic trill as Emily let it clamber onto her lap. Frustration boiled under her skin, making her feel prickly and hot all over.

The Fae woman handed the chain to Emily, showing her how to clasp it around her wrist. "You must always keep a baringbird on its chain, or it will turn wild and fly back to the woods. And they can be quite ferocious when they are wild." Emily nodded, double-checking the chain.

She had no idea, Delphine knew, that she was the one chained, tightly bound to Fae not only by the bargain but by the weight of the spell the magic itself cast over her. How long before she couldn't leave? Was she already too far gone? She had forgotten, again, that she had a home that was not the Fae woman's bower, that she had a family outside of Fae. That this was not her home. Del had brought her back, cajoling her with memories. But she would slip again, and again. Ever further. Ever deeper.

"A beautiful creature, is it not? The hunt captured it, and I claimed it as mine." The Fae woman watched with pride as Emily coaxed the bird into singing. "With time, she will train it to sing any song she wishes. Perhaps she will be a composer of baringbird music—choirs of them are difficult to control, but a gifted chorister can manage it."

"I know what you're doing," Delphine replied.

"And what am I doing? Giving gifts to my daughter? Training her in our ways, in the magic of control and transformation?"

"She is not your daughter!"

"Are we back to this?" The Fae woman gave her a glance that was mostly contempt, with some pity thrown in for good measure. "She is mine. By our bargain and by our laws. How long will you linger here, watching her become ever more so?"

"As long as it takes," Delphine retorted, but she knew the futility in what she was saying. No amount of stubborn grit could change the hold of Fae on Emily.

"She is quite thoroughly Fae's creature already," the Fae woman dismissed.

"She is not," Delphine argued. "She remembers her home. She knows me. She misses her mother."

"That, I doubt. She misses nothing. You can see it in her eyes. She is more than content here."

Delphine hated that the Fae woman was right, and nothing she could say could counter it. Worse, she saw the silver wash of Fae spreading in Emily's eyes, even in her face. "How long, then?" she whispered.

"Not long. If she is not too much part of Fae already, it cannot be more than a day or so away." The look she threw at Delphine was pure malice. "And what will you do then?"

Delphine wavered. She had listened in every corner of the Court, charmed the man in pink into long stories of the Fae world, explored the winding paths of the forest nearest the bone cathedral, searching for any answers that would give her a better option than the gambles before her—trade herself to the antlered woman or try the favor. There was nothing. These were the only avenues open to her, and either could be a trap or a failure.

She left Emily and the Fae woman with the baringbird singing a lilting scale and plunged into the forest. Violet—still strange, to think that the Fae girl had once been her great-aunt—waited by the Spire. A flock of birds like starlings freckled with diamonds called gently in the bracken, but otherwise the Fae woods were silent, waiting.

"I knew you would come back." Violet smiled softly. "I knew you would discern my name."

"Why didn't you just tell me?"

"It's not how it's done. It is forbidden to tell even one's own name, without the long years of bonding to another. Besides, I had to be sure you were who I thought you were, who you claimed to be. Another would not have known the story."

"I very nearly didn't, myself," Delphine replied. "No—not that you're forgotten, or disliked, or—it's only that it is of such a sadness to my aunt Imogene that she didn't want to tell us."

"I see. Imogene." She tasted the name, explored it. The soft smile again. "Tell her I am well."

"You had no way of knowing I'd learn that your earthbound name is your Fae name, too."

The girl shrugged. "I figured you'd find out. Or ask. Eventually."

"It might have taken too long," Delphine said, frustrated. Even this girl, bound to guide her, seemed oblivious to the passing of time and the increasing grip Fae held on her niece.

"Oh. Well, it didn't. And I couldn't just *tell* you how it worked, at the same time I told you the story of how I came here. It would be too close to just saying my own name. And that is forbidden, and blots the usefulness of the name."

"The favor wouldn't work?"

Violet winced. "It would not. And so it would be in vain, you see? Losing my name."

"Is it so great a loss?

Violet sat very still. "For any Fae, it is a great loss. To have the favor used against you, it is a loss, to have your name known by another. For me—" She pressed her lips together until they turned white. "For me it is both greater loss and very little loss at all."

"I don't understand."

"I am outside the Court. I have very little status. So I have very little to lose." She steeled herself before continuing. "But it would likely mean I should never regain enough standing to return."

Delphine blanched, understanding what Violet was saying. What, exactly, she had offered. "If I use the favor, you will be banished from Court forever?"

"Very likely so. Unless someone takes my patronage upon themselves."

"Then what would become of you?" Delphine asked quietly.

"I have lived for some time in the wood." She avoided Delphine's eyes. "I would continue to do so. Besides. The Court is a hard place, you know. It is beautiful, but it is hard."

"These woods are not easy," Delphine said. "Knooks and ryls and trails leading to nowhere and many other nightmares, I'm sure."

"It is true. But I know it well." She shrugged, feigning nonchalance. "Are you going to use the favor now?"

Delphine paused. Of course she had to use the favor. There was no other way, unless she bargained herself to the antlered woman—if that would even work. But with Violet standing in front of her, forlorn eyes cast down on her hands as they plied a woolen thread from her cloak into a hair ribbon, she faltered. Could she truly decide to condemn Violet to a life of banishment, outside even the cold comfort offered by the Court? She gathered herself. Emily was slipping further away by the minute, by the hour. She would use the favor and they would be rid of this dreadful place forever.

Then Delphine saw a single tear slide down the Fae girl's cheek. It flashed like a diamond, like no mortal tear, but it was made from the same grief.

She couldn't condemn Violet for her kindness, for lacking the cruel selfishness of the Court. Violet had bargained away her mortal fate and Delphine found she couldn't steal her Fae potential from her, either.

"Wait here," Delphine said. "I will be back soon."

61

For good fortune on a dance card, spend your old cards on the Fae:
Leave the best and prettiest tied with silk on your window sill and you
shall have your choice of partners.

          —"Old Superstitions for Luck and Love,"
            The Young Ladies' Journal, Fall 1904

MUSIC FLARED FROM the center of the Court, warm and bright, casting its sparks deep into the wildwood where Delphine wound her way back from the Spire. Near the Cathedral, a ring of dancers spun around a glowing light. She looked for the antlered woman, but she wasn't among the dancers. If she was in the Court, Delphine would have to pass by the dance to enter the bone cathedral. She stepped onto the smooth grass of the Court cautiously, stories of wild dancing in fairy rings and intoxicating music percolating up from Lilabeth's stories and the books Father kept on the lowest shelves in the library for her and Alaine.

The books had illustrations of fairies and the shadows they cast as they danced around wicked-flamed bonfires, but the scene outside the bone cathedral was nothing like the storybook woodcuts. There had been overtones of warning, of danger in the books, but where the illustrations were all sharp angles and manic faces, this dance ran bright with sinuous joy. The Fae danced around musicians gathered in the center, who glowed with undulating color and light as they

played. Delphine kept her distance but squinted, making out something like a grand harp, and stringed instruments like mandolins of
various sizes, and a silver-toned flute.

The man in the pink suit seemed to lead the music, plying a steady
rhythm on a hand drum with a beater, the instrument pale and shining like mother of pearl. It winked and gleamed in the light—where
had the light come from? Not moonlight or firelight, but sunrise
shades of pink and lilac, dim blue and warm orange. It seemed to
grow and bend and flare and fade with the movement of the music,
dancing in its own right even as the Fae turned and dipped and
ringed one another. At first Delphine thought each was dancing
alone, then that the dance was carefully choreographed, yet neither
seemed quite right. Hands caught hands in surprising patterns, arms
lifted into arcs when she least expected it, feet flew and halted, and
no one ever blundered into anyone else.

The Fae woman stood at the harp, plucking its strings with a soft
smile on her face. Ever-present worry flared—where was Emily?
Delphine moved closer, scanning the dancing crowd for her niece,
but she was nowhere to be found. Delphine breathed a small sigh of
relief that at least Emily was tucked away in the bower, dreaming of
Fae or home or some place in between where the two met with soft
edges like watercolors.

The dance went on, the pulsing of the drum aligned with her
heartbeat, and the melody of the harp emerged dominant in a half-
feral fugue with the mandolins. It made her want to dance, not like
waltzes and polkas at home, but to let a caged part of herself free.
As she watched the steps of the dance, she slowly intuited it, knew
its next moves. Her feet began to weave in a pattern dictated by the
music, drawing her closer to the mesmerizing ring of dancers. It
parted to let her in. Hands caught hers in the undulating arcs and
rings. She wove and leapt, turned and swayed, always in time with
the rhythm she felt suffuse through her pulse, her very breath.

The pace quickened, the harp strings vibrating and the drum
thick and resonant. Her feet moved faster, and the light and color
pulled nearer, brighter. A riot of light cocooned her, seeped into

her clothes and prickled between her fingers. She laughed. Warmth pooled in her belly, belonging and desire and the dance itself. Each step was joy, each turn ecstasy. Like running through the field in summer, as a child, knowing when to leap because her body told her, relishing the heat and the sweat and the feeling of her own body moving in freedom.

She could move in such freedom forever, running in a current that sprang from some depth beyond the music itself. She closed her eyes.

A dark hand caught hers, firm and unbending. Her steps arrested, a turn half completed, her body tangled and limp in confusion. Around her, the dance faltered. A voice whispered close to her ear. She strained to her it. "What are you doing?" She blinked. The colors faded. The gilded man still gripped her hand in his, the dance regaining speed, dodging them like a stream moves around a rock in the current.

"I—I was—"

"Do not join the Fae dance," he hissed. Over her head, he looked to the Fae woman, still plucking the harp, but with less fervor than before, thin fingers on the harp strings but her eyes fixed in stony silence on the gilded man. He pulled her away from the ring, and her head began to clear.

"I suppose I should thank you," she said shakily as they neared the edge of the wildwood.

He glared at her, golden contempt. "Should? You *should* know not to dance in a fairy ring, earthbound woman."

Delphine flushed. She knew stories of fairies dancing on her own side of the veil, whisking away anyone foolish enough to join their revelry. She had always thought the stories rather absurd—after all, who would willingly join a dangerous circle of Fae? How could anyone have such little willpower or be so foolish? Now she knew.

"I don't know what came over me. I didn't mean to, I only meant to listen, and then I was—"

"That's what she intended," the gilded man replied. "It is nearly impossible to hear the music and not join the dance. And once you join, it is an easy thing to snare you in a never-ending dance that would in short order drive you mad."

"Never-ending? But this is the first I've seen of dancing here—"

"Never-ending for any earthbound who begins it. The drums will infect your blood, the harp your ears, and you will hear nothing else. Your feet will obey only the music." He snorted delicately. "And that would be the end of our planning." He pursed his lips, his mouth forming a perfect bow. "She must know you plan to bargain. She set this trap for you."

"How do you—" She stopped herself. "My plans are my own."

"They are mine, too. My lady bargains with you, I am tied to her fate, and so your bargain with her is, in a sense, with me as well." He held himself apart from her, faintly aloof.

"And what do you think of such a bargain?"

"I am not so taken with you as she is," he admitted. "But I can see why she covets you. You have much potential. To create, to bargain. You must do so in your own world already."

Delphine suppressed a laugh. Her weak watercolors, her failed incursion into Perrysburg society. What potential did that reveal? She remembered the antlered woman's story; maybe the wanting was as much potential as anything else here.

"So it would benefit you. In a way."

"In several ways, yes." He paced the edge of the wood. Nearby, the baringbirds in their cage whispered low and mournful. Even here, the harp strings sang clear and high enough that they beckoned Delphine. She ignored them, but the notes echoed in her chest. "To see *her* power reduced, of course. She has held too tightly for too long. And you understand how a bonding of any kind can draw one of our kind higher. The melding of power, of bargains."

Delphine glanced back at the Court. The dance went on. The music ebbed and pulsed, and she felt it throbbing in her veins, begging her to let go of her tensely controlled body and dance. It would be so easy—she shook herself. "If you all want her gone, why do so many dance with her? Why—"

"We do not *all* want her reduced in power. There are those who have aligned themselves with her, though she will bond with none. Do you see, then, the risk my lady takes with you? Try and fail, and we are brought low." He straightened, the lines of his back corded with muscle, but she saw the fissures of anxiety forming. He hadn't wanted to take this risk at all; if she failed, he was bound to the same consequences as the antlered woman.

"I won't fail. I'll make the bargain now."

He shook his head. "She is watching. She snared you with the dance once; it is like a poison that, once it enters the blood, requires a smaller and smaller dose to do its work. And she will find other ways to thwart you. Do not believe, doeling, that since you have passed unmolested through the Court that you are not being watched. That your movements are not noted. That she could not deploy many more tricks against you."

"Then what do I do?" She was so close, and then she could be free of the Court and the Fae woman forever. She could take Emily and run for the wildwood.

"I will see to it." A small smile curved on his lips, not entirely a warm smile. It stirred, cunning and vaguely cruel.

62

Birdsong is sweet at the close of the day
And sweeter still the song of the Fae
But sweetest is Mother's song at home
Away to bed now, no more to roam
—Children's lullaby

ALAINE HESITATED AS she faced the heavy front door of Orchard Crest. She rarely knocked or waited for an answer; she rarely used this door at all, preferring the rickety screen door off the kitchen. But today she raised the brass knocker and let it fall with three resounding clanks. And waited.

Papa Horatio answered with a soft smile that took in her drawn face and clenched hands and knew why she was here. "Your ma's in the breakfast room upstairs. Ain't eating much, but she's there. You want me to bring up some coffee?"

"I don't think I could stomach coffee."

"Tea then. Mint tea, good for digestion. Good for a lot of things."

"Gran always said that."

"Lilabeth knew her way around a kitchen garden," Papa Horatio said. He closed the door behind Alaine. "I suppose it skipped a generation. Your mother's roses beat all, but your pa never had an interest for herbs. But we've got a tin of mint tea in the pantry, I'll wager."

That was true, Alaine thought as she tiptoed up the curving staircase to the breakfast room. Mother poured her time into roses, not mint and comfrey and rosemary. She was skilled in a particular kind of glamour that had nothing to do with fairies and everything to do with carefully arranged flowers and furniture, carefully chosen colors and words. Now all that magic was as useless as any other.

Maybe it always had been, Alaine considered as she knocked softly on the door of the breakfast room. "Come in," her mother's light soprano answered.

She sat on the chair by the window, cream silk dressing gown and pink silk cushions melding into a cloud. Did she look thinner, or was it just the shadows under her eyes? She didn't look at Alaine right away, instead gazing out the window toward the long slope of Prospect Street slipping away toward the railroad tracks at the base of the hill.

"Hello, Mother," Alaine said, hovering by the door. She had the sudden impulse to go on her knees like a supplicant, apologizing for everything. But she sensed that wasn't what anyone needed.

"Oh, Alaine. We made a mess of things."

Alaine started. "Mother, you had nothing to do—"

"I did. I have everything to do with it. I'm your mother." She sighed deeply and turned to Alaine. "It shouldn't have come to this. I should have seen more for both of you."

"Mother?" Alaine crossed the room and sat next to her, reaching out for her cold hand. "What do you mean, you should have seen more?"

"I never believed you girls could do anything differently than I had done. Find a good man, make a good match." She bit her thin lips together. Her hair fell over her shoulder in a thick braid blending honey and iron. "I taught Delphine everything I knew. I taught her every art, every skill. Piano, dancing, watercolors—"

"All the things I could never learn," Alaine said with a rueful smile.

"And oh, I was frustrated! You never cared to learn—you just wanted to dabble in the dirt with Papa Horatio and learn bargains from Lilabeth." She looked down at her lap, brow creasing. "I thought you'd never make a good match. I thought you'd be an unhappy old maid like Imogene." Alaine kept her mouth patiently shut—Imogene didn't seem unhappy at all, but Mother clearly didn't—couldn't—see it that way. "I was proven wrong with Jack, and I'm grateful. But I thought how..." She closed her eyes, as though in shame. "I thought how *right* I was when Delphine had Pierce Grafton calling."

"Mother, you couldn't have known, none of us could—"

"But you did. I—God forgive me—I thought you were jealous at first, but no. You saw through him. I should have, too."

"No one should have to see through someone," Alaine replied, disgusted. "Don't you see? He's got us blaming ourselves when he's the one to blame."

"I am, too, Alaine. I taught your sister the wrong things, I tried to teach you, I—I was so disappointed in how you're raising Em, I wouldn't tell someone how to raise their child, but—" She caught a sob in her throat. "But I was wrong."

"I was, too, Mother. I—Gran taught me better than this, Imogene warned me against it, but I thought I could do what they couldn't."

Mother looked up, eyes shining with unshed tears. "You can do what none of us could. You're running the orchard, you're a businesswoman. President of the Agricultural Society. I never thought I could dream of anything for you and Del other than advantageous marriages, and that foolishness cost Del everything." She wavered. "And you."

"Mother, Delphine will get Emily back. I know she will," Alaine lied confidently. "She's—she's smart and strong, and none of us give her enough credit. Besides," she said with a poor attempt at a smile, "if anything could prepare someone for navigating the Fae, I'd think the backstabbing politics of Perrysburg would do it."

Mother didn't return the smile. "When they're back, I want things to be different."

Alaine felt a rush of sympathy for her mother. "There's nothing wrong with watercolors and piano, Mother. They're beautiful. We need that, too, you know. But—we need them for ourselves, and for each other, not for Pierce Grafton." She hesitated, then continued,

"Maybe Emily might like to learn piano?" Mother looked up, surprised. "She likes music, I'm sure she'd like to try it out. It's not good for her to be entirely feral."

At that, Mother managed a rusty laugh. "I'd like that very much." They didn't voice the word that ran in a thick dark current under everything they said—*if*. If Emily came back at all.

63

The Fae may claim each bargain due
But may only take the bargain true.
—Folk saying

SEVERAL MINUTES AFTER the gilded man left her, Delphine heard shouts from the center of the dancing ring. The man in pink dropped his drum and pointed. A shadow bounded past the citadel of bone, black waves against the pale walls. A huge cat, Delphine realized as it leapt and rolled on the grass.

The Fae woman's mount. The gilded man must have set it loose, a distraction to give her time free from the Fae woman's scrutiny.

The cat was followed by the unicorn, cantering swiftly into the wildwood, and the giant chicken, who ran toward a patch of brambles and began to scratch. The wobbling gait that Delphine had often laughed at in barnyard chickens was now a terrifying prospect of enormous feet and claws, spurs protruding nearly a foot from the back of each scaly leg.

The dance broke apart, some running toward the mounts, others away in fright, many simply running and laughing as though the whole thing was a great jest. The chicken reared and flapped as a trio of Fae approached it, squawking as indignantly as the hens at home. Still near the center of the Court, the Fae woman let her hands fall from the harp. Her face was schooled in a dispassionate mask, but she was paler, Delphine noted, and her hands clenched into fists. She left the harp and made for the wildwood, the path that the cat had taken.

Now was her chance. Delphine wound her way through the gardens outside the bone cathedral. Despite the shouts and even laughter from outside, it was silent once she passed through the vestibule with its strange washbasin. She didn't pause as she passed a tangle of roses singing in pale harmony and a tree like a weeping cherry, raining ever-regenerating blossoms into a pool of flowers at its roots. The antlered woman rested beside a pool of emerald-green fish. One rose to nip at her fingers as she dipped them languidly in the water.

"I am ready to bargain," Delphine said.

The antlered woman sat up brightly, startling the fish into a flurry of brilliant green splashing. "Very well. I will take you, forever, for my own, and I shall bring a contest of guardianship to the Court."

"No."

The antlered woman's smile vanished as though she'd been smacked. "No? And what do you have of value instead, doeling?"

"I understand what you want. It's not me—" The antlered woman's perfect lips parted to argue, but Delphine stopped her. "Not really, anyway. It's what keeping me here could mean. You want the balance of power reshaped. You want the Fae woman who holds my niece as her ward to be reduced in status. And, I see now, for you to gain status."

"One's loss is another's gain. It is how it is." She shrugged. "But you cannot convince her to free the girl, and I see no other way for you to break her hold on power here."

"The girl is coming home with me. I will use the favor."

Now the antlered woman was shocked, and an ugliness like anger played around her eyes. "You don't know any of our names. You cannot! There is none in the Court who would let you guess, none!"

"But I have guessed a name. Now tell me. How many names do you know? How many of this Court, or any other?"

The Fae woman was silent a long, breathless moment. "None. I know no names."

"Then here is my bargain. I will give you one name, once I have used it for the favor. And if I give you that name, you will take in the Fae girl who lives in the wildwood, as your ward."

The antlered woman scoffed, more like the soft snort of a deer than a human. "The girl? Why? She is nothing, a mistake made by another."

"She does not have to be. Not if you raise her. She could be the third in your alliance. A daughter, bound to you and the golden man. You could reshape the borders of power that way." The antlered woman did not look convinced. "She is clever. She guided me through the wildwood when I first came, and she can ply what she finds there into beautiful things." She held out the comb. "She made this in the blink of an eye."

"It is pretty." She shrugged. "And not without some skill, to render the leaf thus."

"She would learn even better skill from you. And how to bargain with humans and maneuver through the Fae Court." She paused, gauging the woman's interest, which was growing measurably. "Such a bond could change the balance of power here, yes? A bond not unlike that of a family?"

"It is so." She narrowed her deep blue eyes, considering. "But if you can use the favor, you need not bargain with me at all. Why?"

"I don't." She let the words hang between them. "I know why you wished to use me—don't deny it—but you could have used me badly, and you did not. If there is something I can leave you with, there you are."

"Whose name?"

"That I will not say," Delphine said. "Not until I've finished."

"But you will use the favor." She sighed, a pretty sound and a gentle waver of her whole body. "Very well. I will take on the patronage of the wildwoods girl. In exchange for the name."

"The bargain is made."

"Not yet. I desire one more thing in exchange." She rose, languid body unspooling itself. "You do amuse me, doeling. You say I would make a bargain with any—but no, oh, no." She smiled softly, taking Delphine's hand in hers. "You are all life and fire and salt—I would taste of that mortal salt even if it should poison me."

Delphine's heart turned over in her chest, not in fear or revulsion, but because she knew that desire, too. It ran counter to what the antlered woman called mortal salt—it was star gleam and shadow, whispers and linden scent. Delphine had longed since she first stepped into the Court to taste, to savor the Fae world, its power and its beauty. Those manifested themselves in the form of the woman before her, and touching her hand was like holding boundless opportunity.

"I would add to our bargain—one kiss."

Delphine exhaled slowly, desire pooling in her belly. "Tell me. Is it like tasting your food, drinking your wine?"

"It is like that and more," the Fae woman whispered, her breath warm against Delphine's ear. "But it will not entrap you. You are made of stronger stuff, doeling." She pulled back slightly, with a knowing smile. "And you know that I cannot lie whilst I bargain. It is forbidden on this side of the veil, as it is on yours."

"Very well."

"So bargained, so agreed."

"So agreed," Delphine returned in a whisper.

The woman took both of Delphine's hands in her own, marveling with her touch at the calluses on Delphine's fingers where she held pens and paintbrushes too long. She pulled Delphine toward her, and met her lips. It was like nothing Delphine had known—of course Pierce had kissed her, but not with this intensity, this curiosity. Tasting her, testing her. And the fullness of Fae flooded Delphine, purple shadow and pale moonlight, perfume of sandalwood and rose, the bite of autumn wind and the cold rush of spring snowmelt. It was overwhelming, intoxicating, beckoning her to fall headlong in love with this side of the veil.

And yet she did not break away, not until the Fae did.

The antlered woman stepped back, pale and quaking. "Oh, doeling. Salt and fire and a death by iron, you are. But such a sweet death, I would die a thousand times." She lifted her hand. "Go then. And I shall see you but once more, when you deliver me my name."

64

As modern civilization continues its onward march, many have abandoned bargaining practices as relics of the past, ill-suited to the twentieth century, replacing them with better tools, medicines, and of course education.

—*Flora, Fauna, and Fae: A Study in Cultural Geography,*
by Leonard Worthington Wilkes

THE FAE GIRL waited where Delphine had left her, near the Spire. She had climbed a tree whose branches shaped themselves into nearly a perfect sphere. Violet was cupped in the center, toying with a flutter of leaves.

"You came back," she said. She dropped from the tree, hesitant as she approached Delphine. "You shall use the favor, then?"

"I would like to," Delphine said. Violet nodded, bravely resigned. "But something else first. You would like to return to Court, yes?"

"It is better not to think of impossible things." She stared at the ground between Delphine's feet.

"I have made a place for you there." At this, Violet looked up with a start. "You will be under the guardianship of one of the Fae—the huntress with the antlers."

"Truly? I can return, and with a patron?"

"Yes." Delphine hesitated. "I have to give her something in return. Your name."

"Oh—she would have earned that as my patron in any case." Slowly Violet appreciated this. "You are shrewd! To trick her so!"

"I didn't consider it a trick, necessarily—I offered a name. It's all I had of value in the Court, as far as I know—my trinkets wouldn't buy that kind of bargain, I don't think. She took the bargain and didn't insist on knowing whose name she would get."

"Very well, then. She may be upset at first, but I will show her I am a worthy ward."

"Good." Delphine's heartbeat quickened. "Then I'd like to use the favor."

Violet grinned. "It is easy. Say what you want, and ask the favor in my name."

"Is that all? No incantations, no ceremony? No blood?" Violet shook her head with a laugh, and Delphine took a steadying breath. "I want my kinswoman released into my keeping, to return to the human world. I wish all claims to her in this world to be void." She glanced at the girl, who nodded approvingly. "I ask this favor of Violet."

The Fae girl beamed, her face shedding the opalescent veil of Fae for a moment and looking entirely human. "It is granted."

Delphine realized she had spent so much time preparing for this moment that she didn't know what to do next. "Should I go fetch her? Can we go through the door now?"

"Yes. I shall meet you here. Collect your niece and come to meet me."

Delphine went to the Court first. It was nearly empty, but from the shouts and laughter echoing from the woods, she guessed that most of the Fae were still engaged in a madcap chase with the escaped mounts. But the antlered woman and the golden-eyed man sat next to a crystal pool—Delphine was quite sure it was not where it had been before—with their arms interlaced.

"Doeling! You have come to play?" She rose, a swift motion that disentangled her from the man and left him sitting by himself. "We were just deciding what game we should try. He already set a game for the others—oh, they are having a time of it." An indigo fish leapt from the pool—Delphine was sure the fish had been emerald when last she'd seen them. This place, ever reworked, endlessly reshaped.

Delphine glanced at the man, who leaned over the pool with almost-believable detachment. "I've something to tell you."

"Ah. You will give us a moment, my sweet?" The antlered woman stepped closer to the gilded man, dipped her hand in the pool, and splashed him. The water dissolved into a shower of rainbows. "I've decided what game to play later," she said, and he smiled. "But I must speak to this doeling first."

He left with one backward glance at Delphine, nodding once. The antlered woman turned to her, eager. "Well? It is done?"

"It is done. And we're going home." The word tasted sweet and yet not quite real in her mouth. "And I owe you a name."

"And I owe you a home for a foundling Fae child."

For the first time in this transaction, Delphine hesitated. The antlered woman had been led to believe she was getting a name, not of the girl in the wood, but a member of the Court. She didn't know if anger changed the balance of bargains, if this woman's wrath could stand in her way.

"The name is the name of the Fae girl from the wildwood." She swallowed as the antlered woman's eyes widened. "It's *Violet*."

The antlered woman's shocked face melted into amusement. "Very shrewd, doeling. And how you found her name, I shall never know. Well." She smiled, a strange, nearly gentle expression that softened the harsh edges of Fae from her face. "I suppose I may learn, in time."

"You may."

"And now you must go. She will not be pleased when she learns the child is no longer bound to her, and the wind begins to whisper it already. Her cat will not detain her much longer."

Delphine nodded, and slipped out of the palace of bone and down the path to the Fae woman's bower. Delphine expected resistance, or even an army of Fae to careen out of the Court and block her from taking Emily. But the paths near the bower were quiet, and blithe laughter echoed from the archways of bone. No one stopped her.

The silvery door was open, and only Emily waited inside. She played with the chips of metal, smoothing one into a paper-thin sheen of gold under her hand. Delphine watched her for a long moment, watched how her concentration wiped the youth from her face, made her as ageless as the Fae.

"Em," she whispered. Her niece looked up, clouded for a moment, then smiled brightly. "Em, dear, can we go for a walk?"

"Of course, Aunt Del!" She dropped the wavering sheet of gold as though it were a simple plaything. "There is a cage of rainbow baringbirds down this path—have you seen it?"

"No, I haven't. I—I wanted to take a longer walk, Emily. I want to show you the gate to go home."

"Home?" Emily's face constricted into confusion.

"Your home. My home. It's time, Em. This place is lovely, but we don't belong here."

"We could, I think." Emily stood very still, and her voice sounded older than Delphine remembered. "We could belong, in time. Very soon, even. It tells me so. It tells me how to belong."

"Please, Em. Your mama—your mama misses you."

A flash of pain, of memory—and Em slipped her hand into Delphine's. "I'd like to see the gate, anyway."

Heart in her throat, Delphine led Emily down the path, away from the rainbow baringbirds who whistled into the shadows of their cage and deeper into the forest. She spotted the Spire, and picked her way over paths that would lead her there, but Violet wasn't there. Delphine's pulse increased, but she forced herself to squeeze Em's hand and give her a reassuring smile. "We'll go this way, and then I have a friend who will help us."

Emily didn't argue, and examined the twisting trees and silvered leaves of the wildwood with intense curiosity. The path began to narrow, and Delphine forced herself to keep going. Violet must be here, must be waiting. She promised.

It didn't matter—she would find her way to the tree herself, if she had to. The path bent and dipped under a shower of gilt-edged leaves, and as Delphine lifted her head, she stopped.

The Fae woman waited in the path.

Delphine pushed Emily behind her, her hands cold and her mind racing. What now? Could she be stopped, did the laws of Fae restrict this woman? She didn't seem bound by anything, Delphine thought, as she stood unmoving in the path.

"Fool of an earthbound woman," the Fae woman whispered, imperious and unshakeable, but her face was not the immutable mask she'd worn in every encounter Delphine had had with her thus far. "You've made your bargain, have you? Gotten back what you came for?"

"It's not your concern any longer," Delphine said softly, clutching Emily's hand. Her niece's eyes went wide as she shrank behind Delphine's skirt.

"But it is." She advanced, footfalls silent on the silver moss. "You have ruined me, cast me into shame. And now who will save my Court?"

"Your Court? It doesn't seem to need much saving."

The woman shook her head, desperation in her eyes. "I have tried to fortify my world against what is coming. Famine, in your terms. Famine and withering and the deathless mortification of our people."

Delphine held firm to Em's hand. "I don't care what happens to you and your people. Not now."

"Not at all?" The woman's piercing stare, moon-pale in the low light of the Fae forest, forced her to stillness.

"In a sense," Delphine said, halting, "perhaps. But any disaster must surely be of your own making, all your scheming and politics and pride."

"Not in the slightest," the Fae woman replied, ice in her voice. "No, I have bargained and allied and risen in power to avert this. To establish our independence from your world. That was why I asked for cherries, for apples. To create that which might regenerate, might yield."

"Why?"

The Fae woman's smile was triumph and grief at once. "Only I have seen it, seen it for what it is. Your world is ever more bound in iron, ever less passable for us."

"The railways."

"Yes, once it was only the railways. And the bridges, slicing through the rivers. Now your very cities are girded with iron. The doorways which lie too near must close, lest we be poisoned by it. Our paths are cut ever shorter, ever closer. We cannot roam to bargain as we once did. And it will not slow, will it, the binding of your world?"

"No." Delphine thought of farms replacing their horses with trucks, of railways weaving ever-wider webs, of the newest buildings in Chicago and Saint Louis challenging the sky itself, all framed in steel. "No, it won't. The cities will grow, and there will be new railways and new bridges."

"And without our doorways and our bargains, what will we have? We will reshape what is here, over and again, until it crumbles to dust." She wavered, and for a moment Delphine saw fear in her eyes. "With more time, I might have done more. I might have planted orchards to rival yours. But now, you are my undoing and the undoing of this Court."

"I have done nothing that your own people did not wish." Delphine forced back anger at being cast as villain in the Fae woman's story. "That's your own fault. They would have found a way, even without me, in time."

"You should have asked for their help," Emily said suddenly. "If you work together, maybe you can get more done. That's what we do, at our farm."

The Fae woman paused, caught between retort and surprise. "That has not been the way of it, here."

"We are leaving," Delphine said, resolutely lifting Emily's hand in hers.

But Emily didn't move. "Can't we do anything to help them?"

Delphine stopped. She didn't want to help these creatures, tangled in the web of their own politics and glamours and pride. But what example did that set for Em? And what of Violet? She thought of the linden tree, pale and leafless, shorn of its bark like the great oak she had seen, poisoned by iron and cut off from the magic that flowed out of Fae, and the prospect filled her with grief. "We will not allow iron to be brought too close to our tree. And we will still make the usual bargains, as long as we remain the owners of Orchard Crest." She met the Fae woman's eyes over Emily's head. "And that is all we can do."

They left the Fae woman behind as the trail bent and wove through the forest, Delphine barely noticing the brilliant shifting rainbow of flowers and the intricately knotted vines and branches laden with fruit the color of poison.

Violet waited beneath a shower of pale blossoms at the next bend in the path.

"You have come," she said simply, with a broad smile. "You must wish to leave now."

"Yes, very much so," Delphine said. "When you go back to the Court, you will want to find"—she realized she did not have any name to call the Fae who had made her bargain, just the moniker she'd given her in her head, "the antlered woman"—"the woman with antlers, the huntress with the horn."

"I know the woman."

"I've told her your name."

"And was she pleased?" She laughed, a sound like merry birds.

"She was surprised, but I think she is even now preparing a place for you in her own bower. She has plans, Violet. And—you must make plans, too."

"Plans were what *she* did."

"I know. But—but listen to them. Listen to her." Delphine hesitated. "She was wrong in how she made her power, but she isn't wrong about the future, I'm afraid."

Violet nodded sagely. "Very well." She glanced at Emily. "And now you must go. The girl does not belong here, not as I do."

"I am glad I saw this place, though." Emily spoke quietly. "And I am sad to leave. I don't suppose—can we come back, Aunt Del?"

Perhaps it was the proximity to the door breaching the veil, or the time spent with Delphine in the woods, or the release of her bindings, but Emily spoke clearly, and her eyes had lost the haze of the Fae.

"No, my dear. I don't think that we can. But perhaps we will still see a bit of the Fae in our own world."

"You very well may," Violet said. "Now go!"

65

Here's to thee, old apple-tree,
To buds in the spring and roots in the loam,
To the Fae who brings the apples home
— Wassail song

ALAINE SAT ON the porch of Lavender Cottage, looking out over the apple trees that had been her family's stake for fifty years. The late harvest was coming in, long rows of Smokehouse and Northern Spy, laden with heavy red fruit. Crates leaned against trees, stacked taller than Alaine, ready to bear the next wave of the harvest to market.

And Alaine felt empty and thin, stretched by the long weeks of waiting into a dim shadow. If Emily didn't come home, she would sell the orchard. If Emily didn't come home, she would never leave, holding vigil for the rest of her years, peering into her otherworldly mirror to see the daughter she couldn't follow.

If Emily didn't come home, she didn't know what she would do.

"Alaine!" The voice echoed past the apple trees, coming from deeper inside the forest. "Alaine!"

She stood up like a shot. Delphine. She didn't feel her feet hitting the wooden stairs of the porch or her shoes leeching dew from the damp grass, didn't feel the snap of branches against her face at the edge of the forest, only followed that sound like a hound on the scent.

"Del!" she shouted into the hemlock and oak trees. "Del, where are you?"

But she knew already—the linden tree. She ran the paths she knew by heart, dodging tree roots and large stones by memory, coming to a breathless halt in front of the linden.

Delphine sat on her heels in the middle of the circle, Emily in her lap. A faint scent like a spent match lingered in the circle, and the tree pulsed with silver in its branches, but these warnings didn't keep Alaine out. She fell to her knees next to her sister, cradling her daughter's limp body.

"What happened?" She gripped Emily's hand, touched her cheek softly, tentatively. It was cool and damp, her forehead breaking into a sweat. "Did she faint? Did you—are you—"

"I'm all right. Coming through the gate is—it's dizzying, I assume she fainted, but—"

"We should get her home—" Alaine stopped, and caught her sister's hand. "Oh God, Del, I—I—" She broke into sobs and collapsed against her sister's shoulder.

"It's all right," Delphine murmured. "It's all right now. We're home. We're home for good. Now get up and help me, you goat." She shook Alaine gently. "Come on, now. I don't want to stay in a fairy circle any longer than I have to."

Alaine rose on shaky legs, and she could tell that Delphine was no firmer in her bearings, but between the two of them, they slung Emily on their interlaced arms and made their way home.

Alaine lay Em on her bed and curled next to her. Delphine sat nearby. "How long has it been, Alaine? It was—it was still almost as hot as midsummer when I left. And now—"

"It's been over a month," Alaine whispered, voice muffled by Emily's hair. "I had almost given up, Del."

"Alaine, I—" She fell silent again. "Maybe we should get Imogene. Or even Ida, I don't know."

"Why?" Alaine rose on her elbow and smoothed a stray lock of hair out of Emily's eyes. She had kept it neat, after all—nicely brushed out and tied with what looked like a strand of silk. She turned to

Delphine, and her sister's face made her go cold all at once. "Del, what is it?"

"They told me—they told me that if a person stayed in Fae too long, it would—it would do things—I—I'm afraid, Alaine." She shuddered at every breath as she spoke, and didn't take her eyes off Emily.

"You think this is some kind of illness? I thought you said that coming through the door is just jarring—are you sure that isn't it?"

"I'm not sure of anything," Delphine said.

Alaine watched Emily's face, terrified that the peaceful sleep hid something she couldn't understand, would never understand because her daughter had gone somewhere she couldn't follow. She laid her hand on her cheek; it wasn't as cold as before, the paleness receding as a soft flush warmed her skin.

"I think she's just asleep," Alaine said, and she knew Delphine could hear the lack of conviction in her voice.

Her sister hovered over the bed. "If Violet knew, she would have said something, but I'm sure she didn't."

"Violet?" Alaine pulled Emily closer as she lay down again. "Tell me everything."

As Delphine unspooled the tangled story of the Fae Court, and their great-aunt, and a fairy huntress with gilded antlers, and a palace of bone, and a forest of wild magic, Emily began to stir next to Alaine. Not quite waking, but fretful, as though pursued by dreams on one side and the beckoning of daylight on the other.

"So I promised we wouldn't put any iron—or steel, I suppose, or anything like that—near the tree," Delphine said.

"I don't suppose that will be difficult to do," Alaine replied. "I don't want to care a whit for them, but if Violet is there, I suppose I can't help it, a little."

"It was beautiful, Alaine. Horrible and warped and beautiful. I—I never want to see it again, and I would go back in an instant." Delphine stared out the window at the forest. "They said Emily would forget. But maybe—maybe she'll feel this strange twisting in her soul like I do, knowing something else is out there and not being able to see it."

Alaine didn't know what to say, but her attention was quickly diverted to the most wonderful thing she had ever seen or, she was sure, would ever see. Emily's eyes fluttered open, slowly acclimating to the light flooding her bedroom, blinking at the bright, solid realness of her own side of the veil. "Mama?"

66

Come away, O human child!
To the waters and the wild
With a faery, hand in hand,
For the world's more full of weeping than you can understand.
—"The Stolen Child," by William Butler Yeats

EMILY WOVE A handful of golden straw into a knotted ring, Aunt Del holding an identical skein of straw next to her and coaxing it into a smooth wreath. "You've got the hang of it," her aunt praised her. "It's just practice that makes the knots lie the right way."

"Balderdash," Mama replied from her perch on a ladder, head deep in the foliage of an Ashmead's Kernel apple tree. "I've been practicing for decades, and I still can't make anything that doesn't look like a goat chewed it up and spat it out."

"What does it do?" Emily asked, holding the crooked circle up to the sun. It winked as though it was catching the sunlight itself and plying it into a golden ring. Something caught like a thorn deep in Emily's memory, a nostalgia she couldn't ever quite name.

"It was a kind of bargain once," Delphine said. She leaned against the tree, her freshly bobbed hair splaying into a halo of soft waves on the bark. "Before they laid the streetcar tracks so close to Orchard Crest, we'd hang these outside the parlor windows when we were entertaining." She turned her wreath over in her hand. "It made everything seem brighter, prettier."

"Straw did that?"

"No, the Fae did that," Mama replied, still half swallowed by the tree. "They took those in trade."

"Funny trade," Em said. "But if you want, we can hang these in the parlor for the party. Even if it doesn't do anything anymore."

"I'd like that," Aunt Del answered. "It's been ages since I wove one of these—makes me think of Christmastime with Lilabeth," she called up to Mama. "Our Gran would help us make these and hang them in the parlor before Mother's annual Christmas party. I can still taste her gingerbread—dang it, Alaine, watch it with those clippers!" She shook a shower of twigs from her skirt.

"Speaking of, I'd better mix up the pastry dough, or it won't chill in time." Mama climbed down the ladder, leaves clinging to her hair like she was some kind of wood nymph in overalls. "And we should get dressed by four o'clock or so if we want to get seats in the gymnasium. Grandmother finished your dress yesterday. You should run over and pick it up."

Emily nodded. "I will soon. I want to take a walk first—stretch my legs before sitting through commencement."

Mama and Aunt Del shared a look—wordless telegraphs between the two sisters that said more than Emily could ever quite decipher. They had their secrets, Mama and Aunt Del, and all Em really knew of them was that Aunt Del had been married once, a long time ago, and Mama had helped her when she divorced him. That was the fall Emily had been sick—at least, that was what she'd been told, that she'd missed the first month of school because of a fever, even though she didn't remember it. She did remember Mama tilling up a patch of grass in the yard and sowing salt in it.

And she remembered Aunt Del coming to live with them for the rest of that year and most of the next. It was a happy time for Emily; Aunt Del was always willing to have a tea party or cut out paper dolls or practice piano with her. But there had also been gossip and rumor and who knew what else—Moore's Ferry was like that, Em thought, like a sun-gorged snake. Quiet and sluggish and full of venom. It was no wonder Aunt Del had moved to Chicago when Emily was still just a little kid.

Aunt Del sent Em postcards from the city—drawings in faded pastel of buildings that challenged the sky, of the white city left over from the 1893 Exposition, stone lions prowling Michigan Avenue, and the lakeshore, as boundless as the ocean. She kept them tacked up in her room, an ever-expanding collage of potential tomorrows. She could start out as a telephone operator like Aunt Del. She could teach watercolors in the park like Aunt Del. She could work in advertising for the telephone company like Aunt Del, and shop at Marshall Field's, and run the Salvation Army serving doughnuts out of Union Station for the doughboys heading overseas. She could study art and paint strange landscapes of silvered forests and warped branches that spoke to Emily in a language words couldn't, and have her work exhibited and praised in Chicago and New York and even Paris. She could take the train home for visits wearing a modish gabardine dress barely grazing her calves and her hair chopped into a bob.

Or, she thought as the forest enveloped her in a familiar embrace, she could stay right here and run Orchard Crest, like Mama did. The first woman to own a registered farm business in Moore's Ferry, and the first woman to be elected president of the Agricultural Society, and the first woman to lecture on agricultural innovation at the university. One of the loudest suffragette voices in those years leading up to the amendment, and the persistent presence that maintained a chapter of the League of Women Voters for the county. "You can't change things for just yourself," she told Emily time and again. "If there's something wrong, it's more than likely it's wrong for plenty of folks."

The truth was, she wanted both, wanted to drink in the summer haze over the orchard, and the bright frost on the trees, and the pale bloom of apple blossoms every year. And she wanted to leave Moore's Ferry, leave it for the places she imagined beyond the horizons of a town that gossiped about women who bobbed their hair, who had fought women's suffrage like it would poison them, who, increasingly, wore white robes and burned crosses. There was more out there, she was sure, than what made the heart of Moore's Ferry beat. And somehow, in some strange magic that she could never articulate beyond a strange, misty nostalgia, there was more right here at Orchard Crest, too.

She rounded the bend in the path and there it was—the linden tree and its ring of velvety green grass. Its blooms, waxen white, bobbed in the breeze, the scent wan and thin but suspended permanently in a cloud around the tree. She'd been warned away from the tree a thousand times as a child, but she could never quite remember a time when it didn't represent a sort of homecoming for her. It didn't frighten her—though it bloomed in midwinter and the grass never died back, even under a blanket of snow. It welcomed her. It invited her to rest, to dream of all those myriad tomorrows.

Papa Horatio, the family story went, was the last person on Prospect Hill to see a fairy in the flesh—or whatever they had instead of flesh. And he was gone, buried ten years ago. Yet Emily felt a deep-seated conviction the Fae were still here, beyond the bargains Mama still left in the field for good weather and to keep the armyworms out of the branches and the moles out of the roots. You could write that off, Em always thought—raccoons could have eaten the toast they left hanging from the trees at Wassail, birds could have flown off with the ribbons and threads they tied around the trunks. Maybe you could even write off their luck, that their orchard staved off pests when others were overrun, and they hadn't lost a harvest to frost or drought in twenty years.

But you couldn't, Em thought with conviction, write off the linden tree. You couldn't write off the blossoms or the scent like some otherworldly golden perfume. And Emily couldn't write off the exquisite, beautiful pain that flooded her core when she let herself be still here. A longing like being in love, she thought, even though she'd never really been in love—you couldn't count Clarence Whitley, who was all right for going to the movies with, but she drew the line when he tried to kiss her at the Christmas dance last winter.

She pulled a few bits and bobs from her pocket—several bent brass pins, a broken glass bead necklace, and a loop of wool braid left over from the coat Grandmother had trimmed this winter. She left things here—she wasn't quite sure why, except that she could have sworn there were more bargains when she was a child, bargains with silk ribbons and silver pins and beads and shards of glass. She remembered losing a pink silk shoe a few days before Aunt Del's wedding, and trading a trinket made of glass and silk for help finding it, even though Mama swore they didn't bargain in the house, they never had. But she remembered tying silk ribbon around worn green glass, repeating words Mama taught her, cached in memory. So she left little bits and bobs here, things she thought the fairies might like. She wasn't sure why she cared, exactly, except that the thought nagged her—they must have wanted the scraps for something, and if they didn't get them from her, where would they get them?

She brushed a hand against the rich green grass, thicker and softer than anywhere else on Prospect Hill, warmth and a ticklish whisper of gooseflesh creeping up her arm. Then she turned back toward Orchard Crest, where Grandmother waited with her new dress, sheer white cotton with impossibly small pin tucks. She'd wear it for the commencement exercises in the sweltering gymnasium at Moore's Ferry High School, and then for the party tomorrow with her friends, and then— and then who knew?

Hidden behind a veil of velvet shadows pooling beneath low-hanging branches, Violet waited until Em had turned the corner of the path toward the sunlight, then collected the gifts. Wool black as night, glass like ice threaded on silk, and a jangle of pins the color of last autumn's leaves. She held each reverently, the potential of transformation shining in each. The girl had changed, her soft freckled face gaining the planes of an adult's and the sharp timbre of her laugh softening, transformed by the magic of the earthbound that couldn't touch Fae. But something of Fae remained in the girl-turned-woman, a thread binding them together as surely as blood might have. Violet smiled softly, pride in the girl she'd sent from Fae into her earthbound fate swelling like the bloom of magic.

Acknowledgments

For better or worse, this was my pandemic book. I don't think there's any easy way to write a book, and I don't think there's any easy way to muddle through a pandemic. Both can be isolating, solitary endeavors. Both can make for long days when you wonder if you really accomplished anything. The world can constrict to the size of a laptop screen.

The beautiful thing is, of course, we're not really alone—especially not in the endeavor to publish a book. I am fortunate to have an incredibly talented team behind this novel, and I appreciate every one of them.

Of course, my intrepid agent, Jessica Sinsheimer—thank you for guidance, feedback, support, and enthusiasm, which hasn't waned over the course of four books. Nivia Evans, the best editor in the business—thank you for your vision. This book would still be a blob of ideas instead of novel-shaped without you. Angelica Chong, thank you for jumping in with both editing feet! On the managing editorial and production side of things, I don't know what kind of magic Bryn A. McDonald, Susan Eberhart, and Erin Cain work, but things have gone so smoothly, and I know what kind of challenges this pandemic-addled world is doling out—thanks! Laura Blackwell, my patient and insightful copy editor—thank you, and I'm sorry for all the comma splices, for I am so very fond of them.

I may be biased, but this book is beautiful, and that's all due to Lauren Panepinto, Lisa Marie Pompilio, and Stephanie A. Hess, the art and design geniuses. (Orbit has the best covers. They did not bribe me to say this.) And of course, marketing (Alex Lencicki, Paola Crespo, Natassja Haught), publicity (Ellen Wright, Angela Man), and sales (Rachel Hairston)—I appreciate all your work going on behind the scenes.

Acknowledgments

To my worldbuilding, podcasting comrades, Cass Morris and Marshall Ryan Maresca—thanks for challenging my writing every time we talk. Shannon Chakraborty, thanks for reading some early pages and giving me the push I needed to revise in the right direction. And everyone in the writing bunker, there with support and reassurance and a safe place to scream—so many thanks.

Naturally, just when the laptop screen was becoming too small of a place to be, I had a little girl and a not-so-little-anymore girl to snap me out of it (sometimes unwillingly, but you two know best). And it goes without saying (but I will say it anyway, as saying it anyway is a very good practice to have) that I am forever grateful to the support of my husband. Thank you for knowing that the care and feeding of a writer is time and space and for tolerating my nitpicks of Star Trek and for patiently waiting to see the words I'm not ready to share yet.

Finally, for my own grandfather, who bought a few acres of land where an old orchard used to be and built his house and made a life, where nearly a century later I also built a house and made a life and one day wandering the hills thought—but what if fairies?

Meet the Author

Emily R. Allison

ROWENNA MILLER lives in the Midwest with her husband and daughters, as well as several cats, two goats, and an ever-growing flock of chickens. When she isn't inventing fantasy worlds, she teaches writing, trespasses while hiking, and gets into trouble with her sewing machine.

if you enjoyed
THE FAIRY BARGAINS OF PROSPECT HILL

look out for

THE MAGICIAN'S DAUGHTER

by

H. G. Parry

Off the coast of Ireland sits a legendary island hidden by magic. A place of ruins and ancient trees, sea salt air and fairy lore, Hy-Brasil is the only home Biddy has ever known. Washed up on its shore as a baby, Biddy lives a quiet life with her guardian, the mercurial magician Rowan. A life she finds increasingly stifling.

One night, Rowan fails to return from his mysterious travels. To find him, Biddy must venture into the outside world for the first time. But Rowan has

powerful enemies—forces who have hoarded the world's magic and have set their sights on the magician's many secrets.

Biddy may be the key to stopping them. Yet the closer she gets to answers, the more she questions everything she's ever believed about Rowan, her past, and the nature of magic itself.

1

ROWAN HAD LEFT the island again last night.

He had done so quietly, as usual. Had Biddy not been lying awake, listening for his light tread on the stairs outside her bedroom, she would have never known he was gone. But he had slipped out of the castle once or twice too often lately while she slept, and this time she was ready. She got out of bed and went to the window, shivering at the touch of the early-autumn chill, in time to see him cross the moonlit fields where the black rabbits nibbled the grass. Her fingers clenched into fists, knowing what was coming, frustrated and annoyed and more worried than she wanted to admit. At the cliff edge he paused, and then his tall, thin form rippled and changed as wings burst from his back, his body shriveled, and a large black bird flew away into the night. Rowan was always a raven when he wasn't himself.

When she was very young, Biddy hadn't minded too much when Rowan flew away at night. As unpredictable as Rowan could be, he was also her guardian, and however far he went she trusted him to always be there if she needed him. In the meantime, she was used to fending for herself. She did so all day sometimes, when Rowan was shut up in his study or off in the forest and had no time for things like meals or conversation or common sense. Besides, Rowan always left Hutchincroft behind to watch over things. Hutch couldn't speak to her when he was a rabbit, it was true, but he would leap onto the bed beside her, lay his head flat, and let her curl around his soft golden fur. It made the castle less empty, and the darkness less hungry. She would lie there, dozing fitfully, until either she heard the flutter of feathers and the scrabble of claws at the window above hers or exhaustion won out and pulled her into deeper sleep.

And in the morning, Rowan would always be there, as if he'd never left.

That morning was no exception. When she woke to slanting sunlight and came downstairs to the kitchen, Rowan was leaning against the bench with his fingers curled around a mug of tea. His brown hair was rumpled and his eyes were a little heavy, but still dancing.

"Morning," he said to her brightly. "Sleep all right?"

She would have let him get away with that once. Not now. She wasn't a very young girl anymore. She was sixteen, almost seventeen, and she minded very much.

"What time did you get in?" she asked severely, so he'd know she hadn't been fooled. He laughed ruefully.

"An hour or two before dawn?" He glanced at Hutchincroft, who was busily munching cabbage leaves and carrots by the stove. "Half past four, Hutch says. Why? Did I miss anything?"

"I was asleep," she said, which wasn't entirely true. "You'd have to tell me."

She pulled the last of yesterday's bread out of the cupboard, sneaking a look at Rowan as she did so. There was a new cut at the corner of one eyebrow, and when he straightened, it was with a wince that he turned into a smile when he saw her watching.

Biddy didn't think there had ever been a time when she had thought Rowan was her father, even before he had told her the story of how she first came to Hy-Brasil. The two of them looked nothing alike, for one thing. Rowan was slender and long-limbed like a young tree, eternally unkempt and wild and sparkling with mischief. She was smaller, darker, with serious eyes and a tendency to frown. And yet he wasn't an older brother either, or an uncle, or anything else she had read about in the castle's vast library. He was just Rowan, the magician of Hy-Brasil, and as long as she could remember there had been only him and Hutchincroft and herself. She knew them as well as she knew the castle, or the cliffs that bordered the island, or the forests that covered it. And she knew when he was hiding something from her.

He knew her too, at least well enough to know he was being scrutinized. He lasted until she had cut the bread and toasted one side above the kitchen fire, and then he set his mug down, amused and resigned.

"All right. I give up. What have I done now?"

"Where did you go last night?" she asked—bluntly, but without any hope of a real answer.

She wasn't disappointed. "Oh, you know. Here and there. I was in Dublin for a bit, then I got over to Edinburgh. And London," he added, with a nod to Hutchincroft, conceding a point Biddy couldn't hear. In her bleakest moments, she wished they wouldn't do that. It reminded her once again of all the magic from which she was locked out.

"And when did you get hurt?"

"I didn't—well, hardly. A few bruises. I got careless." He looked at her, more serious. "If you're worried, you don't have to be. I'm not doing anything I haven't been doing longer than you've been alive. I haven't died yet."

"Death isn't a habit you develop, you know, like tobacco or whiskey. It only takes once."

"In that case, I promise I'll let you know before I consider taking it up. Is that toast done?"

"Almost." She turned the bread belatedly. "But we need more milk."

"Well, talk to the goats about it." He checked the milk jug, nonetheless, and made a face. "We do, don't we? And more jam. I need to take the boat out to the mainland for that."

This gave her the opening she'd been hoping for. She picked the slightly burnt bread off the fork and buttered it, trying for careful nonchalance. "I could come with you."

"No," he said, equally lightly. "You couldn't."

"Why not? You just pointed out that you've been leaving the island at night since long before I was born, and you're still alive. Why can't I at least come to get the supplies in broad daylight?"

"Because you don't go to the mainland, Biddy. I told you."

"You told me. You also told me it wouldn't be forever. You said I could go when I was older."

He frowned. "Did I? When did I say that?"

"Rowan! You said it when I was little. Seven or eight, I think. I asked if I could come with you when I was grown up, and you said, 'Yeah, of course.'"

She had held on to that across all the years in between, imagining what it would be like. Rowan clearly had no memory of it at all, but Hutchincroft nudged him pointedly and he shrugged. "All right. You're not grown up yet, though, are you?"

She couldn't argue with that. She had tried when she turned sixteen to think of herself as a woman, like Jane Eyre or Elizabeth Bennet or the multitudes of heroines who lived in her books, but in her head she wasn't there. They were all older than her, and had all, even Jane, seen more of life. And yet she was too old to be Sara Crewe or Alice or Wendy Darling either. She was a liminal person, trapped between a world she'd grown out of and another that wouldn't let her in. It was one reason why she wanted to leave the island so badly—the hope that leaving the place she'd grown up would help her leave her childhood behind. Not forever, not yet. But for a visit, to see what it was like.

"I'm not a child," she said instead. "Of that, at least, she was sure. "I'm seventeen in December. I might be seventeen already—you don't know. I can't stay on this island my entire life."

"I know," he said. "I'll work something out, I promise. For now, it's not safe for you."

"You leave all the time."

"It's not exactly safe for me either, but that's different."

"Why?" She couldn't keep frustration out of her voice. "It should be safer for me than for you, surely. You're a mage. I'm nothing."

"You're not nothing," he corrected her, and he was truly serious now. "Don't say that."

She knew better than to push that further. Rowan, like her, had no patience for self-pity, and she didn't want to blur the lines of her argument by indulging in it.

"Well," she amended. "I can't channel magic. I'm not like you. I'm no different to any of the other millions of people living out there in the world right now, the ones I read about in books, and they're safe and well. If there's no threat to them, surely there's no threat to me." She hesitated, seized by doubt. "They *are* out there, aren't they? It really is like in the books?"

He laughed. "What, you mean are we the only people left in the world?"

"How should I know?" she pointed out, defensive. "I've never seen anyone else."

"There are millions of people out there. Of all shapes and sizes, colors and creeds, many of them very much like the people in books. Trust me. Where do you think the jam comes from?"

"I don't know where the jam comes from!" This wasn't strictly true—she knew both exactly how jam was made, thanks to the library, and how Rowan obtained it, thanks to Hutchincroft. But qualifying that would weaken her position, so she rushed on. "I've never seen that either. I've never seen anywhere except the island."

"Well, none of the rest of the world have ever seen the island. So you're not too badly off, considering."

"That isn't the point! I know why the rest of the world can't see us. I don't understand why I can't see the rest of the world."

"Biddy," he said, and the familiar note was in his voice, quiet but firm, that had stopped her in her tracks since she was old enough to recognize her name. "That's enough, all right?"

Against her own will, she fell silent, burning with resentment. It was directed at herself as much as anyone. Rowan rarely tried to guide any aspect of her behavior, and yet when he did she never dared to push back. No, *dared* was the wrong word—that sounded as though she was afraid of him, and Rowan had never done anything to make her so. The barrier came from inside her own head, from her own reluctance to lose Rowan's approval when he and Hutch were the only people in her world. She hated it. The heroines in her books would never care what anybody thought. And she hated most of all the reminder that her world was so small.

Rowan must have seen it, because the lines of his face softened. "Look, Bid—"

"Never mind." She laid down her butter knife and pushed her toast aside, trying for a dignified exit. It felt stiff and childish, only signifying that she had lost both the argument and, for some reason, her breakfast. "It was just a question, that's all. I need to see to the goats."

"All right." Rowan didn't sound happy, but he clearly had no intention of prolonging a discussion he himself had stopped. "I'll be in the study if you need me. We'll probably see you this afternoon?"

Biddy glanced at Hutch, who was watching her anxiously from the fireplace, and managed a wan smile for him. Then she went out the kitchen door, into the windswept courtyard where the chickens pecked. She wished, not for the first time lately, the hinges in the castle doors worked well enough to allow a remotely satisfying slam.

There were three rules to living on the Isle of Hy-Brasil, or so Rowan always said.

The first was to never set foot under the trees after dark. That one wasn't much of a rule—Rowan broke it all the time. It was difficult not to in the short daylight hours of winter. The forest covered most of the island, tangled and grey green and wild, and they often needed to forage well into it to collect plants for food and spells. But certainly there was an edge of danger under the branches once the sun went down. The shadows had been known to misbehave; high lilting sounds like laughter or half-heard music drifted through the leaves when the wind was still. There were things in the depths of Hy-Brasil that none of them would ever know, not even Hutchincroft.

The second rule was to watch out for the Púca, and never accept a ride from it. Unlike the rule about the trees, which seemed something she had always known, Biddy could dimly remember being given this one when she was four years old. She had been picking dandelions in the fields beyond the castle, the summer's grass swishing past her knees, when she had seen a black horse beyond the crest of the hill. There were no horses on Hy-Brasil: She had recognized it at once from pictures in her books, and her heart had thrilled. Its golden eyes had held her, beckoned her, and she had been venturing forward open-mouthed to touch its wiry mane when Rowan and Hutch had come from nowhere. She could recollect very little after that, but afterward Rowan had sat her down in the library for a rare serious talk and told her all about the Púca—that it was a shapeshifter, a trickster spirit who loved nothing better than to tempt unwary travelers onto its back, take them for a wild and terrifying ride, and dump them in a patch of thorns miles from home. She had found the thought more funny than scary at the time, but she had steered clear of any golden-eyed creature ever since.

The third was to never harm the black rabbits that speckled the long grass behind the castle, along the cliff paths up to the ruins. This one was the easiest of all. Biddy couldn't imagine why anyone would want to harm a rabbit.

It wasn't until she was a good deal older that Biddy had realized the fourth rule of living on Hy-Brasil, the unspoken one, the only truly inviolable ultimatum and one that applied only to herself. She was never to leave it.

It took her a long time to notice this, and even longer to mind. Hy-Brasil was hidden from the rest of the world by centuries-old magic, only able to be seen once every seven years and only reached by a chosen few. Nobody had ever come to its shores in her lifetime. As a child, she was curious about the world beyond the sea, but in a vague, half-sketched way, as she was curious about a lot of things she read in books. London and Treasure Island and horses and dragons were all equally imagined to her. She thought she would probably see them one day, when she was old. In the meantime, the island was hers to explore, and it took up more time than she could ever imagine having. There were books to read, thousands of them in the castle library, and Rowan brought back more all the time. There were trees to climb, caves along the beach to get lost in, traces of the fair folk who had once lived on the island to find and bring home. There was work to be done: Food needed to be grown and harvested; the livable parts of the castle, the parts that weren't a crumbling ruin, needed to be constantly fortified against the harsh salt winds; the rocks needed to be combed for useful things when the tide went out. She was a half-wild thing of ink and grass and sea breezes, raised by books and rabbits and fairy lore, and that was all she cared to be.

She didn't know now when that had changed—it had done so gradually, one question at a time wearing away at her like the relentless drops of rain on the ruins by the cliffs. She must have asked Rowan at some point how she had come to the island, but she couldn't remember it. It seemed she had always known the story: a violent storm that churned up the ocean and strewn the shoreline with driftwood; Rowan and Hutchincroft walking along the clifftops the morning afterward; the battered lifeboat on the rocks, half-flooded, with the little girl that had been her curled up in the very bottom. Rowan had since shown her the spot many times at her request. She had been no more than a year old when they found her, with a mop of chestnut curls and enormous eyes, wet through and crying but unscathed. There was no trace of her parents, or the shipwreck that had likely killed them. It was as though the island itself had reached out into the deadly seas and snatched her to safety. She liked to think of that—that Hy-Brasil, which rarely let anyone come to its shores, had for its own reasons welcomed her. It had to mean something. Perhaps she was the daughter of somebody important, a queen or a brilliant sorcerer; perhaps, like the orphan girls in her books, she had some great destiny to fulfill. It made up in some small way for not being a mage.

She could, though, distinctly remember reading *A Little Princess* when she was ten or eleven and stopping short at the realization that Sara Crewe, at seven, was being sent from her home to school. She wasn't sure why this struck her particularly—she had read other stories about children being sent to school, after all, without wondering why it didn't seem to apply to her. Perhaps it was that Sara's father, young and full of fun, reminded her a little of Rowan just as Sara reminded her a little of herself. Perhaps it was just that she was ready to question, and books, as they so often did, crystallized her questions into words.

She'd tracked him down to the library that evening. "Rowan?"

"Yes, my love?" he'd said absently. It probably wasn't the right time—he was up on the bookshelves near the ceiling, balanced precariously as he tracked down a volume about poltergeists. Hutch lay on the rug by the fire, flopped on his side in a peaceful C shape.

"Why haven't I gone to school?"

She thought he focused his attention a little more carefully on the books in front of him, but he might have just been trying not to fall to his death. "Do you want to go to school?"

It wasn't what she had been asking, and the possibility had distracted her while she considered. "I think so," she said at last. "Someday."

"Well, then you will, someday," he said. "It might be a while, though. I'll see what I can do."

It was no different to the kind of thing he'd said before, but for the first time, far too late, she realized what he wasn't saying. He was telling her that she couldn't leave yet, and she trusted that he had a good reason. He was telling her that she would leave one day, and she trusted that too. But he wasn't telling her *why*. He never did.

Once she had noticed that, she began to notice other things he wasn't saying, lurking like predators in long grass amid the things he was saying instead.

She knew, for instance, that Rowan had grown up on the distant shoreline she could see from the cliffs on a clear day, the one she used to think of as the beginning of the world. Actually, it was Inishmore, one of the Aran Islands. Beyond it was the coast of western Ireland, and beyond that was Great Britain and then the great mass of Europe, over which Rowan and Hutch had wandered before coming to the island. Rowan would give her all the books and maps she could ever want, and in the right mood he would talk to her for hours about the countries inside their pages. Yet when she pressed him on any stories from his own childhood or travels, he would turn elusive.

"It was a long time ago," he said once, with a shrug.

"So was the Norman Conquest," she reminded him. "And we were just talking about that."

He laughed. "Well, it wasn't *that* long ago!"

"How long was it, then?" she countered. "I know you're a lot older than you look, because Hutch told me that magicians age slowly once they get their familiars. But he didn't know how old that made you, because rabbits aren't very good with time."

"Neither am I. A hundred years or so? I lost count around the Boer War."

She didn't believe that for a minute. Rowan could misplace a lot of things, but surely not entire years. But she had learned to accept it. It was useless to try to make Rowan talk when he didn't want to. And Hutchincroft, who when he could talk would do so happily at any time at all, knew Rowan too well to give Biddy information that she wasn't supposed to have.

Lately, though, things had been different. It wasn't only that she was getting older, more restless, her eyes pulled constantly to the bump of land on the horizon and her thoughts pulled even further. Rowan had been disappearing more and more often; he was bringing back a lot more injuries than he was artifacts, and some of them she suspected hurt more than he was letting on. Hutchincroft was restless when he wasn't there, on edge, possibly in constant silent communication and certainly in silent worry. It was possible, she supposed, that these things had been festering under the surface of her life for a long time, and she was only lately becoming aware of them. Either way, she could feel a bite of danger in the air like the first frost of autumn, and she didn't like it.

It should have been a perfect morning. The day had unfurled crisp and bright, the kind to be taken advantage of on Hy-Brasil, where wind was common but sun was rare, and she had gone up the cliffs with a rug, three undersized apples, and a battered copy of *Jane Eyre*. The wind ruffled her hair and the grass behind the castle; the black rabbits grazing there, infected with the chaotic joy of it, flicked their ears and jumped in the air. It made her smile, despite everything. And yet she hadn't been able to focus as she usually did. The argument had tainted the morning like smoke, leaving an acrid taste in her throat and a grey pall over the sky. The world of her book seemed impossibly far away, full of strangers and schools and romances when she had never seen anything of the kind. Her self-righteous fury at Rowan's treatment of her gave way, predictably, to doubts about her own behavior, and then to guilt. It was a relief when shortly after midday a shadow fell across the pages.

"Hello," Rowan said. At his side, Hutchincroft nudged her book experimentally with his nose. "What are you up to, then?"

She shrugged, determined not to give him the satisfaction of a smile quite yet. "Not a lot."

"You're not still sulking, are you?"

"I don't *sulk*. You two sulk. I was reading."

"Any good?"

She glanced down at her book. "'It is in vain to say human beings ought to be satisfied with tranquility: they must have action; and they will make it if they cannot find it. Millions are condemned to a stiller doom than mine, and millions are in silent revolt against their lot. Nobody knows how many rebellions besides political rebellions ferment in the masses of life which people earth.'"

His eyebrows went up. "And that's you not sulking, is it?"

"It's Charlotte Brontë, not me!" In fact, that part had been a few chapters earlier, but she had remembered it to make a point. "I'm just reading what she says."

"Well, tell her to lay off." He must have seen that pretending they hadn't argued wasn't working. She heard a faint sigh, and then he settled down beside her on the grass. "Look, I know it's not fair. I know it's lonely here for you. For what it's worth, I'm sure I did say you could come with me when you were older, and I'm sure I meant it. I thought things would be different by now. They might be soon—I'll do what I can, I promise—but I need more time. All right?"

It wasn't, really. But she knew Rowan was apologizing in his own way, and she wanted to apologize too. She didn't want there to be undercurrents of tension and struggle between the two of them, as there seemed to be more and more often these days. There never had been before. Oh, when she was thirteen and a prickly ball of existential angst, she would shout at him that he didn't *understand* her, and he would retort, a little frustrated and a lot more amused, that she was bloody right about that, and she would storm off fuming. But that had been about her own emotions flaring, easily solved once they settled down again. This was about Rowan, and she had enough common sense to see that if he wasn't going to budge, she could do nothing except keep pushing or back down.

And so she nodded, and tried to mean it.

"Thank you." His voice was so unexpectedly quiet and sincere that it caught her off guard. It was as though a curtain had flickered aside, and beyond it she could glimpse something shadowed and troubled. Then the moment passed, and he was stretching and getting back to his feet in one sure movement. "What time is it, by the way?"

Biddy resigned herself to the subject being closed and checked her coat pocket for her watch. "Ah...almost two."

"That late?" He glanced down at Hutch. "You were right. We do need to get a move on if we want to get back before tonight."

"Are you going somewhere tonight?" She made her voice deliberately innocent, and his look suggested he knew it.

"I might be. For now, I'm going out to the oak. Do you fancy a walk?"

She was half tempted to refuse, just to show she wasn't letting him off as easily as all that. But she *did* fancy a walk, and what was more, she fancied their company after her morning alone. So she got to her feet, brushing grass from her skirt.

"It isn't only about me leaving the island," she couldn't help adding. "I worry about you when I wake up at night and you're not there."

"I know you do. But you don't have to, I promise. I can take care of myself. I'm always back by morning."

"That doesn't mean you always will be."

"It doesn't mean I won't be either," he pointed out, which was technically accurate if infuriating.

They walked through the trees, the two of them on foot and Hutch scampering beside them before Rowan scooped him up to settle him against his shoulder. At this time of year, the path was like a dark green cathedral, dappled with sun, and Biddy told the other two about the words the Japanese had for different kinds of light: Light through leaves was called *komorebi*. Her mood lifted, and the trapped, resentful feeling sank back down in her chest where it belonged.

When they passed the familiar track where the elm trees grew, Rowan stopped.

"Think you can get up there now?" he asked, with a nod to the tallest branches.

She sighed. "Honestly, does it matter? When in my life am I ever going to need to get up a tree?"

"You never know," he said lightly. "Does that mean you can't?"

Reluctantly, she returned his grin. "What do you think?"

Children in the books Biddy read were always told not to climb trees and always getting in trouble for tearing their clothes when they did. Hutchincroft, it was true, did fuss over both her clothes and her safety, but Rowan had been teaching her to climb since she could walk, usually just a little higher and on branches a little more precarious than she would have preferred. Sometimes they made a game of seeing how far through the forest they could get without once setting foot on the ground; sometimes they raced to see who could get to the highest branches first. Rowan always won, but she had grown to her full height over the summer, and she had been practicing.

"Good work," Rowan said approvingly, as she made a grab for a mossy branch and pulled herself up to him. "You'll be outclimbing me soon."

She rolled her eyes, pleased but disbelieving.

"No, I mean it! You're clever, and you're brave—that's all you need with trees. My reach is longer than yours, but you're lighter, and you're learning how to use that. You're mostly slower now because you're more cautious than me, and that's probably not a bad thing. Probably."

"Well, it means I'm not going to come back in the mornings covered with scratches and bruises," she couldn't resist saying, "so that's a good thing. *Probably.*"

He laughed. "Honestly, you and Hutch. If you had your way, I'd never do anything at all."

There was an edge to the laugh, and she knew there had been an edge to her words too. He couldn't quite hide that he was in an odd mood: restless, distant, too light and playful when he was talking to her and too prone to frowning silence when he wasn't. He took a great deal of magic from the oak as well, when they finally reached it. As though he intended to use it.

She said nothing more. It was his business, she reminded herself, and he had made it clear that he would answer no questions. If she trusted him—and she did, with all her heart—then that would have to be enough. Until she felt like starting another argument, at least.

That night, when she heard his footsteps soft and light on the stairs, she lay quiet. She kept her gaze trained on her window, until a darker speck of black flashed across the clouds and was gone. Then she closed her eyes, and tried to think of nothing at all.

Biddy wasn't sure what woke her, only that she sat up so sharply in her bed that something certainly had. The sky was still dark, but faint traces of grey and gold glimmered on the horizon. Almost dawn.

She swung her legs out of bed and went to the window. The grass under the castle stretched out dark and tangled beneath them. On it, a square of light glowed from Rowan's study window in the turret. When she craned her neck up, she could see the shutters wide open and a candle burning on the ledge. That candle had been left there for a reason: to guide the raven back from its travels. When Rowan returned, he extinguished it. Right now, like the rest of the castle, it was still ready and waiting. A memory stirred uneasily. She frowned, trying through the last cobwebs of sleep to see what it was that troubled her. She had known he was going, after all.

It was then that she heard a sharp, sudden sound; the sound, she knew at once, was what had woken her in the first place. The warning thump of a rabbit's back feet against a hard wood floor. Hutchincroft.

The cobwebs cleared as if in a sudden gust, and her stomach turned cold.

The sky.

An hour or two before dawn, Rowan had said, when she had asked him what time he had gotten back. He had given her the same answer before, on many occasions. It was one sure thing she knew about his nighttime travels, the more valuable for being the only one: Wherever Rowan went, he was always back an hour or two before dawn.

Now dawn was almost here. And Rowan hadn't come home.